VULNERABLE

VULNERABLE

Amy Lane

iUniverse, Inc.
New York Lincoln Shanghai

VULNERABLE

Copyright © 2005 by Shannon TR McClellan

iUniverse books may be ordered through booksellers or by contacting:

iUniverse
2021 Pine Lake Road, Suite 100
Lincoln, NE 68512
www.iuniverse.com
1-800-Authors (1-800-288-4677)

ISBN: 0-595-33746-5

Printed in the United States of America

To Mack, who is Green and Adrian and more.

To my children, who can't possibly be prouder of me than I am of them.

To mom and dad and mom—look what I did!

To Wendy, who would never forgive me if she wasn't mentioned at least once.

And to Robynne, who had the faith to say "Yeah—it's like an erotic Harry Potter…"

Cat's come in a clowder
Whales come in a pod
Wolf's come in a pack
And so do dogs…
Vampires come in a kiss…
There's a flock of birds
A school of fish
A clutch of dragons
(Can you clutch a dragon?), but
Vampires come in a kiss…
Human's group in Elven halls,
Vampires love to see them fall…
We all come in a vampire's kiss…

CONTENTS

▼

CORY

All alone in the big bad world

If it hadn't been for Arturo, I never would have known what Renny and Mitch were, and if I hadn't known that, I never would have known what Adrian was. And if I hadn't known that, I never would have met Green. I guess, then, I owe a great deal in my life—both joy and pain—to a six foot Peruvian elf, but Arturo doesn't think like that, and I try not to anymore.

The gas station I work at stands between Ophir and Penryn, up on Gold Hill Road. It's perched on top of a ravine, right near the road—it's the only commercial building for a three mile radius. When the sun goes down and the whole thing lights up, it's like a fluorescent sun in a galactic dark spot—superficial, man made, a kind of pathetic island of civilization in what is still, mostly, a rural, farming area. At around 10 p.m., when everyone else in the two non-towns has gone to bed, you can step out past the gas pumps and see the lights of Sacramento making the horizon glow red, and feel like the city is an alien ship, and the rest of the world is really the Emperor Oak trees and the smell of new mown hay and cow manure that's especially present in the Spring. It's a lonely smell, the kind that makes you think *hey—if I died under the blackberry bush about 10 yards yonder, my body would rot, and you'd be able to smell it for a while, but eventually, I would be just another part of the star this-tle and mosquito ponds, one with the decomposed granite. No one would ever know.* It happens to cows and horses all the time, on the bigger spreads. It really brings home the idea that life is fragile, and Mother Nature doesn't give a fuck one way or another.

I know it's not safe for a woman to work graveyards—but it frees me up for school, and that's my main priority. Besides, I get a $.50 an hour raise for working graves, and when you're working your way through college and trying to save up enough to move out of the house, that twenty bucks a week counts. Anyway, it keeps me away from the townies who think going to junior college is just a pit stop on the way to the glamorous world of construction jobs and strip mall retail. It doesn't make me popular to exclude myself from the people I grew up with, but I think eventually it will make me happy.

But I don't feel exposed or helpless or anything. I'm a big girl. I've got the tough chick thing going—you know, a pierced nose, a pierced lip, a line of silver rings up both ears. My hair is short and gelled a lot, and I wear black lipstick. Anything to hide how really unattractive I feel, right? But I took the self defense classes, and my dad took me out to the shooting range and taught me how to use the .22 that Danny, my boss, keeps next to the cash drawer. It was actually a nice bonding moment—Dad told me he thought I looked all grown up holding that gun, and he was proud of his little girl. Working my way through school? Nothing. Shooting the hell out of a defenseless tin can? I'm Annie-fucking-Oakley. Life in the foothills stinks if you're not rich. I'm a semester away from transferring to a real college—can't hardly wait.

So I sit behind the counter of the store, (only occasionally fondling the .22) and do my reading or finalize my labs. I spent half my first year's pay on a lap top and a printer, so I'm not just a tough looking chickie, I'm a tough looking chickie with technology and a plan of escape. It would be absolutely hilarious what kind of mystique you can build in the goddammed witching hour if you're pounding away on a lap top like Beethoven on acid, except, for me, the need for freedom was burning in my chest like cold nuclear fusion and it didn't feel funny at all. And it was in this atmosphere of absurdity and desperation, when I was partially hammered on Red Bull and Vivarin, that I first realized that the hosts of the supernatural were wandering in like the Disney Light Parade of the damned.

Before I met Arturo, they weren't supernatural—they were just regulars. Arturo gets off work at the Denny's in Auburn at about 1:00, and gets to my station at around 1:30. Cigarettes and a six pack—every night. He stands 6'4 in his stocking feet, but he's not gangly or stringy at all. In fact, he's perfectly proportioned, wide chest, narrowed waist, black hair just long enough to curl around his eyes, and o-mi-god beautiful. Terrifyingly beautiful—too pretty to be a man, too **macho** to be gay—so fucking beautiful I couldn't even look him in the eyes for my first year or so on the job. And then one cold night in January, as I studied the counter and took his money, he purposely brushed my hand with his finger—I watched him, it was like drawing a line. My whole body jerked, and I was surprised into looking him in they eyes.

He smiled at me, gently. His two front teeth were ringed in silver, and it only made him more breathtaking. And then, even as I looked, something odd happened to his beautiful features. His eyes...grew bigger, set farther apart, his face narrower, and more triangle shaped. I blinked, hard, and let him distract my vision with his words.

"What is your name?" He asked. He had a little accent, Mexico by way of the UK, and it pretty much made my heart pound in my ears.

"C..." I almost said *Crap,* as in *crap, dude, you scared the shit out of me,* but I was aiming at *semi*-moron this night (instead of the full-fledged type of moron?), so I tried again. "Cory." Whew. Actually my name is Corrine Carol-Anne Kirkpatrick—but that was *so* not coming out of my mouth.

"Pretty name...but it's not yours for real, is it?" He leaned over, so his elbows were on the counter, and his face was close enough for me to smell him. Denny's, grease, and a hint of aftershave underneath it all. He scared me, enough to remember my common sense.

"It's the only name you'll get tonight." I told him, the tough chickie back in place, thank heavens. I went back to studying the counter—or rather, his hand touching my hand on the counter.

"I am Arturo." He said back, touching my palm again, "And I see you every night. It is rude not to look at me when I come in." He sounded angry, and I didn't know how to respond. How do you tell someone that they intimidate you by being beautiful? It's impossible, because to say that would be to call attention to the fact that underneath the white make-up and black lipstick are acne scars, lips that are too full, freckles on a large nose, and an extra twenty pounds that made a mockery of your chin?

"I'm sorry." Is what I actually said. "I didn't think it would matter." I was entranced by his touch on my palm, staring at his blunt, rough finger as though it were the center of my Universe, and my Universe expanded, attenuated, like his fingers on my hand, like the bones in his face. And then he put his fingers under my chin so I would meet his eyes, and I found that I was wrong. His eyes were the center of my Universe. His eyes, that weren't brown or black or anything that would match the dark skin and black hair. They were green. Dazzlingly, swirlingly copper-lightning, bronze and jade green.

"Corinne Carol-Anne Kirkpatrick," he murmured, "It always matters."

"How did you know my name?" I asked, shaken by *everything,* from his sudden notice to his fingers under my chin, to his oddly shaped features that kept swimming in front of my eyes, to his own eyes that were not quite human.

"You told me." He said, smiling. And then he left, just left, with me staring at his broad back and feeling like I couldn't breathe now that his touch was gone from my skin. I didn't look at the clock again for another half hour, and when I finally drifted out of a *total* daze, it was to realize that he had lied. I had never told him my name.

I felt feverish for the rest of the night, restless, achy, almost in pain, right on down through the next day. I went to class, but I was distracted in the uncomfortable wooden desk, and even though I'd done my homework I couldn't participate in discussion because my brain was so very, very, elsewhere. I heard his name in every side conversation I passed, in the wind, in the traffic noises as I pulled up to the school in my crap-brown Toyota. I saw the color of his eyes in everything from the spare patches of grass to the bronze roof on the theatre building to the grey-green skin of the frog that I was dissecting. And the whole time I felt breathless without his fingers on my skin.

I felt like shit that night, but went into work anyway just to see him. He didn't show, and the next day was worse. I had to put my face in my hands to keep from hyperventilating all day. Even though it was Saturday, and I didn't have to deal with class, I still was exhausted by my 10 p.m. shift, just from the effort of not screaming. My flesh felt like it was trying to claw its way out my skin.

By the time 1:35 rolled around I had five people in the little tiny mini-mart of the gas station. When Arturo walked in I was so happy I dropped one guy's money all over the counter and almost sat on the floor and wept with relief. I could breathe again. I could smell his aftershave from the doorway, and *I could breathe again.* I looked up at Arturo and met his eyes, and he had a practiced smile on his face when I did, but something in my face made his eyes widen. I shook myself, shivering like a baby, and murmured "Get out." to the people around me with enough intensity to make my throat burn hot. They fled, for no other reason than the look in my eyes and the sound of my voice, I guessed then—one girl still had her thirty-two ounce soda in her hands, but I would have paid for it myself. I looked up at Arturo angrily, demanding with my eyes that he set me free of whatever it was that possessed me. Concerned, he leaned over the counter again and took my hand in his.

"My sincere apologies." He muttered, doing the finger tracing thing again. "I had not realized…you do a good job, Cory, of masking who you really are. I did not mean to…distress you, by our conversation the other night."

He stepped away from the counter and I felt the tightness between my shoulders, the one that made the small of my back ache and pain and tremble for two days, I felt it go away. I sighed for a moment, and then looked up at him, angry.

"What the hell did you do to me?" I asked, practically spitting I was so mad. "And how in the fuck did you know my name?"

He smiled down at me, gently. I'm only about 5'2—that's a long way down for 6'. "Your name—this building practically shouts it, you are the only heart with any meaning that beats for long within its walls. And what I did…it was…unintentional. In fact, it could not have happened without that thing within you that you don't recognize yet. You do not look, at first glance, susceptible to the night…" He shook himself, as though her were telling me too much, and said "Again, I apologize. I will see you tomorrow, yes?"

"Fine." I muttered. "What *are* you?" I asked after a moment, before he could turn away.

"I'm a child of the Goddess." He said with amusement, and I blew out my breath in frustration. What the hell kind of answer was that? But before I could ask anything else he left, without his cigarettes and 6-pack, for once, disappearing into the blackness beyond the gas pumps almost before I realized he'd walked out the door. I was left alone and feeling very tiny in the almost claustrophobic space of fluorescent lights and beer freezers. I played it all through my head several times, and thought about Arturo. Was I in love with him? After a year of staring at his shoes and two nights of conversation, I certainly didn't think so. In spite of that terrible fascination that he'd held for me, the feeling I got from him now was more…well, like an uncle, or an older brother. Yeah, he was beautiful, but, well, so the hell what? In fact, now that he had walked back through the door, I was losing more and more of my memory of even that terrible, inhuman beauty, or even any lingering tension from that breathless fever that had possessed me so thoroughly for nearly forty-eight hours. I could hardly remember the feeling. And that's when it hit me.

I had been elf-struck.

I didn't believe it at first, but the next night when Arturo came in I could see that he looked *different, other*—something that wasn't human. Don't get me wrong, he was still beautiful, even more so actually, but now his nose looked a little sharp, and those glorious eyes were far too far apart to be human. In fact, the longer I looked, the more angular the curve of his ears looked.

"You're not human." I said bluntly, when we were in the store alone.

"Indeed not." He said with humor. "Do you have a problem with that?"

And the more we talked, the more avuncular he felt to me. "How did you ever pass for human?" I asked him, feeling comfortable with him, now that I realized fully that he was no threat to my nascent libido.

"Glamour." He said evenly. "It's a trait we have—the ability to disguise ourselves."

"We…who's we?" I asked, because I seemed to amuse him and he let me be nosy.

"We're called *sidhe.*" He said.

"She?" He was most obviously a he.

Arturo laughed, looked over my shoulder at someone at the window and shook his head at them, then turned to me. "S-i-d-h-e." He spelled patiently. "I bet we're in a book somewhere." And then he waved to yet another beautiful someone outside the station and was gone.

I scrambled for literature—fairy tales, pagan research, Celtic Myths, Laurell K. Hamilton—everything I was told was fiction, was fact in the flesh in my Chevron mini-mart. According to everything I read, they were the leaders of the elves or fairies—those cute little pictures of the little winged children or the tiny naked women that we see a lot when we hear about fairy land were pixies or sprites—most of my books told me they were lower in rank than the sidhe. The sidhe themselves were the leaders of this fantasy world that had invaded my Chevron station looking for a six-pack—they were the warriors or the scholars, or the poets. And they were tall for mortal men, with attenuated features, and pointy ears and long, triangular faces. Just like Arturo. Oh, yeah, he was a full fledged member of the sidhe…right down to the whirling eyes.

I tried to dismiss that first impression—and my hysteria after I researched it. I mean, I read plenty of books, and it is a little creepy being all by myself at night, but eventually I started noticing more and more of my customers who were, shall we say, a little more than human. That short, homeless guy, with the grime encrusted on his fingers who came in every night for the big can of Schlitz Malt Liquor? His skin was actually *grey*—not just dirty. And, swear to God, under all that stringy *green* hair? There's a third eye. My boss says it's just some sort of big boil, but I know better—no zit is *that* big!

Danny, my boss, tried to talk me out of all of that bullshit—he kept telling me it was sleep deprivation from too many all-nighters, and he had a point—a working student averages about four hours a sleep a night, and that ain't nearly enough. I told him about the elf-struck thing with Arturo, and he said it was just a girl-crush thing, (like he would know!) But it was more than just Arturo— there were just too many other people…things…creatures…whatever, that didn't look human or act human or even *smell* human.

Like the little wizened woman who came in for the shelled sunflower seeds every night? I didn't notice before, because she wears like a dozen coats and she *stinks,* but I think she 's got another set of arms underneath those coats. Her face is puckered and brown, and the gloves on her hands puff up underneath—I'm totally serious, it looks like fur. She's got like two dozen eyes, too—she's, like, part spider—but she wears a big, floppy brimmed hat that gets in her way. I'm sure Danny could explain her, too, but I haven't asked him since that one conversation—for one thing, I'm tired of being laughed at. For another, the more I talk to him about it, the weirder he starts to look to me—shorter, more wizened, and more green than swarthy, and I'm sure enough that I'm right to not want to look any closer at him. I mean, it's not like there's a place out here for real homeless people. When you go out past the pumps at night and look around, all that's there is a moonglow expanse of silver-lit fields and sleeping cows. Where would these people sleep and eat, if not under the shadows of the big granite boulders that pepper the foothills like marbles after an insane throw? Or the blackberry bushes that take over a property if it's left vacant for even a year? No—they're definitely trolls or goblins or something. If they were human, they'd be dead. Human beings are fragile—they couldn't survive, just wandering around the backfields, crazier than starlings drunk on acacia berries.

And not all of the wacko night life is homeless people. There's a group of kids, ten or so of them—not runaways or anything, but small, feral—they've got that heroin-waif thing *down,* along with lots of black clothes and gothic jewelry—but they're really were-cats, of the tom/tabby variety. They come in frequently, especially on the weekends, often going to parties out in Folsom and Granite bay where everybody's doing drugs that are far too good to notice a few extra hip cats hanging out. They're actually very nice, when you get to know them—and they don't do nearly the drugs they pretend to do. They thought I was pretty okay, since I had the hair and all—but chalk up another sub-group of the weird ass community that had started to build up around the Northern California foothills.

Mitch and Renny were part of that group—home grown, like me, but somehow they had escaped into this weird preternatural 'ghoulash', and had carved a niche of their own. They were funny to watch—Mitch was unconsciously beautiful; he moved with the furtive grace of the feral cats that my mom liked to feed and fix. It was a small town, so I knew a little something about his home life—everybody knew he'd been expelled from high school for drug abuse—but it didn't take a genius to spot someone who had been beaten from childhood, and couldn't believe the beatings had stopped. He looked at everything sideways, as though expecting bad things to jump and get him—everything, that is, except for Renny.

Renny had been an honors student, one year below me in school. It was common knowledge that she had loved Mitch since they rode the same school bus together, and that her parents had kicked her out of the house when she told them that she wouldn't leave town to go to college, because she wanted to stay with Mitch. She was a tiny, plain girl, with medium brown hair, a pert little nose, and a mouth that drew itself in at the sides—much like the giant, 110 lb. tabby cat that she turned into as soon as she and Mitch cleared the brush in back of the station and bounded into the night. When they were tabby cats, they frolicked. They played. They bounded.

The first time I saw them turn into cats, I was literally knocked on my ass in surprise. I wouldn't have seen it, I thought, if it weren't for that extra sense that Arturo gave me, with that one, extra-casual touch. The second time I saw them, I had to swallow past the lump in my throat. Some people wait their whole lives for the happiness these two had, when they weren't people. Maybe, I thought, it was worth it, to live outside the world, if you could be just that happy.

I almost missed my chance for that with Adrian.

He'd been driving his glass-pack Harley to the station three or so nights a week since I' d started working, and I'm sure the locals just *loved* all that noise but I really just ignored him. Too high class tough for the likes of me, right? I first *noticed* him about a week after I realized that Arturo's eyes were too far apart and his ears were pointy

I remember that night—mom had been ragging at me all day—*clean your room, when are you gonna get a boy friend, get some sleep for cripes sake— you look like a drug addict, I'm not here just to do your laundry* (like I'd asked her!), *you've got to let something go, you can't do this forever*—the usual. Some of it's well meaning, I know, but when I try to explain to her that it's worth it, these hours, to go to school, she gets this look on her face like she got when I was ten years old and still believed in Santa. Like she doesn't want to disappoint me or hurt my feelings or anything, but Santa's not real and I don't have a rat's chance in a cat factory of getting out of this suck-ass town.

So Adrian walks in and I'm pounding out a paper on Edgar Allan Poe for my English 1B class, and I'm nailing the keys **hard**, because I'm going to get a fucking A on this paper just to prove to her that Santa *is* real, and I'm get-ting a bus ticket for Christmas. It was March now, and I had two months until graduation with my A.A. in Liberal Science, which doesn't sound like jack when you've got a real degree, but nobody I knew from high school was getting one so I was pretty jazzed, and the last thing I needed was another supernatural demi-god like Arturo to come in and give me shit, so the *last* person on the planet I was prepared for was Adrian.

Where Arturo was Latino and lovely, Adrian was…my *God,* how do I describe Adrian? His hair's white-blonde—Nordic looking, right? Six feet or so, (goodness and glory, must they always be tall?)—and wiry, with a face so fine and sharply featured he looked like he'd been carved from ice. He had Roderick Usher hair, gossamer around his face like a spider-web I could pet, and his eyes were blue. Autumn-sky blue. That kind of blue that needs gold to set it off, but silver to shine by itself.

He came in frequently, always with a flavor-of-the-week. He was pale and looked strung out in an appealing *I can stop when my angst evaporates* kind of way. I found out later that this was an act. It's easier for a vampire to fit in with humans if he looks doomed. He talked with a British accent and looked as though he had no way of making a living but leeching the substance out of whoever offered up their resources to him. He wore a shiny black leather jacket that went well with the motorcycle and treated his flavor-of-the-weeks like shiny toys that he'd give away when their batteries died. He was *bad*. Not *good* bad. He was frightening and attractive and a little bit evil. He was *bad* bad.

A month before that night when Adrian first spoke to me, before Arturo had called me on being rude for not making eye-contact, I would have wasted all that beauty by looking exclusively at his lace-up boots and his tight black jeans. But I didn't want to be rude anymore, so when he put the money in my hands for his usual pack of gum I looked him in the eyes and smiled.

He stopped dead in his tracks, grabbed my hands, and leaned over the counter. I should have been scared. I should have reached for the .22 and held it under his chin, right? I was tough. I'd been working graveyards for over a year—we'd been robbed twice, and one of those times I'd fired that gun over the head of an escaping thief to get him to stop before the cops got there. I should have been scared, but his eyes were just so lovely that I couldn't look at them enough, and then what scared me was that I wasn't terrified.

I closed my eyes, swallowed, and then recovered my smile. "Did you need something else, sir?" I asked, my voice like silk on raw wood. He blinked lazily, leaned and smelled me. Really—like Hannibal Lector, smelling Clarice through the glass—put his nose in the air by my neck and sniffed.

"You don't smoke?" He made it a question. An odd, awkward question, but I answered it.

"Nope. Too bad, hah? It would go with the image." I was babbling. I had just gotten used to Arturo—I certainly didn't expect this other non-human man-god to chat me up out of nowhere.

He sniffed me again, smiled a languid smile that didn't quite show his teeth, backed up a little and nodded towards his flavor-of-the-week—I'd seen this one before. She was a pretty town-girl who wouldn't be pretty after she got married at twenty and started a family. If I were not very careful, I could be just like her. I had nicknamed this one Cherry Ice-cream because she always wore red, but looking at her now, I remembered that I knew her from high school—Kim something or other. She was wearing a red party dress this night, and the fluorescent lights with the red dress did not do good things for her skin tone—she looked almost green. "That one smokes. Not a good…taste, you know?"

"Wow." I said, feeling more and more of the tough chickie coming back now that he'd backed away a little.

"Wow what?" When he spoke his eyes were half closed, as though he scented my words, too.

"Wow— that was way too much personal information from someone whose name I don't even know."

He extended a lean hand, with a better manicure than I will ever have. "I am Adrian. No *Rocky* jokes, please."

I didn't want to shake his hand, but Arturo's words about rudeness still jangled on my nerves. Smoothly his fingers slid over mine, and my hand felt both cool and warm at the same time, like I'd slid it into water just a little to warm for a swim, but perfect for a summer bath.

"Cory." I told him.

Again, that smile that didn't show teeth. "That's not your real name, is it luv?" He said.

"What is it about you guys and my name?" I asked, frustrated. 'Cory' had been my name to my parents and through nearly fifteen years of public education, thank you very much, and now these jokers wanted to quibble with my identity like the last nineteen years of my own work didn't mean a damned thing. Besides, *Cory* was a boy's name. A tough name. Corinne Carol-Anne? It sounded too much like someone I didn't know how to be.

His eyebrow arched, and I noticed that the hair of his eyebrow was only a little darker than his skin. Just one more thing on the laundry list of loveliness, I guess. "*You guys?*" He asked. He still had my hand in his, and suddenly his flesh was cold, and then so was my hand. I didn't like his voice now, I realized. It froze my breath in my jaw and made my teeth hurt.

"Arturo." I hissed, and I could swear my breath frosted as it emerged from my stiffened lips. "He asked me my name and he didn't like it when I said 'Cory'".

Adrian's hand warmed as soon as I mentioned Arturo's name. "Arturo." He echoed, in a beige voice.

"Yeah—he comes in every night...in fact..." And the thought made me relax again, which was probably a mistake, "In fact, I've seen you two together..."

He dropped my hand abruptly, captured my gaze easily, and I wondered if he could read the bumps on the back of my skull, he was looking so hard into my brain. "Yeah—Arturo & me are mates, of a sort." With his name out there a third time the whole of my entirely platonic encounter with the not-quite-human man flashed through my head on fast forward, and Adrian cocked his head like he was viewing the film and reading the subtitles to make sure he caught everything. After an hour, or a second, or a year taken out of the ticking of the loud clock on the sterile white wall of the mini-mart, he smiled again, a full fledged smile this time. I had to blink twice before I accepted the fact that his eye-teeth were very, very sharp. Ohmigod—had he really read my mind? *Had I just let a **vampire** roll my mind?* No. Couldn't be. Danny would commit me if I ever told him this.

I swallowed, loudly, and I think he heard me, because his smile both widened at the ends and narrowed over the middle, so I could only see those remarkable teeth protruding a bit over the lip. Cherry Ice-cream walked over in this moment and pouted, pulling at his elbow. He gave her a dark look, and she subsided, looking as though she would cry, then he turned his frightening focus back on me for what felt like another full, breathless moment. Good God, why doesn't he make human men that beautiful? Is it because humans already procreate like hamsters, and more beauty would only make it worse? Everything in my body, parts I don't even have names for, tingled when he looked at me.

His final smile was dazzling, and I felt my face go slack with the force of all that preternatural charm. "What color is your hair, really, Corinne Carol-Anne Kirkpatrick? What color are your eyes?"

"Brown." I rasped, then, embarrassingly, "And the eyes are septic-tank green. The brown's a contact." I was suddenly so scared I could taste my heart beating in my throat. He licked his teeth as though he could too, and smiled that heavy lidded, sniffing smile.

"Sounds...delicious." He murmured, "You should let me see you sometime." Then, too quickly for me to draw back, he pulled my hand to his mouth and touched a pointed tongue to the center of my palm. I gasped, audibly, and snatched my hand back.

"I'm not a snack-pack." I said, trying for anger.

He met my eyes, and they were just as beautiful, but not as scary. "No, Corinne Carol-Anne Kirkpatrick. You're really quite a dish." And then he was gone, Cherry Ice-Cream trailing behind him woefully.

He came in the next night, around 2:00 a.m.—sans Cherry Ice Cream— and bought a 32 oz of diet coke which he never drank. And proceeded to chat me up for about an hour. It was hard to talk to him. He was beautiful—and I'm not. He had that accent, with exotic British expressions like 'luv' and 'bird' and 'is terrific', which did funky things to my knees, and I knew that my voice was sharp, frequently shrill, characterless NorCal, and that I frequently used outdated expressions, like "dude", "as-if", "whatever", and "like". And, to make things even more awkward, he had this look in his blue-sky eyes like there was something crucial he needed from me, and I would never ever see what it was.

But talk to him I did—I told him about school.

"I don't understand." He said bluntly, when I talked about getting out of the California foothills and going someplace big and exciting and new. I was working on a paper at the time, and I found my fingers stilling on the keyboard. I looked at him with humor, and exasperation. "Haven't you ever felt trapped?" I asked. "Haven't you ever felt like your whole life was one little tiny dust speck in the Universe, and if you fought hard enough you could make it the *whole* Universe?"

His face twisted, then, clouded, and I don't know what he was thinking and at the time I was glad that I didn't know because that kind of pain made my palms sweat. "Yeah." He whispered. "I know that feeling." He swallowed then, shook his head, blinked his eyes, and whatever it was he'd been seeing before disappeared. "But not here." He added. His usual self-assurance slid back in place, and I was left shaken by what lay within this man-god, and was never revealed.

At that moment, Renny and Mitch came in. I'd just seen their giant tabby cat act a few nights before, and I was waiting for something in me to recoil from them, because now I knew they weren't entirely human. Didn't happen. What did happen was that both of them looked at Adrian and smiled, a warm, genuine, if deferential smile, and then they…well, they bowed.

And Adrian bowed back.

I was pretty sure my chin hit the counter. Then things got weird. Renny turned to kiss Mitch on the cheek, and then grabbed Adrian's hand and took him outside. My head swiveled, and if anything, my jaw dropped lower when Adrian stopped her short and looked deliberately at me. His face was changing. His teeth grew, his *forehead* grew, and his eyes began to whirl. Renny closed her eyes, smiled, and raised her chin. They were close together, like family, not lovers, but then Adrian met my eyes and lowered his head to Renny's neck and even that changed. Adrian sunk his teeth slowly into the sleek, white flesh above the tiny girl's carotid, and he began to suckle. Renny made a groan that I could hear through the bomb-proof Plexiglas and gave herself to the feeding, writhing against Adrian without inhibition. I felt blindly behind me for my high backed swivel seat because my knees were going to give out, there was a horrible, empty ache between my thighs, and I couldn't look away to save my life.

"Christ Jesus." I blasphemed, and I heard a feral, hungry noise close to me. I spared a glance sideways, and I could see Mitch, holding the flower he habitually bought for Renny with rolled pennies, and staring out the window with adoration and naked desire.

"It's something, isn't it." Mitch growled next to me.

"This flower's better, Mitch." I said automatically, reaching for the special flowers I bought just for the two of them. I had already taken the price tag off, which was good, because Adrian's feeding was nearing its completion, my panties were flooded and I still couldn't look away.

"I love it when he feeds from her." Mitch continued, as though relieved to have someone to tell.

"How can you..." I couldn't even finish asking the obvious question—how could he bear to watch the woman he loved writhe and moan in the arms of another man.

"She's totally turned on when he's done." Mitch said wolfishly. "For that matter," He admitted, "So am I when he's done with me. It's a vampire thing."

Okay. I could believe that. Finally, after the mind roll and staring curiously at his teeth for the last hour, I could believe that. "Why do you feed him?" I asked hoarsely. Mitch handed me four rolls of pennies, and I mindlessly put them in my drawer. I would be two dollars over at the end of the night and have no idea why.

"We're were-cats." He said simply. "All were animals answer to him. Something to do with the change in our bodies—it cleans out our blood, replenishes it quickly—and makes us in tune with the vamps. I think it's the Goddess' way of taking care of both us—it's damned hard to drink us dry." He smiled, a sexy, assured smile that suddenly made me see what Renny had apparently seen since the third grade. "So we feed them. And care for them. And in return, they protect us." He looked up to where Adrian held the limp and laughing Renny in his arms and lapped casually at the blood on her neck. The wound was already closing, I saw, but it was a tender, almost brotherly gesture, and my brain was knotted from trying to wrap itself around the relationships of vampires and their dinner.

"Why…why him?" God, I couldn't talk. I couldn't stand. A little voice in my head was screaming for Adrian to touch me *just like that*. Another voice was saying that if he ever touched me, at all, I'd melt into a puddle and die.

"Because he's our leader." Mitch said, as if that explained everything, and then, with a wholly sweet smile, he ran outside, swept Renny up into his arms, gave a perfunctory bow to Adrian and scooted her out to their old four-door Nissan. After which, I presumed, he would hustle her home and they would mate like lemmings.

Adrian stood outside the Plexiglas after they were gone, and looked at me with a combination of yearning and fear. I looked back, with probably the same expression, and then he turned and vanished into the night.

A week came and went. Then a month or so. The day I usually dyed my hair came and went as well, but I let it pass by. I still saw Arturo every night and now, at different times in the morning, I saw Adrian too.

He made it a point to say something nice to me, every damned time. Often he'd make small talk, try and get me to talk about my family and my dreams and stuff. Sometimes—well, most times— it even worked and we'd go on for hours, but I told myself it made my skin itch. I know what I look like. I know who I am. I'm an average looking, averagely intelligent woman from a lower middle income family who grew up in a hick town. There is nothing exotic about me. I have never been out of my state, much less my country. All I know about the world I have learned from books and my imagination is so dim that I didn't know a six-foot plus elf until he'd damn near bespelled me. My one chance—my only chance—of becoming anything interesting, any*one* exciting, is to get the hell out of the Sierra Foothills and see what is out there. If I wasn't going to put out for any of the other town guys who came in every so often just to see if I was easy, I sure as shit was not going to let someone who had done more, seen more, than I ever would convince me that he saw something in me that was at all 'special'. If I did that, I would get sucked right into this teeny-tiny world that I was struggling too hard to get out of. One night I told him point-blank, that he didn't have a chance.

I had seen him earlier that night, rough-housing with another elf who was trying to pass for a townie. I might have bought the disguise, but as Adrian held the much taller, dark-haired man in a playful headlock, something about the way they were touching each other caught my attention. In a scant heartbeat, the other man's dreadful mullet melted away, as well as the saturnine lines around his mouth, and although I never got a good look at his face, I could see that he was gold and silver, with a waterfall of onyx colored hair trailing down past his hips, almost to his knees.

And the touch—it was supposed to be that rough, testosterone laden, who-gives-a-fuck kind of beating the crap out of each other that really confident men do with masculine grace, but when my heart lurched into my throat, I could taste something more in the touch. It tasted like Adrian feeding from Renny. It tasted like Adrian feeding from Mitch—which he had, come to think of it, made a point of letting me see. Adrian's hand in the other man's hair was casual, knowing, sweetly intimate. These two people had known each other for a long time. And they had *known* each other often.

I swallowed hard, waited for the knowledge that Adrian had slept with this man to destroy that nascent desire that had been growing in the pit of my stomach since Adrian had first walked in to the Chevron station.

It didn't.

In fact, the idea that Adrian had sustained a relationship that lasted longer than a week and continued with respect and admiration made the attraction burgeon uncomfortably under my ribs. And with the attraction came jealousy.

I watched, fighting the swelling in my gut as his friend looked at me from outside, nodded in my direction, and raised his eyebrows at Adrian's happy nod. He looked at me again, and his eyes widened, and he nodded again, this time thoughtfully, and then disappeared abruptly. I mean, in the blink of an eye disappeared. Nope, I thought, trying to get a handle on my anger and dismay, definitely not human.

"Was that Green?" I asked Adrian abruptly when he came in. He had mentioned Green often—I need to ask Green, or Green told me tended to pop into his conversation like a 'Steven Spielberg' would fall out of the lips of the key grip on a movie set. Green was someone big. Green was the person Adrian looked to, when all the shape-shifters and vampires looked to Adrian. Green would need to be called in to check me out, I thought, to make sure I was good enough for everybody's favorite bad/good man-god.

He looked surprised that I would ask. "Not at all." He said, shrugging. "That's Bracken—that's my mate." I had to struggle with that for a minute, because he meant mate in the British sense of buddy, and I had seen, with my own eyes and that weird sense that had been plaguing me since Arturo touched me, that mate took on a new meaning with the two of them.

"And Green?" I asked, still trying to straighten out how Adrian related to the world.

"Green's more than my mate." He said bemusedly. His eyes took on the haze of hero worship. "Green's my savior, luv. He's my resurrection, my redemption. No Green, no Adrian, right?"

I swallowed, hard. Wasn't that how I felt? No degree, no Cory? I'd just disappear, the nameless gas station clerk for the rest of my life? "There's more to us than that." I whispered, wanting to touch him and resisting the urge. "There has to be."

There was a quiet then, in the station, which didn't sit well with either of us. Adrian had entered happily, and I'd come at him all bitchy, and now neither of us knew how to be.

"You're letting it grow out." He said after a moment, pulling his careless, jovial smile out of my frightened whisper. He brushed pale fingers along the ends of my awful hair. "It's looking nice, luv." And strangely enough, I believed that to him, the black ends and the weird roots of my hair really looked better than the dye itself. I should have known then that I was lost, but I never go under easy. "I bet your eyes are lovely too." He said, putting his finger under my chin and trying to get a fix on their color. My eyes looked swampy, like the quarry by our house, in the spring. Even my mother couldn't get a fix on what color my eyes were. I looked away from his Autumn-sky loveliness and didn't let him see them—but I hadn't worn my color-only contacts for days, either.

It was inventory night and I was counting Cheetohs, so I had the excuse of staring at my clipboard avoid his gaze. To his credit, Adrian wouldn't let me get away with it. Everywhere I looked, to the side, to the clip board, to my shoes, Adrian was there—fingers on my chin, hand on my shoulder, pretty, plaintive blue eyes hovering in front of me. But, then, so was the vision of Adrian and every beautiful, preternatural person who had ever walked in my station. "Go away, please, Adrian." I said after a moment. "When I'm done with this I've got a paper to write."

He blew a pink bubble of gum through those extremely sharp incisors, which is no mean feat. "Why do you do that, Corinne Carol Anne?" He asked after a moment. "There's a whole world beyond your books."

"Yep, and I'd like to see it someday—school is my ticket out." Without looking I could tell Adrian had moved from in front of me to behind me, so close I could feel his breath on my neck. He smelled like bubble-gum and leather and something coppery that I couldn't place—and a little of were-cat and masculine cologne. Huzzah for Adrian.

"That's not what I meant." He shook his head. "I see students all the time—they use books to open up their world, not shut it out." He touched my hair again as he said this, and I made a vow to dye it just as soon as I got home. I had a smorgasbord of feelings swirling around my stomach like fog, and I found that the one the surfaced when I lowered the clip board and finally turned my gaze to Adrian was anger.

"Maybe the world expects more for those people than it does for me." I snapped and turned back around to finish my inventory.

"Well maybe you need to find someone who expects the world for you, babe." Adrian said, and it sounded so plausible, so sweet, and I just wanted to cry.

"What are you doing with me, Adrian?" I asked, finally meeting his eyes. I was miserable—I wasn't even smart enough to go to college, or so my parents and my friends and my teachers told me, and here was this man-god, telling me that I had the world at my feet. And I just wasn't worthy enough to take it. "I mean, really." My eyes started to tear, and I had to look away. "You're gorgeous—I'm sure half the state is lining the block to blow you—and you're here with me, and I'm too plain to fuck and too ordinary for food!" I was barely over 5'2"—to me, 6' was hella tall—I'd said that whole speech to Adrian's chest because I didn't feel like tilting my head back. It doesn't matter—I can't imagine that the choices I made later would have been any different if I'd seen the devastation in his eyes at that moment. I don't know if there was a force in the world that would have changed Adrian's choices for him.

There was another silence, then, and I felt like complete crap. This vampire...this *man* had been nothing but nice to me, ever. I was pretty sure he'd given up Cherry Ice Cream—and probably even onyx-haired god—to come in and chat me up. And I'd been a complete bitch. I felt worse than crap. I felt like a maggot—of course he wouldn't want me. I was not only stupid and plain and ordinary—I was mean. What he said next didn't help my guilt any, either.

"How do you know the world isn't wrong, luv?" He asked gently, as though he were asking himself the same thing. "How do you know the only thing keeping you from being extraordinary is the way you see yourself?"

I stood there with my heart beating in my chest, wondering if I should respond to that. He was really a vampire. I had seen him feed. He could smell my blood as it coursed beneath my skin—he told me once that he could even hear my heart beat in my chest from outside the store, and know that it was *mine*. Could he really see things in me that the rest of the world missed? Or did I just need a few more hours of sleep?

I finally looked him in those Autumn-sky eyes, not sure what I was going to say. "I'm sorry." I said simply, meaning I was sorry for what I had said. I don't know if that's what he heard, and before I could gauge his odd and vulnerable expression, Arturo walked in, looking pissed off. He said Adrian's name shortly, sharply, and as he turned away, I could swear the look on his face, finally, was regret.

The two man-gods had a whispered conference back by the beer cooler, and I studied the inventory as though my life depended on it, listening intensely the whole time. Phrases filtered to me over the vague buzz of the stereo I kept on after twelve, things like "innocent", "susceptible", "untapped power", "not your place", and "can't exploit her." These were mostly from Arturo, who appeared to dominate Adrian with both age, an extra four or so inches in height, and, something like authority. Did night creatures have a pecking order? If so, Adrian's rank in the pecking order sat somewhere under Green, and now, apparently under Arturo. It looked almost like a conference between a teacher and a student, or a boss and an assistant manager, and I wondered when Adrian would get promoted, and if I'd still be working in this little gas station on the edge of nowhere when he did. Or maybe it wasn't a supernatural thing at all. Maybe it was just the same street gang leadership that popped up all the time—the meanest and most amoral sons of bitches rise to the top. But Arturo had been nice to me, I thought. And so, for that matter, had Adrian. And they were both, obviously, other than human, and this must mean more than just "back off from the ugly little gas station clerk". Then Adrian began to defend himself and I forgot that I ever had any doubts.

"Fascinating" and "free will" came first, and finally, most clearly, "I won't stop courting her because it's not like that at all."

There was a frustrated silence, and then Arturo asked clearly, out of the blue, "Is that your handiwork out by the blackberry bush?"

I finally looked up and saw Adrian looking surprised and horrified and—hurt.

"God and Goddess, Lord and Lady, *NO,* Arturo." And then he did a curious thing. A thing that cemented his identity with me forever. He dropped to one knee, lowered his head over it, and bared his neck. Right there by the beer freezer, three feet from the slurpee machine. His elbow brushed the rack of Fun-Yuns as he did it.

Arturo stared in pained astonishment, and when he spoke, his voice was hoarse. "Get up, Adrian."

Adrian raised his face to a man who was obviously a superior of some sort. He had a look that was both raw and defensive on his face. "I fancy myself a lady killer, Arturo—not a killer."

Arturo looked away, unable to meet his eyes. "I believe you, but you will still need to answer to Green"

Adrian looked stricken, but he nodded his head in acquiescence, then stood up to his full height and walked out of the store. I heard the motorcycle revved to a maximum rpm and the peel of rubber as he shredded out of the parking lot. I said a quick prayer that he would drive safely—the roads out here are still curvy, in spite of renovation, and there are still one lane bridges that people speed through in big step-side pick-ups. So I said my prayer, and then wondered who would listen to and answer a prayer for a creature of the night.

ADRIAN

A vampire is not an island.

If I'd realized what Cory was going to discover that night, and all the trouble it would cost her, I would have made arrangements to have someone else find it. As it was, I roared out of the Chevron station feeling like shit—a failure at the one thing I'd proven really good at in my life: getting someone into my bed.

But this wasn't just someone; it was Cory.

She couldn't know, in a million years, the sunshine fascination she held for me. There was power in her—something preternatural, I could feel it. And there was all too human passion. And she wasn't swayed by beauty, or fooled by show—she had no idea how rare it was for a mortal to just look at me, and not be afraid, or not follow me like bird follows a pretty light. But even beyond that, there was more—there was a heart to the girl that defied description.

And all that was lost to me, when Arturo said no. Because Arturo was older, and more responsible, and because Green would listen to what he said. Yes, Green would give me anything I wanted, but Arturo's judgment mattered. I was like Arturo's wayward son—his judgment mattered, but it rarely swung my way.

I was in a foul mood when I got back to the hill, and Bracken—who had blown off a date with a pretty townie to look at a gas station clerk through a window—was not much better. We snapped at each other and pounded on each other in the living room until Green called us on the bloody carpet, using the power that he rarely cloaks himself in.

"What the fuck you buggering assholes?" He asked, exasperated, righting a lamp with a thought. "Don't you have something better to do than destroy the house?"

I looked away from him. When he was this bright with his own power, it hurt to look at him anyway—and his human disguise slipped. His eyes grew wide apart, his face narrow and triangular within its curtain of pretty yellow hair. His long body which seemed natural with his glamour became attenuated and otherworldly, and I was reminded, yet again, that for all that I loved him, he was something I was not. And even that was not entirely the reason I looked away.

I was hiding Cory from him. I loved him, but Cory wouldn't understand me and Green—not growing up in this place, where the wrong hair cut is barely tolerated, Goddess help the wrong sexuality. I'd give Green up for a mortal lifetime, if I had to—but I didn't want to hurt him if I didn't have to. And it was hard, telling Green I was in love with a girl. I mean, I love women—I know I've been loved by them. But I didn't know women when I was young. And even when I *knew them,* it was like knowing another language—you could speak it fluently, flirt with it, swear in it, but you never really *think* in it. Well, suddenly, I was thinking in Cory. And not just what it would be like to *be* in her, but what language she spoke, when suddenly you could see into the raw parts of her that she hid with the dye and the peircings and that hideous crap she put on her face.

I didn't have the words to speak Cory to Green, even if he knew to ask.

So I shrugged Green off, mumbled an apology to Bracken and turned to shoulder my way down to my room in the darkling. I could almost hear the look Green and Brack sent to each other as I went. I was wondering which one would be seeking me out later, when I ran into Leah in the hallway. She'd been crying.

"Hey, luv." I forced myself to ask her. We had been lovers once, until I'd given her the choice—slide into that haze of pot smoke and crank that was sucking her down like quicksand, or choose—vampire or were-creature. She'd chosen to be a puma, and ran with that crowd now. Either way, she was mine—my responsibility, my…well, Green wouldn't use the word subject, because he'd been born a Lord and hated that, but that was bloody well what she was. She was mine—she looked to me and I looked after her. It's how we do things here at Green's.

"Hey…" Her voice quivered, and I lay a hand on her shoulder.

"Boyfriend problems, puss?" I asked, and now it was her lip that quivered. My heart sank, just a little. Green was better at this, I thought wretchedly. It was how we had built such a massive power base here in the hills. Green exuded sex, and comfort, and one kiss, one thrust of his tongue down your throat, and you felt like all your problems went away. Lay with him, anytime, ever, and all—or almost all—of what was hurt inside you will heal itself, and if you're most people you feel free to love again. When we'd arrived here in the hills, Christ knew how long ago, it had been just the two of us—that was how we wanted it. But Green protected me, and the two of us protected people who fell in with us, and between the two of us we managed to collect the lost, the lonely, the lovely. Most people would have been excited to lead their own people, to have their respect, and their love. Most people besides me, a dismal voice in my head whispered. Until Cory. Until now.

"He dumped me." Leah was saying, trying to sound philosophical, but her voice was torn and broken, so I was surprised, and both relieved and hurt when she totally broke, sobbing, "I gotta talk to Green…" before she turned and scampered down the hallway.

Smashing, a part of me thought in disgust. Absolutely fucking brilliant. Good enough to sleep with, not good enough to heal. Never had been—it wasn't a vampire talent. Still, I thought sourly, at least I knew which one of the two would be in to see me in a bit.

I wasn't entirely disappointed when Bracken gave a soft knock on my door. He looked unsure, which was not an expression I'd seen much in the seventy-five years since I'd known him. Seventy-five years wasn't long for a high-elf, but it was still a shock to me, sometimes, because he'd been a wrinkled ugly little nipper when he'd been born and he'd grown into this beautiful shining creature who still looked at me with that worship in his eyes.

"Up for company, brother?" He asked, looking in. He'd spent lots of time here, not only as a child, when he'd sneaked in after his bedtime every night to ask me wide eyed questions about being a vampire. He'd also been in as a friend and a confidant, and then, to my surprise as a lover. The first time he'd asked I'd been bloody surprised, damn near wet myself in shock, in fact. But elves aren't humans—and certainly not Green's elves. Sex to Green's people came easy as spots and pints to human children, and Bracken was no exception. He'd had women—liked them fine—but hadn't bunked with a mate, yet, and I was the most logical choice. I was so nervous after he brought it up that I ran screaming to Green, asking for pointers. Green had laughed, kindly—Green was always kind—and then proceeded to give me what he called a refresher course in bunking your mate.

I looked up at Bracken, seventy-five years of companionship and unconditional love standing in my doorway, and thought I'd give up that comfort, ignore that history, push it back to human friendship, with its bullshit code embedded in sports statistics and absolute stark terror of actual animal touch, if only it were Cory looking at me from that doorway, asking to come in.

"Yeah, mate." I said, feeling melancholy creep up into my face like dawn, which was only a heartbeat away. "C'mon in."

"She's out of your league, my brother." Bracken said kindly, sitting on the bed and patting my back.

"Thanks you buggering git." I replied, comforted in spite of myself. "That was Arturo's take too."

"So Arturo warned you off." Brack nodded above me. "I wondered what giant flesh eating beetle crawled up your ass."

"He damn near accused me of murder, Bracken." I murmured, feeling the pain of that accusation all over again.

"He didn't mean it." Bracken assured me, and I knew that he was right but it still felt better to hear it. "He's been protective of that chickie ever since he woke her power up—you know that."

"Uncle Arturo." I sneered. "He's a prince." Bracken began to rub my shoulders and, Goddess help me, I let him. I sighed, and wondered if taking Bracken up on his offer would be considered being unfaithful to a girl who right now probably thought I was a murderer and a complete slut bastard.

"Did you tell Green about the body?" I asked, wishing I could feel guiltier about what was under the blackberry bush, but Green told me once that immortals were attracted to mortals like moths to the flame—so we had to be careful to only let ourselves become attached to them if they were worth dying for. I lived by that law—and self-centered town girls more interested in getting me to score for them than in learning my name were not going to change that.

"No chance." Bracken said. "Leah came in, and then with the sobbing, and then with the 'diddle me, Green, make it all better...'" He finished that last in a high squeaky voice and now I did laugh. She was a good kid, but she was a bleeding vortex of need right now—obviously.

"Yeah, well, we all have a job to do." I said dryly. Bracken's hand moved from my shoulders to my ass, and his long, capable hands slid under my jeans. I held my breath—stupid thing to do, really, since breathing was a habit and not a necessity in my case—and Brack's caress stilled.

"Is she worth all that?" He asked. "Worth giving us all up? Is she that much of a dream girl?"

I gave a humorless laugh, and careful to keep Bracken's hand in my pants, rolled over to my back and let him slide up my front. "You need a girl of your own, mate." I said truthfully, because, while Brack and I might offer comfort and companionship, we weren't ever going to be a couple. We weren't me and Cory. We weren't me and Green. I was pretty sure Bracken knew that.

Bracken gave a strategic squeeze and said, "Yeah, it's a real fucking hardship feeling you up."

My body responded, and I loved that. I had enough bad memories to still cherish the pleasure of someone who cared about me, touching me. Caring about me back. "You know who would be my real dream girl, mate?" I asked, groaning under his touch.

"If you say a man, I'll bite it off." Bracken laughed, unbuttoning my fly and pulling my jeans down my hips.

"No…" He was about to take me in my mouth and I'd taught him well. I had about thirty seconds left to tell the truth before all that mattered to me was cock and come. "My dream girl would love us both." I gasped. Bracken moved his mouth down to my base and then back up.

"You and me?" He asked, surprised, even as he made love.

"Me and Green." I told him, soberly, looking down my body to make sure I could meet his pond-colored eyes. He blinked, understood, accepted.

"You asshole!" he laughed then, "For that I'll leave you hard at dawn!"

He was kidding. I grabbed the back of his head and thrust into his mouth, and he showed me how well he knew me.

I awoke the next night alone, which wasn't a surprise. No one wanted to sleep with a corpse. But the room smelled like me and Bracken, and Arturo was knocking on the door.

"Yeah, mate, make yourself at home." I bitched, and Arturo barged in, rolling his eyes at the messy bed.

"You're going to want to clean this up." He said disgustedly. "You don't have to settle for tweedledum anymore." Arturo loved Brack—Brack was better at being a sidhe than I was at being a vampire.

"Why." I asked shortly. "Who's stepping up for the job?"

"Who do you think, genius." He asked, throwing me a pair of jeans. I shoved a foot in, but I don't wake up quickly, after the day dies, and I found myself falling sideways onto the bed. Arturo stood with his hands on his hips and rolled his eyes.

"Jesus, I can't believe you ever learned to fly."

"I was in the remedial course—what the fuck is the goddamned hurry?" I snapped.

"Your gas station clerk—she dealt with the police last night."

"Fuck." I spat, sitting down abruptly. I hadn't thought of that. No wonder Arturo barely trusted me to tie my own shoes.

"Yeah, fuck." Arturo echoed. Then, surprisingly, "Don't beat yourself up about it—I should have taken care of it too…" He shook his head and smacked me in the back of mine. When I looked at him reproachfully he said, "Jesus, kid, I must really love you, because you fuck up my logic like no one else." I blinked, so surprised to get a compliment from the man, I wasn't sure what to do with myself. Abruptly, Arturo plopped down on the bed next to me.

"She covered for you, kid." He said softly.

"What?" And that I couldn't wrap my head around either.

"The police had her against the wall—Dannin op Creely was there." Cory knew him as Danny. "He said that she totally covered for you—didn't even mention your name."

I nodded. Thought about it, found myself smiling like the child I didn't remember being.

"Christ Mary, Adrian!" Arturo said, exasperated. "Put those things away before you spell me!"

Like I had that much power. Regardless, I dimmed down my smile a little and took off my jeans. "Where's Green?" I asked.

"On a business trip." He answered. Crap—now I remembered. He'd told me the night before, but I'd been so busy beating up Bracken that' I'd forgotten. "What the hell are you doing? You know I don't fly that way." Arturo asked mildly.

"I'm taking a shower." I said, running butt naked like a kid. "I'm taking a shower and brushing my fangs, and the next time she sees me, I'll be done up right."

"She loves you anyway, you fucking moron!" I could hear Arturo laughing. It didn't matter, because the water was on and I was cleaning up for my redemption.

CORY

What's under the blackberry bush?

The curiosity was literally stopping my breath: what was under that black-berry bush? I didn't want to know. I really didn't. I wasn't kidding about that paper I had to write—it was part of the final for my 1B class, and the teacher was one of those people who was really disappointed to realize that the best he'd ever be is a professor in a tiny Junior College on the edge of a hick town. He made disparaging comments about working students all the time—he even walked into my store once, took one look at me typing at the counter and sneered "It figures" before ignoring me while he paid for his coffee. And to top it off, he was a misogynist. I hadn't watched a woman raise her hand yet who hadn't been shut down and ripped up. After the first time it had happened to me I'd kept my hand down, my nose clean, and put Cory Kirkpatrick on all my papers. So far I'd done all right, but I wasn't going to press my luck by turning in anything late at this stage in the game.

But that smell was in the air—the one I'd thought was a cow or a horse or a cat—and it had been getting worse as it had been getting warmer, and I wanted very badly to know what it was that Adrian had not done.

I compromised with myself. First I finished the paper. Then, when the store was empty, right when the air got really cold and the sky began to get the tiniest bit light, I walked down the slight slope from where the station was perched, and investigated the gully with the blackberry bush.

The smell got worse as I approached. I looked behind me, but no one was out—usually there was a good ½ an hour lull between customers this time of morning, and this night was no exception. I wanted to turn back—glory, did I want to turn back—but I thought about that raw look on Adrian's face when Arturo had accused him, and wondered if my face looked like that when my mother asked me if I were dating anyone or my father asked me why I had to spend my money on school, and I knew I had to go on.

I saw the cherry red fabric of her sweater first, then a hand that was blue and gray flopping tranquilly from the bottom of the blackberry bush. Her skin looked faded, as though it were about to become part of the surroundings; color, flesh and all, disintegrating back to where it came from.

I don't remember running back to the station or the phone call that followed it. The cops arrived, and then Danny, my boss, who glared at me. Danny is a short, hairy man who has perfected the Napoleon thing with his eyes—those dirty looks hurt.

I remember telling the stiff, dark-haired police officer that the smell made me look under the bushes. It was a lie. I don't know why I told it. I remember telling him that I knew her from high school, Kim something or other. It was a half truth. I don't know why I didn't tell the full truth. I said that she'd been in the station a month before. He asked me how I remembered that long ago, and I shrugged my shoulders weakly and asked what killed her, and if I could go. He told me drug overdose, possibly, and malnutrition, which I mostly believed, then he asked me the same questions five thousand times.

He kept me there until 9:00a.m.—I was frantic and claustrophobic and nauseous with the need to leave. Didn't he understand that the guy who ran my class wouldn't give me any fucking mercy? The officer (whose name was, appropriately enough, Johnson) smiled blandly, with no sympathy, and told me there'd be other classes. He not only didn't understand, he didn't give a damn. Fabulous—just fucking fabulous. I need a hero, and I get an automaton.

I got to school at 9:30, still in my stupid blue polyester smock that I hated, just in time to watch the rest of the class stream from the room. The professor gave me a superior look over his coffee and his cigarette and wouldn't let me turn in my paper.

I almost cried, and I **never** cry. "It wasn't my fault." I squeaked, feeling lame and defensive, even though this was perhaps the most truth I'd told in the last twelve hours. "I found a body, near my work, and the police wouldn't let me go…"

He looked disdainful. God, I hated that look—he would level it at us, the girls in the class—whenever we'd try to say something really insightful and all our intelligence would just shrivel up and die screaming in front of thirty other people. Something hot ran down my face and into my mouth. It tasted like mascara and foundation and now my eyes hurt really bad because I wear too much mascara anyway and it made it even harder to talk or to meet that damned superior expression.

"If you don't accept my paper, I'll have to take the class over again, and I won't be able to graduate this semester." I was trying for dispassionate and reasonable. I sounded pathetic.

He shrugged. "That's not my problem, miss…" Christ. This asshole didn't even know my name.

"Kirkpatrick." I croaked. "Cory Kirkpatrick." He looked surprised, masked it, shrugged again.

I don't remember in my entire life feeling as desperate as I did looking at his cold, colorless eyes and that practiced, I'm-so-European-not shrug. Something from the evening before pricked my memory. Gracelessly I sank to one knee and bowed my head, looking up at his surprise from under my brow.

"I've worked so hard Professor Jenkins." I said, feeling the dignity seep back into my voice. "Please don't punish me for something that is not my fault." I lifted my hand that held the crumpled up piece of pink triplicate I'd begged from a uniformed police officer at the station. "The case number and the attending officers are written down here, as well as the name of the officer in charge of the investigation. They promised they'd vouch for me if you wouldn't accept my paper—I've worked so hard, Professor. You've seen me at my night job—I work forty hours a week, I take fifteen units a semester, and I still make the Deans list every term. I don't deserve to not graduate because of this. It's just not fair."

For a moment, just a moment, he looked moved. And then he turned around without a word and left me there on my knees, holding that damned piece of triplicate. I heard the classroom door close behind me and grabbed on a desk to pull myself up, feeling numb. The desk toppled, bringing me down on my ass, and I stayed there, sobbing, rocking back and forth and wondering what in the hell I was going to do now.

As I stormed away from the campus my brain shut down and my despair kicked in. Something had to have happened, because in retrospect there were a lot of other options than the one I chose. I could have taken the English class again in the summer. Costly, yes, but worth it. I could have gone to my advisor and contested the grade—I still had proof that there had been circumstances beyond my control. I could have spent another semester at Junior College taking the electives I'd mourned not having the time to take during my degree-or-nothing term of the past two years while I made up the class. I could have not graduated and just transferred—after all, I had been accepted to the State colleges already—I could have just gone and made up the class there. I could have done any one of a dozen things that I was too devastated to see, weeping on the dirty tile of the old classroom. So I didn't do any of them. What I did do that day was walk blindly back to my brown Toyota, ditching my other classes even though that was not the only paper I had due that day. I had no intention of seeing any college campus ever again.

That night at work I was a big fat surly bitch, if I say so myself. It was getting warmer—it was almost May—but I felt cold all night, and clutched my sweater over myself and said nothing that wasn't nasty to any approaching customers. They were used to me by now—it wasn't as though I were a ray of sweetness and light on my best days, and now I was clutching my tough chick routine around me just like my sweater, because I felt like it was all I had. But then Adrian and Arturo walked in shoulder to shoulder, and I felt even my façade of toughness melt away, because damn them both to hell they'd already proved that I didn't even have that.

I was surprised too. The night before I'd had the impression Adrian wouldn't return. They waited until the store had cleared out and I looked at them, clutching my sweater around my too-warm body, feeling as naked as I'd ever been in my life. It occurred to me to wonder if I weren't in the room with a cold blooded killer, and Adrian seemed to read my mind.

"You found the body?" He asked, and I was too numb to lie. I just nodded. "You didn't mention my name?" I shook my head a negative, and he and Arturo exchanged glances. Arturo looked resigned and indulgent, all at once. Like a parent whose going to let a child make his own mistakes. Which one of us, I wondered, was he aiming that look at?

"They said it was a drug overdose." I whispered.

"It could have been, but I'm not sure." Said Adrian simply. "I wasn't there. I haven't seen her alive since…since that first night we came in here.

And I saw you." He meant that. Good Lord, almighty, he really meant that. My heart thawed, all at once, in a red messy puddle, and then it jumped into my mouth.

He came closer to the counter, and I should have grabbed the .22 or at least stepped back, but I just stood there shivering. He stopped then, and didn't try to intrude on my personal space. He just stood there looking, I thought, a little like I felt.

And was that too much to believe, I wondered? I know he's way out of my league, a night-crawler, a man-god, fabulous looking, well traveled, but there's all these stories I've read, about these really good looking men loving these plain women because there's something special inside them…I mean, it probably doesn't happen *often,* but it must have happened *once,* right? And wasn't once, like, a precedent? Couldn't a precedent be followed?

Or maybe he was a blood-drinking, drug-injecting sociopath who could lie really really really well, and who could spot a moon-struck deer mouse like any other good predator. My brain didn't know anymore. My heart had already made its decision.

"Why?" He asked quietly. "I mean, I know it's occurred to you—and you already told me you don't like me—why wouldn't you tell the police it was me?"

I shrugged, just standing there, feeling stupid and weak. Three months, he'd been coming into my Chevron and buying slurpees and flirting with me. Three months. Wasn't that enough? Couldn't you prove yourself in three months?

The silence dragged on, and finally I answered, and I believed the words as they came out of my mouth. I had to. They equaled a decision that would impact the rest of my life, as short as it may be. "I don't believe it was you." I sighed, and he smiled, his sharp incisors showing, but his delight showing too.

He didn't have to lean over the counter then. I moved closer, drawn by that genuine smile. "I thought Arturo told you I was off limits." I said, nervously. I wasn't supposed to have heard that conversation.

He nodded. Arturo spoke from the back of the store. "You believed him, Corinne Carol-Anne. I did too. Not many people would believe Adrian." And like that were enough of an explanation he turned around and left the store. I'd see him again, but suddenly I missed him when he left. It was like being the last two people at a party—lonely and companionable at once.

I looked at Adrian's eyes, beautiful, mesmerizing. Not human. I didn't feel lonely at all. "You'll take me places?" I asked. His answer was important, even though my decision was already made.

"You can't imagine where we'll go." He said, sincerely. He no longer looked vulnerable. He looked assured. He looked happy. Good. It's always nice to see the ones you love happy. He smiled, and doubt and sense and worry all fell away. "You'll enjoy the trip." He murmured, lowering his head.

I closed my eyes tight, like any girl waiting for a kiss. Then I dropped my hands away from my sweater, stood up straight, and relaxed. This really was inevitable, I thought, at peace with my decision at last. Would this be like sex? The only thing I knew about sex was that orgasm is called the "little death." I felt his body close to mine, and I imagined it was warm and I wanted to crawl inside him and curl up and be safe and warm and peaceful. At the same time my skin buzzed and flushed and tingled and I wanted to touch him more than I wanted to breathe. Maybe it would be like sex after all.

Sweetly, feeling beautiful, I tilted my chin up and bared my neck for his embrace.

Adrian

The Blackberry bush as a metaphor.

Shame's off limit for us vampires—it's written in our myths, right? But I don't know what else to call it. I didn't know Cory was a virgin—I didn't even guess, and, yeah, I'm ashamed.

The night after that shocking, tender offering of her pale, sweet neck, there she was in my room, bare limbs wrapped around my body, and everything I'd not felt when tangling with Bracken, or any of the other birds in my bed, was there, humming in the blood beneath her skin. One hundred and fifty years, I'd been making love—and in that moment, with her shadowed, trembling gaze fastened on my face, it was like I'd done it all for that moment, to be inside of her.

And she wasn't afraid of me. And she looked at me like I was everything she'd ever wanted in a lover. When I sunk into her, it was like sinking into salvation.

But salvation has a price, and releasing virgin blood in a vampire darkling is like plutonium in a fusion reaction chamber.

All that power needed somewhere to go.

So I contained it. I know the vamps in the kiss absorbed some, and they thought I was a bloody irresponsible fucking idiot for releasing that kind of heady power in such a confined space, but they didn't know what it could have been, if I hadn't swallowed it inside my skin, because it wasn't just her virgin blood, it was a power, much like Green's. It was based in emotion and strong passions, and Goddess, she must have loved me because if I hadn't had some power of my own, she would have blown me through the roof.

So I was glowing, from love and from power. And in the middle of that, my heart, which beat by the will of the Goddess alone was slamming hard enough to move my chest by my will alone because she was **mine.** My whole life, only Green had ever been mine, and I had been forced to share him after our numbers grew. I was exultant, powerful in my own right, and filled with the power she didn't know she had. The taste of the blood on her thighs was like wine and laudanum and, hell, probably cocaine, like I'd had any of them but wine. It was a sweet, sweet rush, the finest I'd ever tasted.

And it still couldn't compare to being inside her when she loved me.

Was it any surprise I wept blood when I looked down at her, moving with me, ignoring the pain and reveling in the wonder?

When we were done, and I'd seen her eyes go blind and felt her body clench around mine I knew my hands shook, and my voice shook, but I was still holding her within my skin and there was no room inside me for lies.

"I'm sorry." I murmured.

"Sorry for what?" she said, wiggling that sweet, soft, living body.

"You were a virgin." I said, and almost laughed when she blushed.

"I guess you'd know." She said wryly, touching my lips where her blood dried.

The whole hill knows, luv. I should have said it. I should have told her. She couldn't have known what it was that sat within her. No one with any knowledge of power would have given it to someone like me. What I said instead was, "I'm honored to know." And ever, and always, I felt the dawn waiting patiently in the corners of the room, ready to creep in, and knew that with this much power inside me, I had to have her again.

"I know you're good at this for a beginner." I said, making her smile and blush again. Goddess, I could learn to love the slow spread of raw pink spread under her freckles and along her neck.

"Good teacher." She mumbled.

I pulled her astride me, making her squeal, and asked, "Would you like your next lesson?"

She looked uncertain, and blushed again. "I...I read somewhere that a man can't...that you just..."

I laughed, then, comfortable and happy. "Yeah, luv, but I'm not just a man, then, am I? I'm a vampire, right?"

"So?" She asked me slyly.

"So…blood does funny things in vampires." I told her, and flexed myself under her. She laughed and gasped and…tickled me? Was that a woman thing, the tickling? I don't know—it had never happened to me before, not even with Green. What was more surprising than the tickle was the laughter, mine and then hers, and the way she spread her thighs for me without fear, although there had to be pain.

So when dawn came, it was all I could do to try to hustle her out the door, but, being Cory, she wouldn't go.

I blew through her like baby's breath through a dandelion, and my soul left its mark on hers. Forever. In one night, I'd bound her too me for as long as she lived, and I had no words to tell her.

When I woke the next night, to see her there, above me, the relief radiating from every line of her body, I thought it was more of a miracle than my first rising. And I couldn't tell her. Goddess help me, I had no words for her power, no words for the gift I'd given her. No words.

I'm such a bloody git coward.

I longed for Green, who had words, and more than that. I had thought, when I'd taken my girl, mingled our flesh, that it would be glorious because she was mine. But I had loved Green for one-hundred and fifty years, and I hadn't reckoned on that. Because nothing was really mine, unless it was shared with Green.

After I'd risen, that second night, and we both died that lovely little death, and lay there, tangled in the sheets of the only room I'd ever called my own, she rested on my chest, hands under my chin, and touched my blue/white skin like a baby, investigating a new texture.

"What?" I asked, because pillow talk was so easy, and I didn't have to tell her any of the drastic ways her life was going to change if I let her ask me the silly little questions that all lovers should get to ask.

"Where are you from?" She asked, and I could tell that there was more to it than that.

"I have no idea." I said flatly.

"How can you have no idea where you come from?" She looked puzzled, and not at all dismayed by my attempt to scare her away from the subject. Jesus she was fearless.

"I was taken away from it before I had a chance to know where it really was," I non-answered, "But that's not what you really want to ask me, is it?"

"No." Her mouth curved upwards, and I realized that in the last two days she'd gone light on the make-up and heavy on the smiling. She had no idea what happened to her face—all in all a plain collection of features to be honest— when she smiled. It was like turning on the sun. She could have asked me anything she wanted when she was smiling, and it was a good thing she spent so much energy working so hard at not, because I'd be done for. I returned her smile and waited.

"How old are you?" She asked on a pitch of embarrassment. "If you're a vampire you don't age—how old are you?"

I laughed. "Well, I've been dead for a hundred and fifty or so, and I was eighteen, nineteen when I went under."

"You don't remember?" There was something in her eyes—what I wouldn't tell her, she was beginning to guess.

"No one ever got excited about my birth, luv." I told her gently. She nodded her head, measuring me, reading the moment. And changed the subject because she loved me.

"Okay, then," she nodded, "If you haven't lived in England or wherever in a hundred and some-odd years, why do you still have your accent?"

Well, that baffled me, and it must have shown.

"I mean," She continued, "If Madonna could lose her Detroit in ten years, why are you still speaking Brit?"

I laughed helplessly. "I don't know." Although it was a pretty good question. "Maybe it's because we all talk to each other. I mean all of us ex-pats live here at Green's—we all talk to each other, we all listen to each other." I thought about it. "Even those of us who were born here in Nor-Cal speak Brit." It had never occurred to me that that was odd.

"What us?" She asked, all attention. I'd seen her, hard at work at her studies—it occurred to me that she'd just made Green's hill her major.

"Well, vampires—there's around sixty or so of us that live here."

She blinked. "That's a lot of people, Adrian!"

"The house goes all the way through the hill—I figure it holds as many as one of those horrible little rat-box apartment complexes they keep putting up in Auburn."

She thought about it. "That's more than sixty."

I nodded. "Well, there's the fey—probably ninety or so high elves, twenty or so sidhe, and the lower fey...."

"Wait wait wait…" She laughed at me. "You need to give me a crash course in the world of fairie…"

It took me nearly the rest of the night, and made me aware of how much of this I had picked up a little at a time.

The fey was the family grouping (according to Cory—it wasn't as if I had frequented a college campus any time lately), and it was synonymous with the word elf and faerie, but it also was a blanket term—high elves, lesser fey, sidhe—all of them fit under the heading of 'fey'. Immortals. Children of the Goddess. Faeries. Whatever they chose to be called—their names and titles shifted like water, as did their forms and capabilities.

"So what's the difference?" Cory asked. She was wearing one of my plain white T-shirts and sitting cross-legged on my bed,—a huge, King sized thing in light wood that still looked small in the room Green had made for me. My room was deep in the heart of the house, in the place we called the darkling, where the vampires slept. Green and I had designed it so that the light never touched the darkling—any vampire in my kiss was safe if he or she slept in my home.

"That is a vast and complicated question." I told her, trying not to under-state things, and I explained the hierarchy as I understood it. It all seemed to do, I figured, with how human the fey looked. The full sized humanoids were high elves—they had pointed ears, wide set eyes, a good five to twelve inches on me in height, and the sure, bone deep knowledge that they were at the top of the food chain. Their other physical differences varied from individual to individual—anything from an extra digit to a complete lack of body hair could be the mark of the fey for high elves.

"So," she mused, running her hands through her wild, half-dyed hair, "The people who come into the Chevron at all hours of the night are lower fey."

It warmed me that she called them people. "Absolutely." I said, proud of her in ways I couldn't put words to.

"So what's difference between high elves and sidhe?"

"Power." I said succinctly, because it was a sore spot between the high elves and the vampires. Sidhe were high elves—with power. All kinds of power. Glamour—simple disguises like Arturo and Bracken wore when they went and mixed with the locals; terraforming, like what Green used to delve his little kingdom into the earth; climate control, like what we used to keep the grounds temperate in the heat; simple telekinesis. Sidhe could do it all—and often when you didn't expect it.

"So, in the hierarchy of the fey, you've got lesser fey and high elves, who have no power…"

"No." I corrected, "They have powers—but small and, well, specific powers. Like Brack's father—he's a red cap. They're small people, shaped like boulders and earth, and they are really good and sucking blood out of living things."

Cory grinned wickedly. "Works for you, doesn't it?"

"One of my best friends is a red-cap." I agreed. "But, and here's where things get interesting—he's also a sidhe. No one knows how it happened—his parents were lesser fey, and he was born with a high elves body and sidhe powers. Apparently it happens all the time."

I watched her eyes—her best feature—grow wide. "That's really twisted." She said, trying to wrap her mind around the weird genetics of elves. She took a breath and re-evaluated. "So you've got lesser fey and high elves, with specific powers, sidhe with lots of powers—like, ordained to rule by God…"

"Goddess."

"Whatever. And the sidhe have powers specific to their parentage, like your friend who's a red-cap and a sidhe…"

"And Green."

"What's his specific power?"

I had fed from her that evening, and suddenly I felt the blood coursing through my body rise to my face. "He heals." I mumbled.

She leaned forward and put her hand to my suddenly pink face. "Your face is *warm.*" She marveled, and she might very well get all excited about that because it didn't happen to vampires that often. "What's so weird about healing that makes you blush?"

"He heals with sex." I said baldly, and knew my face grew even warmer.

So did hers, and her freckles almost disappeared underneath the flush. "Like, he sleeps with people…"

"Or kisses…" I said defensively, and she arched an eyebrow and I didn't want to take that road. "Anyway, yes. Any intimate contact—and he can heal you. Not just your physical stuff, either, but your head, and your heart…"

Cory turned her head a little, and studied me carefully, with the same look she'd had when she changed the subject from where I came from to the hierarchy of the fey. "That's a very handy talent." Was all she said, then, wickedly, "Want to practice that one ourselves?"

I laughed, and moved across the bed to her, lowering my head to take over her mouth, her body, her soul. And as we made love for the second time that night, I ignored the niggling guilt that nagged at me because I'd managed not to tell her that I'd marked her, for better or worse, as a part of us all.

I made love to her, and showered with her, and kissed her goodbye, loving her more than I'd thought possible and at the same time longing for Green to help me make it right.

GREEN

What he can't heal

God, Goddess and other, what a day. Green threw open the door to his many-roomed wooden home and began to disrobe. His white canvas brief-case went on the glass table in the entryway, his white brocade coat on the maple coat rack, other clothes, also white in linen and silk, cascaded over the white tiles as he padded to the back bedroom. He returned to the living space, bared feet padding on the hard wood floors, still naked but pulling a wooden comb through yellow, yellow hair that fell past his hips. He had a body of alabaster perfection—as did all the sidhe; David, but leaner, six feet, five inches of skin so pale and hairless that it must be touched to be believed. In a bound and a swirl of sunshine colored hair, he leapt across the pale wood floor and landed on his white brocaded couch.

The couch looked out the bay window that wrapped around three quarters of the hill wherein the house itself resided. The living room was immediate to the front entry, and most of the activity of the house passed through it, but it was really only a fraction of the place itself. Green had built his hill like the fairie mounds at home, with the addition of the darkling—which had no windows— and a giant car port in the basement, that had used to be a stable back before there were cars. The wrap around window itself overlooked a canyon, silver in star fall, looking cooler than it actually felt outside. The immediate grounds before the drop off managed to stay 65 or so degrees Fahrenheit…but only people who'd been invited there knew that for certain.

Green stretched on his couch, innocently sensual—the brocade was fine, and satin, and his body appreciated even the tiny prickling of the linen in the bottom of the embossment. His clothes were finely made, always, but nothing—*nothing* was better than being naked. All elves felt that way, and Green was a high elf, all sensations intensified. Food was better, skin was better, sex was better. High elves have it *very, very* good.

The phone rang, and he sighed. There was a price to pay for being one of the most powerful preternatural beings in Northern California. Answering the phone 99% of the time, whether or not one had been on a six day road trip to check out various investments, was part of the price.

"Green." His phone voice was very So-Ho gone yank, because he found that was most effective, but the accent changed depending on his mood. He'd been alive for a long time—accent was all a state of mind.

"Green...Green, its Arturo." Green felt his eyebrows arch to his hairline. Arturo sounded panic stricken. Tall, deadly, easy-going Arturo—panic and Arturo were as likely a match as salt and honey.

"What's the matter?"

Arturo laughed, almost hysterically. "The matter is all over me." He all but giggled. There was a breath, audible, strong and controlled, and Arturo started again. "The were-kitties...the babies...they were we were standing at the gas station, just talking...and Mitchell just...just exploded, man. Adrian and I just stood there, taking his report and all of a sudden Renny changes...right there at the station—and takes off...she stopped at the bushes and mrowlled, sort of desperate, and Mitchell looked at her...surprised, you know, and then...he just...exploded...all over me...all over Adrian..." In the background, Green became aware of retching noises, and a low, miserable voice, swearing to ward off hysteria.

"Wait a bit, mate...who the fuck is that in the background..." Green demanded...Arturo was shaken, obviously, but it didn't sound like one of his people there, and he, Arturo should *know* better than to let an outsider hear.

"Cory." Arturo said..."She's Adrian's."

"Since bloody when?" Green was indignant—he'd been out of town *six days*...and he didn't want to think about Mitchell, a sweet kid with a harsh past and a girlfriend who'd followed him into the preternatural half life just to keep him clean. He especially didn't want to think about Mitchell's innards apparently dripping off the walls of the Chevron mini-mart.

"Since she covered up a body to protect Adrian…dammit Green, *focus.* I need you here, man. Cory's hooking up the pressure hose, but something did this. Something *bad,* and there's a half-grown kitty out there who needs us."

Focus. *Good boy, Arturo, that's why you're my second.* Green took a deep breath. "I'm exhausted—I have to take the bike." He said, breathing deeply and thinking, finally.

Arturo choked on a breath of his own. "That's fine, man. Adrian's got to be in bed by dawn—sometime before then." The phone clicked dead, and Green swore, not sure which was harder to wrap his brain around—Mitchell Hammond, dead, or Adrian, in love.

The ride through the foothills should have been beautiful, full of trees and red dust, and a warm, pine smell that was home to Green now. It wasn't. After the white leathers had come on, so had the responsibility and Green was surprised to find himself *very* angry.

There weren't that many preternatural beings left. Maybe too many by mortal figures, which calculated none at all, but the world was losing its sense of *wonder.* Books helped to hold back the encroaching tide, but as man exploded over the planet, and scientific knowledge obliterated superstition, a harsh and constant light was being shed on beings too fragile to even view the dawn. To lose one of them—a recruit, even—destroyed by magic, was a dreadful loss.

By the time Green got to the Chevron station, the only being he could see was a short, plump girl dourly hosing out the concrete near the pumps. She must have been doing it for some time, he thought, because the station was immaculate—and the water was running clear. It wasn't until he got close to her that he noticed the delicate features under the make-up, the full lips, and the penetrating hazel eyes. He also noticed her pallor, and her shaking hands. This must be Cory.

"Can I help you?" She asked, voice dull and contained.

"If you're Cory," He said, "You don't look like Adrian's type."

"Type O." She shot back, "I'm a universal donor."

In spite of himself, Green felt his lips quirk. "Where's Arturo and Adrian."

Cory looked out past her shoulder. The station perched rather precariously on the edge of a hill. If a person were to go over the curb away from the road, he would find himself rolling through scrub on the way to a rather nasty ditch filled with blackberry bushes. It was a favorite haunt of some of the more…unwashed fey.

"Looking for their cat in the bushes." She said dryly. Green watched her shudder, and looked at her sharply. "Renny is a friend." She said hoarsely. "Mitchell...Mitch...well, Renny loved Mitch." She met Green's eyes, and he could see the toughness that had held her up waiver, then fall. "Please help her. All she ever...she's never had...she needs you guys. She signed on so someone would have Mitchell's back. She needs...she needs you to have her back." She looked away then, deliberately shifting the hose so that Green would have to move. He watched diamonds tremble on her lashes, move down, taking a heavy dose of make-up with them. And could think of nothing to say. Drawing on the resources he saved by riding the motorcycle instead of walking the twenty-five or so miles from home, he *moved*. To Cory, it must have looked like magic, he thought, but he could tell without looking that she never looked up from the power hose, as it finished obliterating what was left of Mitchell Hammond.

He expected Adrian and Arturo to be pounding through the bush, but as he tripped over a crouching, listening Arturo and threw a high velocity tumble into a blackberry bush he realized that both his captains were smarter than their general.

"Jesus..." He heard Arturo swear. Coming from a mostly Catholic country, Arturo had no problem mixing Christianity and pagan origins. Gods were gods after all. "Green, brother man, you okay?"

"Peachy." Green snapped, pulling thorns out of his waist length braid. His skin was tough—he'd started out as a wood elf, after all, but still, lots of little scratches could *hurt*. And the leathers, of course, were going to need to be brushed.

Arturo blinked for a minute, and a reluctant laugh was forced from him. "What the fuck were you doing?" Arturo stretched his body out of the bushes—he was wearing what looked like borrowed sweats on the bottom and nothing on top, and to Green's relief he wasn't covered in gore. Cory, he surmised, had stepped in, and Green was grateful. Arturo was six feet, four inches tall—which was tall for a Mexican, but short for an elf. Even so, Green always felt a trifle diminished when standing next to his second—Arturo could have been a leader of his own territory, and a damned fine one, but for reasons known only to Arturo, he chose to stay in NorCal. He chose to stay with Green.

Green chuffed, bit back his pride, grinned ruefully. "I was planning to shift through the bushes quickly—I *wasn't* planning to shift right over you, mate."

Arturo twisted a smile. "My plan was better."

Green nodded. "Damned straight, it was…any sign of her?"

"I'm right here." Both elves jumped, and turned to see Adrian walking towards them through the star thistle, holding Renny against his side. Adrian too was clean and wearing sweats too tight on his bottoms and nothing on the top. His chest was cleanly muscled, and Green found himself wondering when Adrian had started working out. "I heard Green crash and knew it was safe." She murmured. Green held out his arms and she rushed to him.

The preternatural community in NorCal was pretty large, in relation to other areas of the States—Green had between two and three thousand people under his aegis at any given time. But his job was to protect them all—any one of his children could have rushed to him like that, buried him or herself under his chin and burrowed next to his skin. However, Green had a soft spot for Renny.

Mitchell Anderson had become a were-cat by accident—his brother, who had become one on purpose, had been a habitual drug user—and a slob. Mitchell, at fifteen, had picked up a dirty needle and the ability to turn into a 180 lb. tabby cat when the moon was full—or when he was angry, or when he was aroused, or when it was dark and he just felt like eating mice. Renny had been in love with Mitchell since the two had been in second grade. She'd been the teacher's pet, the good girl, and he'd been the bad boy who'd loved her. When he began his career as a rather bemused were-kitty, Renny had been the only person to not dismiss his behavior changes as too much drug use. Once he'd trusted her with the secret, she gave herself to him—unconditionally, taking his change as her own, and they'd been inseparable ever since. She'd given up dreams of college for Mitchell, dreams of a white wedding and a perfect home. And she never once looked back. She and Mitchell had made a life for themselves living on menial jobs and a lot of faith, and Renny never once looked back. Green, who knew that sidhe living almost anywhere but in Nor Cal would have dismissed people like Renny and Mitchell as peasants, had learned enough in his 1800 years to be both humbled and awed by love like that.

Renny wrapped herself into Green's arms, whispering "safe…Mitch we're safe…" against his chest and Green's heart cracked in two.

They couldn't untangle Renny from Green long enough to put her on the back of the bike, so Adrian drove them in Arturo's Caddy while Arturo waited for Cory's shift to end at dawn. Green watched covertly from the back of the car as Adrian and Cory said good-bye, shamelessly listening to their conversation with senses far sharper than a mortal would suspect.

"I worry about you, every day." She said, her delicate, freckled face scrunched a little. "I can't...you *die* in my arms, Adrian—you're so vulnerable..." She turned away. Dashed a hand across her eyes, and turned back to him, looking cranky at the same time she brushed ink stained fingers across his bare shoulder. Even from his distance, Green could see Adrian's skin rippling in reaction, his pulse throbbing (too weakly, he noted) in time with hers. "We're too new," she was saying, "...and I'm too alone, and you're too precious to me to have to hose you out of your basement before the cops get there, okay, Adrian? You say Green's your guy—well you make sure he knows that you are fucking *important*. Got it?"

Green had known Adrian for over a hundred and fifty years, and he had never seen that curve to Adrian's neck or that softness to his jaw aimed at a mortal before—man or woman.

"He's got my back, Corinne Carol Anne..." Adrian was saying gently...and now Green had to fight not to turn away, because he knew what Adrian was going to say, and it was intensely private, and it was about *him,* Green and Adrian, and the mortal had become very important to Adrian and Green didn't want to see this hurt him.

"Me and Green—we're...we go back, right?" Adrian was saying. "He takes care of people. And I love you so he'll take care of you." Green sighed. Not too much revelation. Not yet. Good. Adrian could still lose her—and Green didn't think even *he* could help with that sort of pain.

Cory murmured something else into Adrian's chest, but Green had turned away now, and was watching the moon set. Arturo came up next to the window and murmured, "That wasn't nice."

Green swallowed, looked up at Arturo's inscrutable face, nodded. "It's my job, mate—make sure you all don't endanger yourselves—or your hearts."

"Certainly." Arturo agreed, "But that wasn't why you were listening."

"What would you have me say, Arturo?" Green snapped. "It's never been that way, with Adrian and me—you know that. It's the nature of my job—and he's always had others."

"But not this time."

"But not this time." Green agreed. "I'll...I'll miss him, that's all." Arturo nodded, wisely silent, and the two of them tried studiously to ignore the last of the goodbyes between the two new lovers.

They couldn't see the sun yet, but the air had the smell of dawn as they drove, so Adrian gunned the motor through the thick morning of the foothills. Renny had fallen asleep even before they'd left the station, and Green intended to make sure she stayed that way for a good twenty-four hours. But that brought up another problem. The silence in the car had been troubled, tense with things both men knew but neither wanted to talk about, but Green breached it anyway.

"Adrian, mate, you eaten yet?"

"Shit." Which meant no, apparently. "That's why we were meeting Mitch and Renny in the first place."

"It's all good, Adrian, I don't mind."

There was a quiet. Green hadn't let Adrian feed off him in years—most sidhe felt it was somehow perverted, because vampires and fey so rarely met, much less mated, and Green tried hard to keep the peace between the vampires and the elves. But they were alone now, and ever astute, Green had noticed Adrian's pallor. If Adrian didn't feed before he slept, he'd wake up drained and hungry—not hungry to the point of being crazed, not hungry like a newly bled vampire who was likely to feed on his own family, but still, they all needed to think, and when nightfall came again, Adrian wouldn't have time to chase his dinner all over the foothills in an attempt to get satiated before he got down to business.

But there was more to it than that. Feeding was an act of intimacy among vampires, often related to sex and lovemaking. Although Adrian had frequent lovers, and was considered, by mortal standards, to be promiscuous sexually, he *only* fed from friends or lovers. Unless driven by need, Adrian was rarely a promiscuous feeder. Fairy blood, elfin or otherwise was rich, ambrosia for a vampire, not iron based, as humans, but sugar based, like the sap of strong young trees. For Green to offer, when he *never* offered, was a gift. It was a parting. It was a benediction.

The caddy spun quickly through the winding of hwy 49—less windy now than it had been even five years before, when three summers of dust and roadwork yielded roads a little easier on the queasy stomach, and Green found himself in a half-dream on the final stretch of road. In his mind's eye, he saw a boy more than a hundred and fifty years before, nineteen, imprisoned, a concubine for the captain of one of the vast wooden ships sailing the sea. Green himself had been an émigré, eager to flee the thinning forests of Great Britain for the promised gold of California. He'd hoarded his energy for years, a scrap of worship, a drop of honey at a time, in order to escape Oberon's grasp, and in the end, he'd managed to make it across by the simple method of exporting lime trees—a source of power for elves on their own— to a land inhospitable to such niceties. The captain had been *very* solicitous when Green had offered the profit of two trees of the freight in exchange for sleeping on the roof of the cabin instead of the stinking quarters below, even to the extent of offering his boy to Green.

And that was when Green had decided the man had to die. Because the boy was filthy, starved, chained like an animal, ready to be raped at the captain's beck and call. He'd outgrown his "girlish" looks long before, and what glared out of a mat of what should have been white-blonde hair was very old, very adult, and very *very* bloodthirsty. Keeping his face expressionless as he accepted the captain's offer was one of the hardest things Green had ever done.

That night Green showed up to the sunless hold where the creature was kept with food, a bucket of water, and a suit as fine as his own. The boy—a slave as long as he could remember—didn't hesitate to gulp the food in savage, ripping bites, and he submitted to the bath as any good slave should.

And then Green seduced him. He started by combing his hair, which, untangled, hung to his waist. He pulled the strands between his fingers, smelling them fresh from the lavender scented soap he'd brought with him, and waited until they were dry enough to cascade across his arms. And still, the boy sat, glaring, waiting for the force, the penetration, the violation.

Green didn't oblige. He bathed him again, this time using the warm water he'd heated at the room's small brazier during the first, rougher bath—the boy needed another— but he also needed to see that Green was no threat. And this time Green was blatant. He touched the boy tenderly, his hands soft, and he kissed the places he'd touched in a whispery, tormenting way that only the fey could achieve. He teased the sensitive places on the body, waiting for him to ask for more, and never making him beg. At first it was slow going. Over ten years of slavery had taught the boy to ask for nothing at all. But Green was skillful—the fey often are. He was gentle when touching the boy's manhood—he made it thrust, made it pound, made it *prove* its masculinity, and then he allowed the boy his way with Green's body. He was brutal at first, but Green didn't mind pain. The point was, Green allowed him, and that meant the boy could heal. That was what Green did, after all, heal with his sex. And as the boy's anger worked its way through their sex, the anger changed, morphed, became passion. And, an eternal surprise to Green, what had started has healing, and turned into violation, finally became love.

There were immortals who allowed themselves to decay often know *nothing* but debauchery and sensual pleasure, but Green was not one of those. He'd had countless lovers in his life (most of them female)—and he had *loved* all of them, in his immortal way. And Green admired courage. One look from those angry, sky colored eyes and Green was lost. One night with Green showing him love as he had never had it, and the boy was found.

As the sun rose that morning, Green held a boy in his arms as he climaxed, and loved a man as he wept with the joy of pleasure and freedom.

When Adrian had sobbed himself dry, the two plotted how to keep that freedom. And of course they planned revenge…

Green's memories were disturbed when he heard the tires of the Caddy crunching on the white gravel of his road. The front door opened and the black leather seat in front of him tilted forward, allowing him to maneuver Renny into Adrian's arms. She didn't want to go, clinging stubbornly to Green's leather shirt until he overbalanced and ended up sprawled gracelessly on the gravel while Adrian knelt next to him and looked into her frantic eyes and willed her to sleep in that deliciously subversive way that vampires have. When she had quieted, boneless and inert, Adrian stood and took her from Green so that he could at least stand up. They deposited her in one of the many spare bedrooms—this one next to Green's own room so that he could hear her if she woke. By mutual consent, they collapsed onto the sofa in silence.

A minute passed, then two. Looking out into the canyon the two men could see the sky lighten, just a fraction. Dawn was coming. For Adrian, Death was tiptoeing through that window on were-cat's toes.

"If you're hungry," Green said at last, "It'd better be now." Because now, with Cory, moments had come to mean something to two men who were accustomed to not notice the passing of years.

Adrian moved then, breathing softly, covering Green's body with his own and tracing Green's pulse as it beat against the skin of his neck. Green looked up into those smoke colored eyes with a sense of joy and a sense of loss, so bitterly commingled that he couldn't tell which one was causing his eyes to water.

"You're sure this is okay, mate? I could wait until tonight—Cory'll be here, and I haven't fed from her lately…

Green shook his head, arched his back and pressed his fluttering carotid against Adrian's incisor. Adrian sighed, happy, and the motion caused him to sink softly into Green's sweet flesh. The ichor began to flow, and Adrian began to suckle. Their bodies tightened against each other, convulsively, hardening, heaving, as the act of feeding rose to its climactic conclusion, and then shuddered in completion.

They were still for a moment, their breaths blending in time. Adrian chuckled, giddy, Green knew, from feeding off Elven blood. "Shit, Green…I don't have time to shower…"

"Let me." Green asked, pulling the hair—shorter, now than it had been, cut to layer and to curl, but still stunning in its paleness—from his lover's face.

Adrian was one hundred and sixty-nine years old. He had enjoyed count-less lovers, and every form of pleasure imaginable. And still, the blush was in character. "Aww, gees, Green…"

Green chuckled at his discomfiture. "We don't have time to talk about it, mate…but she 's a nice kid…and if you're fixing to keep her for a while," meaning forever, "…no—don't interrupt, I saw the first mark, even if she didn't—then let me do this for you. Consider it a wedding gift."

Adrian all but giggled at that, and Green noted over his shoulder that the sky was increasingly light. With a sudden move, that cost him most of his energy reserves he *shifted,* pulling Adrian in his arms with him as he leapt off the couch and blurred down the hall to the darkling quarters.

Green's hallway veered from the Eastern facing windows directly north, directly west, directly south, and directly west again, straight into the hill upon which the house was built. Nearly twice the size of the outward portion of the house, the "darkling" began midway through the hallway, so that, even if the entire house sheared off the side of the mountain—taking a good por-tion of earth with it into the canyon— there was no way that a vampire in the quarters would be disturbed and destroyed by their deadliest enemy. In fact, if Adrian had been truly careless, he still would have been safe after the first turn in the hallway, and Adrian was *never* careless.

Green carried his friend down the hall easily—preternatural beings as a whole seemed to come with preternatural strength— and set him down gently in the bathroom, his back against the wall, leaning his head on the closed toilet. As he ran the bath, Green noticed the small changes to Adrian's bathroom that spoke volumes—make up, lots of it, rinsed underwear, a neatly folded pile of jeans and T-shirts that *could* have belonged to a man, but they were sized for someone smaller, and rounder than most men. Cory had been here, already, then, in his absence. He fought off the twinge of jealousy, and went to help Adrian undress, but Adrian had noticed the direction of his glance.

"One of the town girls I dated a while back died, earlier this week—I don't know what from. I don't think it was drugs, but I can't tell, you know? Cory found her body in that hollow below the gas station—she's sensitive—she *saw* Arturo, and then others, and then knew me—really knew me. I'd been hitting on her for weeks, Green, and she kept saying no, and I got interested and then I realized that there was more to her than I'd ever looked for in a girl, and then she found Kim..." He'd been blathering, still drunk on faerie blood, and now he just stopped.

"And..." Green prompted, shucking off his friend's pants and giving him a hand in the tub.

"And nothing. And she left me out of it completely to the cops. I don't even think *she* knew why at the time, but when I asked her, she looked all surprised, and then her eyes got big, and...and *dammit,* Green, she believed the best in me. I hadn't given her any reason to...but she knew, without me defending myself, she just *knew* that I hadn't done it. The only person on the planet to ever give me that, Green, was...was you..."

Adrian looked up at Green, his face more naked and helpless than his body even, and Green found himself smiling gently. "It was destiny, mate. She'll be okay, then. If she can love you like that, given so little, then you'll be fine." Adrian looked down at the water, relieved, and smiled back up at Green, his whole heart, his whole incorruptible soul in that smile, and a comfortable silence born of a hundred and fifty years of companionship fell in the little yellow tiled bathroom.

By the time Green had laid Adrian in his bed, and shut the reinforced door, Adrian had cried out in pain and gone limp in Green's arms, and the first ray of sunshine had flooded the front window of the living room.

Green woke up a couple of hours later, startled by screaming. In a blur he rushed to Renny's room, only to find Renny was still out cold. Still disoriented, he ended up in the living room to find Cory rocking herself and sobbing in the middle of the sunshine streaming gloriously in through the window.

He stopped, abruptly, not knowing how she'd receive him, and she glared up from under a shock of dyed black hair with brownish roots, mascara running down her face in gloppy streams.

"I'm sorry." She muttered, but she didn't sound sorry. She shouldn't, he realized, part of him amused. Her screams had been genuine, and so had her sobs. Brave girl, strong girl. Good, he thought, nothing less for Adrian.

"Don't be." he told her, still balancing on the balls of his feet. "You had a shock last night, there's no shame there." Green was his people's leader, he gave them punishment, livelihood, and succor. It was all he could do not to comfort the short, plump human crouching on his sofa.

Her mouth was full, and it twisted a little, almost as bitter as Adrian's had been, all those years ago. "Sure there's not. That's why I'm out here, and not back with Adrian, right? Because I'm so fucking brave." There was self-loathing there, and Green knew exactly where it came from. He couldn't stand there at the entrance to his hallway for another moment.

His weight sank into the couch at Cory's feet, and she eyed him, not with suspicion, exactly, but with a carefully neutral expression that twisted his heart. She may not look at Adrian that way, but Adrian, it seemed, was her only exception. This child was injured, hurt in her still beating, human heart and Green's whole being screamed to comfort her.

"I started as a wood-elf, you know." He said after a moment. She looked at him, startled, and he realized that he'd mistaken the shade of her eyes. In the washed out lights of the gas station, they had been a muddy hazel, but here, surrounded by sunshine and warm wood, they were really a stunning shade of green. Grass green, Ireland green. Ah, *Adrian—you're choice will be my undoing.* "I like cool greenery—I probably would have been more comfortable in Canada, but there were too many French émigrés in Canada, and I didn't want to impose. Adrian, also, needed somewhere to hunt, and there seemed to be a plethora of vampires there, also, and he was too new, too powerless, to subject himself to all of that. But I like sunshine, and trees, and Adrian wanted to see gold—real gold, and power, and so we ended up here."

"How long ago was that?" She asked, her voice barely there.

"That was back in 1849. We've been here ever since." He kept his voice neutral, but he still saw her flinch.

"That's as long as Adrian's been a vampire..." a laugh escaped her, and it was not a happy sound.

"It's pretty young for a vampire." Green assured her. Tentatively, he reached out and pulled some of her hair from her eyes. She didn't seem to notice.

"How young is it for a wood elf?" She asked, surprising him.

"Embryonic." He responded. "I'm more than ten times that old...if that's even a math problem."

"I don't think my calculus teacher would approve." She murmured, and this time her smile was a little more real. Her face was heart shaped, and her lips were full. Green's heart thumped, his blood ran a little faster, and he felt his eyes sheen with tears. *Dammit, Adrian—she's so young.*

"We won't tell him." Green smiled back. "But the point is, I've been alive for nearly two-thousand years, and I don't sleep in the darkling. I don't stay with Adrian, and I don't stay with the other vampires in the kiss. It's not cowardice, Cory. It's love. We don't like to remember those we love as corpses. For the day, that's what Adrian is—it's not fair to expect yourself to want to stay with him."

There was silence for a moment, then she twitched her head sideways, enough to make complete eye-contact, and Green was startled yet again. It was a very shrewd and perceptive gaze she turned his way.

"People we love—you love him, don't you?" She asked.

Elves weren't allowed to lie—none of the Goddess creatures could, not even the were-creatures or vampires. It was more than a point of honor with them—untruths resulted in nausea, headaches and overall wooziness. But since they all had to disguise themselves from the human world, they *were* very good with evasion. "Over a thousand beings of every kind report to me, Cory. I love them all."

"But you're not their lover." She said bluntly, and as tired and as heartsick as he was, he still evaded once more.

"You'd be surprised." He said dryly. Obviously Adrian had not explained the intricacies of Green's rule here in the foothills.

She gave him a droll look, and he re-evaluated that assumption. "I mean lover, not healer." She responded without flinching.

"There's not much difference here." He said evenly.

"It's been a shitty night." She said mildly. "Please don't split hairs."

He had enjoyed sparring, but she was right. "What is it you want to know?" He said finally.

"You and Adrian have been true lovers for a long time." She said again, and in spite of her youth, Green couldn't have denied her a straightforward answer. Goddess, she was relentless.

"Very much so." He replied, and looked sideways at her to see how she would react. Green liked to call anything North of Marin County the Northern California Bible Belt—it was a very conservative area—redneck country. And Cory was so very obviously home grown—he worried—desperately—how she would take that information. Would she reject Adrian out of hand because Adrian and Green's idea of love differed radically from her own? He so much didn't want to see Adrian hurt. And after two minutes with the girl, he so much didn't want the same for himself.

She smiled a little, put her hand on his arm, leaned into him. "Good." She said quietly. "Cause it sucks to be alone…"

Green wrapped his arms around her then. His relief at being able to offer comfort was a tangible thing, seeping from his body, and his happiness that she would let him was contagious. Not surprisingly she began to tremble.

"Renny loved Mitch so much." She whispered against his chest. "So much." And slowly, her body was taken over by sobbing as powerful as the surf, and almost as rhythmic. Green held her against his bare chest, soothing, her, whispering to her of green things, and wildflowers, and bright sunny days with cool breezes, and peace.

They fell asleep there on his white brocaded couch. When he tried to move she whimpered and clung, much as Renny had done, but Adrian wasn't there to seduce her with his gaze so Green ended up staying. She was plump in his arms, and young, and pleasing, he remembered thinking once, so he clung to her in turn, and slept until early afternoon. He awoke when Arturo shook his shoulder, and he looked up into his friend's whirling eyes groggily, trying to put things together.

"Renny…" he asked softly…

"Still sleeping." Arturo confirmed. "I just woke up, but I thought we should talk while…"

While the innocents were sleeping. And that included Adrian. Adrian had been Green's friend longer than Arturo, but Arturo was an older being altogether, stronger, and more able to lead. Adrian had been a child without a childhood when Green had found him, and Green's experience—and financial finagling—had allowed him a hundred and fifty years of deprived childhood. He may have called Adrian a second, but all three men knew who would take over should anything happen to Green.

Green nodded and disentangled his body from Cory's, rolling smoothly over the back of the couch. He was naked—as he always was when he slept, and hoped Cory had been too distraught to notice. Arturo had been around too long to care.

Green padded around his kitchen, snagging a piece of fruit here, a glass of milk there, and then he rummaged under the counter to pull out a bag of trail mix, which he began to shovel into his mouth ravenously. After a couple of mouthfuls he smiled sheepishly at Arturo and nodded towards his bedroom, shaking his tangled hair out of his eyes. It itched at him, his hair, but when he'd awoken he'd been starved of energy, both from his exhaustion the day before and from being Adrian's snack. He shook his head again and sat himself cross legged on his bed, nodding to Arturo who straddled a chair by Green's desk.

Green closed his eyes blissfully and crunched another mouthful— trail mix had been around forever…but whoever had added M&M's to the mix of fruit and nuts had been divinely inspired.

"Wha' 'oo fin' ou'?" He mumbled around his breakfast.

Arturo looked at him, exhaustion dulling the brilliance of his copper-blue eyes, and incongruously enough, smiled, showing the two silver crescents that capped his teeth.

"Rough night, brother?" He asked.

Green smiled back, his cheeks still full, and swallowed. "It is when you're dinner." He replied, following up with another mouthful of food. Arturo just shook his head and sighed, standing up abruptly and moving around the room as he spoke. "I went out to Folsom, where Raymond lives, to see if Mitch had been there the night before—no dice." Arturo picked up Green's favorite wooden comb and sat behind him, tsking impatiently when Green tried to turn around again. He continued talking, while Green ate in bemusement. Arturo's proclivities were strictly hetero—although he passed no judgments whatsoever. His taking the moment to do something as intimate as brush Green's hair was a gift. Much like Adrian's feeding the night before. Green, fearless leader, was being handled—cosseted even. It was odd, that, and a little irritating, but mostly full of the wryness of warm fuzzies. Arturo had been some sort of minor god, in Mexico, around the same time Green had been born. It wasn't often that a minor god waited on a minor wood elf, voluntarily, out of loyalty and even a macho sort of affection. Green would have died before he rubbed it in Arturo's face.

"I couldn't find Mitch's brother, Ray—I couldn't find their room-mate. I couldn't find *any* of the kitties. Hell, I couldn't even get their freaking cell phone numbers, Green. The whole lot of them...just vanished."

Green felt his stomach turn, the trail mix sitting there for a moment like cold gravel. "Did you check...basements...shrubbery...sidewalks...that sort of thing mate?"

He heard his second draw a deep breath, hand Arturo's next few passes through his hair were not exactly gentle.

"No." Arturo said after a moment. "But it would have been hard to miss."

"Right." There was quiet for a moment. Arturo made to plait the hair, but Green shook his head.

"I'm showering in a bit—don't trouble yourself." Pause. "Thanks, mate."

"De nada." Arturo replied, returning to his original place, straddling Green's office chair. Green resumed his dogged munching, now more because he knew he needed the energy than because his stomach was doing much in the way of demanding.

"Did you see *anything*...anything at all?"

Arturo shrugged, laughed a little, wry and helpless. "Just a bunch of flyers for a rock band—one of those little local ones, you see them stapled all over telephone poles downtown. A few for *Giant Pussy*—Elvis' band." Elvis was a were-cat as well—he and Mitch had been infected by the same needle. They had both loved the irony of the dirty joke. "A few for Raymond's club, and a whole lot for some band called *Sezan.*"

Green choked, spraying peanut bits everywhere.

"Jesus bleeding Christ, mate...give me that name again?"

Cory

Sidhe wakes in confusion.

I woke up completely when I heard Green spit up peanuts all over his bed. I'd been halfway there when Arturo woke him up, but I didn't want to make things awkward, and they would have been if he'd been aware that I was aware that he wasn't wearing a goddamned thing.

For someone who'd just lost her virginity four days before, recognizing someone else's perfect body was *not* kosher.

But to my credit, I hadn't known nor cared the night before, and all Green had *ever* offered me was comfort, and shit on fire, did I need some comfort.

I didn't have many friends. Renny and Mitch topped my short list. I wondered if Mitch ever knew that I bought the special roses—the three dollar ones, with vases and ribbons and everything—and passed them off as the cheapies. It was worth a few bucks out of my pocket. Mitch's expression was so heartbreaking when he made his 'secret' purchase, and Renny's smile, when she got her flower, would have shorted out the sun.

I'd had to hose Mitch's innards out of Adrian's hair, and Arturo's as well. Adrian had been eating people for one and a half centuries. Arturo was some sort of Aztec god, who'd had virgins sacrificed to him and everything and both of them looked on the verge of tears, on the verge of throwing up. I passed right over the verge and puked all over the bloodied concrete, and the two of them had held me up, and kept me from sinking to my knees in the gore.

Mitchell Anderson had been a recovering drug addict, a high school drop out, and, some would say, a four time loser. But he had loved in a way that few men have the purity of soul to achieve, and he was my friend. I had mourned him last night, and I had mourned my own innocence, because now I knew I lived in a world where someone that sweet could die in an explosion of blood and gore that no one should ever have to see, let alone experience. And Adrian had been dead when I needed him most, and Green had not.

Adrian had been dead. I didn't even realize I loved him until, six nights ago, I realized that I would believe in him. Lie for him. Trust in him. And now the thought of Adrian dead had me completely unglued.

But it had been worth it. He had kissed me that first night—carefully— delicately around the fangs, and while my heart was still thudding in my ears with it he had taken my blood. I thought that touch couldn't get any better than that, but then the next night we'd made love and I discovered it could.

Just laying there on Green's absurdly fine couch I found myself squirming with the memory. His skin had been white as marble, clean and soft over hard muscles. Touching him had made me feel honored, and the way he touched *me*...I had never believed I was all that. I had never believed I was special. But if Adrian could touch me like that, could weep tears of blood while his body moved in mine, could clutch me to him as though I would save his soul, then maybe there was some truth to the idea that there was something in me that all the mortals in my life had been unable to spot.

But knowledge like that, from someone immortal, like Adrian, does come at a price. Adrian kept me up all the next night. In the first hour there had been, ever so slightly, pain, and blood—blood he'd licked from my thighs in a way that made me not care about shedding it. Then there was pleasure, and intensity, and, after a while, fun. Laughter. Joy. We'd bathed together, and he'd slid into still rumpled sheets that smelled of our sex, but he wouldn't let me follow.

"You'd best go, luv." He said, a tiny frown wrecking that "leave it or lay it" expression he habitually wore. "This freaks most girls out—and I want you to come back."

I'd been surprised. I'd told him that I loved him. I thought he would know that I meant it, so I was hurt when I told him I'd stay.

"Promise me." He said. "Promise me, then, that even if this is it, that you don't want to see me after this, that you'll at least tell me. That you just won't let me think that I have you, and then pretend you don't know my name?"

He was agitated, serious, that perfect face anxious and young. I promised him, smiling, bent to the bed to seal the promise with a kiss. But even as our lips brushed, the sun rose, and Adrian died.

I felt it, that moment when his soul left his body. I felt it blow through me. For a moment I saw with his eyes as it went, saw our bodies together, his in bed, almost artfully arranged, mine static, kneeling by him, stunned.

It never occurred to me, even as I trembled, wept, and fled from the room, not to return to him the next night. It didn't occur to me once not find my way back to Green's enormous house and make my way through the basement to the nest of rooms buried in the mountain. It never crossed my mind to not be there standing over his bed, even as he awoke. It didn't occur to me that we wouldn't make love frantically then, before he drove me on the back of his Harley, to my job. Not once did I think of regretting that I loved a vampire, and that I'd let him take me in every way he could.

But I finally knew why he would ask.

A noise from the hallway broke into my thoughts, and before I could even sit up, I was surrounded by three figures that, in my wildest dreams I wouldn't have imagined.

One of them was, surprisingly familiar—and close up, he was just like Green—impossibly beautiful, fine boned, pointed ears that it seemed only I could see, and eyes so wide apart and so large that he was obviously something other than human. His knee length braid was black, and his lips were thin and cruel, but if Adrian said Green was a high elf and a sidhe, then so was this guy. He laughed at me, and the sleep still in my eyes, before I could even focus on his face. I knew him, though—I'd seen him once, that night outside the station—and I'd never forget Adrian's hand, resting on his hair.

The one in the middle was everything the tall one was not. He was short, misshapen, his face brown with broken blood vessels networking his nose and cheeks, and lumps of flesh that made his features look like a Picasso painting. He had hair like dirty cobwebs, and you could see patches of stained scalp peeking through. His back was hunched, and his flesh between his chest and his (eek!) large groin was folded over and over again, like a stack of pancakes. I could see this because the only creature of the three standing around

Green's couch who was wearing any clothes at all was the third one, and she wasn't wearing much.

She must have been a pixie, because she was as short as the misshapen goblin man next to her, but she was perfect—violet haired, delicate, proportional, exquisite. She was wearing a lacy slip thing, and if I were still in high school, I'd guess she'd be a total snob, but now, watching my reaction to the three of them around the couch, her expression was kind.

The short, ugly man began to snuffle me. I didn't make a sound, but I backed myself against the couch, trying not to be frightened. It felt like a dog or a cat, making friends, and I was not even surprised when he backed up and grimaced at the tall, beautiful one. "Green." He said, nodding certainly, but the tall one narrowed his eyes, and looked at me with a barely contained fury. He knew, I thought. He knew that I should not smell like Green at all. As though it were a formality, he bent at the waist to put his nose almost directly in my crotch—I suddenly regretted taking my jeans off and sleeping in one of Adrian's T-shirts and my little girl's cotton panties. I *did* squeak now, but it didn't seem to bother mister "I'm so beautiful I shatter glass."

He stood straight and shook that straight, raven colored mass down his bare back. "Adrian." He said with some authority, and I raised startled eyes to him. He smiled at me, slyly, and I wished that at least Adrian's corpse were in the room so I could crouch over it and snarl *mine.* The short dumpy one looked puzzled, and bent down to sniff me again. I brought my knees up to my chin, wrapped the afghan that Green had draped me with tight around my body and snapped "Adrian."

They looked at me in surprise—it talks!!! "Adrian and I..." I tried gamely. "But something awful happened and Green rocked me to sleep..." And suddenly, that air they had, like tormenting me was just such a hoot, disappeared. The charming little pixie with the purple hair came closer to me and looked distressed.

"Don't mind them." She said, "They've been playing this game almost since Bracken was born." She smiled fondly at the tall, beautiful one, "And Crocken's a bit put out because he was wrong, that's all." And with that she bent to kiss the short, dumpy one on the forehead. To my surprise, he raised his face and caught her mouth in what proved to be a truly embarrassing embrace. The pixie laughed, and sighed, and looked at the ugly, misshapen goblin so besottedly that I found myself taking another look, and then, when his horrific appearance didn't seem to change, I tried their tactic. I closed my eyes and inhaled, through my nose. He smelled like earth. Clean earth, rotting logs, diamond sparkle streams, sunny meadows, and animal haunts. I opened my eyes and found him looking at me shrewdly. I smiled at him, brilliantly, because it was a good smell, and maybe a handsome one as well. Crocken grinned back, through a truly awful set of pointed and dirty teeth, but the smell was still comforting, so I didn't mind.

Bracken shifted somehow, and the look he sent me now was measuring. "What happened." He asked, and his voice was clean and sharp like a knife. Bracken, I was beginning to suspect, was nobody to dick with. I looked involuntarily to Green's room, where, I hoped, Green *hadn't* choked to death and he and Arturo were coming up with a plan.

"I can't tell you." I told them, feeling immeasurably childish. "Green and Arturo…they'll tell you." And I was relieved, heaven help me, because I didn't want to relive it one more time.

The pixie nodded. "That's fine, dear." She said reassuringly, and I realized that for all her sex-kitten appeal, she was doing her best to be maternal. I smiled back at her. Little mama, proud of her six foot six stud-muffin with the voice like steel knives.

"No, it's not." He said after a moment. "She knows why Renny's here alone. Where the fuck is Mitch?" His voice got louder and I stood up right there on the couch and shushed him.

"For crap's sake, shut up. I think Adrian had to spell her last night, and I *know* she needs to sleep for a while before…before she faces the world…" I'd figured this part out for myself—I saw the panicked way she was clutching at Green when they'd gotten into the car, and I knew that nobody slept more than twelve hours without a sedative. Adrian had told me he could do it. He'd *offered* to do it, the night before last, when he'd taken blood from me again, but I wanted to remember. Those fangs, sinking so sweetly into my neck, the total trust of letting him feed…the smell of his arousal as he suckled from me…just the thought of it made my panties wet, all over again. Then Brack started to sniff the air and eye me dubiously, and I realized my mistake. We'd been close—with me standing on the couch we were eye to eye—and suddenly he was a lot closer, and I would have fallen backwards over the couch if he hadn't locked a hand around my waist and locked me to him, my cotton covered crotch to his bare, uncircumcised groin.

"Not good enough." He hissed, and everything I remembered about being a tough bitch came flooding back to me as I brought my knee up to his unprotected balls and grazed them, before slamming my head into his nose.

"Back off, asshole." I grated, trying not to crumple myself as I counted stars, but it was okay, because his nose was bleeding and he was simultaneously trying to hold his arm over his crotch and staunch the flow of blood at the same time. If I hadn't been standing in a house full of supernatural beings that might come and eat me because I pissed him off, I'd find the whole scene absolutely hilarious.

Apparently Crocken and the little pixie-mama didn't have any worries about being dinner, because they had no inhibitions about laughing uproariously. Brack, egged on by his parent's laughter, forgot his pain and lunged for me as I stood up on the very back of the couch and balanced precariously as the whole seven foot brocaded monstrosity threatened to topple. Brack reevaluated my position, and made for another lunge when the couch went over, and I found myself falling gracelessly into a pair of lean, lovely, male arms, and tangling in a whole mess of glorious yellow hair.

"Morning, Green." I grunted into the stillness left by the clattering furniture, and I felt his chest shaking silently with laughter. Next to him, Arturo was not so silent about it. Green didn't put me down, and the whole next ten minutes happened while I was held in his strong, masculine arms. I was already wet from thinking about Adrian. Being this close to Green didn't help. Fucking groovy.

"Morning Corinne Carol Anne." He replied blandly.

"Call me Cory, Green." I responded in kind.

"I don't think so." He shot back cryptically, and then continued to the three fey I had already met, as well as to others, emerging from the hallway and the stairs after being alerted by the clatter that something was up. "Bliss, go check on Renny, would you?" He nodded to the little pixie-mama, who had quickly sobered up when he'd arrived on the scene. "She should be waking up sometime in the next few hours—and we need to talk to her. But Bliss…" she turned to him, raising a perfect brow, "Make sure there's a truckload of tenderloin and a giant cat box for her when she wakes up, because she's going to want to change and she's going to need to eat." Bliss nodded thoughtfully, and Green turned to Arturo.

"How long we have until sunset, mate?"

Arturo looked at the sun and the clock. "Five hours, twenty-two minutes."

"Three-thirty? Crap." I said, "Green, shitfire...I've got to call my parents..." Green's arms locked around me tighter. "It can wait." I squeaked.

Green nodded. "Okay then. Everyone...we have everyone?" He turned his neck and body, and I realized with some surprise that he was naked, holding me in his arms, and talking to what felt like a zillion...well, *people* who had gathered in his living room, in most stages of undress, and nearly all stages of inhumanity. There were beautiful Caucasian ones with long flowing hair, like Bracken and Green, and imposing Latino ones with copper lightning eyes, like Arturo. There were tiny black humanoids with vast afros that appeared to hold beings as large as themselves and ugly, lumpy ones like Crocken. There was a rainbow of pixies, but none of them had Bliss' maternal countenance. Wow—honestly, in the last five days I'd only rushed up the stairs to Adrian's rooms. Just how big was this house?

"Ernie's missing." Said one of the tiny black people. This one had corn-rows down to his?her?heels. The voice was actually larger than the person. "So's Todd, Eve, & Jack."

"Hell." Said Green, as he exchanged a glance with Arturo. "One of you will have to fill them in." There were nods of assent, and Green backed up to the kitchen table so he could make eye contact with the suddenly crowded room.

"There's been a death." He began, and had everyone's absolute attention. Even Bracken stopped glaring at me and holding his balls, and straightened up, putting a Kleenex that pixie-mama gave him to his nose. Green spoke, and what started as an informal gathering became a wake.

"Last night, at the Chevron, Mitch Reynolds, were-cat, Renny's lover, guitar player, friend." He said this list, and the others nodded in time with him, and I felt my eyes water again. He didn't say *junkie*. He didn't say *drop out*. He didn't say *loser*. God, I thought, looking at the various faces of loss, Mitchell had some true friends. I looked up at Green, capturing everyone's attention, making them all feel his pain, and I realized why Adrian was so sure he was safe with Green. Green took this personally. Green loved all these people. Green was theirs—their defender, their leader, and apparently their provider. Suddenly Adrian's status as head vampire in this little dictatorship seemed much less secure, and Green's role in it seemed much more necessary. It didn't bother me that Adrian wasn't head blood-sucker at vampire central, but I wondered if Green realized why Adrian wasn't all that he could be. I don't think it mattered. I looked over my shoulder and saw Arturo, listening to Green's eulogy with rapt, devoted eyes, and knew it didn't. Arturo could have been a god. He chose instead to be Green's right hand man. This was a kind of love I had not reckoned with, and needed to think about, because sure as hell's afire, sleeping with Adrian put me in neck deep with Green.

Green finished speaking for the dead, and began to address the questions evident on every inhuman face. "I don't know how Mitchell died. According to Arturo and Adrian—and Cory, here, he simply exploded." Everyone winced at that. "Everywhere. Cory had to rinse his remains out of the Chevron with a power hose." I felt my gorge rise again, and fought it back. I had thrown up last night and not eaten since. The idea of puking again made me feel light headed. Maybe it was a good thing that Green didn't put me down. "Arturo went to Raymond's place, and the were-kitties were gone, so we need to do a couple of things now, to see what happened. And to balance the scales, if they need it."

Nobody complained, not once. Green had the little ones look after Renny, but made sure that some of the bigger, troll-like creatures would be around when she woke up—he guessed she'd probably change immediately, shock and grief of remembering taking over her intellectual overrides in a heartbeat, and as a hundred and five pound house cat, odds were, she could eat some of the little ones pretty quickly if they weren't sharp about keeping her contained, but the trolls looked purposeful, and, I noted, protective of the smaller ones so I had no worries.

A group of the larger, more human looking ones were to check in with all of the were, fey, and vampire establishments all over the area—Folsom, El Dorado, Nevada City, Colfax, even Truckee and Fort Bragg all had a delegate running down to the garage to pick up a vehicle and blaze out of there. Before they left, Green added something that disturbed us all.

"Okay—people, while you're out there, keep your eyes and ears open for the name *Sezan*. Got it? It's an old name, and it could be hunting for Adrian and me…if you hear it, *don't* reveal yourself, yes?" They nodded, serious, and Green reinforced that they protect themselves first, and himself and Adrian second. "And people…" His self confidence faltered for a moment, his eyes tried to look down, but I was in his line of sight, and I caught the frustrated, wry look he gave himself when he remembered he was still holding one hundred and forty pounds of little old me and had to look up again. "People…I'd take it as a personal favor to me that you don't mention this name to Adrian until I have a chance to do so…nothing off the cuff, nothing in the hallways…I need to tell Adrian first, yes?" They all nodded, some of them cast surreptitious glances at me, but they all nodded their full appreciation of what he was asking. My heart warmed a little. So they all loved Adrian too. Very, very, cool. But now Arturo, Green, and I all had a secret from Adrian. Very, very not cool.

The room cleared out, and there I was, caught in a sex elf's arms until he put me down again. He stood lost in thought until I started to tickle his ear to get his attention.

"What, Corinne Carol Anne?" He asked me, still thinking hard.

"So I'm Cory to them and my whole biblical nightmare of a name to you?" I asked annoyed. I didn't expect an answer—Arturo and Adrian hadn't given me one—so I just went right on. "Can I get down now, Green? Brack's left the room, and I don't think anyone else is going to pound the shit out of me, so I can pretty much fend for myself." He snorted, and looked down at me wryly.

"You can pretty much fend for yourself on any level." He replied, setting me on my feet. To my humiliation my legs threatened to buckle, and he scooped me up again and nodded to Arturo. Arturo started rooting through the refrigerator as Green righted the couch with his foot and set me down on it.

"You haven't eaten, you lost most of your lunch last night, and you've been a steady donor for a good week." Green assessed after he'd sat himself on the love seat adjacent to the couch. "You need food, you need sleep, and you need Adrian to leave your pretty neck alone for the week…he can feed other places."

I scowled at him, even though he was right at that last part. "He doesn't, like…" I flushed, "He doesn't have to sleep with everyone he feeds with, does he?" I hadn't had the nerve to ask Adrian this—so much seemed to be off limits with Adrian.

Green shook his head no. "He will want to be friends—it's an intimate thing, after all, but sex is usually just a side benefit." I flushed some more, but I was satisfied with that. Then Green had to go and throw me a curve ball. "And Corinne Carol-Anne, you're moving out of your house and taking a few days off work."

I was *almost* so angry I couldn't speak. "What the fuck is this, a goddamned cult!" I snapped. "Do I have to shave my head and hang out at airports? I need my job you asshole…besides—it's *my* job. And my parents…" I trailed off. I was nineteen. I had been planning to move out as soon as I started State College next year, but that didn't mean Green could dictate to me now.

Green laid a hand on my shoulder, and I felt my thready heartbeat even out. At that moment Arturo dropped a plateful of food in my lap that included sliced ham, sourdough bread, grapes and a small bowl of trail mix. My mouth started watering, and I realized that actually taking a bite of the food on the plate *was* more important that ranting at Green about my loss of freedom. At least until the meal was over.

"This isn't a cult, Corinne Carol-Anne." Green said quietly as I chewed. "But it is a family. You were a witness to a death in our family and we need you here to help. Don't worry about your job...I'll tell Dannin op Creely I need you and he'll let you go for a day or two. Besides—you are exactly where you need to be, at the station, to help us gather information. Just not right now. You need to regroup."

I almost choked. "oo no 'anny?" I asked through a mouthful of ham.

Green's lips twitched. "Well, Corinne, I do own the station, and Dannin is one of ours."

If I had kept chewing then I *would* have choked. It made perfect sense, actually—the little Chevron was in the middle of nowhere. There was no reason for it, no demand—the demographics were all wrong to put a gas station there. And, ever since Arturo had touched my hand over five months ago I had been seeing the odd side of the supernatural—fey, vampires, sidhe, were...all of them seemed to circulate through that Chevron station. I nodded, the whole thing hitting me at once, then resumed chewing. After all, Green was the provider—he owned the house and put food on the table—it made sense that he had an independent source of income. After a moment, I swallowed.

"What about my parents?" I asked. "I mean..." and I blushed. "I mean, it's not like I wasn't spending some time here anyway...but, well Adrian and I hadn't talked, like, commitment...or residence, or anything. I mean...it's obviously the kind of place people can crash for, like, years...but why me?"

Green looked at me frankly, but his next words were evasive. "Because you're useful, Corinne." I must have looked surprised because he went on. "You're smart, you're accepting, you're observant. We need humans on our side—very few of them know about us, and that's good, but it's also a handicap. Whoever did this to the were-cats—they were able to circulate a lot more freely than, say, Crocken or Blissa. There is power in you that not even I know how you will use," I waved this part away, thinking it was that whole 'you are more powerful than you know' hippie new age crap, but the next part hurt unexpectedly. "And you're not going to be working the Chevron forever, are you?"

I looked away, trying to hide my mortification. "What else would I do?" I said quietly, and suddenly Arturo was looming over me like Zeus with lightning eyes.

"You didn't." He thundered at me, and I instinctively moved back against the couch.

"My professor wouldn't take my paper, Arturo." I told him defensively. "I failed the class...I got mad, and just...left. That was, like a week ago. Finals start tomorrow—and all my papers are late."

Arturo stepped back, scowled at me, and did a double take. "A week ago...Kim." I nodded, embarrassed. "You were late to school because the cops held you for questioning about Kim."

"Yeah." I said shortly. "So what?"

Arturo and Green exchanged glances. "So it's our fault." Green said after a moment. "Arturo?"

"I'm on it, Green." Arturo said. Then he turned to me. "I'm making five phone calls, Corinne Carol-Anne, and then you are going to finals tomorrow with your late papers—which will be accepted. The rest is up to you." And he spun on his heel and disappeared.

"Jesus." I breathed, watching him stalk away. "Can he really do that?"

"We can do that." Green told her. "I make quite a bit of money, Corinne, and have quite a bit of pull..."

"And some talent at mind control." I snapped.

"That too." Green agreed. "But I won't use it on you. I'll just tell you the truth. What happened to Kim—yes, Arturo told me—indicates that someone's after Adrian. What happened to Mitch indicates all of my people are in trouble. You're right in the thick of it, and the safest place for you to be is here. Your parents can be pawns against you, and then you can be used against us. I would prefer not to ever put Adrian in that position, wouldn't you?"

I glowered at him. "That's emotional blackmail."

Green smiled gently. "I don't really work like that, Corinne Carol Anne. But I usually do get what I want." And suddenly he was right there, next to me, kneeling by the couch, making me look into his wide-set green shadowed eyes, using his lean fingers to tilt my chin up. "Hey, sweet, it's not so bad as that. You will have autonomy here. And care. And, when you've finished your education, guaranteed employment, should you need it. I know it feels like your life made a left turn somewhere—that's true. But that's what lives do—and once you let Adrian anywhere near your wheel, the vehicle's not going to end anywhere you expected it to, yes?"

Adrian. That's who it came to, wasn't it? I smiled, a small smile. "It s not like there's a shit load of windowless rooms for sale, is there? You're right. My life did take a left turn. I need to catch up, that's all...but you can't tell me what to do all the time, right? I mean...if a girl's going to move out, she's not going to move in with her big brother, right?"

Green laughed, delightedly, and I felt myself warming to my toes. I could see back into his mouth, his even teeth, and the smooth column of his throat. No. Not a big brother at all. "You're a grand girl, Corinne Carol Anne." He said standing, and, thank God, backing his naked self up a step. "We will find ourselves dependent on you, mark my words." He padded towards his rooms and looked back at me. "I'll get some of your clean clothes from Adrian's room, and you can shower first. Then give Arturo an hour of rest, and he'll take you out and about."

"I've got my own car..." I started, and he looked surprised nodded.

"You're right, sweet. I want you and Arturo to run some errands for me and you're right—your car would not be recognized. I've got tending to do here, but I want you both back by dark. Now don't argue...we don't have much time, yes? I want some information before Renny wakes up—and Adrian. And Corinne? You may want to find some time tonight to study for finals." He added before disappearing around the corner.

"I don't need to study." I called out. "I've got those classes nailed." And his delighted laughter faded down the hall.

I didn't need to study, which was a good thing because I didn't have time anyway. Arturo popped up from his nap like it had been straight eight instead of a scant two, and we were on our way. My parents' place in Penryn was first and I wish I could say it was worst.

Arturo pulled into the overgrown field which was flanked by a raw wood fence. They owned at least three acres, but none of it was tended. I had to blink twice because it seemed so far removed from Green's house and my life of the last week that I almost forgot I lived there. When I told the wiry, distracted woman tending the neat garden in back, and the tough, tattooed trucker under the car in the driveway, I couldn't believe I had ever lived there at all.

Mom was thrilled, casting surreptitious glances to where Arturo stood smoking by my little blue Honda. Daddy just stared at him, flat eyed, asking me if that Mexican guy was going to support me. I tried to explain that he was a friend, and that I was just rooming with other friends, and that Adrian was the guy I was dating…nothing washed. They wanted to meet Adrian and they didn't like Arturo, and given Arturo's even gaze I was sure the feeling was mutual. Pretty much all I could do was pack my clothes (a few boxes), the quilt my gran made me before she died, and throw in my boom box, c.d.'s, laptop, books, and a pathetic bunch of stuffed animals that I had accumulated over the last few years. I told my mom I'd be by to visit, and she just got all moony. I told her graduation was in a week and I'd probably be walking—she didn't even hear me.

As Arturo pulled away, past the strung out rows of little houses on big properties, I was pretty sure that it was that indifference that made my eyes water. I stared out the window, watching blindly as the properties became better kept as we approached Auburn-Folsom via the little back roads that I knew and loved, pretty sure he didn't know what was on my mind. I'm wrong a lot.

"They do love you, Corinne." He said after a moment.

"They just don't know me." I murmured, disappointed.

"They will." He said surely. "There will be a time when you will need them, and they will understand."

I turned to him quickly—he looked so *grounded* sitting at the window of the car, I couldn't hardly credit he was really a six-foot South American elf. "What do you know?" I asked, a suspicion tugging at me.

"Very little." He replied, without getting defensive. "But parents of children such as you have been lost and found many times in many years. More often than not, it ends well."

I didn't know what to say to that, so I said nothing. But in an odd way, I felt better. I guess humans don't offer many surprises after 2000 years.

We drove the back roads to Auburn/Folsom road, past the newer strip malls, and took the old bridge over the dam to old town. We weren't going to cruise the new outlet stores, or the spanking new venues that had been built to cater to Intel's veritable city of employees. Our next ten stops were the ten crappiest gas stations in Folsom. I was looking for the same sort of thing I'd seen the night before. At least those were Green's words. The image they conjured wasn't nearly so vague.

"Green doesn't own these, does he?" I asked, the third or so time I ran into a bathroom looking for police lines and too much blood and ran out after finding God knows what. My Chevron was immaculate. We kept the concrete clean, the stupid little flowerbeds in the front cheery and bright, and the bathrooms *spotless.*

"No." Arturo answered, looking balefully out of the car. He hadn't ventured into any of the bathrooms. As of yet I hadn't ask him why—but his look, designed to wither anything within a twenty yard radius—told me something was up.

"Why not?" I asked, slamming the door in a temper. "And why am I doing this and not you?" My car wasn't air conditioned, and the temperature was in the high nineties. I was wearing shorts and a T-shirt, but I could feel my legs sticking to the vinyl seat even as I moved to put on the seat belt. Arturo looked cool and unruffled, which totally pissed me off. But at my comment, he turned a scowl in my direction that told me he felt the same.

"Nobody knows you here." He growled. "And you're mortal. I am not—and anybody who knows about us will know that."

"But you're not happy here in the car…" I asked.

He turned his attention back out to the ragged bushes on the side of the station. "The gas stations and in'n'outs are the perpetual hangouts of the young, the rootless, the night dwellers who have yet to find a home in the night. The young were-cats of our area practically live in these places, Corinne Carol-Anne. They are known to talk to me, to defer to me. You've seen it. You recognized it in Adrian, and even in Renny, Mitch, and the others. If I'm seen looking for these people, they will remember me. They will blame me. And if someone is responsible for this, they will connect me."

"And yet you're here." I said shortly. Just because he was in my car instead of his own didn't make him any less visible.

"Yes." He said mildly. "Green wouldn't risk you with anyone else. Besides, while I'm waiting in your car, my glamour will hold—once I get out, speak, touch hands, it will get harder to maintain. I could do it, but this way is safer."

"Glamour." I echoed, although Adrian had told me what it meant.

He turned to me, smiled, as he started my car. "Look at me, Corinne Carol-Anne—what do you see?"

"A six foot Aztec elf who got his teeth capped." I responded quickly.

I heard his low chuckle. "No—look at me—not who you know I am, but at what I look like."

I tried again, and remembered thinking how grounded he looked as we left my parents place, and I saw it.

I saw nothing. His eyes, instead of being the color of old and new copper, were plain brown. His face was handsome, but in a fading, aging way, not the breath stopping beautiful way I had seen since he'd first entered my store. And his ears weren't pointed anymore. Glamour, I realized, to make him less than glamorous.

"Shit." I breathed. "You're doing that on purpose."

He smiled at me, for a moment letting the glamour drop. "Yes, of course I am…I've worn it all day. I'm surprised you didn't see it come on…but then, you all but forgot my original appearance from the first time Adrian spoke to you." As it hit me that he was right, the glamour reasserted itself, and I saw him looking normal and human beside me. He'd been just that beautiful, I realized, the entire time Adrian was chatting me up in the back of the Chevron. But I hadn't seen it. I'd seen Adrian.

"Can Adrian do this?" I asked, curious.

Arturo shook his head negative, negotiating a tight turn in with my stiff little steering wheel so smoothly I wondered if he could glamorize my car the same way he did to himself. "He can hypnotize—vampires are famous for it. He can make them forget he's fed on a victim, make them want to be fed on. He can put to sleep, or minimize pain, or make somebody think they want him when ordinarily they wouldn't find him attractive." He paused, just long enough to make me wonder. "But he's done none of these things to you."

I smiled a little, a self satisfied, confident smile that I wouldn't have had a week ago. "I know that." I said smugly. "I told him to go piss up a rope for two months. If he was going to fuck with my mind, he would have done it two months ago." But in my mind, that's not what I was thinking. I was thinking of Adrian, his face slack and raw and passionate, and his eyes closed tightly as he bared his body and self to me, taking my body to places it had never been. I was thinking of two tears of blood, rolling down his cheek at my surrender. These things could be faked; I wasn't naïve enough to think that they couldn't. But they hadn't been. I was woman enough, now, to know that for certain.

Arturo looked at me, grinned, and the glamour dropped away for a moment that left me breathless at his beauty. "That's not what you were thinking." He said, his voice both feral and amused.

"I'm not going to ask how you know that." I responded tartly, flushing to the roots of my hair. He said nothing, turned the wheel and pulled into the next stop & rob. When I thought back on this conversation later, I would realize that he never answered the question about why Green didn't own any gas stations in Folsom when he apparently owned at least four in any of the neighboring towns. The scene at the gas station wiped it from my mind.

There were onlookers—there are always onlookers. This time they didn't have anything to look at. There was yellow tape in a giant half circle around the front half of the AM/PM. The reason it wasn't around the whole thing is that the front door and overhang stopped the blood. In June, in our part of the foothills, the stench was overwhelming. And still the people gathered, to stare, white faced, and wonder. I didn't need to stare—I'd seen the whole show first hand.

I had gotten out of the car in order to get a closer look, and I had just spun on my heel to go report to Arturo, when I felt a hand on my shoulder and an unfortunately familiar voice saying "Isn't this a sweet coincidence…Cory, isn't it?"

Oh sweet Jesus. "Officer Johnson?" I asked pleasantly, feeling my palms sweat. "What—don't you have someone else's life to ruin?"

"Don't be dramatic, sweetheart." He said snidely, "Besides—I'm not talking about a goddamned English exam, I'm talking about murder."

"I almost flunked out of school because you kept me for three hours about a drug overdose I knew nothing about…now who's being dramatic, Johnson."

"Yeah." He said, and for the first time a trace of human anger crept into his voice. It made me like him just a little bit more, dammit. "Well this isn't a goddamned drug overdose, and that wasn't either."

I looked at him, surprised and more than a little bit shocked. He looked away, the color over his cheekbones going from olive to dull red. He hadn't meant to say that.

"Well," I said after a moment, "What was it?"

He was still rattled, because he shouldn't have said what he said next, and it was a good thing, because my face must have been a study but he never looked up. "Exsanguination." He said shortly. "Complete blood loss."

"Jesus." I breathed, truly horrified, but not for the reasons he thought. He looked up. "X-files shit." And he nodded, distractedly.

"So's this." He added.

"Who died?" I asked, hoping his distraction and his horror of it would loosen his tongue even more.

"Don't know." He said shortly. "Don't have a body." He looked surprised again, as though he couldn't believe he was saying all this shit to me, but at that moment another officer on the scene hailed him, and as he turned to answer I wriggled out of his hold on my shoulder and disappeared into the crowd.

I jumped into the car and barked at Arturo to drive, only to make him pull over to the side of the road two minutes later so I could throw up.

GREEN

Other Deaths

It was not quite dark by the time Cory and Arturo got back to Green's place, but all hell had already broken loose.

As they stepped off the landing and back into the bright wood and vaulted ceiling of Green's living room, they were almost overwhelmed by the noise. In the fading light of the sunset, the actual sight was even worse. The littles—tiny, usually invisible fey whose powers varied—were chittering in panic and chasing the rock trolls and nymphs, who were in their turn chasing a giant tawny housecat who was carrying another little with the cornrows in its mouth.

Green, who was running into the room even as they entered, noticed the shadows under Cory's eyes, and the grim set to Arturo's mouth as they stood at the entry way, and swore to himself. Another death. He could smell their anguish, and, radiating from Cory, an urgent sort of distress, a question she didn't want answered. And a desperate need for comfort. *Christ, she was young!* He thought, not sure who he as angrier with—Adrian for dragging her into their midst, or himself for feeling his frayed nerves knitting themselves together, just at the thought of being able to once again offer her comfort. But first they had to get the little one away from Renny.

Cory, apparently, had the same idea. She scanned the circus from the doorway, her eyes narrowing in thought, and then she crouched, and waited. When Renny made her next pass around the room, Cory jumped in front of the large tawny mass with her arms outstretched—and was immediately knocked down by one hundred plus pounds of were-kitty. The odd parade that had followed Renny stopped short, plowing into each other when they tried to stop.

But at least Renny stopped. Growling low in her throat, and pinning Cory with her forepaws, she sniffed at Cory's throat, pulled back her whiskers, and hissed around the limp body of the little creature in her teeth. To Green's immense relief, the little lifted her corn-rowed head up, just long enough to wink at Cory, before she again flopped listlessly in Renny's mouth. The relief was short lived, however, when Renny dropped the tiny one, and sniffed again at Cory's throat. A mewling sound, all the animal and none the girl came out of Renny's mouth, and as he inched slowly towards the fragile tableaux, Green could see Cory's eyes tear up. Unobserved by either were-cat or human, the tiny one ran away, and Green moved in to touching distance behind the were-cat.

"We'll all miss him, baby." Cory said hoarsely, and Renny let out a howl that rattled the windows and all but popped the ears of the people in the house. Then she lunged for Cory's throat.

Quicker than sunset, Adrian rushed in, even as Green's stronger than human fingers grasped at the were-cat's fur. In a blur he tackled Renny, pinned her, took her down. Green reached his outstretched hand towards Cory to haul her up, and side by side they could see Adrian, pinning the were-cat with his gaze alone, catching at her humanness with his own inhumanity.

"Renny, dammit, he's *gone*. Gone. Goddess, baby. We can't change that. Now change…***change*** dammit. You've got to feel this like a human…*In the name of the Goddess, Erin Alexis Joyce, you **will** take your human form and grieve.*"

Green could see Adrian's fury—and his outright alarm. His fangs were out, his eyes glowing red, and the strength and the speed of the vampire were on him like a glowing blue aura, but Renny wasn't weak willed as a girl, and wouldn't give in to her grief easily as a were-cat. She howled at him, and Adrian snarled back. Renny pulled her back claws into position underneath Adrian's belly, and Cory's frantic scream of "Renny, no!" rang in the ears of the frightened, gathered assembly of fey and vampire alike. But Adrian was older and wiser than that, and like any good predator, knew how to subdue his prey. His jaw extended, his fangs flashed, and a with groan of hunger, he sank his teeth into the were-cat's jugular, and began to feed. Renny's snarls of rage turned to whimpers of pleasure, and then she began her change. In a shimmer and glow, and a queasy slide of fur to flesh, Renny was naked underneath Adrian, crying out in an orgasm of blood and change and grief. Adrian's frantic suckling stilled then, and he swallowed one last time, and rolled to the side of her, gasping for breath as Green lifted Renny's still spasming body off the floor and into his arms.

With a weak mewl, Renny turned into his chest and began to sob. Green cuddled her and looked at Arturo helplessly. His people needed leadership, they needed Arturo and Cory's information, they needed to plan. And Renny needed him—needed healing that only Green could give, that he was made to give. After the foreplay that Adrian's feeding had given her, she was aching and needy, and craving the healing of flesh that Green excelled at. He looked over at Adrian. That flying tackle had surprised him, as had Adrian's forceful insistence that Renny return to form. It had been strongly and wisely done, that—Green forgot, sometimes, that Adrian was not still the same terrified boy he had met in the hold of that ship.

Adrian was still sprawled and stupid after the climax of feeding, with Cory crouched over him, looking rueful and concerned at once. That question she'd had, hovering around her body like its own entity, had evaporated, but the anguish was still there, temporarily glossed over by her concern for Adrian. Half blind with satiation, Adrian reached out for a hand, and she gave it to him, the other one smoothing that white-blonde hair from his lovely face. The moment made Green's chest hurt, and he turned away, catching Arturo's eye as he did so. Renny made another urgent mewling noise, and Green buried his face in her hair, whispering to her to wait…wait…he would come…

Arturo was at his side in an instant. "I'll be done in an hour or so." Green murmured, "I'll hear your news then. Is Grace here? Good—have her make dinner for everyone—make it formal, downstairs, and tell Adrian that I need his people to feed lightly—we'll need them to hunt tonight."

Arturo nodded, then caught Green's arm as he turned to leave. "The boy did well tonight."

Green grinned and the smile lit the room. Renny's frantic wriggling eased, temporarily, and all eyes, including Adrian's and Cory's, turned towards him before he pivoted lightly and moved from the room.

Over his shoulder he called, "The boy was amazing. He always is."

Green heard Grace careening through the kitchen at top volume over an hour later when he emerged from his bedroom. Knowing Grace—and the mood she was bound to be in, he tried valiantly to just slide down the hallway and not catch her attention. Grace was having none of it—at first sight of him she blurred past her helpers—a gift both vampires and fey had been given—and caught him at the bend of the hallway. She lay hold of his shoulder, and, he was sure, if her temper had had it's sway, she would have lunged for his throat. Considering that Grace was 5'10" of lanky, red-headed vampire, the threat could have been very real.

"It's a good goddamned thing I had shit in the fucking freezer, Green—order a banquet at a moments notice, will you? You let Brack and Ernie shop again, and your next cocksucking banquet's gonna consist of pizza bites and goddamned frozen fucking burritos."

Green smiled charmingly and pecked Grace on the cheek. Inside he could feel her melt a little, and he patted her bottom for the final thaw. Before her change, Grace had been a thirty-something stay-at-home mom—who'd been dying of breast cancer. Adrian had found her on hunt one night, staring at the moon and looking so wistful, he'd said, it had wrung his heart. Grace hadn't been Adrian's only 'saved' child, but she had been, perhaps, his favorite. He'd pulled Grace over, and since then she snuck into her daughters' dreams every night, letting them know that mom had done all she could to be there for them. But in Green's house, she reveled in the freedom of a colorful and imaginative vocabulary. She didn't eat food anymore—like all vampires, all she needed was warm blood—but by heaven, could she cook.

"I'm sure it will be fine, sweet. Is everyone down there, yet?"

Grace nodded, and before Green could leave, she grabbed his arm again and shook him gently. "I saw Adrian and Cory, Green. Too goddamned innocent to get out of the rain, both of them. How are you going to manage them?"

Green looked at her thoughtfully. A politician she was not, but she could muster a mixed species group into a crafting, cleaning, or cooking army of formidable proportions. And she was also extremely perceptive.

"Adrian can do fine on his own—did you see him handle Renny?" Grace nodded. "Good—and Cory's rather remarkable on her own—she's got enough untapped power to blow up a city, I think. Remember, you're native to this area, and pretty amazing at the preternatural scene—what makes you think she won't be?"

Grace smiled grimly. "Because I had almost twenty years of growing up on her, that's what. And I'd had to face my own death for nearly a year, before Adrian came. I'd been married for nearly fifteen years, and given birth and all that great and wonderful bullshit that gives a woman perspective on things like, say, monogamy and sex versus life and death. She's a baby, Green. Shit—she was a fucking virgin, did you know that?"

It didn't surprise him—but it apparently surprised Grace. He didn't even want to know how she would know, but she filled him in anyway.

"The whole kiss could smell it, that first night they were together. Made us nuts...let's just say there were a lot of anemic rednecks with some pretty goddamned erotic dreams that night."

"Did you call him on it?" Green asked, wincing at the imagery, but agreeing, still, that it had been unwise.

"It wasn't his fault—honestly, he didn't know." Grace said, shaking her head. "Cory...you know—she's got the hair, and the make-up, and the attitude—had him fooled, right up until...you know. Otherwise, I think he would have been more careful. He was certainly embarrassed about it the next night...he's already marked her."

The abrupt change of subject didn't faze him, because he could see it coming. "Yes—I can tell." Green had seen it—that subtle psychic impression that marked Cory as property. One mark gave them an emotional bond—she could tell if he were happy, or sad, and vice versa. Two gave them a physical empathy—body aches, desires, tastes, all would be shared. Three, and their thoughts would echo in each other's heads, until they didn't know where one of them stopped and the other one began. Four, and she'd have his immortality, and his life would be tied to hers. Vampires could go for a thousand years without caring enough about a mortal to offer a mark—it took incredible courage to be that vulnerable.

"But Green—that's crazy. She's just a baby...she doesn't..."

"She's the same age Adrian was, when I saved him, Grace. She's the same age he was when he became a vampire. She's old enough, and strong enough, to decide for herself, and I won't take that away from the both of them. And you need to stay out of it as well."

"Oh, really? Even when you want the both of them so bad you almost feed me with your sex?"

Green turned away, then turned back to her, the beginnings of anger in his eyes. "That's between me and me, Grace." He said sharply, not denying it.

It must be pretty obvious for her to notice it after seeing them all in the same room together only once.

"You think I' m the only one to notice?" She asked, making him wince. Damn, he was nearly 2000 years old—how old did he have to be before he stopped making a fool of himself over mortals—or vampires?

"Well isn't it my business, that?" He asked, still trying to swallow his anger.

"As long as it doesn't hurt those of us who get to live with you—Green— you're our haven. You're our safety. You need to keep your goddamned balance, or the rest of us will lose our fucking minds…and the best home most people here have ever had. I've lost home. I know how that hurts. I won't put these people through that if you can control it by putting a lock on your Johnson."

"My *Johnson* is exactly where it needs to be when it needs to be there, Grace." Green hissed, "And you would do well to remember to whom you are speaking." His voice was as glacial, and his eyes were flat and hard and angry. He had pulled his power around him, and he vibrated with the brilliant greens and shadowed browns of forest and meadow and pond. Grace looked away in a combination of contrition, hurt, and awe. Green pulled rank so rarely, it was easy to forget that he was a high elf of the last forest, that he was descended from the court of Oberon, and that he had parlayed forty stolen lime trees into a fortune of both magnificence and bounty—bounty that he used to run his own court in dry, barren area that by rights should have driven the fey out long ago.

Her voice, when she spoke again, was a deferential whisper. "My apologies, Lord Green." She murmured. "You're right—you're old enough and wise enough to not let such matters affect what you do here." There was a quiet, and he allowed his power to seep from him, becoming, simply Green again, and not Vernal Green. "I worry for you, as well, Green." Grace said, quietly. "If Cory is everything you think she is…the three of you may be okay…but if she's weaker than that—more set in her ways…no actual preternatural power…I don 't want you hurt, hon. I don't want any of you hurt."

Green turned to her, trying to muster a reassuring smile, but Grace, ever perceptive, had latched onto what he had said when he was in his fury. She touched him again, her flesh cold, like all vampires, but full of a human warmth he felt himself crave. "It was hard," She said kindly, nodding towards his closed bedroom, "Being with Renny?"

He set his jaw carefully, trying to not show weakness, knowing it was useless. "There is a giant hole in her soul, Grace. My body isn't going to fill it. She told me some things—important stuff—but she fell apart again, and wept, the entire time…she'll heal, but…but *Goddess*…Goddess, why?" He shook himself, eased away from her, then bent and pecked her on the cheek again. "We'll answer that question. I swore to her, I swear to you…I will not be foresworn." And then he made his way down the hallway, past the hall to the darkling, and down the stairs to the banquet room.

The banquet room was actually the first part of the house to be built. In those days, Adrian had slept in a coffin shoved (post-haste, as it were) into the side of the mountain, and Green had fashioned the room himself. His hands had cut the trees, tenderly, curing the wood, and polishing and sanding until his hands had bled, then toughened. Elves do not bleed lightly, and their blood, when shed, tends to give all it touches a magic to it, and so it was with the room. The floors were polished wood, and brass lamp fittings accented the vast space. A table big enough to seat over a hundred full grown beings was parked in the center of the room, and smaller satellite tables radiated out from that vast center. A wrap-around window looked out to the West—the bottom counterpart to the top wrap-around window. The house really was big enough to wander through the center of a small mountain. Green's living room caught the first rays of the dawn, and his banquet room saw the last light of the dusk, and Adrian was kept safe, nestled in the heart of the hill.

When coming down the stairs, Green heard what should have been happy sounds of his people, enjoying their own company. Some of the laughter was forced, and the gaiety was subdued—they were worried, he could tell. As he looked out across the floor he saw all their forms, bent, lumpy, straight, clean, tiny, huge, hairy, bare, all of them beautiful to him, but it was Adrian and Cory, near the head of the table, who caught his eyes first.

She was looking overwhelmed, but pleased. Her eyes flit everywhere, often delightedly. Sometimes, her entire face would light up with recognition, and she would wave at someone she no doubt recognized from the station. Adrian sat next to her, his head inclined to take in her every reaction. He had fed deeply from Renny, and his eyes glowed with health and with interest…and with arousal. Just watching her, her reactions, her delight, even the narrow eyed suspicion that she aimed at him occasionally, seemed to charge Adrian with light.

Green stood at the top of the stairs and drank in the two of them like liquor. Cory, her attention everywhere, saw him first, and her smile was both shy and wondrous. Adrian saw her glance, and her smile, and his smile was a twin to hers. *They were in danger,* Green realized, the instinct sure and certain within him. He grinned back at them, no trace of sorrow in his gaze at all. He would keep them safe. That much he could do for the both of them. He *would* keep them safe.

It took him a while to draw near them. His people were upset and on edge, and he needed to reassure them—and everyone was concerned about Renny. After his hour alone with her, he was already drained. By the time he had made his way to the head of the table, where he sat between Adrian and Arturo, he was exhausted. Grace was at his side immediately with a plate of eggplant something, and a smack on the head.

"Care for yourself, leader." She hissed, and he frowned at her. She pointed imperiously at his fork. He shoved a few bites in his mouth, swallowed, and turned his head in time to see Grace do the same for Arturo. Arturo returned the favor with an affectionate—slow—caress on Grace's generous bottom. Grace swatted at his hand irritably, not giving him a backwards glance. Green caught Arturo's eyes with a raised eyebrow. When Arturo returned the look, Green shrugged.

"I thought you didn't like vampires, mate." A long ago prejudice, revealed over too much bad wine, he wasn't sure if Arturo would remember. But the rueful expression on the other man's face showed that he did.

"When I was a god," Arturo returned mildly, "She would have been my goddess."

"And now?"

The rueful look deepened. "Now, she won't have me."

Green was dumbfounded. "Won't have you? That's odd…"

Across the table, Cory made a sound between a giggle and a snort. Her water went everywhere and Adrian spent a few minutes tapping her delicately on the back If he had actually pounded on her, her ribs would have caved in.

Arturo and Green watched her, expressions bland, until she could glower at them. "You *would* think so." She eventually croaked.

"So, you meet the woman while you're running up the stairs for a quickie, and you think you know her so well?" Arturo asked, irritation in his voice like static in a cat's fur.

"Not *her...*" Cory coughed again. "But women...women who look like me and Grace...us." She made a face, knowing she was saying it badly, and Adrian bared his teeth, a feral growl coming from his otherworldly toes.

"You...are...beautiful..." He hissed.

Cory flushed, looked away, looked back at his glowing eyes, and Green saw Arturo look away, embarrassed. Green couldn't have turned his head if Arturo had dragged him away, kicking and screaming.

"Only to immortals." Cory said gently, looking to Green for confirmation, then catching Arturo's eyes.

"She was a housewife for fifteen years, Arturo...she had babies, got fat, and ran around without make-up because there was too much to do. You guys see all that and, well, you worship it. Most human men...well...they don't see it."

"Her husband did." Adrian said quietly, and Cory nodded in agreement.

"That makes it even harder." She told Arturo. Then, unexpectedly, she reached across the table and laid her hand on his arm. "Arturo—you've got to give her time. You've got to convince her that you're sincere...it might take a while."

"It only took you three months." Adrian said dryly.

Cory looked back at him, over her shoulder, and grinned unrepentantly. "I'm young and easily led astray." They both laughed quietly, and Arturo looked away again, obviously feeling as though even their laughter was too private for him. Green simply gazed at them, and smiled.

They ate, and Green received reports. It was not done formally, but it was done completely—between Green, Arturo, and Adrian, every name of every preternatural creature in most of Northern California could be recalled. Green knew mostly the high elves, the sidhe, the greater powers, and some of the were-animals; Arturo knew the fairies, the sprites, the boggles, the trolls, the brownies, and most of the fey that were never seen by human eyes; Adrian, of course, knew the vampires, but he was also the specialist of the odd-man-out—the one were-cougar in Truckee, the family of shape shifting bears up in Lassen, or the disenfranchised fey children who had slipped away from their parents but who still stayed in contact with their extended family in the foothills. Between the different beings coming to talk to the three of them, lounging indolently and powerfully at the head of the table, a complete picture was formed of the state of affairs for Green's people. The news was both troubling and insightful:

Only the Folsom were-cats had disappeared, but *all* the were-communities were skittish. The tiny fairy that had flown to Lassen had almost been eaten by the family of bears before they had seemed to recall who she was and why she wasn't dinner.

Three of the vampires that usually nested in the darkling were missing— two men and one woman. Of the three, one of them had taken his belongings. The others had shown every indications of returning to Green's Hill.

The sprites—a particularly fragile type of smaller fey— were becoming, even as they all sat to break bread, more and more erratic, buzzing frantically, becoming higher and higher pitched. All Arturo could glean from them was "notes...high..." before they would disappear. Finally, before the meal was out, Arturo stood and ordered them all to "safety"—a place they all spoke of, but none of the higher elves knew. To Cory's shock, and everybody else's relief, all of those small, translucent, flitting bodies simply vanished.

Of all the news, Arturo's and Cory's was the worst.

"Great Goddess...and you don't know who?" Green asked, when they told him about the crime scene at the am/pm.

"No." Arturo said, and Cory looked at him woefully.

"There's more." She murmured, and the three men, as well as Grace and Bracken, who had joined them shortly after reports began, looked at her. "The vultures...and the cop." She said quietly, and Arturo nodded his head for her to continue. She grimaced, obviously not at home in the center of attention, but told her side of the story. "We pulled over at the side of the road so I could..." she flushed, "To throw up, okay? I don't eat people; I've never seen a human sacrifice...I had to blow chunks...any problems with that?" She glowered around the table at four perfectly bland—and very sympathetic faces, who all nodded that no, there was nothing wrong with losing her lunch. Grace smoothly pulled the now-empty plate away from Cory and handed it to one of the other kitchen helpers—a mid-sized, cerulean haired sylph with a sly face and quick hands.

"So anyway...I was losing my lunch near this field outside of Granite Bay, and there was this horrible...roadkill smell...I looked up and there were vultures...Arturo and I walked in but...but it was all over the trees. There wasn't even anything for the vultures to..." She shuddered, her pale face going even whiter, and Adrian ran his hand soothingly up her back. He whispered something in her ear, and she shook her head and shrugged, looking at Arturo from under a glower. Arturo looked at her blandly, then made eye-contact with Adrian.

"She fainted." He said, in answer to Adrian's question.

"You bastard." She spat, but without heat. "I told you I didn't want anybody to know."

"So tough." Adrian murmured. "Now tell us about the cop."

She looked at him with something like shame. "Why doesn't Green own any of the fey gas-stations in Folsom?" She asked, as though at random.

Adrian smiled, his fangs retracted, his eyes barely dampened. "Because another vampire rules there, in Folsom." He shrugged, embarrassed. "I never wanted…power, Cory. It came. Green promised me safety, I promised a few were-animals safety, Green promised a few elves safety…this whole hill started with me being Green's friend, and both of us protecting the little ones…it just came. Some bloke wanted to be all big and bad and rich…I told him fine…as long as the fey were free to come to Green, Lake Clementine's closer for a swim. Green agreed to stay out of Folsom, as long as the were and the fey were free to come to us."

Cory touched his cheek, remembered there were witnesses, said, "That's fine. That's what I thought. But…but I had to think it through…because…" she swallowed, and looked supremely unhappy. Her eyes were fixed on a spot of nothing past Green's shoulder, and she swallowed fiercely. "The cop said that Kim had been exsanguinated. He recognized me from the crime scene— wanted to know why I was there, and he was pretty sure the two things were related. I think they are too…but for a minute, maybe…for a minute…"

Adrian looked stunned. "For a minute you doubted me."

"Yeah." There was a silence at the table.

"When did you stop?" Adrian asked, his voice neutral.

"When I saw you with Renny…" Cory ran her hands through her hair. It was too long now, to make it stand up in spikes, so it merely looked disheveled. "Look…" She said, then turned towards him, looked him in the eyes. "Look—I know what vampires do." She pinned her fierce gaze on Grace, who merely arched her eyebrows, then on Arturo and on Brack. Lastly, she fixed her gaze on Green. "I know what you do. I know what you may have had to do in the past, when you started—it was probably a vampire eat human world back then—I get it, okay? But…" And she looked down at her hands now, which had magically entwined with Adrian's fingers. Her fingers tightened convulsively—she had been forgiven. "But nobody who could calm

Renny down that way, could make her become human to…to grieve…no one who could do that would be capable of murdering an ex-girlfriend just because she got in his way. I had to see you again…but once I saw you, it made sense…"

She turned, intense and still ashamed, but making eye contact because what she had to say was urgent. "Adrian—whatever is happening…they're after *you.*"

Adrian usually sat very, very still—his heart didn't beat, his lungs didn't need to function—he was, for all intents and purposes, dead. But at Cory's words he sat back and took a breath. "Me? Why would someone want to be after me?" He laughed at it, looked at Green and Arturo to share the joke, and rolled his eyes when they didn't.

"C'mon, people…I'm a minor consideration here…I'm not the leader—I'm not really a second. I'm the pain in the arse you all put up with. The only one who takes me seriously is Cory—and that's because she doesn't know any better…"

"Shut up." Cory snapped, and stood. "Stop it. That's not true—or it is—but not the way you see it. I just counted over three hundred…people…whose well being was reported directly to you. You just told me yourself, that whoever it is in Folsom was threatened enough by you to make Green forfeit his property there just to keep your nose out of his business. I take you seriously because there *is* something serious about you. And this is aimed at *you.* At *you* and *your* vampires. This is *your* food supply that's exploding all over the foothills. I know that's a special thing…you guys just don't feed from anyone, do you? Not if you can help it?" She looked at Grace who shook her head no, and at Adrian who also conceded. "This is aimed at *you.*"

"She's right." Green said quietly, before Adrian could deny it again, and they all looked at him in surprise. Green sighed. Renny had told him a few things, as they had lain together in the darkening room, all of them corroborating Cory's gut instinct. All of them needing to be told. "Here—let's move into the other room." He said, but to his surprise, Adrian vetoed him.

"No—whatever needs to be said can be said here. You've been hiding something from me—everybody has. Nobody who reports to me told me the complete truth—but they told you, didn't they, Green?"

Green looked back, aristocratically as he could. "Yes, they did."

"What is it? What do you think I'm too weak to understand?"

"It's bad, Adrian." Green told him truthfully. "It s…it's something you'll want privacy for."

"Fuck privacy." Adrian growled, standing up. His eyes were glowing, and his fangs were out. "I'm not a child, Green. I wasn't a hundred and fifty years ago…I'm not one now. What is it?"

Green held his temper, because Adrian was right. He was used to shielding his friend—it was second nature. Apparently, Green thought ruefully, true love brought responsibility. Who knew?

"The were—cats saw a band last night—Renny said they had a sound—a real "sound" like nothing any of them had heard before."

"So?" Adrian was still upset—his eyes were still brilliant, glowing with power and anger; his fangs were still out, and his chest heaved as dragged oxygen into his lungs that he didn't really need, but just seemed to feed the fire of his temper.

"So," Green echoed, breathing deeply, "The band's name was *Sezan.*"

Cory got to him first; although the whole table saw his knees buckle. The other two or so hundred beings in the room had watched his anger with interest. None of them watched his undoing—in the ten heartbeats of silence between the time the name passed through the room with its dark smell of power, and the time Cory wrapped Adrian's arm around her shoulder and chafed his cheek in panic, they had quietly left the room.

"He's dead, Green." Adrian whispered, sinking slowly to the ground like a spent balloon. "You promised me…he's dead…we watched him die…we heard him scream…he's dead."

Green came to his other side, sat by him, took his other hand and rested his chin on Adrian's shoulder, so close their faces almost touched when he turned Adrian's to face him. "He's dead, mate. He can't hurt you any-more…but someone out there is trying. This is hard—I know it…but you've got to think. Whoever it is went after your last girl…just to get to you—what will they do with Cory then, when he finds out that doesn't work."

"Ouch." Cory said in a small voice. "Adrian, ouch, you're hurting me." Her voice seemed to sink into Adrian's daze—he turned shell shocked eyes to her, and looked at their locked fingers. He released her hand and as quickly caught it again, and rested his cheek against his upraised knees. Two crimson tears leaked down his cheeks and onto his black denim jeans.

"Corinne Carol Anne," he whispered into the silence, "By all that's holy, what have I let you in for?"

CORY

Colors Stolen by Moonlight

Green's gardens were beautiful by moonlight. They encircled the house...I mean the hill, which contained the *entire* house. The hill itself was one-hundred percent Northern California Foothills—dry red dirt, tall pine trees and short Manzanita scrub. It could be worse—Ophir (where I work) would be all dry brown grass and sentinel oak in about a month.

But Green's gardens—damn. Like something out of a book—fairy tale green, grass so soft it was like kitten fur under my bare feet. When I was in high school our band took a trip to the Bouchard Gardens, in Canada, and I thought the pain of all those colors would make my heart splinter into a thousand pansy seeds. Green's gardens were better. The flowers were as exotic as orchids, and as plain as the wild blood roses that entwined the stone wall around the property. The colors were as deep as passion and as translucent as bubbles in sunshine. The grounds were foggy and misty, and they encircled the hill like my legs around Adrian's hips. They just felt perfect.

In moonlight, where every color was silver and shadow, they were like the promise of daylight after a thunderstorm.

It occurred to me, as I sat next to Adrian in the utter, windless silence, that this was the only way Adrian had ever seen these gardens. I had seen them in the sunshine, and he never would. He would see colors stolen, by moonlight, from lights inside the house, but never, ever, in the full glory of the sun. That thought alone made me cry, when watching him come unglued, even in both mine and Green's arms, had kept me strong.

And still we said nothing. He crushed me to his chest while I wept, and when I was done, he told me everything.

"I was a slave." He said at first, kissing my hair. He breathed in, deeply. I knew he was smelling me—his sense of smell is pitch perfect. He told me once, when he was courting, that he could tell when I was working because he could smell me from around the corner. My scent must be comforting, I thought, because although his strength was very carefully shielded, I could tell that if his arms convulsed, I would be squeezed to dust. My hand still ached from when he had lost control earlier. A name. Sezan. What was in a name?

"I was a slave in a ship—for years, all I saw were sailors…one cock after another…I did what they made me. I hated. I hated them all…I would dream about biting, chewing them until they were screaming pulp…and so much blood. A man could bleed to death, from a nick in the groin…"

His voice was dreamy now…I knew, if I looked, I would see his fangs, and his eyes would be glowing and half lidded. Blood and revenge—a vampire's strong wine. He breathed sharply, through his nose. Focused. Continued, in a cold way. Impersonal. As though this had all happened to someone else.

"So I was their toy—filthy. Beaten. Probably pox ridden—I was always sick, by the end. They offered me to passengers, if they paid money, and were so inclined. One day, the Captain offered me to a handsome gentleman, who was transporting himself, a large box, and forty lime trees."

"Green…" And it was all there. All of it, right into place. Adrian's status— a leader, but not. His relationship with Green—an equal, but not. The way they both adored each other, and the way Adrian worshipped Green. It all made sense—all of it. Everything except the way Green looked at me, that is. He should have hated me…he should have resented all I was to Adrian, and all I promised to be, between them. Or he should have dismissed me…after all, I was only mortal, one of many. But that wasn't what I had seen in his face tonight, as he came down the stairs…not at all. What I had seen in his eyes had been more like…hunger.

"He…he rescued me…" Adrian was sounding uncomfortable now. I turned to him, feeling fierce, and angry, and protective—of both of them. I was nineteen and mortal, and even I knew that love didn't always come wrapped in a pretty, pink and blue heterosexual bow—not if it was to matter. I knew that love, any love, was important.

"He loved you." I said to him, my whisper fierce as I sat on my knees and held his face between my hands, willing him to understand. I could see it, now, the pain, the joy that they felt in each other. The scene itself played out behind my eyes, as though I had been there, in a stinking hold of a long ago ship, where Green had discovered an abused boy...my boy. "He probably bathed you, because you both are always so careful about that. He probably made love to you—made you want it, instead of fear it. I bet he let you use him, so you wouldn't be angry anymore. And he made you free. He loved you. You don't have my permission to profane with shame. You never will."

It's hard to look an aroused vampire in the eyes for any length of time. Like Arturo said, hypnotism is a vampire's oldest gift. Their eyes glow and whirl, and suck at your soul. But Adrian's red glowing eyes were looking into my plain, mortal green ones as though I were doing the same thing to him. As though I were pulling him out of a swamp, with the force of my swamp water colored eyes. Time slowed down, for both of us. I could count the heartbeats in my ears, could hear the breaths he didn't need to take.

"Do you know the story of the first vampire, Corinne Carol-Anne?" He asked, his voice hoarse.

"No." I said. I would have shaken my head, in the silver light, but I didn't want to look away from his eyes.

"Let me tell you." He begged. "I'll tell you about...about *him,* and his death, soon enough, but you need to know this..." He looked away for a moment, closed his eyes, kissed me, with his eyes closed and his soul on his lips. "This story is why I...why I chose to be who I am. Green told it to me, the morning after we made love. It's just...Goddess, Corinne—you are *Goddess,* through and through...you need to know that. All that is lovely in you, and wounded in me...is in this story...will you hear?"

I nodded, and he took off his leather jacket and laid it on the ground, and we stretched out there, in the moonlight, side by side, facing each other. I could feel the heat, radiating from him, from his feeding, and it kept me warm. His voice, as he spoke, would sing song at times, and I could hear Green's voice through him, telling this same story to a frightened boy who had just learned how to love:

"After God made the heavens and the earth and the creatures, Goddess liked to come down into the world and *be.* She would be flowers, and earth, and trees and sky. She would be cats and dogs and snails and butterflies and monkeys and horses and *everything.* She birthed the sidhe, and the fey, and the shapeshifters, and she would come down and be them as well. The world was her playground, and she would just come down and *play* in every form God had given her. One day, she came to earth and took the form of a man, and she met a boy, and she loved him. They fucked like rabbits, for months, and God saw them—and was a bit surprised. He hadn't really designed the package like that, yes? He called to Goddess, and she left the boy, and told him she'd be back before the sun went down. She and God had a conversation—(*I just bet they did,* Adrian added on the side. I smiled and told him to keep telling the story.) But God decided that she was right—what was joy and love could not be wrong, and sent her back down, with his blessing. But it was after sun down, and the third, the other, had come to the boy, and whispered "shame", and the boy believed him. As the sun sunk low the boy hung himself for shame. Goddess came back to earth in time to see night steal to earth, and his body swinging from a tree. In her grief, she cut him down and gave to him what a God or Goddess should *never* give without thinking things through…she slit her wrist with the same knife she used on the rope, and fed the boy her own blood to bring him back to life. But the boy had been dead, and God was angry, because that *was* a rule, and he had *not* sanctioned the action. But he could not undo it, either. So he told Goddess that the vampire was *her* creature, and that he would not listen to its prayers. He told her that he could not abide the creature's face in the light of day, so it could only live by night, or else it would burn to ashes, as it should have at its death. All this he said, as the newly born vampire was suckling from the wrist of the man whose form the Goddess had taken, and she grew distracted, and could not sustain the body. It toppled over in death, and she fled to find another, so that she could be with the boy, and teach him what he would need to know in order to survive in his new life. When she returned (as a woman this time), she found the other, the enemy, with him. The enemy had whispered to the boy of blood and lust until he bathed in the gore of the body she had offered. She was horrified, and her new form wept. Her tears fell on the boy, and drove out the other. They cleansed the boy of the deed, and the shame, but the enemy had done his work. If not made carefully, a vampire will feed on those closest to him when he first awakes. Because we are feeders of blood, we are susceptible to evils of the flesh, and of the whispers of the enemy. But this is the Goddess' gift: We are allowed to live without shame, if we are brave enough to do so…and act of what pure emotions we can afford.

Such is her gift to all her beings, to were, sidhe, fey, and to women and men too, if they are not too blind to see."

I cried, of course. But it was a beautiful story—and imagining the telling, from Green to Adrian, from Adrian to me—it was perfect. And so was the lesson.

"No shame." I said, with wonder.

"No shame." Adrian repeated, and grinned, flashing fang. We stayed like that, silent for a moment, before I asked, "What time is it, Adrian?"

This time his fangs were not so friendly. "Two or so…"

"Tell me." I commanded, and neither of us doubted that it was a command. That seemed to me to be the power of the story—I told him no shame, as though I were the Goddess. He heard her words from my lips, and there was my power. It was a good thing. It was equality. It was terrifying. For the moment, I ignored it.

"The box of dirt," He said, "Was really a coffin."

"I knew that." I murmured.

"Hush…" He kissed me, I returned it, and he spoke again after a moment. "Green was not the only émigré coming to America…After that first night, Green took me out opside…dressed me well, pretended I'd been there all along. Nobody recognized me…and I hated it. I hated the open. I *hated* the ocean. It was huge, and vast, and ready to swallow me in all that sunshine, and all I could think of was that, one word, one glance, and I'd be back in that stinking hold, being sodomized by some fucker who thought he was a good Christian and I was a piece of meat. I got the shakes after half an hour, almost started to weep, for Goddess' sake. Green took me back to his room, and we sat…just sat, for hours, while the ship rocked and rocked…the sun started to go down, and I felt free again. I ran to the porthole, and pressed my face out…and said 'Green, I want that. I want the dark and the stars…I want the power to never be anybody's toy again. I want to be the player.' And Green told me the story of the first vampire. He made me wait until the voyage was over, until he let Lucian bring me over. He tried, repeatedly, to pull me into the sun. I couldn't do it. And…and I knew that Green was immortal. And that this was my only way to be immortal as well…"

"It was important? Immortality?" I asked because earlier, in Green's hall, I had been made supremely aware of my own mortality. The other beings there, most of them, wouldn't die unless they chose to. Vampires—they could be killed, by sunlight, by too much bloodshed, by decapitation—but it was difficult. According to Adrian that one night, the fey were just like the Green Knight, they could be decapitated, and come right on back smiling at you.

"I was dying." Adrian said simply. "I told you...I was pox-ridden...not small-pox, but syphilis...I'd been chained in that hold since I was barely old enough to remember my mother. Another five or so years, and I'd have been mad...and then I'd have been dead."

I touched his face, and he captured my hand. Oh...oh my Adrian. He'd been so proud, so cocky, when he first walked in to my damned gas station. But still I'd known. I'd felt...somewhere inside him...had been this. But it hadn't prepared me. It hadn't prepared me for his life...for his reasons to be what he was now. For the sacrifice he must have made, inside himself, to tell me.

"Who knows all this?" I asked him.

"You." He said. "Green."

"Arturo?"

"No."

"Oh." It was inadequate, but it was all I had.

He smiled. "I love you too." He moved quick—too quick for me to see. In a moment, I was under him, and he was kissing me again. But it was too close to dawn, and there was much more. I pulled back, breathless, and he nicked my neck, ever so slightly, and began to lap at what welled up there, like a kitten, licking the last of milk from its whiskers.

"So...you decided?" I moaned, because even this, vampire foreplay, was about to bring me to climax.

"Obviously." He smiled, very self-satisfied, and I let him touch me...my breast, my abdomen, and just the feeling of his hands slipping under the waistband of my cut-offs brought me. I shivered, and grunted, and rolled to my side again and pushed him off.

"Dammit..." I hissed, turning back towards him and making him look at me. "You're stalling. Say it, Adrian. Tell me about this man...tell me why he scares you...and I'll make it better. I'll love you until you can't remember his name anymore, I swear...just tell me."

He stood up abruptly. I would have been hurt, but I'd watched him move for months...he wasn't being dismissive; he just forgot, sometimes, that he was supposed to be still, and cool, and vampiric. All those years, I guess, trapped in the hold of a ship—his body needed to move, when it could. And he was nervous.

"I killed him, Corinne Carol-Anne. Captain Sezan. Not as a vampire...like I said, Green didn't let Lucian bring me over until we actually made port. No...what I did was worse. Much worse." He stopped pacing, turned to me in the moonlight, looking silver and magnificent—and tortured. What would be worse than being eaten? Than being ripped apart by the groin tendon (which is what I imagined Adrian had done to him at first.) How bad could it be?

"Have you ever read *Goblin Market,* luv?" Adrian asked, out of the blue.

"Christina Rosetti? Girl goes to the market, tastes fairy fruit, pines away wanting another taste? That one?"

"Aye...do you remember the end?"

"Yes...her sister had the fruit smeared all over her mouth and her body, so the one who was dying of want kissed her sister...lapped the fruit off her face, and was healed."

"We did that. But not on purpose."

I shook my head. "I don't understand..."

He sighed, and stood, hip-cocked, looking out into the darkness beyond the gardens. "Fairie sex." He said, and I could tell, even from a distance, that his face had begun to flush. Adrian. Damn...after the life he'd led, he could still blush.

"Fairie sex?"

He blew out a breath. In some dim part of my mind I wondered if he realized how human he was when he was embarrassed. I would never tell.

"Fairie sex." He repeated. "Elves, sidhe, etc. It's like...if you steal a taste of them, you *will* pine and die, if you do not receive another..."

I frowned. It sounded like enslavement...and Adrian and Green had been 'stealing tastes' of each other for decades. "Even now?" I asked, nodding my head towards him.

He shook his own head. "No, no no...*stolen*...or, sometimes, inflicted. There must be something non-consensual about the exchange." He frowned at me, remembering something. "You've felt it, luv...remember, Arturo's first touch?"

I shuddered. I remembered. If Arturo hadn't come in the second night, I very well might have clawed the flesh off my body, trying to assuage the ache...Oh my God. Oh dear Godess. "Yeah..." I said, "But that was accidental—he touched me, with power, and didn't realize I'd be susceptible…I mean…you couldn't do that to someone who…who rapes little kids for kicks, can you?" He flinched, and so did I, but I was distraught. He hadn't candy coated the truth, and spitting it up left just as much bitterness.

"Only if they steal the kiss." He said, not meeting my eyes.

"Christ." I murmured. "You and Green…" I couldn't say it. Even knowing they'd been lovers…but this had nothing to do with love, and everything to do with calculated murder.

"'Exchanged essences.'" Adrian euphemized. In this context it made me queasy.

"And then you let…" He interrupted me, which was good, because I wasn't sure I could say it.

"There was no 'letting' about it." He hissed. His body shook in the moonlight. Vibrated at a frantic pitch, and I couldn't be sure he wouldn't fragment into rage and disappear into the moonlight, cold, white, silver anger. "I was going to stand up to him—I thought I could…fuck-it-all, I thought all I needed to do was stand up to him, just once. I told Green I could do it—I made him stay in his room because I **swore** I could defend myself. Goddess…I was so wrong. But I told him…Sezan I mean. In fact I gave the cocksucker a chance for mercy that he didn't deserve. I said 'I do not consent to this. If you do this, you will suffer what I have suffered, and more.' He looked surprised. I don't know if he knew I could speak—he thought I was some dumb fucking animal that crouched in that hold waiting for him. And he grabbed me—I fought for my fucking life…I swear to the Goddess, Corinne Carol-Anne, when I went into that hold, I thought I would win. I thought I could fight him off. I told Green I could—I swore to him, that I wouldn't let it happen again…" Adrian swallowed, almost lost himself, smeared red across his face with his sleeve when he wiped away his tears.

"It doesn't matter." He choked. But oh, God, it did. "What matters is that he didn't take me easily. Not this time. Not knowing what I knew—about love, about what Green said would happen to him—about everything. I said without my consent, and I meant it. After Green and I first made love, there was nothing we could have done that would have stopped what happened after he raped me again. So I fought for all I was worth, but Sezan was bigger…that fucker was always bigger…" That last was said on a whisper, and he sank to his knees, and my heart broke. I wouldn't waste my pity on the man who'd done this to Adrian. He hadn't suffered enough. Adrian had suffered through his death for one hundred and fifty years, and Sezan had lived it once.

I held Adrian, I rocked him against my chest, I wept with him. And still, he kept talking. "He screamed for days. His own men tied him down, called him mad…he shrieked, and babbled, and tore at his own flesh…he escaped his bonds and ripped out his own eyes…ahh…Goddess. He ripped out his jugulars and bled to death, screaming "boy" the whole time. Fifteen years, my whole fucking childhood, and he didn't even know my name."

His face was covered in bloody tears, and I kissed him through them, not caring about the sweet copper taste on my tongue. He turned to me with something like a whimper, and I kissed him again. Our tongues meshed, and I cut mine, deliberately, on one of his fangs, and heard his growl of complete arousal as he sucked the blood from my tongue. He ripped his own jeans in two…vampire strength, and made tatters of my own clothes, and shoved himself between my thighs with enough force to leave bruises for a week, and I didn't care. Because when his body was in me, and he was growling my name, he wasn't in the hold of that ship. He wasn't listening to the cries of a monster who had arranged his own horrible death, and made Adrian suffer through it. He was fucking *me*. He was inside *me*. He loved *me*. He was the possessor, the master, the beloved, and he was mine and I was *damned,* I was *thrice Godess fucking damned,* if anything was going to hurt my Adrian again.

So I let him take me, there on the grass, and I thrust and growled too—and snarled curses in his ears, urging him on. He bit my neck, and drank deeply, and when I bit his, hard enough to taste my own blood, he sighed and shrieked, and came, and so did I.

Our breathing stilled. (He still breathed while we made love, always. Human still, our Adrian) I heard my heartbeat from inside him, inside me, and realized that I was exhausted. As I slid into sleep, I whispered, "Mine. You are *mine.* Nothing will hurt you again." And the last thing I remember was the smell of our sex and our blood and of night in Green's garden, before I closed my eyes.

GREEN

A Show of Power in the Moonlight

The lovers in the garden were as unaware of the watchers from the house as they were of the blinding aura that surrounded them, or the fact that their bodies glowed, near to blazing, and translucent

There was a bubble to their aura, a shield. It had a clamped down, straining look, as if the maker of the shield had to struggle to put a cap on it, but it was there. Green stood at the window of his room shaking with the effort of shielding, and of watching them. He was both aroused beyond endurance, and in shock. Arturo and Grace rushed in behind him, as he knew they would, excited and angry.

"Dammit…did you feel that…"

"Be at ease, Arturo." He murmured. "I shielded it to inside the grounds."

"But Christ Jesus…" Grace gasped, and Green noted, hardly surprised, as Arturo wrapped his arms around her from behind and, literally, made her breathe. Vampires didn't have to breathe…but when their chests were nearly crushed concave by power, the feeling must be awfully reassuring.

Arturo looked out across the lawn and abruptly sat down on Green's bed, dragging an unprotesting Grace with him. "My Goddess, it's her." He said, and Grace made a surprised noise before she laid her head limply against Arturo's shoulder.

"It is indeed." Said Green quietly. "One hundred and fifty years I tried to heal that wound…this child does it in one amazing fuck."

"Holy holy holy hell…" Arturo's shock was nearly as large as Green's own. "If I hadn't touched her hand one night, none of us would have ever known…"

The lovers had stilled below him, and with their climax, the glow and the aura faded abruptly. Green noted the time unhappily. He and Arturo would need to move quickly and soon in order to keep Adrian and Grace from a vampire's fate. "We'd have known, Arturo. She would have failed her class, gotten stuck in this town, and gone mad…she would have taken out a post office or fucked an entire town into stupor…but we'd have known…its better this way, you think?"

A small smile played at Arturo's mouth. "I'd have to agree with you there, brother." Grace slid, bonelessly into his arms, and he shook her gently, but in vain. Green shook himself, preparing to *move,* and move quickly. "I'll get Adrian, you get Grace." He said, as he shifted to blur out of the room. "But leave Cory to me…she thinks of you like an Uncle, Arturo, and no girl wants her uncle to see her as she is right now."

And he was gone before Arturo could ask him what it was she thought of Green.

CORY
Continuing Education

It was early morning, and Green was shaking me awake, and I was exhausted. "Go the fuck away…" I mumbled, only to find my universe upended, and myself face to face with an ass that tied for first for most beautiful in the nation. "Crap, Green…don't you ever wear clothes?" I wailed. Then the world righted itself and I was stood—butt naked myself— in front of a mirror, and I shut up.

"My God." I swore. My face was caked with dried blood. It matted my hair and my chest, down to my groin. There were even red smears down the front of my thighs. My hands shook as I raised them to my mouth, and I felt the world do a violent dip and wheel beneath me. Green caught me. He was getting good at that.

"Adrian's tears?" I asked, my voice small and helpless. I had not been prepared to see myself like this. I looked…pagan, and brutal, and all sorts of things a woman at the cusp of the millennium doesn't imagine she could be. I scared the hell out of myself.

"Adrian's tears." Green confirmed, dropping me back on the bed. "And your blood, too, I think. And Adrian's…which would mean both yours *and* Renny's. All in all, a bit of a mess."

"I need to shower." I mumbled, trying to hide my head in his chest. God. I was in his room, in his bed, which means he must have picked me up off the ground pretty much as I was right now…covered in blood and…and other things…and naked. Adrian had fallen asleep with me…Christ! "Adrian?" I squeaked, in panic.

"In the darkling…don't worry. You healed him, we kept him alive." Green said briskly, setting me down on his bed again.

In a frantic wash of shame I grabbed for the covers, but his hands stopped me. He sat down next to me, and, given my line of vision, I didn't want to fight with him any more. "Go away." I whispered. His arm went round my shoulders, and I jerked away from him in shame.

"Don't." He whispered into my hair. "Just listen. Look at yourself and listen." I did look at myself, at the brine-washed blood that coated my body, at the stickiness that wept between my thighs. I felt the puncture marks at my neck, the sore place on my tongue, and the bruising on my hips and thighs, the scratches on my back, and knew I'd inflicted the same. Sweet Goddess, what had I become? If Green hadn't been there I would have wept, but I didn't want his comfort. I did, but I wanted him too, and I didn't want to want him, after the way I had needed Adrian last night…what did that make me? My God…I was two weeks short of being a virgin…what did all this make of me?

"Stop." He said into my hair. "I can almost hear what you're thinking…and the words are all bad. You're thinking thoughts of shame. You're thinking words that you've heard belong to girls who give their bodies with contempt and dishonor and it's not fair. You are not those things. What you did last night…" He laughed a little. I saw that lean, fine-boned hand sneak under my chin, lift my face (with some difficulty) to face his own. His too-wide-set eyes were lovely, many colored green shadowed havens for all of my fear. I sank into them, and his words sank into me.

"I'm a healing elf, Cory. I heal with my body—I heal with sex. I'm good at it. Without me, Renny would have died last night, of a broken heart and broken dreams. Grace would have waited for the sunlight, the first day she missed her children. Blissa never would have conceived Bracken, and Crocken would have pined away for the thing he could not give her. It's who I am—it's where my power goes, and it's where I get my power. And as good as I am, and as much as I have loved your lover, I couldn't heal him. Last night you did. Adrian has been carrying that burden for one hundred and fifty years. It has sat on his shoulders, and he has run from it in the same way he ran from responsibility, and a belief in himself that could have redeemed him. And you healed him. I watched him, as I carried him to his room this morning, and the black, empty fissure that sat in his heart is closed. That's a wondrous thing, Corinne Carol-Anne—ye ken? You know? Do you know how I've longed to close that—the things I've given, the things I've stolen, just to fill that fissure with love instead of loathing? And you did it. One night. We watched you…no…no…don't pull away." He murmured, when I would have. We? Who we? That's the *last* time I get laid in a public place, I thought miserably, but Green wouldn't even let me have that.

"We had to, love. I won't apologize for that…you summoned enough power to cleave the moon last night…didn't know that, did you? I needed to shield it. Whether you know it or not, me watching was more important than your dignity, so suck it up and hear me out."

I summoned a rusty chuckle…"Go, healer, go…" I murmured, and was rewarded by being pulled next to his smooth skinned, muscled body. Since I was falling slowly into his eyes, I watched them crinkle at the corners, and felt the whole moment thud to a halt of want. So I wasn't a slut…oh really? His laugh rumbled up through his stomach and against me, and all thoughts of shame fled.

"You'd tempt anyone, love." He said softly, "But now is not the time. You need to know you have power—in fact, you need to know you're a player in this little war I think has started. And you need to know you're a target."

I squeaked. I was a gas station clerk. I wasn't a goddamned immortal. And I wasn't a goddamned target.

He nodded, and I felt a shame that had nothing to do with sex, and everything to do with making him say these things without active participation. *That* shame I could fix.

"That's stupid." I snapped hoarsely. "Unless I'm armed, I'm pretty goddamned harmless."

Green's attention sharpened. "You can use a gun, Corinne Carol-Anne?" He asked.

"Yeah…working graveyards, you have to. I've been taught to use pretty much everything…"

"Licensed to carry?"

I shook my head, starting, again, to enjoy the feeling of being next to him. "Not at all."

He nodded, sagely. "We'll have to fix that. But until we do, Arturo or Bracken will shadow you." I opened my mouth to protest, when suddenly, in a quick movement, he swept me up into his arms again. "But first," he said,

"The showers…you've got 15 minutes to get dressed and out the door, or you're going to miss your finals.

I bitched the whole goddamned time. I bitched about his presence as he reached in and lathered my hair. I bitched about how rough he was as he took a scrubby and scrubbed me clean—in a purely non-sexual way that managed to piss me off even more. I bitched about bodyguards and people driving me from place to place and I bitched about his insistence that I was important enough to guard. I argued about having power because any moron could see I was as mortal as the other goombahs attending Community college, and I bitched about the clothes he made me wear because instead of going through my own stuff he'd had Arturo borrow them from Grace and they were five sizes bigger than I am, and it wouldn't matter if he'd gone through my own stuff, because I would have bitched about that too. I bitched about the fact that we couldn't take my car, and about Arturo maybe but hadn't I kneed Bracken in the balls less than twenty-four hours ago and he was going to make my life a *joy*.

I fought him on **everything,** and I still ended up, scrubbed clean and pretty, with my wet combed hair slicking back against my head, next to Arturo in Arturo's blue Cadillac, sending fulminating glances at Bracken who was getting ready to join me. Two little hovering things popped up in the air next to Green as he belted me in and gestured to Bracken to fold his long body next to mine. They dropped my backpack—complete with laptop and printed copies of papers I hadn't printed yet—into my lap. I scowled at Green, and he laughed and patted my cheek, and gave me a look that let me know, under no uncertain terms, that this wasn't over.

"You'll be exhausted, Corinne Carol-Anne—you'll need to eat plenty of protein, so let Arturo and Bracken feed you. Think well—and good luck, you'll need it because you didn't get a chance to study. One of them will be with you at all times."

"Fuck you and your little dog too." I snapped, out of patience.

He smiled, and his eyes were warm, and sensual, and dangerous. "I have no 'little dog'", he said pleasantly, "So you will have to settle for me. Later. Remember you have finals tomorrow, too." And with that he whirled, and that glorious, sunshine colored braid swirled around behind him, and Arturo backed out of the driveway. He was wearing, I realized in shock, a towel wrapped around his waist, and it made a tent. It was a long, silent, drive to

Sierra College, after that. I'd spent all my energy bitching at Green—I didn't have anything else to say.

Arturo did. Somewhere between Forresthill road and Highway 80 he started casting surreptitious glances at me. By the Newcastle exit, I was out of patience with him too.

"What?" I snapped.

"I did not see you." He said mildly.

"See me what?" I asked, feeling dense.

"See you naked, and covered with Adrian's glory." He sounded wistful and put out, and I felt my whole body blush for about the hundredth time in the past half hour.

"Oh." What else was there to say?

"Green thought that would be important to you, so I wanted you to know." He was so damn proud; I couldn't even get mad at him for sounding like he *wanted* to have seen me. But I did pick up on Green's involvement in this weird ass conversation.

"Does that bastard have to control *everything* on the whole fucking planet?" I asked querulously, ignoring the fact that, yes, irrationally I *was* glad that Arturo hadn't seen me as Green had seen me this morning.

"No." Brack answered me judiciously from my other side. "Only the fucking that happens on his corner of it." He wasn't being flip.

"This conversation is over." I said helplessly, and for once I got the last word.

I passed three of my finals, but honestly, I'm not sure how. I remember entering the classrooms, because it's hard to forget something like that when you've got two 6'plus bodyguards flanking you. I remember turning my papers in to my professors, then writing forever, and then staggering out to be caught between Arturo and Bracken. They stuffed hamburgers down my throat and hauled me to my next class. After the last of the day's tests I have dim memories of being carried to the car in Arturo's arms, mumbling calculus formulas against his chest.

I woke up an hour before dawn, after fourteen hours of sleep. I was in Green's bed, and Adrian was kissing my temple—it was his smell that woke me first, then his cool lips against my skin. I turned my head into his, and woke up fully with his kiss. He broke away from me after a moment and gathered me to his chest, and I sighed, happily. I went to kiss him again, but he shook his head and pushed me reluctantly back to his chest.

"Green's orders." He said, and I chuffed in exasperation. His eyebrows puckered, kindly, and he stroked the hair back from my face. "You knackered yourself, Cory luv…"

"It's our life…" I grumbled, and his eyes narrowed.

"It's your life." He stated flatly, "And you used considerable life force healing me…you don't know what a thing it is you gave me, Corinne Carol-Anne. The lightness of heart…it's like the moon is brighter, the air smells sweeter…it's like…"

"Forgiveness?" I supplied gently, when he trailed off. He smiled, and it dazzled me.

"Yes. Forgiveness. But I'd never been able to feel it before." He took my hand into his, kissed it. "That takes a lot of strength…that took a lot of your strength. You needed to sleep. Green was right."

"I'm starting to hate that about him." I growled, and Adrian pinned me with a hard glance.

"You don't get it…I don't blame you for that—you're so new to this world…but you need to get it. You **healed** me—the way Green heals. Not in a 'new age' psychobabble kind of way…a true physical act. You did it with sex—but that's probably not the only way you can do it…Cory—you're one of us. You're a child of the Goddess—you have her powers, you love her child…And as such…well, Green **does** have a say in your life. You watched us the night before last—he's a King. You don't like that word in this country, I know…but it's the one to use here. He rules us—he cares for us…he knows about power and the Goddess in ways we have yet to learn…he holds us together. You answer now to him too."

I was too stunned to answer. He kissed me, and, for the first time, spelled me with his eyes, and I slid into sleep again. At seven the next morning, I repeated the whole day again, but with different finals, and without the bitching. I awoke the next morning in Green's bed again, fully rested—Adrian hadn't even woken me up the night before. I was blazingly, viciously, spectacularly mad.

"You're my **KING!**" I shouted at Green as he walked into the room. This time I was up, and dressed (he'd gone through my stuff after all…I'd spent the last two days in my own clothes). I had muttered to myself through the shower, and paced myself into a fury. I must have been angrier than I ever anticipated, because my yell knocked Green on his ass—literally. Behind me I heard a window break, and as I turned in surprise I heard a whirring sound, and was knocked on my own ass. Green hovered above me, his stunned, exasperated face inches from mine.

"What is it I have done to you, Corine Carol-Anne, to deserve to be so accosted by power in my own home?"

"I'm sorry." I said, reflexively. But it was true, I realized after a moment of breathing in tandem with the muscular body above me. Anger is one thing—destruction is another. I had no intention or wreaking destruction on this person. When my mad was over, I had planned on remaining friends. Green's eyes narrowed and I swallowed in honest contrition.

"I was mad, Green…but I didn't want to hurt you…"

He laughed wryly. "Bullshit." He said after a moment, and he stood and let me stand. "You wanted to hurt me because you didn't know you could."

I thought for a moment. "Fair enough." I murmured. "But…damn, Green…I never knew I could…" and at that my knees buckled, and I looked up at him from the ground again. I was at a loss. I remembered another scene in this same room, two days earlier, and I wrapped my arms around my knees. I was more than *at a loss*. I was **completely lost.**

"How long will this last?" I asked after a moment.

"Forever." He said immediately. Silence descended, and I gazed sightlessly into the room. It was a good room—light wood, simple lines. The blanket on the bed was a home made quilt, with a bear claw pattern in dark greens and blues and reds. Very masculine. Very Green. The front window—what was left of it—projected out, and was almost as big as the one in the living room. Green liked light, I could tell. Adrian, child of darkness, Green, king of light. He was still behind me, I realized. I wasn't ready to speak. I'm not sure how much time passed before I did speak again, but the sun had moved, just a little bit, and the shadows of the willow trees that bracketed his window had moved with it.

"I don't understand." I said.

"I don't either." He answered. "It's not really to understand, is it? Just to accept."

I didn't have an answer to that, so I just sat there, staring outside, while tiny creatures with translucent wings fixed his window. The sun continued its westering course across the sky.

GREEN

Hearts make a sound when they break.

Adrian was making him crazy.

"She's just sitting in there?" He asked for the third time.

"Just sitting." Green affirmed, looking up from the kitchen table. Grace had made ravioli for dinner, and Green was finally getting to it. He'd been up to his ass in business calls and e-mails all day—he did, after all, have several businesses to run, as well as his inquiries into Mitchell Hammond's death.

"Why can't I go in there?" Adrian burst out, whirling on the carpet so fast that his black leather boot ripped it down to the pad. Green glared at him in annoyance. It wasn't like Adrian to forget his strength. From the moment he'd awakened, suckling from Lucien's throat, Adrian had been thoroughly respectful of his gifts as a vampire— and, as careless as he was to women's *hearts,* he was respectful to his gifts as a man, as well. Green remembered her small voice, as Adrian had bruised her hand two nights ago. Cory made him forget so very many things, Green thought wryly watching Adrian try futilely to pull the carpet back together, but learn so very many others. It was a fair trade off, he knew, but that didn't mean Adrian wasn't going to drive him mad before it was made.

"Leave it be." Green told him, mildly, "The sprites will take care of it." The sprites, he knew, would be thrilled—Cory's shattered window that morning had been the most excitement they'd seen in years. Grace ran too neat a house for them to get that much work.

- 105 -

"Damn." Adrian stood and ran a hand through his hair, ruffling the pale strands to form breezy curls. It looked better when he was done mussing it than it had beforehand, Green mused. Damn indeed. With a sigh, Green took pity on his friend, and went to the marble counter behind him to dish up some ravioli and salad.

"Here, mate." He said, giving the plate to Adrian. "Go in and set it down, answer any questions she might have. Don't touch her, don't kiss her, don't speak to her…what she's doing is important."

"Important? She's sitting there…staring out the fucking window like she's in a space ship and it's the window to earth."

Green nodded. "Very apt." He murmured. "She's watching her old life disappear, Adrian. She had a specific idea of what life would be like, and now it's going to change, and not even I can tell her how." Goddess knew he had tried— Cory had stalked out of the room a half a dozen times that day, asking him questions. Each time he had looked up from the computer desk that took the corner from the breakfast room, and answered as best he could. He would hardly even finish speaking before she then stalked back to his bedroom to ponder the answers. *Am I immortal, Green? I don't know—that usually requires something voluntary, some sort of test. Can I use this to hurt people, Green? Anything can be a weapon, Cory. Can I just ignore it and pretend it doesn't exist? Sure, luv, if you want to lose your sanity—you've enough power in you to off the whole of South Placer County and half of El Dorado if you've a mind for repression.* Cory hadn't liked that *last* answer at all. But a question at a time, she'd been re-arranging her self and her future to fit her knew knowledge.

"She's just got to put that picture together in her head again— and she hasn't had very long to do it, really." Green finished, after Adrian stared woefully at the plate in his hands for a full minute.

"I want to take her riding." He said after a minute. "No sex—just a ride, tonight on the motorcycle. It will do her good, Green, I swear it."

Green looked outside to the darkness. There was a full moon, and beyond his gardens the air smelled of buckeye flowers and bottlebrush and oleander, and it was that temperature and humidity that made you feel like you were swimming through it, and it was the most refreshing swim of your life. And power—the air was charged with power and magic…it was the full moon before midsummer night, but still…she would feel it on her skin. She might even be able to do something with it, if she were in a mood. And she'd be with Adrian, so she'd be in a good sort of mood.

"Why not, mate?" Green said after a wistful moment. He'd spent nights like this on the back of Adrian's motorcycle. He knew what Cory would experience, and he longed for it just as he longed for her to have it. "No sex, though, Adrian—not unless you're back here—preferably in the darkling, and Grace and I know about it. She almost made the sky light up the other night—not a thing I want to have happen again."

"Right." Adrian agreed whole-heartedly. None of Cory's protests from Adrian, Green mused. Adrian had never had a temper.

"Give her a moment to talk to you first, right mate?"

"Will do." Adrian affirmed, starting for the door.

"And don't talk to *anyone*...not with this whole Sezan thing out in the open, and the were kitties missing. We're also missing some of the equines and not a few canines—the shape-shifters have been hit hard with whatever this is."

"We'll be careful, I swear. Just us...honestly, Green, you'd think I was twelve or something..."

"You'll let her eat first, won't you? And don't snack on her—not tonight."

"I'm not a complete bastard, Green." Adrian replied mildly, shaking his head. He flashed a crooked smile that both showed his teeth and hid his fangs. It made him look endearingly young, terrifyingly innocent. "Don't worry, okay. I'll take care of our girl."

And with that he went through the door. Green heard her voice, murmuring, and Adrian's, murmuring back. Something inside of him made an actual glass-cracking noise—and before he could convince himself that that it was his imagination, Blissa and three of the other nymphs danced through the hallway and into the living room.

"We heard that." Blissa said, sweetly.

"Heard what?" He asked, genuinely surprised.

"Heard your heart breaking." Said Grace. Grace was a strong vampire—she had heard the sound of a broken heart through two stories and several rooms, but nothing in life or death could make her 'flit'. She was a few steps behind the nymphs. "Now come on—they have to go through here to get outside, and we don't want to make this a party. Green felt small hands over his body, blatantly erotic hands that, he knew, could make him come in two minutes flat—or in two hours, depending on the mood. He was their healer, and all of them had been hurt at some time or another. He was a *very* good healer—and a very good teacher, as well. And suddenly he was weary, and in a cold ocean of pain.

"Okay." He murmured. There were sighs as the nymphs herded him into the hallway, and he felt Grace's arm, strong, companionable, and with an earthy, attractive sensuality that Adrian had seen first, but that Green had nurtured, around his shoulders on one side.

"Arturo will be jealous." He said, weakly, feeling noble. He loved Grace—well, he loved them all, the vampires, the elves, the fairies, the sidhe. But if he hadn't been any of those things, if he had just been a man, he would have loved Grace as a friend. And Arturo, as well.

"Arturo's an elf first, a jealous suitor last." Grace said dryly. "He'll understand like no on else will." And with that she pushed Green into the darkling, down the hall and into her room. Green had insisted on giving her one of the larger rooms, but she had still made it a homey place, with a crafting corner, a sewing machine and huge boxes of yarn and fabric where other people would have an office and a computer. It felt like comfort, and the bed was deep and wide, and the nymphs were busy with Green's clothing. Grace wrapped her arms around Green and kissed him thoroughly, without fang, until he sighed and melted into her flesh. She pushed him back onto the bed, and, kneeling to one side, kissed him again while the nymphs went to work with his bare skin, and his sensitive groin. Green felt the cold that had crept up on him when his heart had broken recede, and his whole body began to heat up with, if not passion, then at least the warmth of friendship and gratitude.

"Now shut up, healer," Grace said, before Green lost himself in sex and the honest pleasure of friends, "And let us heal you."

Green woke up in his own bed, feeling thoroughly sexed and a little disoriented. Arturo was sitting on his bed, looking at him thoughtfully.

"She said it was a 'bachelorette fling'." He said, as soon as Green's eyes could focus on him.

"Is that what it was?" Green croaked. "I could have sworn it was a pity-fuck...but I've never had one before, so I couldn't be sure."

Arturo grinned, looking self-satisfied. "As long as I wasn't the one to have to say it."

Green looked away, for once embarrassed about something that the sidhe took for granted. "She's lovely, mate—you're a lucky man." And then, before

Arturo could answer, Green asked the painful question. "Where'd Cory sleep? I almost didn't recognize my own bed."

"Partly with Adrian," Arturo began, "Really sleeping—they got in around four a.m., and she was pretty much asleep in his arms, then partly in her own room."

"I don't know if I ever got around to showing her that she had one..." Green began, and then, through four walls and a separating hallway he heard her gasp awake. From the look of Arturo's face, Arturo had heard her as well. Green rolled out of bed quickly, and for once donned a robe, and they both hurried towards her room.

Cory was standing next to the bed bent legged and ready for action, wearing an outsized T-shirt and white cotton panties. She had the look of someone who had sprung from bed before she was truly awake, and was waiting for her brain to catch up with her body.

"Did you hear that?" She asked, breathlessly, putting Arturo and Green both on alert. "It was a cracking sound...like an echo or something...just now...didn't you hear that?"

"I don't fucking believe this..." Green murmured, and Arturo shot him a sharp look. Green grimaced back. "Nothing important, Cory, luv...just some idiot, playing around with elemental forces."

Cory blinked, focused on the two men in her room, and sat abruptly back onto the bed, feeling safe. "What day is it?" She asked muzzily.

"Friday." Arturo told her, a smile playing with his impassive features.

"Do I work today, Green?" She asked, not sure how long his imposed vacation lasted.

"Not until Monday." Green told her, waiting for what would come next.

"Am I supposed to do anything today?" She asked, honestly at a loss. Green felt for her suddenly. Her whole life had been cut loose from normal—one night she had been a gas station clerk, living at home and beginning a new love affair, and within five days she'd had her entire life put into the hands of a virtual stranger. And Green still had tasks for her to complete.

"Arturo's taking you to apply for a permit to carry a weapon, and then you've got a trip to the shooting range—but that's not for a couple of hours."

"And before that?" She was waking up now, he could tell. The strangeness of being answerable to Green for her actions was settling in. There had been a faint irritation to that question—as though she expected him to have planned her life out, and resented the hell out of it. He'd put a rest to that if he could.

"I don't know, Cory—you're grown. Do whatever you want—I've got work to do, and I need Arturo until you leave for the permit. Enjoy your day, luv—if you need anything for your room, ask Blissa. Between her and Grace, the house is pretty well run."

Cory looked around the room—it was a lovely space, the same light wood paneling that graced the walls of the rest of the house, plain but good, and the waxed hardwood floors that shone everywhere else. Green could see the impulse strike her before she opened her mouth.

"Thumbtacks?" She asked suddenly.

"On my walls, are you high?" He shot back. "I cut that paneling with my bare hands. If you want to hang a picture, simply put it out by the wall you had in mind, and the sprites will take care of it—in fact, you're the most excitement they've had in years. Anything else?"

"Food?" She asked, cautiously.

"In the fridge." Green affirmed. With a smile, and a peck on her cheek that he couldn't refrain from, he turned away from her. She'd puzzle out a place here, he was sure of it.

CORY

Guns and Other Weapons

It is reasonably easy to get a gun permit in my neck of the woods. A trip to the courthouse in Auburn, a written statement about working nights in an isolated area and voila! It all would have been like silk, if Officer Johnson hadn't been there.

"Feeling insecure about something?" He asked me, while I was standing at the counter, filling out the paperwork. I looked up at him, annoyed. I had spent the morning setting up my room, more pleased than I cared to admit. Green's home was lovely, and my gran's quilt looked more at home than it ever had in my parents' pre-fab doublewide. I loved being there, I realized, as I watched the sprites hang my framed copy of *La Belle Dame Sans Merci*, with Renny prowling around their waists, rubbing against them every so often. I didn't want to love it—it was very un-independent, un-twentieth century for me to take so quickly to Green's forced invitation to live in his giant flophouse for the preternatural. But take to it I did—and the other residents, it seemed, took to me. I had been halfway done with my unpacking when Blissa and two other nymphs, Dree and Lait had come in and started to fuss with me as well. Before I knew it, I'd been sat down and, well, *groomed*. The last of my dyed black hair had disappeared in a few snips of golden scissors, and what was left was a pixie cut of my own blonde-ish, brown-ish, red-ish hair, that looked, for me anyway, stunning. So, if I were to answer Officer

Johnson's question truthfully, I would say that no, at this moment, I was feeling insecure about very little.

"Night work is risky for a woman." Was what I did tell him.

"But you haven't been working nights." He said pleasantly. I scowled up at him. He was out of uniform today, leaning casually against a the counter in jeans and a white T-shirt, and I have to admit, if I wasn't spending my nights with Adrian and my days with the rest of Green's household, I'd find him quite attractive. He had dark hair, straight, and parted in the middle, a bold nose, and brown eyes that crossed just the tiniest bit. And he was tall—taller than Adrian even. But he was looking at me in that way again, like I was something to be pitied, a stray to be set back in the kennel. I didn't like the way he looked at me. I didn't like his questions. I didn't like him.

"I took some time off." I told him. Casually, I looked towards the back of the room, where I knew Arturo and Bracken were waiting for me. Arturo looked in my direction and nodded, so I knew he was there if I needed him. "It's allowed." I murmured, and went back to my paperwork.

"You didn't just take time off, I understand." Johnson was saying blandly. "You were given time off by the man who owns the station—and a number of other businesses. He called your manager directly, and made sure you wouldn't lose seniority of even pay for it. That's a pretty big favor." For a gas station clerk. He didn't even have to say that last part, I heard it loud and clear.

"He's a pretty nice guy." I said sincerely. And then I got mad. I had been mad at Green two days before, and had knocked him on his ass. So I knew now, that my temper did something important. This time I controlled my mad a little, and turned the tables on the oh-so-disdainful Officer Johnson. "Does this discussion have a point, Johnson, or are you making small talk because my new haircut looks just swell."

"My name's Max." He said sweetly, "And the haircut is terrific. But I'm talking about something serious here."

"And that would be?" I looked up from the paperwork now, and pinned him with my eyes, willing him to tell me everything I needed to know.

"Five more of those huge, grisly, awful spots. Our coroner estimated that there was enough gore in each one to account for a human body, but he found evidence of animal hair as well. No one, human or animal, has been reported missing. The coroner keeps saying there's something wrong with the blood, but he won't give us a direct answer as to what. But I know they're human…I had an informant, nice enough guy, looked like a rat, snickered when you called him Ratso. Should have been a transient, never was. Always had money, food, clothing. Nice guy—I used to watch him give food to transients—usually apples. I went to his corner and found one of those damned gore spots. They're all over the fucking county, and I want to know why."

His voice was rising, and I could hear my own fear echoing in it. With an effort I took a breath and clamped down on my mad. There was a fuzzy sound, like the kind your hand makes when it rubs over a television screen, and suddenly it was a lot easier to breathe. Officer Johnson took a deep breath, but I saw, to my surprise, that even as my emotion drained, his remained in his bright eyes and flushed face. He had cared, I thought sadly, for the giant were-creature he called Ratso. I didn't want to know that. It made it harder to dislike this asshole.

"How did you do that." He demanded, suddenly, furious with me.

"Do what, Officer Johnson?" I asked mildly, turning my face to my paperwork so he couldn't see the pleasure or the triumph in my eyes.

"I just told you more than I told my damned Lieutenant—you looked at me and I spilled it—how did you make me do that?" He really was slipping, because by now, people were starting to look at us, and he didn't notice. He reached out and caught my arm, pressing enough to leave bruises, and I felt my mad come on again. With an effort I breathed, and looked up and caught Arturo's eyes, telling him to stay back now. His own eyes had narrowed to slits, and I could see that he and Brack were an eyelash away from shouldering their way through the crowd of people in the court house and making things much, much worse.

"I don't know what you're talking about." I said mildly, thinking about the cool of Green's eyes, the way they seemed to calm me whenever I was upset. When his hand just tightened, I thought of his gardens instead, and when his hand dropped, I sighed in relief. "Its okay, Officer Johnson." I murmured, visualizing Green's gardens. "You'll find out what's happening. You'll get the bad guy." Pretty gardens…brilliant yellow flowers, pink and fuchsia and blue, rioting for attention. Silver by moonlight. "I only wish I could help you more." This last was the truth—those gore spots represented my friends and Green's people, and I would dearly love to see them stop appearing. But with the truth, came, unbidden, my moment of truth with Adrian in Green's garden, and the spell I seemed to be weaving over Officer Johnson changed in tenor. He had almost been calm, his color normal, and his head nodding in time to my words. In a heartbeat of my memory, all that changed, and his hands were both around my arms again, and he was crushing my mouth in a kiss that might have been sensual, if it hadn't been brutal. I slid my foot down his instep, and shoved him back when he gasped in pain.

"What the hell are you doing?" I hissed; my control over myself and my power was gone.

"I saw you." He hissed back, "In my head, I saw you, fucking some guy with blonde hair, outside for the whole world to see."

"So you wanted to be next?" I snapped, and then I snapped. "Let me tell you this, Officer Maxwell Johnson." I said, loudly. "I would rather fuck a man who's been dead for a hundred and fifty years than fuck you." He gasped in shock and backed up. People began to discreetly wander out, writing on their paperwork as they went. I didn't care—this bastard had screwed with me one time too many. "I would rather fuck a guy who used to sacrifice virgins than fuck you. I would rather get on this floor and bone the asshole I kneed in the balls on Tuesday, than fuck you. So if you want a glimpse of what you saw in that garden, go fuck yourself." Arturo and Brack were at my side before I finished speaking.

"Who the hell are these guys?" He asked in confusion. We were having a full-blown scene now, but since the room was empty now, it didn't seem to matter.

"I'm the guy who used to sacrifice virgins." Arturo said mildly.

"I'm the asshole who got his balls crushed." Brack added. They both smiled. It wasn't pleasant. "And you need to leave."

Johnson shook his head, hard, as though trying to clear his vision, and my anger faded abruptly. He looked like a guy who had just been beat over the head with a sledgehammer, and I had swung the damn thing. He was a snob and an asshole, but he also liked some poor guy named Ratso, and he wanted to make the world a better place.

"Give us a second guys." I murmured to the boys. They looked at me, unmovable. I sighed. "Fine. But I'm about to share some family secrets, so you guys can't get mad 'til I'm done, fair enough?"

Arturo didn't look happy, so I tried again.

"Officer Johnson has found five more, 'spots', Arturo...one of them was a friend of his...he would like some help finding what's happening."

"That's no concern of ours." Arturo lied, flashing his silver caps.

I pulled him away from Johnson and Brack, watching nervously over his shoulders as they eyed each other like enemies. Bracken, with his knee length braid, looked thrilled and vicious to be eye to eye with a boy in blue, and I wondered if they had met before.

"He cared about the guy, Arturo." I murmured, "And I just mind raped him—I didn't mean to, but I did…and I feel like I owe the guy, okay?"

"He wants you, Cory." Arturo growled. I laughed.

"He thinks I'm white trash—he just read my mind at a bad moment— otherwise he would have needed a body condom before he touched me."

"We've managed to stay under official radar for hundreds of years…why should a mortal I've known for six months change that?"

I shrugged. "Because no one will believe him except us—and the other way around. I'm telling you, the guy's not doing this for glory…he's doing this for some guy named Ratso…" I broke off when I saw the look on Arturo's face. "You knew him."

All that macho manhood—all that anguish. It was horrible to watch. "I brought him from Brazil with me, two hundred years ago." Arturo murmured, heart-broken. "He was a capybara. He was a friend." He swallowed, and I grieved for him. "Tell this fuckwit what he needs to know. Brack and I will wait at the door." With that, Arturo stalked towards the door, gathering Brack with no more than a glance. It was just Johnson and I again, in a white tiled glass room that was painfully empty.

I swallowed, and kept my distance from him. "You're looking for druggies." I said, remembering his casual assessment of Kim, lying pathetically under the blackberry bush. "Look for people who live like drug-addicts—but aren't. Look for people who live under the radar—and who will hate and avoid you like the fucking plague. Those are your victims."

"Who did this to them?" He asked, voice cracked.

"If I knew, they'd be stopped." I told him mildly, knowing that neither of us wanted to guess how that would happen. "But for now, our only lead is the local music scene. Look for a band—or a man—named *Sezan.*"

"That's it, *Sezan?*"

Just hearing it twice made me shudder. "If you knew what that name meant, to some of us," I told him, Adrian's face from that night in the garden dancing before my eyes, "It would be more than enough." I swallowed, and gestured towards him imperiously—even I knew it was arrogance—and said "Now get the hell out of here. Go. I have a busy day today, and you are not in my plans." And with that I turned around to my paperwork and filled in the last two lines, and my signature—Cory Kirkpatrick. When I looked up again, Maxwell Johnson was gone, and Arturo and Brack were right behind me, close enough to lean on when I was finished. So I did.

"Nicely handled." Bracken said later, as we were driving from the shooting range. I'd fired nearly fifty rounds from the .22, and another forty-six from the Sig-Saur 9mm I didn't think I'd ever actually use. When I first started using a gun at the Chevron, Danny told me that a .22 did plenty of damage—that little bullet ricocheted around in there until it hit something vital and turned everything else into goo. But Arturo said that anything fey or vampire or were could take five to ten times more damage than a human being, and keep coming at me with super speed and a nasty smile, so we figured a 9mm would make a whole lot more goo. My arms ached, and my heart too, because I'd fired at enough man shaped targets with really big holes coming out of them to have the reality of my situation sink in. Something awful out there might be after me. And I might just have to kill it. Better it than me, right? But still...it gave me the chills.

"The gun or the cop?" I asked him wearily. We'd brought Arturo's Caddy this time, and it had a lovely air conditioning system. I was enjoying sinking into the leather in the back and just getting cool. Early June in the Sierra foothills—mid-nineties to low one-hundreds. Standing in the middle of the prickly brown field at the shooting range had been a sweat-fest.

"Both." Brack replied after a moment of thought. "The gun will take more practice...but the cop used a considerable amount of power. You were fairly delicate, for someone who didn't know what she was doing."

"You mean I whammied him, but I did it nicely."

Brack snorted a small laugh. "Pretty much. Let's just say I've seen power used far less considerately, and with less passion behind it. Like I said, nicely done."

"Thanks." I replied shortly. It was a decent compliment, I would return in kind. "By the way...I'm sorry about the whole...knee in the nuts incident."

He looked at me from the front seat, surprised. "Don't be. It's the first thing you did that gave me hope that you weren't just some hick who got lucky with Adrian."

Oh. Well. "You're still an asshole." I told him, feeling good about it.

"I do my best." He said smugly. Arturo cocked an eyebrow at us, and said nothing.

I talked to Green about it the next morning. Not too early because Adrian and I had been out to the wee hours the night before. We had driven down to lake Clementine, and I had gone skinny dipping. You haven't lived if you haven't gone skinny dipping in the middle of the night in the foothills. Green agreed with Brack that the whole thing with Johnson the cop had been "nicely done." He also told me sternly that we would have to have some long training sessions with my so-called power before I used it again and that was fine with me. What I did to Johnson still didn't sit right, even if, I realized, I had done things like that before. The second time I had seen Johnson at the crime scene, he had told me more than he should have—I hadn't known it then, but that had been my doing. I knew it now, and it made me wonder…

"Green—have I always been able to do this? Play with people's minds, I mean?"

He thought about that for a moment, blanking his computer screen and turning towards me to give me his full attention. He had a very nice little work-station in the corner of the kitchen and the living room, and I realized that he did quite a bit of work there. It hit me then, that he really was a business-elf—he must have to do some amount of work every day, to keep up with the interests that supported all his people—he had to have some form of support to keep him up to his armpits in trail mix and kitty litter. That being the case, for about a heartbeat, I wondered why he didn't have a study, but in the time it took him to answer, I had it figured out. If he was in a study, he couldn't keep the pulse of his household. I'd seen a workstation in his room, and I was pretty sure he used it, but during the day, he could see the comings and goings of his giant den of fey, right from where he was sitting. Good leader, I thought, very good.

"Yes and no." He finally answered, breaking into my thoughts. I looked at him, annoyed. He smiled back, wickedly. Green was very appealing when he was wicked. Green was very appealing anytime. It was disturbing how very appealing he was. How could I find Green this attractive, when I knew, without thought or doubt that I would kill or die for Adrian? It wasn't just an "if I wasn't with someone else right now" attraction. It was an "I'd kill or die for both of you as long as I could have you" attraction. It was starting to make me queasy—but only when I was alone. When I was in the same room with either or, it all seemed very copasetic.

"I wasn't able to do it when I was trying to get out of the Chevron to take my finals." I pondered.

"You were desperate." He replied, seeming very sure.

"I wasn't able to convince my English 1B teacher to take my paper, either."

"You were desperate then, as well." He said this like it made sense. It didn't.

"Well what good does something like this do me if it doesn't work when I need it!" I snapped. Arturo heard me from the kitchen, where he was making a plate for us, and he grinned, also wickedly, and also appealing. But Arturo just didn't have the same hold over my emotions as Green. I wrinkled my nose at him, and he chuckled outright.

"I didn't say that." Green shook his head, then stood and paced. He was wearing clothes, for once—or jeans at least. Thank Goddess for that—truly. For a while there, it felt like I was surrounded by naked men with boners, and while some women may dream of that, to me it was damned embarrassing. Green cocked his head, looked at me closely, then smiled as though he liked what he saw. I flushed, and smiled back. Green could do that to me. "Tell me, Corinne Carol-Anne, how did you feel when the cops wouldn't let you leave, or your professor wouldn't take your paper?"

"Pissed off." I said shortly, and he arched an eyebrow. It had been a quick answer, but not an honest one. I thought it over, carefully. "Powerless." I said after a moment, and he nodded.

"You felt guilty after your moment with Johnson yesterday afternoon— why?" He knew the answer. So did I for that matter, but I still felt awful about it, and it was hard to say.

"I felt like I'd...abused him somehow." I said slowly, looking away. "Like I'd taken advantage of him...and used my power all wrong."

Green nodded his head, apparently satisfied. "To use power, Corinne, you need to feel powerful. You need to be aware that you can do something. I'd told you that you possessed some abilities, and you believed in them and consciously used them—it came naturally. Those other times you'd felt as though you had no recourse—nothing to stand on. You didn't use power because you didn't know you had it. You only use it when you realize it's there."

"How very zen." I said dryly.

"I try." He grinned back. He turned back to his workstation and sat down, and I continued to look at him thoughtfully. He was genuinely a nice guy— nothing I had seen since that first night had changed my mind about that.

But he obviously knew how to use power. I'd seen Renny chasing around in were-cat form, and occasionally as a human. There was a sadness in her eyes, in the slight curve to her shoulders that might never truly go away, but she would live. For a while there, I was afraid she wouldn't, and I was fairly sure that every time her emptiness threatened to overwhelm her, she ended up in Green's room, in his bed, and he kissed her and made it better. This house and these grounds alone were a testament to Green's power. For five acres in any direction the grounds were a cool, misty garden, full of rioting color and streams that seemed to begin and end in nowhere. Only the dome of the house itself consisted of the red dust and dry pine trees that made up this part of the foothills, after the sentinel oak and scorched straw gave way to it back around Auburn. Nothing in this part of the country resembled Green's land—even in temperature, which, in June, should have been in the nineties. In fact, the mound *over* the house, *was* in the nineties. But around the house proper, it was a cool seventy-eight Fahrenheit.

If that wasn't use of power, what was? But it wasn't *abuse* of power. Even taking Renny to bed wasn't abuse of power. In fact, I'd seen him, once, after she'd been with him. He'd stumbled out of his bedroom half blind with exhaustion, red-eyed, almost weeping, and Bliss and a host of other nymphs, sprites, whatever the hell they were, had swarmed around Green, well, purring was the best I could phrase it. And suddenly he hadn't looked so haggard anymore.

So I was beginning to understand—I was new to sex, myself, but I was beginning to understand its nature:

Sex was love—if you were lucky.

Sex was healing—if you were good.

Sex was release—at the barest minimum.

Sex was power—in any form.

Green wielded sex—with affection and kindness and an honest goodwill towards those who sought him out for protection and companionship. It made sense, I told myself. *Everyone* was attracted to Green. I was no exception. And the fact that I was sleeping with Adrian only made the attraction stronger—both the men had an easy familiarity about them—friends, lovers, family. I was just sort of pulled into their circle. It was comfortable there, I realized. Kind. Kindness is underrated.

"What are you thinking?" He asked suddenly, and I had to shake myself aware. I had been, I realized, staring at him as he worked.

"Kindness is underrated." I said truthfully.

He grinned again, more wicked than ever. "I'm not always kind." He chuckled, then made a shooing motion with his hand. "Go away, Cory—I've got things to do, and you are way too distracting."

I stuck my tongue out at him. "Are all the were-folk accounted for?" I asked.

Green shook his head no. That had been their priority, for the last two days—they were finally at a place where they could be reasonably sure that anyone *not* accounted for was probably dead. It had taken a toll on all of them—the vampires especially.

Although it's pretty hard for *people* to get attached to their food, it's pretty easy for vampires. Because the were-folk replenished their blood supply every time they morphed, they were an ideal part of the vampire food chain. And because they didn't weaken or die off, they were also usually very good friends. Adrian seemed to know every victim of what had been called (with a certain grim sense of humor) the 'greasy spot syndrome' personally. Mitch had been the first victim we knew of. Part of our little jaunt to the river the night before had been so Adrian and his crew could feed. There were always parties down at Clementine this time of year—especially on the weekends. Adrian, Grace, and a host of around twenty to thirty other vampires just slid into the crowd, and…lets just say the party got *really* interesting for a number of the young rednecks whooping it up. Feeding *is* a sensual experience, and there were a number of people who woke up this morning missing clothes and no small amount of dignity—but with some *very* erotic memories. I took a certain amount of satisfaction in watching the homo-phobic captain of my high school football team go off in the woods to get high (or so he thought) with a very beautiful, very *male* buddy of Adrian's. I bet he had a few surprises last night that he would prefer to forget this morning.

That had been about the time I had wandered to the lake to swim. Uncomfortable doesn't even begin to describe the sensation of being in the middle of a hallucinogenic vampire orgy—and knowing your own personal vampire was out in the middle of it without you. Of course Adrian found me after he had eaten, but even then, I wasn't about to make love in the middle of the lake, in the middle of the night, amid the sounds of moans, and grunts, and sighs that made up the feeding orgy. Don't get me wrong—it did turn me on. But it was also creepy and strange and perverted. I wasn't ready for perverted or slutty yet. I was still surprised enough to find myself turned on under normal circumstances.

But the whole weird experience would have been unnecessary if the were-folk hadn't either gone underground or been killed, because in the natural scheme of things, the shape-changers fed the vampires, and the vampires protected them. The fact that they had all been blind-sided by this attack, this *plague* didn't sit well with Adrian. It didn't sit well with *anyone* at Green's place—Adrian's people were obviously the target, but Adrian and Green were so closely aligned that everybody felt under attack—sprites, sluagh, trolls, nymphs, vampires, brownies—everybody. And everybody felt angry. Arturo, Brack, and I had canvassed the rest of Folsom the day before, and all of Foresthill this morning, and I knew of six other parties hitting Auburn, Colfax, and Loomis. The dead ends were both mounting and insurmountable. Flirting with Green just reminded me that everybody was under pressure, and made me wonder what would happen if the pressure blew the lid off of Green's little faerie hill.

"I bet I'd find out more if I went back to work." I said abruptly. I didn't realize how quiet the room had become until I saw Green jump, then glare at me. "Well I would." I finished defensively.

"It's possible." He acknowledged, shaking off his startlement, and looking back at his paperwork. "But I'd like two more days to see if we can't get this thing under control before we send you back out there."

"You know…" I was going to say that just because Kim had been killed didn't mean that I was a target next, but Green looked up at me in an honest mix of irritation, exasperation, and what looked a lot like sexual hunger. I was so surprised by his intensity that I literally fell backwards into the couch, doing a back roll to land on my knees looking over the back of the couch at him.

"You know what?" He asked, too angry to look surprised or even amused.

"A swim sounds like a good idea." I squeaked. It hadn't until just now, but it was a good recovery. "Arturo—Rattlesnake Bar and Beals Point haven't been checked out yet."

Arturo looked from Green to me, standing in the kitchen with plates of food in his hands. Grace cooked for everybody at night, and Arturo just seemed to take over for her during the day. I hadn't even thought about the incongruousness of a giant South American man-god taking over the domestic chores until he stood there with a little apron on and a pained expression on his face. "Can we eat fir…nevermind." He sighed, set Green's plate down in front of Green, and turned around to pack us a lunch. I scurried off to find my suit and a towel.

Brack came with us. At first I was annoyed at him, but as he sat in Arturo's Caddy wearing cut-offs and a pleased expression I realized that following me around for this last week couldn't have been a picnic—especially when what he really wanted to be doing was killing whoever was responsible for Mitchell and the others. Finally we were going somewhere he might actually enjoy.

Rattlesnake Bar is really just a series of short peninsulas jutting into the uneven bottom of the lake. They're covered with crab grass, gravel, and dust, but at the waters edge there are usually little shelves that make nice stepping points into the water. It's the kind of place where people should wear river shoes—because there's mud, crab grass, dead cat fish, broken bottles and worse on the bottom—but nobody ever does. It's also the kind of place where you can swim out for twenty or thirty feet and still feel weeds growing up from the bottom to wrap around your legs. I'd been swimming in Folsom Lake and Rattlesnake Bar for most of my life, and the weeds had never creeped me out. Until now.

Maybe it was the company. There is something clammy about a man's skin in the water—I don't care what all the romantic movies show, it's just not appealing to touch. But it was also the fact that these weren't high school friends, or flirts or dates or anything else like that. They were bodyguards, and even in cut-offs, with water slicking back their hair, they didn't look in the mood to frolic. They were also, I realized uncomfortably, both grown and older than I was.

They'd dragged me, half conscious around Sierra College. They'd held my arms and helped me learn to shoot. And my perception was still that Adrian and I were children, and Arturo, Brack, Grace, and the others were adults. I was wrong, I thought now. I was in a world where age didn't matter—Adrian was one hundred and fifty years older than I was, and seventy five or so older than Brack. Green, who I found so very appealing, was almost as old as the legend of Christ. It was all such a reality adjustment that I couldn't do it. For a moment, watching Arturo and Brack on the shore toweling off, I couldn't make my mind fit around the company I was keeping.

In a move I would have been proud of if I'd seen it, I flipped around and headed for the far end of the cove, swimming as fast as I could. When I tired, I lay on my back and stroked lazily in the shady water, looking at my skewed vision of the sentinel oaks against the brutally blue June sky and tried to find a little peace. With my ears in the water, blocking sound, and the sun pushing the shadows over me, dappling the water the whole summer felt just a little less dazzling. When I glanced over at the boys again, they looked like regular people—they looked like friends. I stretched vertically, treading water for a moment, preparing to swim back to my friends. It was then that I felt a weed wrapping clammy fingers around my ankle and pulling me under.

I kicked hard and sharp, thinking that it *was* a weed at first, but the pull was too strong—too bony to be a plant. Water closed over my head and I pushed hard, breaching just long enough to pull in air before it had me down again. The lake was, at most, twelve or fifteen feet deep here, but murky, and I looked frantically above me as the shaded light clouded over with green water. My heart echoed in my ears and I felt something very much like helplessness swamp over me. The water closed further, faster. Then I looked down.

His eyes burned red and his face was bloated and dead from being in the water, but his grip was strong around my ankle. His hair was shoulder length, and somehow terrifying as it swirled around the sagging flesh of his face. He smiled, and his fangs extended, looking as smug as a walking corpse could. Mother Fucker—try to drown me and smile like that—Adrian was going to fucking kill him. My mad hit me like a freight train. With a scream that cost me air I probably couldn't afford, I wrapped my hands around the bony hand on my ankle and pushed against him with all of my angry will…

And exploded out of the water, shrieking, his hand still attached to my ankle, arm dangling limply below it.

As I fell a good ten feet back into the water, the dead flesh combusted, burning around my leg and causing me to scream again. Frantically I clawed my way towards shore. Bracken met me halfway there, latched his arm under my armpits and dragged me to land, then lifted me and carried me to the Cadillac, whimpering in pain. The hand and arm were gone, disintegrated into ash, but my ankle was on fire, and I didn't even want to look to see if it was blistered, cracked and blackened, which is what it felt like.

Suddenly Arturo exploded out of the water, right where I had been, and in his hand was a human head, held by a handful of dank hair. The head exploded as soon as it hit sunlight, but Arturo didn't scream in pain. He just glared balefully at the burning mass writhing in his grip before it fell out of his hand, turning to ashes and disappearing into the water. As he glided back down towards shore, the rest of the body floated up behind him and immolated just as quickly, but the look on Arturo's face was enough to make me forget even that.

"Mother fucking son of a..." And then he lapsed into what was probably ancient Aztec or something, because it sure wasn't the Spanish I learned in high school. He touched down on the beach and walked towards Brack and me, controlling his expression to look like something less fearsome and a little gentler. It made me feel better to know he'd do that for me, but then Bracken shifted me in my grip and my vision went white with pain as my ankle brushed my leg.

"Gonna barf." I whispered, then tilted my head and threw up on Brack's feet. He set me on his lap and brushed my hair back from my head with something like tenderness. I reminded myself not to give him shit about it later, and then whimpered and turned into his chest. "Ouchie." I whispered, and knew Arturo had moved closer to look at my wound.

"Ouchie." He agreed grimly. Strong fingers gripped my chin, soothed my face, and I turned to meet those amazing copper lightning eyes that had first seduced me into this strange world I moved in now. He looked like the fairie godfather I'd always wanted but never had. "Cory, I'm going to take the pain away, but I have to touch it first."

"Swell." I whispered. "Arturo, you can fly."

"Yes." He nodded, a small smile touching his lips. "And so can you." He turned away.

"How did I..." I started to say, but then he touched my leg, and the world exploded into pain and bright light, and I passed out.

GREEN

Dirty Little Cookies

She was asleep now, for which Green could only thank the Goddess. She had apparently awakened on the trip back and her pain, when Arturo had carried her into the front room, had been excruciating. Not that she had done much more than whimper and bury her face in Arturo's chest. Green had tended the wound—it had been blistered, down through several layers of skin and a thick layer of flesh and fat. If Cory hadn't actually landed in a lake, the hand around her ankle would have charred until her foot severed from her shin, and the damage would have been irreparable. As it was, when Green touched her, she had shrieked once, then fainted again. Green then breathed on the wound, waited until the damaged flesh had sloughed off, then kissed it, lapping a little at the freshly flowing blood. After a moment or two the blood flow had been staunched by her skin, growing back a layer at a time to cover her exposed flesh, and her leg looked normal again—straight and clean, with a wide, jagged band of white skin where the original wound had been. Green had then fallen limply to the couch next to a pale and shaking Brack while Arturo put Cory—without a word from Green—into Green's own bed.

Arturo emerged from Green's bedroom then, and flopped listlessly onto the couch next to Green. The three men took a ragged breath, and sighed it out.

"I'm glad she's okay." Bracken said after a moment. "I would have hated to have to explain that to Adrian." Arturo nodded in sympathy, then shuddered himself. Green could tell that it was more than Adrian's anguish that Arturo had feared.

"What the hell happened." Green asked after a moment.

"It was a vampire." Arturo said, certainly. "Under the water, in the shade—the sun didn't touch him until we dragged him to light."

"I didn't know they could even be awake in the day." Bracken said, wide-eyed.

"Some of them—the older ones—if they've given up all their humanity, it can happen." Green murmured, absently before looking sideways at Arturo. "But none of ours have given themselves over to the other—who was he?"

Arturo shrugged, and thought hard. "I've seen him before—a couple of nights ago, right before Mitch died. He was talking to Pete and Marcus—but they didn't seem that impressed."

"How did he burn her like that?" Green asked, then felt thick when Arturo explained it to him.

"It was great, man." Brack put in enthusiastically. His earlier lethargy had disappeared, and something—fear, adrenaline, worry, was revving in him big time. "She swam to the other side of the cove and just as we realized she was under for a while, the water starts to boil—this big ass fifteen foot radius of water, and she comes *exploding* out of it, with an arm attached to her ankle. Do you have *any* idea how much power that took?"

"Not as much as you might think." Arturo interrupted. "The vamp had been there for a bit—his flesh was rotten, right? He was still alive when I went under—I didn't know what he was at first, and was trying to pull his whole body out of the water—his head came instead."

Green looked at Arturo, nose wrinkled. "Eww." Arturo nodded, and Brack bounced off the couch like Tigger. "It was epic…Arturo flew out of the lake, the head burst into flame—the body floated up behind him—it burst into flame…then…"

And suddenly Brack flopped onto the couch again, all of his enthusiasm gone. "She was hurt. I mean, really hurt." He turned tortured eyes to Green. "I didn't think I'd like her enough to care about that, you know? But she was *hurt*. And she was so brave in the car, Green—didn't scream or anything. Arturo took some of the pain away, but…Goddess…Green—I'm not gonna steal Adrian's girl or anything, but, you know, I've got this protective thing…I'm starting to think I'd kill anything that hurt her…" Brack's body went still, quivering with rage. "In fact, I'm wanting to go find who ordered this and rip him apart..."

Green took a good look at Brack. The boy's eyes were whirling—he had eyes like swamp water, literally, with grey dapples and brown spots, and swirling green irises. He was wound way too tight for Green's liking. Green knelt before him, leaning into his space, putting his forehead against Bracken and breathing deeply. "She's okay." He said after a moment, when he felt Brack's heart beat time to his own. "She's okay, and we'll find who did this. But no one needs to die right now, 'kay Brack?" Bracken's even breathing lapsed into shudders, and Green wrapped his arms around his body until they subsided, then lay him down on the couch in a spelled sleep.

Then he stood and paced the floor, whirling towards Arturo. "This is not good." He said after a moment, scrubbing his face with his hands. "This is not good at all. Six were-creatures, gone. Adrian's ex-girlfriend, killed to frame Adrian. And now they're after Cory." He felt his own eyes whirl, just as he knew Brack's had. "They're after them *both!*" He ground out, and his heartbeat spiraled out of control. Arturo would stop him, he thought, desperately. Arturo had to stop him from spinning into fury. But Arturo was pacing too. Arturo was furious and frightened and angry, and his heartbeat echoed in the back of Green's throat, faster and faster. If Arturo couldn't be strong, his emotions would become wrapped around Green's own, and between the two of them they could rush out and do something foolish and panicked and brave that might get them both killed. But Green couldn't stop it. Couldn't stop his fear and his anger from swinging faster and faster, in an arc of panic and love and pain that was screaming to be cut loose. Arturo grunted, turned, pounded his fist through the wall behind him, and Green knew he was pulling his friend, his second, into his madness with him, and that none of them could afford to see that. Abruptly he turned from the room and stalked out the front door, slamming it behind him, leaving Arturo staring after him.

Fifty years before, when the foothills had been sparsely populated—and certainly not exclusive and expensive—another vampire had challenged Adrian to the death. Adrian had laughed at him, invited him to Green's, shared Adrian's then favorite lycanthrope, and told him he could have Folsom. Adrian, being Adrian, could pull this off, with a sweetness of smile, and a hearty handshake, and never look back. Crispin, the head vampire of Folsom, initially lived in a cave in what was now the new Empire Ranch development. But it had been just that—developed—and Crispin had been forced to move. Green had known this, but Crispin had kept to himself, for the most part, gathering his followers. They were a rougher, less benign crowd than Adrian's—but since they didn't outright murder, rape and pillage, Green and Adrian hadn't bothered to find out where he lived. After the first attack, he had made it his business to know where Crispin held court—but it hadn't been easy. While Arturo and Cory had been scouring the countryside, Green had been scouring the Internet. At his first hit, a site talking about aspiring local rock bands, he'd sent a few sprites in to make sure—the sprites had not returned. He'd been planning to give this information to Adrian tonight—but it couldn't wait. *Green* couldn't wait.

The house itself couldn't have looked less imposing. Built in the hollow of a hill, about half a mile from East Bidwell Street in Old Folsom, it was a depression-era structure—solid wood, crappy grey paint, most of it peeling, with a small sitting porch and a peaked, shingled roof. The lawn was overgrown but not brown. Cared for, but not trimmed. Green shuddered to think of what slithered through it. He was driving Adrian's Harley and it echoed loudly off the street as he drove up, and he could feel the eyes of the locals peering dourly out of the shades in the adjoining homes. Of course they wouldn't expect anything odd to happen there—all of the *really* strange things happened at night, while they were all in a bespelled sleep. The moment Green's foot touched the gravel, he could feel it. The booming vibrations that came up from the hollow center of the hill and through his boots. Vibrations that spoke of power. He could almost laugh in frustration—Arturo and Cory had driven down this street half a dozen times—but they had never walked it. Even Cory could have felt this if she had walked on this particular street. The house itself was about a quarter mile from where the third "greasy spot" had been found. It was two miles from Ratso's corner. Green wanted to weep with the perfection of it. Perfection may not necessarily be guilt, he reminded himself as he stalked up the stairs two at a time. But it was at least a stepping off place to see who *was* guilty.

The front door was open, with only a screen hiding the rest of the house from view, and Green's sense of caution returned. The inside consisted of a darkened room—it had no ventilation or air-conditioning, and reeked of paint fumes, because it had been spray bombed to perfection. The word *Sezan* was featured prominently in every motif, as well as various figures exploding, dripping with blood. The artwork was twisted, disturbing, and brilliant. The only thing that kept the room from being completely unbearable was a small fan, swiveling lazily on the floor, and open windows in the front, coupled with an open door behind the living room, leading from the kitchen to outside. There was a hallway, and what looked like a set of stairs leading down, although he was on the ground floor of a one story house. In the living room itself, two people lay together on the broken couch against the wall, copulating languidly. Underneath the spray paint, Green could smell their sex, and the drugs that lay unheeded on the scratched table in front of the couch.

The fury boiling through Green was almost a high of its own. It made him reckless and calm and confident. Without knocking, without even clearing his throat, he strolled through the door—literally through; with the anger came power. He could have walked through a steel safe and kept going with the gold in his arms with what he was feeling. Soundlessly he dropped onto the couch and watched them, passionlessly, until their act was completed.

The boy was young, he mused. Younger even than Cory—certainly younger than the woman who rode him. Even stoned, his every touch was full of wonder, tenderness, amazement. Sex was new to him, Green realized with a touch of pity. Drugs were new to him as well. A new recruit, Green thought sadly. His anger stilled a little, as he watched the boy climax artlessly. The girl, more experienced, angrier, rode him ruthlessly until she was finished, then leaned her head against his chest and grunted.

"Getting better at this, baby. Soon you'll be a pro."

The boy smiled, his enlarged pupils and narrow face making him seem almost alien in his serenity. "That'll be nice." He mumbled.

"No, it won't." Green contradicted pleasantly from his seat at the foot of the couch. He watched as the girl turned towards him hostilely. Her face was not pretty, he reflected. It could have been—nice planes, nice angles—but her expression was not flattering towards it, and the curl at her lips looked perpetual. Her hair, also, was dyed a distressing color of coral that didn't look good with her skin tone.

"Who the fuck are you?" She spat, standing up and adjusting her skirt and tank top. Always ready for action, mused Green—he didn't see a trace of bra or panties in the cluttered room.

Green smiled, ironically but winningly, and stood. "I'm someone who knows that you never want to do professionally what should only be done for love." He murmured. "At least for love of the act itself, yes?" He aimed this last at the boy who had stood, and was trying his best to fasten his 501's around his naked hips. His shirt was slung around his shoulders—he'd been using it as a pillow. Thin, thought Green, but rangy, and built. Give him ten years, and he'd be tall and muscular. Poor baby—seduced by this coral snake. What a boy wouldn't do for a little sexual satisfaction—they were distressingly easy targets for evil, that way.

The kid's concentration was touching, and with a paternal sigh, Green grabbed his shoulders and turned him so they were facing, then bent down and buttoned the boy's jeans. He looked at Green bemusedly, even more so when the contact caused his jeans to tighten. Green stood and tousled his hair. "Don't worry about it, Junior." He said, a smile in his voice. "Even good boys forget to keep their fly done."

The young man smiled back, sweetly. His eyes were a soulful brown, Green remarked ruefully. He was pulled back to reality by the coral snake's sharpened nail, scraping down his T-shirt at the shoulder. He caught her hand before the nail could reach skin.

"Like I said before, faggot, who the fuck are you?" She asked. Green regarded her coral colored manicure serenely. Poison there, he mused. Wolfsbane, oleander…something else, something preternatural, designed to suck out his will.

"I am not to be trifled with." He replied, keeping his voice pleasant. With a slow, deliberate touch he dragged his finger across the top of her nails, ignoring her gasp at the faint blue light that canceled the poison. "So tell me, coral snake," he continued, grasping her chin between his fingers and scrutinizing her face intently, "Are you Crispin's creature, or Sezan's?"

The girl squirmed under his regard—Green knew it couldn't have been pleasant. Just touching her made his skin tingle with the conflict of forces, good and evil. She may have been small and petty and mean, but she was still potently evil. Green was man enough—and sidhe enough—to know that evil had its own attractions. He dropped the hand on the chin, but still he kept her wrist imprisoned in his grip, and her eyes level with his own. The young man, puzzled, made a move towards Green, as though to protect her, but Green stilled him with a single touch on his chest. He heard the kid grunt, in surprise, in confusion, and moved his hand up, still without looking, to stroke the side of his face. The boy stilled, will-less, quiet, happy to be near Green.

"So…" Green intoned, willing her to answer. His will was quite powerful.

"Crispin gave me to Sezan." She murmured. Green could see them now, on the side of her neck. The pinpoint scars that came with being a frequent donor. Cory would have them soon, thought Green a little sadly. Green had his own, long faded now, where his two recent wounds sat.

"Interesting." Murmured Green in reply. "Were you a bet, a bribe, or a bauble?"

The girl smiled, then, bitterly, and Green wondered if that moment hadn't been the moment of coral nail polish and electric hair for her. "I was a bribe. Crispin gave Sezan a lot of bribes at first."

"Hmm...and now what does he give Sezan?" Green asked, voice still pleasant, hand still gripping her wrist. The young man still stood at Green's back, so Green ran his hand down his body, slowly, suggestively, and the boy leaned into his touch like a kitten.

The girl looked down, a poisoned tear escaped her eye, and ran with mascara down her face. "Tribute." She said softly.

Green nodded. It was the answer he'd expected, with more pain, perhaps, than he'd anticipated. He let go of her wrist and caught her chin again, pressing his lips together with hers in a blue lighted kiss. He felt her poison seep away from her pores, and planted a 'gift' of his own. "So, Tribute," He named her, as he pulled away from her kiss, "The next time you see Crispin, give him that message for me, will you?"

She nodded, looking at him with elf-struck eyes. "I can only do that if Sezan allows me to." She told him blankly.

Green raised his eyebrows. The compulsion he'd cast had been fairly strong—apparently Sezan's compulsion was stronger. It was almost overkill, to burden the little coral snake with such a command. Sezan was either very new at this game, or very paranoid about the things he thought of as his. "Well then," He told her seriously, "You will have to give the message to Sezan, yes?"

"Yes." She answered, and he gave her a tiny push on the chest, sitting her down on the couch behind her. A sound behind him made Green turn around to the kid, who was gazing at him adoringly.

"You want something, don't you?" Green asked kindly, and the boy nodded unhappily.

"You don't know how to name it, do you?" He continued, and the boy shook his head, biting his lip. Green raised a tender hand to a stubbled face. Poor baby—probably an artist, someone sensitive, misunderstood, frightened of life. Not a child anymore, and yet easily sucked into this house, with its unholy leaders, its cruelty, and its pain.

"I'll tell you what you want," murmured Green, allowing the kid to lean into him. Their lips touched, and Green pulled back. "You want love." They touched again, retreated. "Acceptance." He whispered, finding the taste of the young man sweet, still, like a chocolate dropped on the floor. A little dirt there, yet the chocolate remained. "Safety." And with a moan the boy pulled Green into a kiss, and Green crushed him against his body, being generous with his arousal and his tongue. And he flooded the boy with protection against the coral snake, and any other poison that may have been flooding his veins at the moment, filling him with it, until Green knew he would see the place for what it was, and live to tell the tale. The young man gave a little half sob, and fell to the floor in a second climax, bemused and frightened.

Green crouched down by him, pulling off his own T-Shirt, and using it to wipe off the fluid that now covered the newly buttoned jeans. "I give you acceptance and safety boy." Green told him, dropping the shirt into his lap. Then he stood and tousled his hair on the way out of the door. "All you need to do is ask."

He made a sound, and Green turned back to him. Their eyes met for a moment, but the younger man looked down, clasping his knees against his chest and rocking back and forth, shaking his head.

"Any time, boy. My name is Green. Ask around—you'll be able to find me." He turned back at the door.

"By the way, Tribute," He said carelessly before he left, "Where does Sezan play? When does he play next?"

"He plays at *Granite Horse* tonight." She responded, still blankly. Poor baby, he thought again in sympathy, caught between two compulsions of such strength. She'd be lucky if she survived with her mind.

And with that thought he stalked to his motorcycle and gunned the motor, disappearing down the street wearing a helmet and a pair of jeans, his smooth-skinned chest white enough to reflect the glare of the sun.

CORY

How Not to be a Gas Station Clerk

I awoke once to the sound of raised voices—Arturo's and Greens—why would they be fighting?—and then a fuzzy feeling, like pulling a static-ky sock off your shirt, and then I was sucked right back down into sleep again. When I awoke again I was in a tangle of limbs, so much so that I had to fight my way to the surface, gasping for breath. I found two thick braids, one dark, one fair, crossing my body, and Adrian's eyes, staring at me in concern, as he hovered above me about a foot from the bed.

"Jesus," I murmured, "Can everybody fly here but me?"

"You can fly." Arturo said from the foot of the bed, "You just can't control it."

That did it...blonde braid—Green, dark braid—Bracken, fuzzy red hair over Green's hip—Grace, voice at the foot of the bed—Arturo, purring noise—Renny..."Get off me!" I yelped, feeling suddenly claustrophobic. Eight pairs of eyes regarded me from various positions on the bed, sleepy and stunned. I inhaled, to keep from screaming, and tried again.

"Everybody here who has *never* seen me naked, get up right now." To my complete chagrin, nobody moved. My horrified eyes met Adrian's, and he was smirking. Damn that night in the garden, anyway!!!

"Everybody here I never *wanted* to see me naked, please get out of this bed!!!!" They took pity on me then, and everybody except Green got out of the bed, slowly. Green I let pass, because not only did he look wiped out but

- 133 -

everybody in the room including Adrian probably knew I didn't mind if he saw me naked. But it didn't matter, because after Brack unwound his braid from my hips and knees, I felt like I could breathe again, but I wasn't telling them they could go back to their original positions, nope, no sirree, no way.

"Whew." Adrian came down gently besides me then, and hugged me gratefully. I leaned into him, happy beyond words to have him there. It occurred to me, poignantly, that there was much of my life that Adrian would not have, and I burrowed closer to him, frighteningly near tears. "What is everybody doing here?" I asked, when I was sure I could speak clearly.

"Worrying." Bracken replied dryly.

I burrowed into Adrian's shirt again. "I'm actually without words." I murmured. Adrian laughed at me, then, and I was absurdly comforted. If Adrian could laugh at me then I was still me in this weird world. I was still human.

"Like that'll ever happen." Green said sleepily.

"You healed me, Green." I said, still turned into Adrian's shirt. He smelled good. He smelled like soap and clothes softener and testosterone and *vampire*. I thought I could devour his smell alone. And tantalizingly, he smelled like Green, and I could eat that up with a spoon too.

"And almost killed his damned fool self." Arturo bit off. He sent an unfriendly look at Green, which, to my surprise, Adrian echoed.

"What the fuck were you thinking?" Adrian asked him, and I was surprised. I was even more surprised when everybody else—including Brack and Grace—sided with the two men, and glared at Green, who looked away meekly.

Adrian surprised me again. He grabbed Green's shoulder and turned him to face us. "I'm serious, mate." Adrian said, his face twisted by dismay. "What the hell was that, walking in there without us? You were *alone*...what the fuck're we for, if you're going to do that?"

"Where'd you go?" I asked, but Green wasn't making eye contact. "Where'd he go?" I asked Arturo, and his copper-lightning eyes practically set my hair on fire.

"He went to Crispin's. The other vampire. He went to Sezan's."

My jaw dropped. "Where..." I started to ask.

"Between Natoma and East Bidwell—half a mile from the 7/11." Arturo bit out.

"But we were just there..."

"We never walked the land." Arturo shook his head, disgusted. "Green said we would have felt it, if we had ever walked the land."

"That's not your fault." Green told him.

"Just like it's not my fault that you went haring off there alone? You wouldn't have gone if I..."

"If *we*, Arturo." Green bit. "It was the both of us—you were obviously upset, and I let you get carried along with me. I had to walk away."

"Right into the mouth of the fucking dragon!" Adrian snapped.

And now *I* was pissed at Green. "You just walked in there? Without us? Why would you do that, you asshole?" I found that I was not just angry—I was hurt. I felt like we had failed him, and he had taken the whole thing into his own hands.

And now he looked at me, his eyes not soft and comforting but hard and bright, like emeralds, or ice caverns in a green sea. "They *hurt* you." He ground out. And suddenly the room was silent. I felt Adrian touch my knee, feel lower, felt his hand on the still new skin of my calf, and he was tender. His hand was trembling.

I swallowed. "But I'm not anyone." I said, in a small voice, not meeting any eyes. "I'm not anyone, and you're Green. They need you." I looked up at him now, and at Adrian and Arturo. "Your people need you—all of you." I should have sounded impassioned, but I wasn't. I was just quiet. It was truth.

Green laughed and shook his head, and Arturo too. Adrian regretfully touched my face, but it was Brack who finally spoke.

"Well, Cory, I guess it's pretty obvious that they need you too."

I was without words, again. "I'm nobody." I said again. Meaning it.

Green laughed then, bitterly, but warmly, and Adrian followed him, without the bitterness. Arturo joined in, then Brack, then Grace, and even Renny danced about, smiling in that way that big cats do. So that answered that, I guessed. Not nobody. Me.

"Who was there?" I asked, suddenly. "What did you find?"

Green sighed, and sat up. He looked in need of a good "healing" himself. I wanted to do it, I realized. I wanted to run my hands on him and feed him my energy in the worst way. I breathed in Adrian's smell, deeply, reassuringly, but even that still smelled of Green.

"Sezan—whoever he is—is definitely behind this." He said after a sigh. "There's artwork there—terrible pictures, spray bombed all over the walls. Whoever he is, he isn't being subtle about it."

"And people?" Adrian asked.

"Two." Green smiled, a twist to his lips, and sensuality. I shivered, and I felt Adrian do the same. One hundred and fifty years, they had known each other. I shivered because I wondered about that smile, Adrian shivered because he knew. "One was quite evil." Green continued, "A poisonous little coral snake, all set to bite."

"So you defanged her?" Arturo asked.

"And mind fucked her as well." Green added. "It wasn't pretty—someone had laid a pretty stiff compulsion on her—I had to work to get her to do what I asked."

Mind-fucked—it was too close to what I had done to Officer Max. "Did you mind fuck the other one?" I asked sharply, but Green just looked at me, all understanding. That could get irritating, but it wasn't right now.

"Nope." And still that smile. "Him I seduced."

I found myself smiling back, fully, knowing I was wearing all of my newly discovered sex in my sunshine smile. "How'd he taste?"

"Like a five second rule Oreo..." he said thoughtfully

"A five second rule Oreo?"

"A little dirty, but still sweet..." We smiled at each other then, and there was heat there, extraordinary heat. I felt Adrian's arms still around me, and knew he was growing hard with the wanting of the both of us.

Arturo cleared his throat delicately. "And what of Sezan?" He asked.

Green looked at him sideways from suddenly feline eyes, and then looked back at Adrian, and then at me. I couldn't turn my head to gauge Adrian's expression but I had the feeling something important had been said. "If he's still playing tonight, I want to be there."

"Playing?" Brack asked.

"His band is playing at *the Granite Horse*." Green explained. "But I left something...unpleasant, with his little coral snake. If she delivers the message, he might not be up to the night, which would be fine too."

"Why fine?" I asked.

"Because, my little vampire slayer, if he's out of commission, he won't be doing whatever he's doing to make our shape changers explode, and then we might have a little chance to work on keeping you safe. Because you're *very* powerful, dear one—and I can't afford to let that much power sit at home while the rest of us go out and fight bad guys. I need to train you up a bit, before this mission—and therefore, a little time would be just fine too."

"Powerful." I said after a moment. It made sense, an awful sense, but sense nonetheless. "A powerful what?"

Green looked thoughtful. "A powerful sorceress…witch…being…just powerful, I guess…"

"Jesus." Grace snorted from the back of the room. "A powerful woman, for one—and we're going to clear out of here and let you deal with your woman things—food is on in an hour, any and all help will be appreciated." And like that, the room was clear, leaving Green and Adrian and I alone together. Green was still lounging against the bed's headboard, and I was still nearly in Adrian's lap. I scooted, taking Adrian with me, until I was close enough to reach out and touch Green's cheek, which I did.

"How mad's Arturo?" I asked, seriously.

"As mad at himself as at me." Green answered, capturing my hand and closing his eyes.

"That was really stupid—you know that, right?"

He opened his eyes, looked at Adrian, looked at me. "I'd do it again, in a second. No one goes after you two. Not Crispin, not Sezan—whoever he is— not the other himself. No one."

Adrian reached out, put his hand on Green's leg, and we all gasped. The lights dimmed, then brightened, and I heard a sound that popped my ears. I went to drop my hand from Green's cheek, but he seized it, kept it there, and seized Adrian's hand as it rested against his thigh. He made eye contact with both of us, and I felt almost suffocated by the power that roiled through me, the room, the men whose bare skin touched mine.

"This is us." He whispered. "This is love, and want, and power—preternatural and personal. This is us. You two need to decide what to do about it—but you need to know what we are…"

I needed to scream. I turned my eyes to the window, his lovely bay window that looked into the night, and opened my mouth and my eyes, and screamed. What came out was sunshine, bright, teeming with life, full of seeking, fertile fingers. Adrian shrank from me, shrank from that ray of death, and even as I was overtaken with it, I took care to point it out into the night. As my head tilted back and my sunshine scream burst forth, I could see Green's people, flocking to it, dancing, glowing with health, and then he released us, and I fell against Adrian, aghast.

We sat there, still, breathing hard, aroused, and watched outside that window as Green's gardens ran riot, unfurling, blooming, flowers multiplying infinitely. What had once been lovely and peaceful was now gorgeous and alive, fertile mayhem that would all but engulf the house and the porch before it was done growing. In the morning, an army of Green's people would have to dig out cars, lawn furniture, and some very indignant gnomes and nixies. All we could do at that moment was watch in awe. And wonder what came next.

News came next—Grace had called *the Granite Horse,* to find out what time Sezan's band played, and was told that the lead guitarist had come down with the flu. A sigh of relief passed through the three of us, still sprawled on Green's bed, and Grace must have known we'd be unable to answer questions about the wonder that we had just performed, because she asked none.

Dinner came after that. The three of us were too drained to participate in the fixing, of course, but Blissa had been busy that evening, after I had been injured, and Green had been up to powerful magic, so there was means and need for a formal dinner. I enjoyed the formal dinners in the vast, dark wood dining room under the house proper. They reminded me of Camelot, and fairy tales I had read as a child, except, instead of being one of the serving wenches as I had always imagined myself, I was at the head table. As much as I complained of my own insignificance, nothing could counter my joy—as well as the awesome weight—of being one of those at the head table. There was a savory irony in the fact that when I had accepted Adrian, I had thought I was loving the frog, but in reality, he was to all intents and purposes, a prince of an underground kingdom. And he kissed much better than a frog.

But the irony was overwhelming, as well. I watched Adrian taking a report from Marcus, a short, wiry, dark-haired vampire who gave me shy, sideways glances as he told Adrian that there hadn't been any shape-changer fatalities or disappearances reported in the Fair Oaks/Carmichael/Citrus Heights area. I was going to ask him what was wrong, when he had stopped talking, but that was when he sank to one knee and bent his head. I had seen Adrian perform this gesture, and I had tried it, clumsily, but I had never, ever, in a thousand years, imagined that somebody would perform this obeisance to me. I was speechless. Then, when I looked around and saw that every vampire in the room was performing the same gesture, I was horrified.

"Adrian..." I murmured, "Wha..."

"Stand up, luv." He said softly.

I didn't have any better ideas. I stood, and so did Adrian, who looked around, and spoke so that his voice carried. "Corinne Carol-Anne Kirkpatrick," He said clearly, "Vampire slayer, bringer of sunshine and death, my love, we name you, we honor you, and we will protect you. Those who would do you harm are not among our number. So I say, so say we all."

"So say we all." And it wasn't a murmur. It was a whisper of power, a thunder of acceptance, and I realized that this was a ritual of power, more meaningful, and possibly more binding, than any marriage ceremony I had ever attended. I was being married to Adrian's Kiss. As much as making love to Adrian, to being responsible for another being's death, as yearning for Green and reveling in power, this was a binding of me to a life I had not dreamed of, or even believed in. I bowed my head and thought of Green's eyes, and Adrian's touch, and sent these through my voice.

"And so I accept." A whisper of wind blew through the hall as I breathed out, that gained in power until it stirred the hair of every being in the room. The vampires cried out, and some of them wept blood. When I turned to Adrian, I saw that his eyes were wet as well.

"Wha…" I started, but he shook his head and held me close to him, as the hall erupted into applause.

"Your breath, your voice…" he murmured, against my hair. "You smelled like sunshine and flowers in bloom, and things that we will never see again."

I whimpered with the pain in his voice—in all of their voices—then turned to those who were now my people and bowed. The applause threatened to last all night, and I was suddenly very overwhelmed. "I'm no one." I said quietly, as I sat down. "I'm not who they think I am." Adrian didn't hear me—he wouldn't have understood anyway, because from the time he had walked into the Chevron station, I had been his world. As difficult as that had been to understand, this was worse.

Green heard me. He stood gracefully, offered me an elbow, and waited as I gathered myself and moved towards him. Adrian looked up from a discussion with another vampire—this one from West Sacramento, and as new, I thought, to all of this, as I felt—and nodded at the two of us. Green bowed to the assembly, and so did I, and together we exited up the stairs. When we got to the top, I didn't know where to go.

"I'm not tired." I blurted to Green, and he smiled. When he smiled, the clean lines of his face were interrupted by creases at the corner of his mouth, and dimples. I liked that very much.

"Neither am I." He said, "But you were feeling overwhelmed."

"You weren't." I responded.

"This is a small gathering, compared to the fairie rings of Oberon and the Tuatha de Danaan."

I felt my eyes getting big, and suddenly wished I was back down in the assembly. At least Adrian had been born after the Industrial Revolution. And Grace, I thought faintly, Grace was barely old enough to be my mother—we were practically children together, compared to the man looking at me with that amusement on his face.

"I don't understand." I murmured. "How can you be older than all of us, but understand us all better than we do ourselves?"

Green shrugged, simplicity itself. "It's what I do." He replied. It was a line from a really bad movie, I remembered. I had laughed my ass off at it.

"Is there a television anywhere?" I asked, out of the blue.

"There's a big screen right there in the front room." He responded, his smile widening. "And DVD's and videos."

"I hadn't noticed." I said thoughtfully, looking at the widescreen plasma television, concealed behind a panel. "Do you have a preference?"

"*Lethal Weapon,* 1, 2, & 4. "He said promptly, "But not 3. I hate the third one—horrible script. Either that or *Shakespeare in Love.*" I found myself giggling. Unable to reply, I followed him into the living room, giggling like an imbecile. I giggled while he put the movie in, (*Lethal Weapon 2*) and giggled during the previews, and giggled while he made popcorn, during the whole first scene with the car chase. But at the end of the scene, he sat behind me and gathered me to him, putting the popcorn in my lap, and my body stopped convulsing, and the giggles eased, and my mind stilled. It could have been magic, I thought, right before I was pulled into the movie, but I was pretty sure it was just Green.

I fell asleep during *Lethal Weapon 4,* but it was okay, because Adrian came in then, fresh from feeding, and sat on the couch with us, watching the screen flicker in delight. I realized, waking up a little, that Adrian and Green both loved movies, the same way little kids like movies, unabashedly, delightedly, with their whole heart. The thought made me weepy, so I closed my eyes against it, and waited until Adrian took me back to the darkling, only a few hours before dawn. He had been planning, I realized, to work on correspondence in his room—he had a computer there as well, and ran his own tight little ship, just like Green's, but smaller, and his computer hosted a lot more porn sites. But I awoke, and spoke before he had a chance to leave me alone in his bed, and he lay next to me and we talked.

"What happened tonight." I asked him.

"You killed one of us today—we were paying you honor for it." He replied.

"I don't understand."

He shrugged, and smiled. He looked young, I thought, tracing the curve of his lips with my forefinger; young, and amoral, and dangerous. And he loved me. He nipped at me playfully, capturing my finger between tongue and fang. Sucked on it, for a moment, released it, seized my hand and did the same for the other fingers. He'd had a long time to learn how to do this, I thought muzzily. He was really good at it.

"You're distracting me." I accused him, but not with any real anger.

"I'm playing for time." He admitted. "It's nothing that goes well into words."

"They're all we've got." I told him.

"But not forever…when you get the fourth mark, we'll share minds, at will…"

I sat up in bed. "The fourth mark? What about the first mark…Adrian?" He was looking away from me…and he didn't look amoral anymore. He looked ashamed. What did it take to make a vampire ashamed.

"It was an accident…" He began.

"An *accident?*" I felt my mad beginning to come on, and, I realized, after turning Green's garden into an Amazon paradise, ripping the arm off a vampire and flying, being wounded and healed, and that weird little party downstairs, I wasn't ready to be mad, not physically. But my emotions were another matter altogether.

"An accident." He said firmly, capturing my gaze. He was doing something hinky, I could feel it, but my mad went away, and my mind was left open, accepting—but mine and no one else's.

"Thank you." I told him. I meant it.

"I'd say any time, but you won't need me to do that often. You've had a long day…a couple of them, actually. And my hours don't help…"

I smiled then, a little. "Yeah…vampire's hours…they're a bitch."

He flashed a little fang—and told me about the marks. "So the first mark was an accident." He finished. "I…you were there, when the daylight hit…and wherever I go, I went through you, and I left a part of myself there."

"You humble me." I said softly.

Disturbingly enough, my words didn't make him happy. "Then you're really going to like this next part…"

GREEN

The Powers That Be

Green found her curled up on the end of the couch. She had dragged the quilt off her own bed, and was buried in it, in spite of the sun that pierced through his window. Already, the rest of the household was stirring, and with a wry twist to his mouth he remembered her first morning in his house. He didn't want a repeat of that. Preparing himself for the wave of want that would sweep through him, he swept her up in his arms, passing Crocken and his fellow Red-Caps, shovels over shoulders, on their way outside to start hacking through the tremendous growth that had finally stilled during the night. Crocken looked at the sleeping child in Green's arms and shook his head. He turned to Green, ignoring the almost comical back-up of fey behind him.

"C'mon, Da…" Brack complained as he rounded the corner, then caught sight of Green and stopped in respectful silence.

"She'd make a strong Queen." He said gruffly, and Green arched his eyebrows in surprise. He'd always run a pretty open ship, but the number of people butting into his personal business lately was fairly disconcerting.

"Mind your own business, Da." Brack hollered from the back, pushing his way through the other Red-Caps. He pat them on the head, affectionately as he waded—they were his uncles and cousins, and he shared their gruffness, and their violence. When he reached Green he grimaced in annoyance.

"Don't mind him." Brack murmured. "It's all cut and dried—he doesn't recognize Adrian, you know?"

Green shrugged. "Her status is her business, Crocken." He replied. "She doesn't even know what that means, yet."

"She was quick enough at accepting it from *his* kind." Crocken harrumphed.

"They both love Adrian, Da." Brack interjected. "You won't turn a King to a Red-Cap by dissing what they both love…"

"What the hell kind of word is that?" Crocken asked, turning to his son. Brack defended himself, cannily winking at Green and hurrying his father through the living room and out the door. Green stood patiently by as first the Red-cap brigade, then nymphs and mid-sized fey paraded by him. Eager for the chance to show off, they saluted their leader, singing and whistling as they went by, and breaking into a variety of fractured grins when Green returned the gesture with a nod of the head, or a smile. Cory didn't stir the entire time, and he wondered if he'd ever tire of holding her. He was stronger than mortals, true, but it was something more, something uniquely Corinne Carol-Anne Kirkpatrick, that took the burden from carrying her limp body. As the smallest of the fey disappeared, carried on the backs of Renny and the other fifteen or so members of Renny's clowder that were sticking close to Green's house for safety, Green looked again at Cory's sleeping face, and saw that she'd been crying as she fell asleep. He also saw the second mark, glowing from the fresh fang marks on her throat.

"He told her." He murmured.

He put her in her own bed, which still had Renny's imprint and a few tawny cat hairs at its foot. He sat next to her, looking around at her room. It had been her space less than a week, but already it glowed with her. He could be carried into the room blindfolded, and know, he thought. There were her prints on the wall, and the quilt that she dragged around like a child would, of course, but there was more. When he closed his eyes he saw the warm brown/clear blue of an autumn morning. On the edges was a brilliant sunset orange pink. This was Cory, he thought: earthy strength, clear blue dreams, a nascent sexuality that was beginning to emanate strongly from her body and her aura. It should have clashed, but it didn't. It contrasted. For a moment he closed his eyes and allowed himself to sink into her. And felt it, right there, the deep purple of the vampire marks, two of them, now, making her glow with Adrian.

Something moved in Green, something unpleasant and dark. He didn't mind seeing Adrian's colors there—in fact it both moved and aroused him, to think of Cory's colors mixing equally with Adrian's. But he wanted his own. He wanted Cory in his own soul. He wanted his soul in hers. And he wanted Adrian back.

He had to smile a little at himself. If he had stayed, all those years ago, in England, or had gone to Canada where most of the other high elves and sidhe had gone when they emigrated, he wouldn't be in this dilemma. High Elves and the sidhe, the fairest of the fey and mightiest of the strong, didn't often give a damn about monogamy. They had centuries to themselves—who could be faithful for centuries? Men often had problem being faithful for *weeks* at a time, so elves just didn't bother. They were as free with their bodies as they were exciting and addictive lovers—a trait that nearly did them all in after Christianity took over Europe. But when they did bother with monogamy, it bordered on obsession in a way that the Bard only *hinted* at in *Midsummer's Night's Dream*. And when they did obsess, it was with mortals.

Of course, they hadn't ever figured on vampires, Green thought wryly. Vampires had been a legend to the elves, and vice versa. The vampires had lived amongst the human cities to hunt, and the fey had lived in the rural areas and the woodlands, having only periodic interaction with humans, until the Industrial Revolution had pushed the fey closer to the night hunters. A few of them had even become prey—of each species, since not all the fey were bipedal herbivores. As far as he knew, though, he and Adrian were the first lovers—and Green's Fairie Hill the only combination of elvin conclave and vampire kiss to exist in the world. But then, Adrian had been human first, and had become a vampire in order to follow Green to immortality. And Green was one of those elves who took human lovers obsessively, loving them through old age and dust. The two of them were well matched to create a form of government unheard of in the preternatural world.

This brought him back to the event that brought Cory into his life at the beginning. Mitchell Hammond. Sezan. The death of his people. And how a weapon to fight their destruction had fallen neatly into his lap. Gently he stroked Cory's forehead, his hands rifling through her short, strawberry-blonde hair. So young. So strong. *Ah, Cory, luv,* he thought, *we're all using you.* Adrian had made her his queen, and now Green would have her too.

She must have heard him think because her eyelids fluttered open.

"Hey, Green." She said, her voice raspy.

"'Lo, luv." He replied, keeping his hand on her forehead.

"I'm the Queen of the fucking Northern California vampires. I'm two marks away from complete power, and being some sort of human vampire crossbreed liaison." She told him, as though she had memorized the speech.

"I know that."

"I had a hard enough time being me when I just wanted a bachelor's degree."

Her voice was pitching querulously. "Go back to sleep, sweet." He told her, continuing to stroke her brow, and willing her to slumber. "When you wake up, I'll show you how."

"You assholes have to stop putting me under," she murmured, closing her eyes.

"You have to learn to stop us." He whispered, and kissed her temple. Then he bounded out her bed to dress and go join the red caps.

Arturo had recovered much of his humor when Green got outside. Part of it, Green knew, was the fun he had ordering the fey around—Arturo had an autocratic streak a mile wide. The other part was anticipation.

"This is powerful magic, brother." Arturo was saying as he grabbed hold of a gnome's kicking legs and pulled the creature out of the baby's breath that had engulfed him. "She's going to do us proud."

Green frowned. "She's not a weapon, Arturo. Adrian's already got her in over her head—I don't want to terrify her."

Arturo stopped and glared at the chaos around them. "Look at this, Leader. We've got something going after our people, and here's this little girl who can take him out—are you seriously telling me you'll let her just sit at home when this comes to a head?"

Green smiled, bitterly as it were. With a careless wave of his hand he ordered a pair of rose bushes to cease and desist. Meekly the plants stopped rioting up the wise old maple tree that was the centerpiece of the garden and shrank back to their original size. "I don't think she'd let us do that." He murmured. "She still mourns Mitchell, and watches over Renny like a mother hen—she won't want to be left home. I'm just saying that she had a purpose before she came here, and we shouldn't put any obstacles in front of her ambitions if we can help it. And her power's a complicated thing—look at this, with all your eyes, Arturo."

Arturo scowled, then closed his eyes for a second and breathed deeply, then looked up at his leader. "This isn't just her." He said thoughtfully.

Green shook his head, and made another pass of his hand towards a once-placid little gladioli bed. The flowers shrunk to normal size, but their Technicolor blooms remained stubbornly day-glow. "Nope."

"I mean, it's mostly her, but it's you and Adrian too...you're all tangled together here...it's almost..." Arturo shifted his stance uncomfortably, then, in that curiously macho way men have, rearranged his body to fit more comfortably. He looked at Green in alarm. "You three didn't have that much time." He said incredulously.

"We touched, Arturo—that's all. Adrian and I, Cory and Adrian, Cory and I...we all touched. And this happened. It was pure sunlight—if she hadn't thought carefully she could have destroyed Adrian with a scream."

Arturo swallowed, and looked blankly at a tiny, butterfly sized fairy that was trapped in a Morning Glory vine. She shrieked indignantly and he reached out and freed her. "Damn. That's complicated."

Green snorted. "Tell me about it. Christ, Arturo—I wanted her. I think I may love her. But that's a hell of a thing to pull on a kid. She's already damn near Queen of Night—what could she be if she were Queen of the Day as well? I don't know if I can do that to her...it's not bloody fair."

Arturo looked at him, narrow eyed, while he ripped handfuls of the furious baby' s breath out of the ground until it behaved. "So you're telling me you're not going teach her how to use all this?"

It was tempting to say no, he wouldn't, but Green looked at the crowded yard. The werefolk were crammed into his home, onto his grounds, leaving jobs and families and staying in their morphed forms for days at a time. If they stayed too long, they could get stuck there—or at least lose some of their most obviously human characteristics, such as their eyes, or their herbivorous back teeth.

With a sigh he blew out towards a waist high patch of lawn, and watched it as it mowed itself in the wake of the passage of air. A dozen sprites climbed out from the fallen grass leaves in relief, and began to haul them away. "Well, now, brother, I didn't say that..."

Arturo grinned ferally, and Green snarled back. Cory would approve of that fierceness, he thought, and began to put his back into his work.

Cory toddled out in mid-afternoon, then sank to the ground with a sigh to watch them work.

"What did you do to me?" She demanded grouchily. "I was *not* that tired."

Green snorted. "mmm...should we count the ways you were drained of energy last night, Cory luv?" He moved to where she was seated and plopped down next to her. The yard was nearly back to normal now, and his folk were resting. He himself was tired from his work—both the physical and the metaphysical. He watched under his eyelashes as she eyed his body, shiny with sweat, and wriggled her bottom a few discreet inches away from him. He laughed then in a way that was all man, and then laughed louder when she wriggled again, uncomfortable with her reaction.

"We will talk about *that* later." He said, without a trace of repentance. "But for now, I want you to close your eyes a bit, and tell me what you see."

She looked at him, levelly, but didn't argue. Her eyes closed and she leaned back, letting the sun bathe her face with careless joy. "I see gold and red." She said after a moment.

"Very good." He murmured, then caught her chin between his thumb and forefinger and lowered her chin, until her vision would have been parallel to the horizon. "Now what do you see."

"Blue." She said promptly. "A really nice blue—like the sky, but cleaner and colder. And brown—you know that dark brown like chocolate, but with more red?"

Her descriptions were rich, he thought. Studied, in depth. Specific. Good.

"And what else?" He prompted.

"Adrian. And you. And the Sunrise."

Green snapped to attention. "I beg your pardon?"

"Colors like you..." She struggled. "Purple, like the sky before dark. Green, like gardens in England...it doesn't take a genius to figure out this is us, Green." She snapped, opening her eyes and glaring at him. "Except that whole sunrise thing...what the hell is that?"

Green looked at her, disgruntled. Quick. Damn, she was quick. He wondered who had ever underestimated his Cory—and what it had cost them. With calculated slowness he put his hand on the inside of her knee—she was only wearing shorts, and the skin to skin contact made her gasp.

"Close your eyes." He ordered.

"But..."

"Close your eyes." He repeated patiently, and covered her face with his other hand, rising on his knees to squat in front of her as he did so. Then he moved the hand at her knee to her thigh. He heard her whimper. Then he trailed it up to the inside of her thigh, and ever so softly stroked the skin at the crux of where her thigh met her body, and he heard her moan. Then...

"Ohhhhhh...." She murmured in wonder. Then she shot out a hand to dead center on his chest and pushed hard, glowering at him as he flopped backwards in the grass and laughed some more.

"Real goddamned funny, Green." She hissed. "How do you know Adrian won't kill you for that."

Green grinned. "Two things, luv. One, I'm incredibly hard to kill. Two, he loves me almost as much as he loves you. Now I said we'd talk about this later and I meant it, so let's get back to work, shall we?"

"Work..."

"I'm teaching you how to use all that energy in that lovely head of yours, yes? Now tell me the things you've done so far, eh?"

"Well..." she said thoughtfully, shredding a grass leaf as she spoke, "I knocked you on your ass..."

"That you did." He grinned.

"Now hush and let me finish...I..." she blushed, "I healed Adrian, I ripped a vampire's arm off, and I did...this." She gestured to the garden. "Except I didn't do this alone, I needed you and Adrian to do it."

"Quite right—and remember that. There are probably some things you can do in *gestalt* with other people that you can't do by yourself, so learn not to rely on those things, eh?"

"I never do." She said sharply, and he felt his fingers itching to smooth her hair back. She hadn't brushed it yet, but it looked amazing sticking out all over her head like that, and all he really wanted to do was smooth it down for her. Ah, well, he sighed, then did it anyway, and pulled his hand back just before the expected slap. "Behave." She said mildly.

"I'm the King of this particular Faerie Hill, Cory. The standards of behavior are mine to judge." She opened her mouth to retort, but he got there first. "Now close your eyes again and think about colors."

She did as she was told. They worked hard for the next few hours. Imagine a color. Make it change. Superimpose it on another color. Think of the world as your coloring book. Make it what you will. This is how you change appearance. Now listen to the world. Listen to the sounds of trees, the heartbeat of birds, the whispers of worms—now sing in time. Now sing some Sheryl Crow and see what happens. This is how you change substance.

Green saw Adrian emerge just around moonrise. He laughed silently at the sight of Green's garden dancing in time to *Sweet Child of Mine* and walked quietly behind Cory and sat down. The song was a cover of an old guns n roses hit, but Cory's throaty alto did it justice. Green was sitting cross-legged, facing her, watching her face intently, but he met Adrian's eyes over her shoulder and they shared a soul-deep look of understanding and want. Then they realized that she had altered the lyrics.

He's got eyes of the bluest skies, after a summer rain...
I hate to look into those eyes and see an ounce of pain.
His hair reminds me of a shower of gold, but when I touch it I find
It's softer than love's own whispered words
And strike's my lover blind...

"I'm the one with the blue eyes, right?" He Asked, dropping behind her and wrapping his arms around her shoulders.

"Don't you know what color your eyes are?" She asked, leaning back into his arms. When she stopped singing the garden went back to normal—sort of. There was a prevalence of dark purple in the flowers, and the green— always lush and lovely, was so deep it almost breathed.

"Mirrors, darling...vampires and mirrors?"

Cory made a strangled sound, almost a laugh but not. "Then how are you so well groomed?" She snorted.

Adrian blinked. "I guess my friends have always been my mirrors."

"Well, hon, you have good friends." She chuckled, "You really are gorgeous."

He laughed then, and nuzzled her neck, but his eyes met Green's as he did so. The moment went from playful to serious, in one throb of Cory's blood underneath Adrian's incisor. Green felt himself go hard, in that one moment, and he watched, entranced, as Adrian lowered his head and sank into Cory's flesh, still while Green sank into his eyes. Green knew what was coming next, erected a shield over the three of them without thinking, and then just watched.

Cory moaned and leaned into Adrian completely, not forgetting that Green was sitting there. She knew he was watching as her once crossed legs straightened and stayed parted, but instead of closing him off, pretending he wasn't there, she embraced his presence. She abandoned herself to Adrian's feeding, knowing that Green was watching, trusting that she would still be safe. Her breathing quickened and Adrian moaned, and her body bucked and a grunt and a muffled scream wrenched from her throat as Adrian groaned in their completion. And his eyes never left Green's.

Their bodies lay then, lax in silvered dark, and Green leaned over Cory's body, carefully, to lick her blood off of Adrian's lips and teeth. Adrian closed his lips then, captured Green's tongue, and Green's knees gave a definite wobble. Cory's hands came up to his bare shoulders and began to explore the vulnerable area below his collarbone, before moving to his flat male nipples. He captured her hands, and pulled reluctantly away from Adrian, noting as he did so how their sexual repletion had dimmed but not eradicated the magical little pop'n'zings that had ping-ponged through his bloodstream the last time they had touched.

"Later, children." He murmured, kissing her hands with lips and tongue that still tasted of Adrian, and of her on Adrian's lips and tongue. "Later—tonight is for rest—we have things to do tomorrow." It was gratifying to hear them both whimper as he stood up and moved to walk away.

"What's tomorrow, Green?" He heard her ask. She sounded as though she were pulling her thoughts together from a great distance. Good.

"Tomorrow you go back to work." He heard her murmur of surprise, but kept walking, savoring their sounds of beginning love-making in the darkened garden. He made double sure his initial shield would hold, then walked through it, and the sounds disappeared. Soon, he promised himself. Soon.

CORY

Smile at the Nice Man

It felt weird to go back to work at the Chevron station. By 3 a.m. I had come to two conclusions—one was that there were **no** preternatural people out at all, and the world was a scary place without them. What had once been a teeming meeting place for trolls, brownies, were-animals and elves was now strictly humans only—and the dead of night was *really* the dead of night. The other conclusion was that I was not the same person I was two weeks ago.

I stood there, behind the counter, listening to the regulars asking me how vacation had been, and wondered if my life had ever been this small. Had there ever been a time when counting cigarettes had occupied more than a fraction of my brain pan? Had there ever been a time when I hadn't scanned the population, wondering who was preternatural and who was immortal, and who was just like me? Had there ever been a time when I hadn't realized that being just like me was a lot more than a pierced eyebrow and a bitchy attitude? Had I ever thought Arturo was nothing more than a night cook at Denny's? The thought humbled me. Arturo was so much more than a night cook at Denny's, just like Adrian was more than a flamboyant party-boy. And, even I could reason the rest. I was so much more than that "tough chick" persona that had kept me safe for so long. As I helped yet another regular, one who smiled and kidded me and asked me where my tan was, since I had been on vacation and all, I felt that tough chick crumble around me, falling at my feet like a tattered prom dress.

I smiled at the regular like a real human being, and saw the older man go all moony and slack jawed as he pushed out of the double doors. I could almost smell his wonderment, and knew that in that moment, with that smile, I had been his favorite niece, his best granddaughter, and the first girl he had ever kissed, all rolled into one. I could do that with a smile, I realized. Who needed to be a bitch?

Bracken sauntered in and I erased the smile from my face. It wasn't that I was mad at him, but if I just suddenly buckled and turned into a complete Pollyanna, he'd probably die of shock. They *all* might. I figured I might ease into this "I'm not *really* a bitch thing" slowly—it would be more comfortable for us all.

"What the hell did you do to that old man?" He asked gruffly.

"I smiled at him!" I couldn't hide the defensiveness in my voice. "He was nice."

"Smiled at him?" Brack looked scornful. "He acted like you gave him a brain-wipe...what the hell did you smile at him for?"

"He was nice." I said again, and I felt myself getting mad. What the hell was Brack doing here anyway? I mean I *knew* what he was doing—he was my fucking bodyguard—because Green was afraid I'd suffer another attack while I was feeling out the customers for the currents of the night. But he didn't have to be *in* the store. "What the hell are you doing in here anyway?" I added, pleased with my crankiness. Too much change was not necessarily a good thing.

"Apparently making sure that you don't spill power like water...Jesus, Cory, what the hell do you think you're playing with?"

"I smiled." I said again, weakly. "I didn't use any power—I just...I just got tired of being bitchy and thought he was a nice old geezer and I smiled..."

Brack began to laugh, slowly at first, but it grew, and he ended up sliding his ass down by the frozen snack freezer, leaning against it weakly. "Goddess." He chuckled. "Don't you have any idea what real emotion is? Don't you ever wonder why we all spend ninety percent of our lives cloaked in glamour? Real emotion *is* power. Jesus, God, Goddess and kin...no wonder you ended up at Green's...you could have killed somebody with a smile."

I looked at him sourly. "I'm a fucking freak of nature, and you're my god-damned identical fucking twin." I said with deep conviction.

Brack went into another paroxysm of laughter, and that's where he was when the vampire came in.

Not just a vampire—this was a vampire who didn't mind *looking* like a vampire, which was frightening in a whole new way. All of Adrian's crew could still pass for humans who work the night shift. They sheath their fangs unless they *want* you to see them, and they dim the brightness glowing in their eyes, or even wear sunglasses at night. They keep their claws withdrawn and their clothes impeccably neat, so that no trace of their feedings rests on their collar or their front, or their sleeves. Some of them even use make-up to hide their unnatural pallor. But not this vampire. This vampire had whirling eyes and the extended jaw and deep grooves carved into his musculature that showed that he wore this face all the time, and not just when he was feeding. Even so, he had blood and dark matter dripping down his chin and onto an already blood soiled shirt— this vampire had fed only seconds before, and he wanted know it.

Bracken was still sitting next to the ice-cream freezer, tucked between a rack of potato chips and the cold-locker itself, so the stranger didn't see him. He wouldn't have anyway—he was busy forcing his ice-cold presence on me.

"You Adrian's bitch?" He asked from dripping crimson fangs, and I had a sudden sick notion of where he'd gotten that blood...the only one near enough to feed on had been that poor, besotted old man, who had left here happy, and apparently got dead.

My hands closed on the gun behind the counter, and I had it drawn with the safety clicked back before he could walk another step. "You have no idea what a bitch I am." I hissed, my mad coming on like a freight train, thank the goddess. "Get the fuck out of here."

"I'm here to leave a message, dear," He said nastily, and turned the full force of his eyes on me. Adrian could bespell me with his eyes and his voice because I loved him. Green could do it too, for pretty much the same reason. But I had no idea how happy I was to be a powerful fucking bitch-sorceress on wheels until he turned his terrifying red-eyed glare on me and instead of becoming his mind-fucked-blood flunky, I got mad some more.

"So leave it." I said defiantly, and then he got mad back at me.

"In your blood." He murmured, and was flying towards me before I could even blink.

I fired the gun. I didn't close my eyes, I kept them on the target, and I pushed at him with all my will and magic but he kept coming so I fired the fucking gun until my hands ached and I shoved at him some more in my head and he went flying back against the beer freezer and exploded into a cloud of blood and flesh and bone. The bone especially was nasty—it acted like shrapnel, and I felt a piece rip my shoulder open as the blast of the dying vampire knocked me on my ass.

When I came to, Brack was hauling me to my feet looking worried and amazed at the same time.

"Get up, chickie...the cops are on their way—someone saw the old man's body—it's right on the road and everything."

Cops. Max. Shit. "Am I alive?" I asked groggily.

Brack brought a worried thumb up to my cheek and pulled it away, smeared with blood. I winced. Some of that was mine. There was a wide big pain in my shoulder, and I looked at that and almost passed out. Brack caught me as my knees buckled. Oh, God...I was going to be sick. I leaned my head over, but Brack gave me a little shake, and I managed to pull my stomach together.

"Can't do that, Cory—not now." He said gruffly. He looked worried again, but like he was trying to hide it. Big brother Brack—who woulda thunk it? "You've got to go greet the police..."

"Okay, sure." I rasped. Christ, I hurt. Now that I looked at my shoulder, I could see it was pumping enough blood to make even Adrian sick. My vision started to go black again, and Bracken looked at the wound hard. It didn't close up, but the blood congealed as I watched. This time my knees did buckle and Brack's with them. Together we slid slowly down the back of the little clerk's chamber, our bottoms hitting bottom with twin thuds. We were still sitting there when Officer Max walked in and passed out.

I didn't think he was going to pass out at first. He looked at the walls with that stoic cop's face that's both daunting and reassuring, and then he looked at me. I smiled greenly, and his eyes took in all the blood, and then the wound at my shoulder, then they rolled back in his head and he went over like a ton of bricks into the officer behind him. His back-up man caught Max, dropped him like a rotten squash, then turned and retched right behind the door, and I almost laughed into the warm, blood-saturated summer night.

"Look, brother." I said to Bracken, who grunted. "It's a midnight showing of *Abbot and Costello Meet Dracula.*" A rusty sound came out of Brack's throat, and I had to turn my tunneled vision towards him to actually know he was laughing.

When my eyes cleared again, Adrian was there, and for a moment my brain blurred with the strangeness of him. I knew he had been out and about, checking bars and gas stations and hangouts for his people, but I had not been expecting to see him tonight. I certainly had not been expecting to see him in my Chevron, when I most needed him. Was it only a month ago that he'd been here, I'd been afraid, and he'd been mysterious and I had lowered my sweater and raised my neck to greet him? There was a whole history of love and knowledge between us since then, and now I was afraid, but not of him, for him, and I was in danger, not from him, but because of him. Life was so strange, I thought as he looked at me, assessing my injury. To my surprise he bent his head to it and licked it, making the blood flow just enough to hold the wound closed with his hand, and I gasped with the cessation of pain.

Then, he called to Brack, who was still sitting on the floor, weak, I thought, with the healing he had given me, and told him, "Okay, brother— you need to move away from her for a moment, then do your thing—right?"

Brack nodded queasily. "Sorry, A'—I did what I could to stop the bleeding, but the call…"

"Is strong, I know." Adrian's voice was pure compassion, and I realized that I didn't know what he was talking about. "Brack's a Red Cap." Adrian said to me. "He can call blood—it's his gift. With all the blood in here, and your wound—he had to close himself off from his power to heal you—he could have made you bleed to death if he hadn' t concentrated very, very hard…"

I could have said something then, about Bracken not being the best choice of bodyguards, if he made any wounds I had worse, but he was looking very ill, and I realized that my wound was very bad in the first place, and that was part of the strain on us both. He must have liked me, just a little, to go to all that trouble not to kill me, I thought with a certain amount of satisfaction. Maybe it wasn't so bad being the twin sister to a freak of nature.

"Is he the reason the vampire exploded?" I asked weakly. As Bracken moved towards the beer cooler, which was now coated in blood, bones, and big sticky bits, I felt better. Then he stopped, and looked at me, and scowled very very hard, and I could feel my wound closing. He didn't heal it completely—not anywhere near what Green could have done, I knew—but he did make it so I could stand with only grey around the edge of my vision, and not black blurring everything I saw. But as soon as he stopped scowling and Adrian let go, the pain returned, and I felt my knees wobble again before I grabbed Adrian's hand and pulled myself up with sheer stinking will.

Adrian was looking pained, before he shook his head wryly. "Another one, luv? It's a good thing you're on our side. But no—we just go out differently, that's all. If we live in blood, we tend to die in it. If blood is food, but we live in the Goddess, then that's a different death altogether…this bloke must have been very, very bloody, to go out quite like this…" He looked at Brack now, who was looking like he was feeling better. "All right, brother—do your thing—Cory and I are going to go tell some lies." I looked behind my shoulder as Bracken walked to the beer cooler and began to hum, for lack of a better word, and then to my horror the gore that coated the freezer began to ripple, then to run across the glass, then onto the floor, then towards the bathroom where the floor drain was located. It looked odd, like a big ripply river, and I pulled away from Adrian, and was abruptly sick in the corner.

"Oh gees…" Brack muttered. "I knew that was coming."

"Then you should have warned me." Adrian grimaced, but he got me a bottle of water and a little tube of toothpaste, then held me gently as I cleaned up. As if the smell of blood hadn't given the place enough of a stench.

When I was ready, Adrian gently turned me towards the policemen, who, I noticed, were now propped up back to back, chins resting on chests. He had obviously put cop number two under before he'd woken us up, and I had time to be surprised. Had Adrian always been this competent? Had he always been this clear-headed? This Adrian I hadn't seen before—was this leadership because of me, or just the part I had missed, because I got to see sweet, vulnerable Adrian all the time. I remembered what Adrian had said about telling lies, then, and I grabbed his hand before he got to Officer Max.

"We need to tell this one the truth." I told him. I had told him about my encounter with Officer Johnson before, half way fearing that Adrian would go haring off the next night to eat himself some pork, but he had surprised me that night too—instead of being angry, he had been amused. I'd kidded him, then, about having an ego the size of the state, but he'd shaken his head and said "No, Cory luv—it's just that I trust you, right? And you've got a lot of big guns in your holster—you'd be able to fend off anything he threw at you. I'm just looking forward to seeing you two do the dance, that's all."

"What if he tries to dance me into bed?" I'd asked tartly, feeling miffed—I don't know why, it's a stupid girl thing.

"Well, then I'd rip off his dick and feed it to him—but I think he's an honorable man, your officer Max—a prick, but an honorable one. He just needs to learn what dances you'll take, and which one's you've reserved for me."

Now, as I held Adrian's hand and looked at the unconscious officers, I wondered if he would remember that he didn't want to kill the nice policeman. He looked at me, quiet, clearheaded, and again I was surprised. Competent. Able. A natural leader. How much of a human being had been lost in the hold of that ship, I wondered painfully. But then, how much of it would have matured a hundred years after his death.

"This one can help us." I said. "We need some help—that old man is out there, and they've lost some time, and Max is unsure enough about the world right now to believe us and to need someone to turn to about this shit. And he really wants to get the guy who killed Ratso—he seems to feel like he owes him something. We can use that."

Adrian regarded me steadily. Vampires don't blink, and as his pupils widened to hunting mode, even with his thought, I found myself becoming unnerved. I didn't fear for myself, but I had seen enough blood tonight. He finished thinking, controlled his eyes, smiled, and his face gentled to *my* Adrian again. And that connection that he'd planted in my body flared to life, and I suddenly knew what he was thinking. He was worried about me, I realized, and something inside me relaxed. I was the center of his universe again, and the thought shamed me. I was the one who kept saying he had larger concerns. But that didn't stop me from enjoying, even privately, the thought that he had been worried for me. I worried about him every sunrise—turnabout was only fair.

"All right, luv." He said, putting a dry hand on my face. He hadn't fed tonight, I realized, and felt bad. "We'll do it your way, some, right?" I nodded, and felt my eyes start with my first tears that night. Trust was a beautiful thing.

I walked over to the unconscious officers and began chafing Officer Max's wrists. "C'mon, Officer Max," I murmured, "Time to wake up you unconscious prick..."

I watched as his eyes fluttered open, rested on me, almost started out of their sockets. "Christ, Cory..." He sputtered, scrambling to his feet and almost pitching forward and taking me down with him. That would be bad, I thought, scowling. The last thing we needed tonight was me and Officer Johnson wrestling about on the bloody floor in front of my demon lover. Determinedly I stood and supported Max's weight, and tried not to look as the floor queasily continued to clean itself up.

"Focus, here, cop-man." I hissed. "This is important; we need your help, and that man outside needs justice. Stop staring at me like I'm a walking corpse and go talk to your partner there." He was very muscular—and very heavy. I was relieved when he started taking his own weight to himself. His nearly cross-eyed gaze sharpened, and he squinted at me, as though trying to put together a jigsaw puzzle in his head.

"What am I supposed to say?" He asked crankily. "How in the fuck do you explain this?"

"Look—tell him to take Adrian's statement. Then Adrian's going to go outside and tell him some lies, and I'll stay in here and tell you the truth, then you're going to meet him and tell him what he wants to hear—only hurry!" I said this last on a strangled breath, as I caught the time on Max's beat-up black-rubber digital watch. 4:15. *Christ,* how could it be 4:15—I couldn't even place the time when the vampire had walked in…how long had Brack and I been out?

"Bracken," I squeaked, "…Jesus, Brack, when does the sun come up?" I asked as Max walked outside to do what I asked. I was way too weak on too many fronts to keep the panic out of my voice as I called to the elf behind me.

Brack looked up at the wall clock behind the register and swore—his voice shook too, I noticed. "One fucking crisis at a fucking time, Corinne Carol-Anne." He said harshly. "We've got half an hour before we have to shove him in the beer freezer or the trunk of your car or something…"

But both of us knew that either one was risky. *Dammit.* Adrian was always so careful…if this attack on me had been designed to make him vulnerable, then it had certainly succeeded.

"What does that matter?" Max asked when he came back in. He looked lost. I saw all of him then: his swimming eyes, the concern for me that had been shocked out of him, his careful avoidance of the river of gore being herded across the station like a giant liquid sheep. Lost indeed.

"Adrian will die if he's outside at sunrise." I said wearily, "So you need to listen, and not question and I'll give you a number you can call me at tomorrow, deal?"

And to my surprise, Max nodded, and blindly thrust a notebook in my hand where I scribbled Green's number. So lost. Maybe we all were, I thought miserably.

"A vampire came into the Chevron at...well, I don't know when." I began. "He said he was going to leave a message in my blood, so I drew the gun on him, and he rushed me. I fired, and he exploded."

"But your shoulder..." He murmured, and I was absurdly touched. Big super-cop man—I bet he hadn't had a wound this bad. And here we were, this was my second.

"Shrapnel." I would have shrugged, but not much was keeping me on my feet. "Bone fragments, force...sort of an undead grenade, I guess."

Max looked at me, skeptically this time, and I noticed some color had crept back into his cheeks. Well, at least one of us was feeling stronger.

"Look behind me, Officer Johnson." I snapped, "And tell me what you see." The river of blood was trickling now, but it was still marching to Brack's dry humming. So now I knew what a Red-Cap did. And now, if his white face was any indication, so did Officer Max.

"Gotcha." He rasped. "Undead grenade. I'm buying it...but what about that old man..." And now he took on something of a greenish cast.

I looked down. "I...a customer..." I smiled at him and he loved me, and then he was dead. "I think he was a sacrifice—a reward—maybe just in the wrong place at the wrong time." And a small part of me began a mourning wail that I couldn't stop. Innocent. He had been innocent of all this. He'd been a harmless old man in a blue flannel shirt and I had smiled at him and he had fallen in love and now he was dead. "Where did you find him?" I asked.

"He was lying right in front of the station...he's missing his head."

I had thought nothing could make me feel worse—how's that for arrogance? "Swell." I whispered. There was silence, and my heart still grieved. Movement, reassurance and queasiness in the same touch. My shirt grew wet again with fresh blood, and I looked up at Bracken, both grateful and nauseous.

"Hush." He said quietly, and I looked at him in surprise. I hadn't said a blessed thing. He held two hands to his chest—I suspected if he actually touched me again, I would bleed out, this time to death. "In here, Cory. It is more mete that others grieve." He backed away from me then, and went outside to tap Adrian on the shoulder. I thought hard, shut down that wail of grief in my heart, felt something of myself die quietly with it. Innocence, I mourned, looking outside as Adrian and Brack furiously discussed Adrian's safety; innocence had nothing to do with sex.

"What will you say?" I asked Max, to keep him away from the discussion outside.

"Say to who?" he asked back, looking where I was looking with narrowed eyes.

"Your partner, moron." I was remembering the last time there had been a murder here. They'd kept me until nine in the morning—would they do the same thing now? I didn't think I could face that...I felt my world swaying and I put my hand out for the auto maintenance shelf and got Max's chest instead. Nice chest. Lot's of muscles. Warm. You didn't get warm from Adrian. I heard a surprised grunt and focused. With an effort I moved my hand from his chest to the shelf next to me.

"First, Cory," Max said, moving his solid body next to mine and helping me sit down on a shelf, "I 'm calling an ambulance, and we're getting you to a hospital. We can talk about the rest there."

"No." I said. "No. You can't. They'll ask questions."

"To hell with questions." He bit out. "You're going to pass out...you've lost a hell of a lot of blood."

Couldn't argue with that. "But not all of it is mine, though." I protested weakly. "There will be hella questions." I looked outside, saw the lightening sky, saw Adrian and Brack still arguing. Adrian cast a desperate look through the window and saw me sitting there, not looking good, and I thought maybe it would be the hospital and questions for sure.

Then I saw him, walking alongside the station, and my relief was so palpable it made my wound ache just with thought. The ache was good, I thought muzzily. The ache was better than the cold. Green. He literally picked Adrian up by the back of the collar, and I heard a holler and a thump, and knew Adrian must be in the trunk of the car. Arturo's caddy, if they were thinking. And then Green was in the doorway, looking at me with a mixture of fury and worry that almost did me in right there.

"Goddess, luv." He said, bending down and picking me up into his strong, strong arms. "We're not being careful enough with you."

"Take me home, Green." I whispered against him. He was wearing a T-Shirt, I thought vaguely. Green was dressed. How often did that happen? To my horror I felt myself coming completely unglued.

"First things first, Corinne Carol-Anne." He said gently. Then he bent his head and breathed softly on my shoulder. The last time he healed me, I was unconscious, and I was not prepared for the oddness of the world, of my body's own rebellion as tissues re-knit and blood pathways regenerated. I almost felt worse when he was done than beforehand, and apparently so did Green, because his balance wavered, and he sat down hard on the shelf I had just vacated.

I looked at him in worry, but he just smiled grimly. "Need to re-think that whole bodyguard thing for Bracken, right?"

I shook my head. "No—I'll keep him." I whispered. "I'll just try harder not to bleed."

"Works for me." Brack said, coming in to the station, too weary even to toss the Cadillac keys in his hands. "Our boy's all locked up, Green, but I'd wear a garlic overcoat come nightfall."

Arturo was right behind Brack, and his smile as he looked at Brack was almost as grim as Green's. "I'll have Grace make you one." He said, and for some reason that struck me as funny. I giggled weakly into Green's chest.

"Hiya, Arturo." I mumbled. "How was Denny's."

"Sticky and stinky," He told me, kneeling next to the two of us, "and too full of the wrong sort of people. Sort of like here." He looked up at Officer Max with unfriendly eyes.

"Your friend believes this was a smash and grab job with a fatality. Brack has made it look so. The perpetrator is in his forties, white, with salt & pepper hair and two missing teeth. Do you remember all of that, supercop?"

Officer Max glared back. "There's no way we can make this fly...and what about her?" He jabbed a finger at me and Green. "You're just going to take off—she needs medical attention."

"I'm much better now." I murmured. I lifted a hand to my shoulder, still sore, but lacked the strength even to grab the stupid poplin shirt. Green did it for me, ripping the rest of the torn cloth, exposing my shoulder, brown from my little journey to the lake, but with a wicked pink scar running from arm-pit to collar-bone. "See, Officer Max? Two more and I'll have a matched set..."

He didn't look reassured—he looked appalled. "Two more? What the hell happened to you between Friday and Monday? Tuesday." He amended. He sagged suddenly, hunching down by me, looking bewildered, and still so lost. "Cory, what's after you?"

He was talking to me, and I answered, but I think everybody else in the room wished I hadn't. "Not me." I murmured. "Adrian. I'm Adrian's bitch." I giggled. "Woof woof...bitch, get it?"

Max's eyes narrowed, and he looked at every man in the room—Arturo, Brack, Green, and I saw him doing math, getting answers, rejecting them. I would have gotten indignant, if I hadn't been fading out—I bet he thought I'd slept with everyone in the room. Bastard.

"I haven't fucked any of them, you asshole." I said with conviction, struggling to sit up in Green's arms but not succeeding. "And as long as that's all you think this is about, you'll never find out who killed the kitties, or Ratso, or that poor guy outside. I told you where to look, and we still got there first, and now they're getting back. Either do what I'm telling you to do or get the hell out of our way, but either way, Officer Max, get rid of your prejudices they're killing you..." I had been mad for a moment, it had sustained me, and even Green perked up a little, but it didn't last. I sank back into Green's arms, burrowing for safety, but he wasn't done with me yet.

"Any of *them*..." He spat. "But I saw you...in my mind...I saw you with that guy outside..."

"What guy?" Arturo asked smoothly. He stood in a motion, and was now pressing Officer Max back with sheer physical presence. "Your partner doesn't remember him...and you don't need to either."

"Stop!" Green said, and it surprised me as well as everybody else. "Stop, Arturo." He repeated, standing up with me still in his arms. "Let Mr. Johnson remember Adrian—and Adrian and Cory. I think it's important that he does."

Arturo nodded, looking rebellious, but Max looked at me then, and his eyes were tortured. He regretted it, I realized. Regretted that morning when he could have been my hero but chose to be an asshole instead. Fantastic, I thought to myself as the world turned gray, I couldn't have planned it better if I'd tried.

GREEN

Taking Care of Business

Green himself called up Max Johnson and asked him to accompany his party to *the Granite Horse* in four days. He didn't tell Cory of his decision—for one, she was still sleeping after losing so much blood. He also didn't want to hear her complain about it—because, dammit, they needed all the help they could get.

He had been counting were-folk when a car with a brick on the gas pedal had tried to crash through the hedge that bordered his garden. It had been easy enough for Green to "push" the vehicle off the road and into the pine studded canyon below, but the car had been rigged to blow up—just a little bit of C-4 and gasoline thank you very much, and Green's people had needed to leave the sanctuary of his Hill to clean up the mess before the authorities saw it. And that was when Green heard Arturo's call for help in his head.

Two men had burst into Denny's—they had tried to make it look like an armed hold-up, but every bullet had been aimed at one of Arturo's people—elves he had brought from South America when he himself had emigrated. No one had been killed except the perpetrators, but they had been rigged to blow—just like the car and Adrian's were-people—and Arturo hadn't had a Red-Cap to help him clean up the mess—or the minds—of the nine civilians who had been eating breakfast at two in the morning at Denny's.

Adrian had been flitting about from bar to bar, checking on the fringes of their organization which is what he did best, when he had heard Arturo call him in panic, and he'd been fully involved in the mind-sweep at Denny's. So all three of them had their hands full when they felt the vampire die. It had been a painful, bloody death caused by both magic and violence, and it was a reasonable certainty that the psychic vibrations had ripped through the Sierra Foothills just like the deaths of Arturo's two hold-up men. Only with Cory's vampire, it was worse, because he had been a strong son-of-a-bitch, and hadn't been meant to die like the hold-up men had been. Adrian actually flew all the way from Auburn to Ophir—no small distance, for a vampire trying not to be spotted—while Arturo had, by necessity, finished cleaning up the mess at Denny's, fretting the entire time. Green had *moved* to be at Cory's side as quickly as possible, and arrived as soon as Arturo had. They found Adrian, dealing calmly with the mind-wiped policeman while the sun flirted with the horizon like an extremely skilled harlot. There had been no small amount of adrenaline coursing through Green's muscles as he seized Adrian by the scruff of the neck and shoved him into Arturo's trunk.

All in all, the attack had been organized, vicious, and deadly. It had been meant to both reveal Green's people and hurt them, and most especially, it had been aimed at devastating Adrian. Maybe even killing him, by his own neglect. And Cory had, yet again, nearly died. The last thing Green felt like cosseting was a narrow-minded, sexually frustrated, arrogant policeman who hadn't recognized Cory's value when he'd had the chance and was making their lives miserable because of his own goddamned mistake. But Cory was right—Sezan, and what had once been Crispin's organization, had become too huge, and too frightening, for Green to refuse any source of help.

That's what he'd told Arturo when he got off the phone. His second was glaring at him with accusing eyes.

"The police…" he said, appalled.

"No, not *the* police." Green corrected. "Cory's policeman. There's a difference."

"The difference wants to get in her pants." Arturo spat. It was mid-afternoon. The vampires were sleeping—Adrian was in Arturo's trunk which was far into the depths of Green's multi-car garage. The rest of Green's people were reinforcing magic perimeters, or finishing the clean-up of the explosion and brush fire at the bottom of the adjoining canyon. It was hot, outside of Green's hill, and the sprites, Red-Caps, and assorted fey had to return frequently to Green's hill for water and rest. The were-folk were under strict orders not to go *anywhere,* and all in all, the hill was under siege.

Green's mouth quirked grimly. "Well, yes, but it's still a difference, you think?" He turned away from Arturo and shuddered. "Damn, Arturo. Damn it all—I don't want to live through a night like that again."

Arturo nodded agreement, but added, "Better than dying in it, you think?"

Green sent him an appalled look, but Arturo shook his head. "You've had it easy, here, leader, you know that, right? Fights for territory are common in almost every fey-run venue there is, accept here."

Green blinked. "I hadn't realized…"

Arturo laughed, a full laugh. "You and Adrian—you two have no idea what a mind-fuck the two of you are. I myself came here, all hot and bothered, and ready to take you on—you remember?"

Greem shrugged. It had been nearly forty years before—the sixties—a blessed time for an elf whose specialty was sexual healing and worshipping the Goddess. "You were pretty intense…"

"And then you got me stoned, and shared a bottle of homemade wine and I woke up in one of your spare bedrooms with a couple of the finest nymphs ever birthed from a tree and thought "Could I make a better home than this?"' And I couldn't. So I chose to serve you instead."

Green felt humbled. "A gift I've never taken for granted." He said truthfully.

Arturo shook his head. "No, you haven't, ever." He agreed. "But you have no idea what a rare thing it is, to meet a leader who will inspire that kind of gift. To meet two—because Adrian does it too, in his own subversive, play-boy sort of way. So this is new to you—but it happens."

Green knew—he was a cosmopolitan elf, he had business deals across the country. He did *know*. But he had never appreciated that it could happen to him. "Well, no offense, mate, but we need to fix it so it doesn't happen to us anymore—because this is no way to live."

Arturo nodded agreement. "I'll give you that, brother—that's why I stay." He yawned, suddenly, hugely, showing off the silver caps in his teeth that were, he admitted, pure vanity.

"Bed." Green ordered imperiously. "Crawl in with Grace, sleep naked with the piskies—I don't care what your choice is, mate, but you need to recharge."

"Agreed." Arturo said mildly, "If you'll do the same."

Green nodded. "As soon as Adrian's up—I don't want all three of us out of commission."

"Will you at least work from your room?" Arturo insisted. Green had placed Cory there, gently, while Arturo had taken Bracken to the Red-Cap quarters so his mother could fuss over him. Brack's efforts to not kill Cory with his own natural call for blood had been pretty damn heroic, for an elf who had initially hated bodyguard duty with a passion. Green would draw energy from being in the same room with Cory, simply because she cared for him. It was good, sometimes, to be a healing elf.

"Deal, mate." Green agreed, then shooed his second off towards the darkling.

He spent the next six hours making phone calls and e-mailing like mad. Businesses, all in order, ready to be passed on to Adrian, Arturo, Grace, Cory, Brack, Blissa, Phillip, and on down the line, in case things went more bizarrely wrong than even he could imagine. He was not going to let his people alone, without recourse or aide, on the off chance he should be taken out while defending his territory. At 8:45—Christ, the night was short in the summer— he felt the vampires stirring in the darkling, and slumped weakly against his computer in relief. Sleep. Rest. Restoration. Adrian found him, asleep on his keyboard, shortly after that. When Green woke up again he was undressed, curled up with Cory in his arms, and it was morning.

There was a post-it on his computer that read "Not if I can help it, mate."

"What's it mean?" Cory asked through a mouthful of trail mix—there had been a coffee can of it next to the bed when they woke up, and they were both eating ravenously. Arturo had put her in one of Green's ubiquitous white T-shirts, and it fell to her knees, but she didn't seem to notice.

"It means he doesn't want to admit the worst may happen."

She scowled at him, and he felt a moment of panic that he might have missed that expression forever. She'd been so weak, when he'd healed her— he would never take that gift for granted—ever. "What does *that* mean?" She asked crankily.

He sighed, shook his head, reached for a comb to pull it back. She brushed the crumbs off her hands and gestured imperiously to the comb.

"I'll brush, you talk." She began to comb, not ungently.

"It means I was putting my affairs in order, in case this affair ends badly...leaving the businesses to people...it's important. Too many of our people look to this hill for sanctuary, we can't afford to let the government confiscate the property…there can be no invaders on this land."

Cory thought about this for a minute, jerked the comb through a particularly nasty tangle and then smacked him on the head when he turned to protest. He wondered if she'd inherited that gesture, mother to daughter…and then wondered about her family, and if they were missing her yet.

"Adrian doesn't want you to do that?" She didn't believe it, clearly. Green didn't blame her. Adrian had shown her his best side, these past weeks—he'd been competent, able, clearheaded. Adrian wasn't always on his best behavior.

"Adrian doesn't want to admit I can die." Green told her. "He likes to think that never aging is some sort of guarantee…"

"But you are hard to kill…" She asked, apprehensively. Mortality would mean something to her, he thought. She had killed a vampire the night before—a supposedly immortal being, and she had nearly walked away unscathed. Mortals were frightened to have their cozy view of life intruded upon by grim reminders of the alternative.

"Harder to kill than a vampire." He told her reassuringly. He turned then, and grabbed her hands, making sure he had her complete attention. "Harder to kill than you, Cory luv…maybe you should think about what that could mean, staying here."

Her busy hands stilled for a moment, and he could hear honest contemplation in her silence. Then she resumed. "I 'm targeted either way, Green—Kim was, and she meant nothing to Adrian…this way, someone's got my back."

He felt himself relax, and didn't realize how worried he was, that she would change her mind and leave them, when so much of their energy and will had been bent on keeping her alive. He nodded, as though he expected her answer, but thought he should add at least one more thing.

"Very well then." He murmured. "But, Cory…I made provisions for myself, and those for Adrian, and Arturo as well…is there, perhaps, something you've left undone that you might want to remedy, before we take our trip to *the Granite Horse* this week?"

Again, he felt her hands still. She had been dividing up his hair to plait it, but the sections fell out of her suddenly numb fingers, unheeded. When they took up their actions again, her hands were decidedly shaky. "I might…" she started, and there was a long pause before she continued again. "I might want to go see my parents again." She murmured.

To say goodbye, if things didn't go well. He understood—it was why he'd spent six hours working the night before, to say goodbye to his people, if things didn't go well. He tried not to make it any more of a big deal for her, this very young, fragile, human, than it had been for him, the old, nigh invincible immortal. "Would you like me to drive you, luv?" He asked casually.

Her face worked, and he could see that she both really, really wanted him there, and that she would really, really rather not have him with her at all. Her dilemma was solved for her when Arturo walked in with the cordless phone in his hand. He looked a little sheepish.

"Cory, it's your mother...she's got some mail for you, from colleges you've sent to...she wants to know if you can come get it, and I told her we'd be by on our way to target practice."

Cory looked non-plussed for a moment. "Target practice?" She said faintly.

Arturo's eyes narrowed, and his jaw clenched, and Green saw for the first time what the morning before had cost him in serenity. "Target practice." He replied grimly. "You're the only one of the day-folk who can hold a gun without risk—we need to make sure you nail the next one before he gets close enough to damage you."

"Target practice." Cory repeated, sinking to the bed. Green pointed to the phone in her hand, and she raised it to her ear dazedly.

"Yeah, mom." She murmured. "We'll be by today...Arturo, I guess...and Brack...he's a friend. No...neither of them is more than that...Well I do have a boyfriend...sort of...He works nights..." then, cautiously and mildly alarmed, "No—he's not a cop, why do you ask? He has? When? Why, what did he say? Well, it looked worse then it was...I'm fine. Yeah—I'll be there in a couple of hours. NO!" This last with an alarming emphasis, "Do not tell the cop I'm going to be there...Because I don't want to talk to him, that's why...No, I haven't done anything illegal..." She winced with that last one, looking a little ill—strictly speaking, it wasn't killing if your victim was already dead. "He's just butting his big fat cop's nose where it doesn't belong...Yes, I know he seems like a nice young man...He is a nice young man, but he's not *my* nice young man. Can we talk about this later? Yes...yes I'll be there." Sigh. "Yes, we'll stay for lunch...uhm, mom? No meat, okay? Because I asked nicely? Thank you..." She clicked off the receiver and looked sourly up at her audience.

"I don't suppose there's a chance that sounded sophisticated and adult, is there?"

Arturo grinned, his first real smile of several days. "No—in fact it was very human."

She sighed again, looking even more depressed. "Coming from you, I'd have to say that's pretty much worse."

Arturo laughed outright, and she scowled up at him. "Laugh all you want—you've met the woman—my mother probably thinks chicken is a vegetable." Arturo's horrified look seemed to mollify her, and she looked at Green with sorrow on her face. "Don't take this the wrong way, Green—but you'd probably think better of me if you never met my parents...I'll take Arturo and Brack instead."

Green stood and shook his completed knee length braid behind his back. Cory did good work. Then he moved to the bed where he bent and kissed her on the temple, knowing she fed off his touch as he fed of hers.

"I respect your decision." He said sweetly, "But anyone who birthed and raised you can't possibly be all that bad." And then he buttoned his jeans and left, bare-chested, to go check on his kingdom.

CORY

Secrets and Lies

Lunch with mom was both better and worse than I expected—for one thing, Max showed up. He sat there, in the kitchen which just screamed "pre-fab double-wide" and ate my mom's chicken salad while I pulled out some plain lettuce and sunflower seeds for the boys. Mom and dad were making painful conversation with the three men, and trying awkwardly to cover for their first mistaken impression that I was going to live with Arturo.

"I told you he was a friend." I hollered from the refrigerator. I'd put on denim shorts and a T-shirt that morning, and I caught Max appreciating the view. I scowled at him, and gestured to Arturo with my nose. I don't know what Arturo did next, but my next view of Max was far less appreciative. Prick.

"But being a friend means so much more these days." Mom said, "And I know you had plans to go off to college." I straightened, and looked at her—really looked at her. I had thought, a week ago, that she and my father were really clueless about me and my life. But I guess being self-involved presumptive prick wasn't Max's exclusive territory. They were worried about me—they were worried about my plans for the future. My mom's plain, lined face said it all, and my dad's awkward, polite silence towards the three strange men in his kitchen said more. Dad usually slept on the weekdays, I realized belatedly, because he drove at night. This was *special* to them. They wanted to make sure my future was in order. I swallowed. My future had never been fuller of promise, nor more in doubt than it was right now at this very moment.

Somewhere from the bottom of my toes I mustered a smile—a real smile, full of love and appreciation for what they were trying to do. It was as genuine and as powerful as the one I had bequeathed on that poor old man, and I didn't care if it bewitched them or ensnared them or whatever, as long as they would always remember me just like this.

"I'm fine, mommy." I said, no irony at all in my voice for the endearment. I put the lettuce down on the counter and moved to kiss my mom's cheek. "Adrian's a nice guy—I'll bring him by some time—when he remembers his manners, he's charming, and when he doesn't, he's still really good to me." I aimed my smile at my dad, and watched his worry ease away. Ahh…a part of me thought, before I squelched it, this is how you did a mind-wipe. "Don't worry, daddy." I said sincerely. "You raised me smart—I'm not doing anything I don't want to, and I'm not going to waste what I've worked for, okay?"

They both smiled, and looked down, hiding shining eyes. I finished making the salad, and sat down with the boys, chattering about colleges and maybe going to Sac State instead of the Bay Area choices that had responded in the packet mom handed me. I told them about a major in history, or maybe in biology, because I hadn't made up my mind yet, and they asked me "why not business" because they were, after all, practical people, and I told them gently that I wasn't going to school for practical reasons, but to see the world in a certain way, and they seemed to be happy with that. Max tried to interrupt twice, both times about the murder/robbery at the gas station, and both times I stepped on his foot and glared at him, and oddly enough, I think the glare hurt more.

He did prompt mom to ask, though, and I told my first real lie of the day. (The little one about not doing anything illegal didn't really count. Dammit—there's no law against shooting the undead.)

"Danny was the clerk that night, mom." Arturo looked at me, grim and disapproving, so I backtracked a little. "I mean, he's the guy who talked to the reporters." I felt a little better then, and wondered when the little white lie had suddenly become such a big dark deal. "The station's owner is going to get new security—he's really unhappy with what happened." All of which was true, but mom was still worried.

"But, gracious, Cory—you could have been killed."

"I'm tougher than I look." I said truthfully. And then, suddenly, a thought from nowhere: "Mom—where are your people from? Where are dad's?"

"Welsh & Irish, honey—Irish on your father's side, Welsh on mine. Where do you think a name like Kirkpatrick comes from? Literally, its Patrick's church. Look at the town names round here—Auburn, Loomis, Colfax, Ophir, Penryn—they're all names carried over from England, Wales & Ireland when California was being settled in the late 1800'ds—I thought we'd covered this when you were in the fourth grade."

Oh. "Oh." Oh indeed. From England—just like Adrian. Just like Green. It explained a little—maybe I was descended from a long ago elf, a sidhe, slumming with the humans or something. If the high elves and sidhe originated in that section of Europe, then maybe there was a reason for my freakish explosion of power. It was better to dwell on that than on the fact that I'd just lied to my parents and might never see them again.

Soon after that we left. I gave my mom a longer hug than usual, and realized that she felt thin, and slight, and mortal. Did I feel that way to Green, I wondered? How did he bear to be near me, knowing I was so fragile? Even my dad, who had always seemed to be wiry and strong, and impervious, felt brittle and slender. It was a good thing I had a legitimate reason to leave, I thought, swallowing hard, and smiling at them both again with the whole part of my heart that wasn't broken and panicked. Arturo had booked a good 2 hours of target practice at the firing range in Auburn, which my parents fully approved of, and I think it was that commitment alone that got me out the door, waving as I left.

I personally didn't know if I was going to have the strength to hold a gun, not to mention the fact that I didn't want to have a blessed thing to do with it after the other night, but life was finally starting to get interesting and precious to me. I figured I'd stick around for a while, and the gun seemed to be part of that. In fact, I sort of wished I had the damn thing with me when Officer Max rounded in on me.

"You told them nothing." He said, grabbing my shoulder from behind. Brack and Arturo were in front of me in half a heartbeat—faster than human speed, actually, but Max seemed undeterred. "You lied to them." He hissed between the two men, "You flat out lied!"

"Only once." I qualified sourly, squinting between the two men's shoulders. Brack was about two inches taller than Arturo, I noted out of nowhere. "Yes, I do have a conscience, and lying makes me feel like shit. The rest of it was true—Danny *did* talk to the press. Green *is* taking extra safety precautions…don't you know the truth when you hear it?"

"But I thought…" He said, and his voice trailed off. I looked at him closely. Twenty-five? Twenty-six? Compared to Adrian, he was a baby. And so, so lost. He looked at me miserably. "I thought you'd tell them the truth…and then I'd know…"

"Oh, baby doll…" I murmured. I didn't want to touch him—he looked pitiful, his eyes swimming with unshed tears and uncertainty and worry. I was afraid he'd take any gesture the wrong way, and that would be wrong to do—not to Officer Max, who tried so hard to always do the right thing. "We're fighting a war." I said softly. "It's under your radar—it always will be, right? Someone out there knows about something that happened in 1851, and they're mad at Adrian, and they're getting back…it's like…like gangs…only quieter. Anyone affiliated with the gang is a target…"

"And you just left your parents…"

"There's no affiliation by family." I told him sadly. "It's more complicated than that."

"Gang activity is illegal in this state." He told me, drawing himself up and trying to look official, and I laughed at him, but gently.

"I'm not talking crips and bloods, moron." I said, laughing. "If you can't figure out what kind of gang we are, you're dumber than I thought." I tapped Arturo and Bracken on the shoulders, and let myself into the Cadillac. I was tired of this conversation. Hell—I'd been wounded twice in the same week, and was staying up late being a vampire's girlfriend. I was just plain tired.

"Cory…wait…" I opened the window as the boys got in the front of the car. "Who is Adrian?" He asked, and I could have said any number of things, but I knew what he was asking, so I guess I couldn't have.

"He's a vampire." I said softly. "I love him very much."

And we left him in the dust, looking stupid and depressed. I knew how he felt.

GREEN

An Elf's Got To Do...

The Granite Horse was bigger than it looked from outside. It was clean, reasonably well lit, free from cigarette smoke, and the warm-up band was folksy-bluesy and marginally talented. If it hadn't been for the twisted emanations of power that were making Green's folk both nauseous and testy, it would have been a decent place.

Green surveyed the crowd apprehensively—it was an odd mix, mostly preternatural. He saw a many of the Folsom area vampires, ghosting soundlessly in and out of the nocturnal mortals who often frequented such places. They were looking unhappy, he noticed, and gaunt. There were *no* were-folk. He was surprised at that—he had assumed that the "greasy-spot" syndrome would have been confined to his people alone, but apparently the word had gotten out. Mitchell's brother, Ray, had shown up in Green's garden the night after the attacks, sobbing soundlessly about what they had already known—*Giant Pussy* had performed for *Sezan* two nights before Mitchell died, and after that, Ray remembered changing form, and staying a large were-cat for nearly a week, out of fear.

Ray wasn't as smart as Mitch—he'd spent that time wandering around the foothills, fishing in Lake Clementine at night, and eating the scraps of the campers that swarmed over the place this time of year. It had taken him seven days to find Green's house, and by then he'd been gaunt, distracted, and nearly paralyzed with fear. And then Renny had seen him, in human form, and had nearly split her skin with the drive to change form and rip his throat out. Fortunately it had been night, and Adrian had been there, and he had fed deeply from her again. Ray had looked at the supine were-cat purring in Adrian's arms, smiled greenly, and said "I guess she'll always blame me for Mitch." Then he had passed out, and the entire household had been on the alert to keep Renny away from an unconscious Ray for the last three days.

But the entire incident had pretty much confirmed what Green and Adrian already knew—the word was out, in the were-community, and the word wasn't good. Now, seeing the starving vampires, Green was not just concerned for his own people, he was outraged for Crispin's as well. Adrian walked up beside him, looking devastating in black jeans and a leather jacket and growled "I'll kill him," in Green's ear. Green was apparently not the only one who was angry.

"They all look hungry." Cory said nervously from the other side of Adrian. She looked tired, Green thought, and noted Adrian looking at her with concern. Working at the Chevron had been right out, but she had been training her heart out for the last three days, learning to use powers that less than two weeks before would have seemed impossible for her to possess. She'd woken early, with Green, drilled extensively in the garden, since it still reeked of her power surge from the week before, and then gone to target practice in the heat of the afternoon. She came home and napped in the early evening, waking around nine, when the vampires awakened, then stayed with Adrian, as wide awake as she could manage, meeting the other vampires and familiarizing herself with the hunting-wolf hierarchy that made up vampire politics. She acted, during those meetings, very much in charge of herself and of them—fully assuming a mantle of responsibility only Green, Adrian, and Arturo would have assumed she could fulfill. It was only after those meetings that she came unglued—first with Adrian, when he swept her off to bed and to sex and to feeding, and then to Green, who woke her in the morning and asked her what she had learned.

"I'm Queen of the fucking Vampires." She'd complained that very morning to Green. "And I'm apparently the fucking Queen of the Vampire," she added wryly, "But it sure would be nice to know what my major is going to be."

"Queenship, or fucking?" Green responded, straight faced, just to see her laugh. She did, but wearily—so, so wearily. He was sitting next to her, in her own bed where he brought her from Adrian's every morning. She didn't ask—but she did look around gratefully when she saw where she was and that he was awake with her.

"You know," she said this particular morning, "It's getting so I can tell how badly my night before went by whose bed I wake up in, and who's with me when I do."

"Really?" Green took to stroking her hair as she spoke. Her head was pillowed on her arms, and she had to look sideways to see his face. It made her look rumpled and sly, he thought, and it didn't take a sexually-driven preternatural elf to know sex had been sweet and slow the night before.

"Mmmhmm…" she murmured. "If I've come two inches from death, I'm in your bed with half the freaking household. If all is well and Adrian and I have made love, it's just me and sometimes you. If the night went somewhere in between, it's some compromise between those two extremes."

"D'you mind?" He asked, all antennae sharp.

"Not at all." She murmured, sliding back into sleep. He decided to let her. "It's just not very human of me, that's all."

He looked at her now, human, mortal, vulnerable, and remembered that conversation. He had a sudden, unreasonable impulse to make Adrian take her home. *She doesn't belong here.* He thought miserably. *We expect too much from this fragile mortal.* But she turned her face to him though, as if she could read his thoughts, and smiled.

"I'm fine, brother." She said gently. "I got to sleep in this morning, remember."

He felt his face go grim and purposeful, and he leaned carefully across Adrian and touched her hand. "I'm nobody's brother, little one." He said politely, and saw her uneasy, sexy frown at Adrian, who winked back at her in turn.

"Okay, leader." She murmured, pulling her hand back and looking around. "Why are they starving the vampires?"

"What the hell are you talking about?" Said Max from Cory's other side, and she groaned.

"What are you doing here?" She practically whined, and Green suppressed a grin of his own. She sounded very human now.

"He asked me here." Max groused, looking sourly at Green. Green leaned across the bar, in front of Cory and Adrian and extended his hand.

"I don't believe we've been formally introduced." He said pleasantly. "I'm Green, and you are Officer Max, and we don't like you but have invited you anyway. Be nice."

Max stared at Green's hand, openly hostile. "Make me."

Green smiled, and it wasn't pleasant. "Cory love, could you move out of the way, please? I believe Officer Max made a request."

Cory, looking a little panicked, elbowed Max in the ribs and stomped on his foot at the same time. Max pulled his arms up protectively and pitched forward slightly, bringing his hand in contact with Green's, and Green took it in his own, looking ironically at the youngest member of their little party.

"Nicely done, luv." He murmured.

"I try to only kick the shit out of vampires." She returned. "Bad ones who hate me." She added hastily when she saw Adrian starting to crack up. "Max, this is Adrian—you've sort of already met."

"She's too goddamned young to be here." Max panted. He took the extended hand this time—Cory was stronger than she looked.

"So are you." Adrian returned pleasantly.

"I'm over twenty-one." Max responded indignantly.

"Really? Any one under seventy-five, I can hardly tell the difference. Now stop being a buggering git and get your head in the game."

Max blew a breath out. "Fine. So what in the hell were you talking about."

"The vampires." Cory murmured, nodding in the direction of a couple of greasy haired, gaunt cheeked men and women hovering nervously together. They had an aged quality, as though they were in their early twenties, but hard living made them look forty. "They look like hell—someone hasn't been letting them feed."

"They're junkies." Max spat dismissively.

"Was I ever that blind?" Cory turned to Green and Adrian in despair.

Adrian shrugged, all cheekbones and arrogance. "I don't know, luv—you kind of studied my boots for about a year."

She sighed. "Look closer, Officer Max. They're not smiling with their teeth—I've seen junkies, they're all teeth, and they don't smile at all. These guys are not shaking. They're not shifting stance or staggering. If you observe closely, shit head, they're not even breathing. And watch—every time the waitress walks by their noses flare and they practically lick their lips. I bet if you got close their eyes aren't dilated *or* pin-point. They're just really, really intense. And glowing red. And it's the middle of fucking June and these people are pale as snow on crystal."

"They're junkies." Max said flatly. "And these two assholes have slipped hallucinogens in your Kool-Aid, little girl. You don't belong here."

Cory's eyes narrowed, and her chin lifted. Then she smiled, and Max looked uneasy. She was short, just under Adrian's chin, but she stood on tip toe and bumped his chin, gently, with the top of her head. As quick as that, the air with filled with an unbearable intimacy, and Green's eyes went towards the group of vampires. Their heads tilted up, and their eyes went to half-mast, and their noses went in the air, sniffing delicately. Max had noticed it too, and his eyes grew round and afraid. He couldn't hear the conversation between Adrian and Cory, but Green could, and so could the vampires.

"What are you doing, luv?" He asked playfully.

"Touching you." She murmured back. Something in her smile, her voice, and Green knew she knew she was on display.

"Mmmm…." Adrian murmured, kissing her forehead. Then he kissed his way down her nose, brushing her lips, nipping her chin, in a long sensuous line as she tilted her head back, exposing her throbbing carotid to his tongue. He traced the vein there, and she groaned softly, and this time Green knew she had half forgotten their danger, and all but forgotten their audience. But, more significantly for Max, anyway, the rest of the "junkies" had turned their heads towards the pair at the bar, and Max took a step back until he was practically trapped, when he saw them struggling to control their fangs.

"Hey, there, friends." Green said loudly, forcing joviality into his voice, "Get a room, eh?"

Adrian and Cory both shivered convulsively and took deep, shuddering breaths. They took a step back, breaking the physical connection, and Max and Green watched as the room full of vampires struggled to get themselves under control, some of them actually weeping dry tears from desire.

The four beings at the bar sat for a moment, breathing tensely, until the force of that red-eyed regard faded, and the band played their last song and people applauded and the room returned to normal.

"Not junkies." Max admitted softly. "And you seem to know exactly what you're doing."

"Apparently not." Arturo said sourly, coming from Max's left. He moved across Cory, coming to talk to Green and Adrian. "If she knew what she were doing, she'd try very hard not to rouse a room full of starving vampires. Why is Crispin not letting his people feed?" This last incredulous, angry. It was inconceivable to the group from Foresthill that someone could be in charge of this many people and not give them sustenance.

"We will feed, pixie." Said the vampire who had just walked in front of Cory and Max, openly dismissive. "We will feed on you." He was tall, with a Roman nose and black hair in a widow's peak. If he didn't look depraved and jonesing, he could have been very attractive. Behind him, Cory strangled a laugh, and it came out as a snort.

"She's manner-less meat," the vampire went on, "But she will not live long." Cory snarked again, and this time her nervous humor was catching because Adrian made the same sound in the back of his throat, and so did Arturo. Widow's peak seemed a little put out that his threats didn't have their desired effect, so he looked disdainfully down his nose at them and flounced off.

"What the hell is wrong with you?" Green hissed. "We're not here to piss these people off."

Cory sobered up immediately, and met Green's eyes with a confidence he hadn't seen before. "No one feeds on us." She said firmly. "And I'm no one's meat."

Green began to feel infinitely better about the entire expedition. He took a deep breath and reassessed the room, noting Grace and Phillip getting a cold reception where they stood, nearer the stage, and watching as stage managers came out and replaced the sound equipment. Green frowned for a moment, wondering why a club this small would need such an extreme amount of amplification equipment, when he was interrupted by a tentative tap to his left. He turned in surprise to the young man with the limpid brown eyes who had been so ardently engaged the week before. Green could hardly recognize him now—for one thing, at their last encounter, the young man had been happy.

"Green?" The tremor of fear was unmistakable. "You're here...God...I thought I'd never see you..." He clenched his eyes shut, and Green saw him fight back tears. "Tribute." He hissed. "She had another name...but she couldn't remember it after you left...and she kissed Sezan..." The shaking intensified, and Green looked around in alarm. He saw several of Crispin's people eyeing them with evil little smiles tweaking their starved lips. Something sick clenched in his stomach. Cory's bravado was heartening, but these people had something *planned.*

"Green…" The kid said, "This is a *trap*. Sezan got hurt *bad* by Tribute, and he…he said he'd never do it to one of us, but he…" And now the boy was weeping freely. "God, Green…please get the hell out of here. Take me with you. Please." The boy was miserable, shoulders shaking, nose running, and Green had a sweeping feeling of such ill will and danger that he was almost physically sick.

He turned to Adrian urgently, and then house lights went down, the stage lights went up, and *Sezan* walked on the stage. Next to him Adrian whimpered, ever so slightly in his throat and instinctively Green reached for his hand. Next to Adrian, Cory had done the same, Green could tell because of the sudden surge of power that passed between them. He almost groaned aloud. Of all the stupid things to do…he tried to release Adrian's hand but Adrian was gripping it so tight that if he were human he knew the bones would crush. He must have had some awareness of Cory because she had her teeth gritted tight, but wasn't making any other sign of pain. Unable to shake Adrian, Green looked up on stage at the man who had caused so very much chaos.

He was short and slender, with skin so olive it was true green. He wore his magenta hair shoulder length, and Green wondered if he was the only one who could see that was his real hair color. His teeth were long, and narrow, and pointed and his face littered with pock marks and ill formed, with chunky, jutting cheeks and a low forehead—he was quite easily the ugliest immortal Green had ever seen. But there was a charisma about him, as he launched into the opening number. It was a hard rock number, sort of a cross between *Def Leppard* and *Good Charlotte,* and wholly original. The opening chords made Green's skin jumpy somehow, and the feeling grew worse when Sezan opened his mouth to sing. To Green, it felt as though all of his blood vessels had just kicked it up a notch, pumping harder, faster, all in dizzying accompaniment to the music coming from those overblown amplifiers. Sezan blurred into the back of a tunnel of sound, and Green began to panic.

"Adrian—mate, you've got to let go…" Green shouted against the buzzing of sound. "It's not him…"

"I know." Adrian whispered. "It's not him—it's worse."

"Let go…fuck it all…" Green was frantic now…something was pushing beneath his skin, something augmented by the coursing power between them. He felt physical pain starting at his innards, and his vision began to go red. At that moment, two things happened simultaneously.

The first was that Officer Max, seeing Cory's pale face and clenched teeth, grabbed her hand to yank her away from Adrian. At the exact same time, the kid on Green's left grabbed Green's free hand in an attempt to physically drag Green from the room.

The pressure in Green ceased abruptly, leaving him panting and sagging against the bar. Then, every light in the room exploded, the electrical equipment sparked spectacularly and went silent, and the only sound left was Cory, Arturo, & Brack, swearing fluently into the dark as every other creature in the room dropped heavily to the ground as though they had been shorted out with the lights.

CORY

Not Dead, Sleeping

After the lights went out, the purple-headed moron on stage started to shoot at us with something. No, not a gun…after target practice for a freaking week I know what a goddamned gun looks and sounds like. This was the shit I do in my head—this was power.

Brack, Arturo and I said "Fuck" at about the same time Green said "Shut the fuck up." And then I dropped to the ground. I would have liked to think that I was dropping because I was that smart, but the truth was, Adrian and Max had passed out on either side of me, and neither one of them was letting go of my hand. Just as well. I'd heard bones snap when Adrian had held my hand—loudly—it was part of the reason Max had grabbed me on the other side, but everything on the left side of my body was numb now, and I wasn't sure if I wanted that pressure to let up. As it was that all too familiar feeling of hurt/nausea was welling up inside of me. If it wasn't for the asshole on the stage throwing lightning bolts or whatever the hell those things were at us, I'd be happy to be quietly sick and pass out. I was getting good at passing out. I was starting to enjoy it—you couldn't worry about how to stay alive when you were unconscious. Instead I pried my hand out of Max's much looser grasp and grabbed the gun I'd strapped to my ankle with a little leather harness Grace had sewn for me this week.

It was an unlicensed .38 I'd borrowed from my father during my little visit—don't ask me why, but part of me was pretty sure I didn't want the same slugs here as I'd left in the beer cooler at the Chevron so I'd jumped when he'd offered it to me quietly, when mom couldn't hear. I'd practiced firing one handed, but I sucked at it, so I wasn't surprised when all I hit was the drum set and the back wall. It didn't matter. Purple haired asshole spat something in a language I'd never heard, and then Green retaliated. Green swore better in magic-elf, I guess, because there was a chartreuse colored explosion in the general direction of the stage, and Sezan, or whoever he really was, took off running, his legs far apart, his swearing vicious.

The four of us who were still conscious in the room took a hesitant breath then. "Christ." I murmured, "Where'd he go?"

"Fucked if I know." Green murmured weakly from the dark to my left. "I just gave him a giant hard-on on the edge of release—it should last a couple of days—heaven knows what he did with it."

I was in agony, and frightened, but that still cracked me up. "What?" I asked.

"Do I look like a warrior-elf? It was the best I could do on short notice." He said testily. I snickered then, and it came out more like a moan, and his annoyance vanished. "Brack, Arturo—call some of the sprites, we've got work to do."

And with that, small fey bodies appeared, illuminating a very creepy looking room. As we had noticed, three quarters of the room's population was vampires—and they were all unconscious. Unconscious vampires don't breathe. A room with a hundred corpses—ick. The humans were also unconscious—breathing, but out cold. In fact, I realized vaguely, I was the *only* conscious human. Green made a move to shove Adrian off of me, and that almost changed.

Green swore, viciously—but it came from far away, and a haze was blocking my vision that just made the room full of unconscious vampires look worse.

"He broke your fucking hand...Jesus Christ...Adrian, you manky buggering git asshole fuckhead, you broke her hand..." I'd never heard Green swear at Adrian like that. It would have been gratifying, but Green was prying Adrian's fingers off of mine and I just felt queasy and miserable with pain. Several sprites flew down to illuminate, and I could hear their concerned chirping over me. It took all the maturity and patience I had not to tell them to fuck off. I was suddenly aware of Brack behind me, propping himself at my back to make sitting easier, and I felt his gentle fingers on the gun in my right hand.

"Safety that and put it in my holster, will ya?" I asked, and he did so, never stopping the gentle hand in my hair.

"I thought your shots were off." He said gently. I got a look at his face, and realized that he had red smears starting in the corners of his eyes, and from his nose. Christ, I thought, shuddering…what *happened.* But we couldn't think about that now.

"I suck one-handed." I said instead. "I need to practice." Then Green managed to pull me free from Adrian's death grip, and I went blind with pain again. We must have been getting good at the whole pain thing, because Bracken had an empty pretzel bowl at the ready when I threw up, after which I leaned weakly back on him, and watched Green marshal his thoughts. Brack handed me a glass of water, and I felt better after I'd rinsed and spat and swallowed a little of it.

"We need to get them out of here." He said at last, gesturing helplessly. With an effort he stood up, then bent at the knees to pull me to my feet while Brack pushed. Stars spun in front of my vision, and I wondered if the room full of dead vampires would look less creepy if I wasn't passing out. I took a good look at Adrian, then, his marble skin almost blue, his eyes closed like a sleeping child's. His skin on mine had been rigid and cold. My chest went tight and I swallowed hard. Nope, I thought. Any way you sliced it, it was pretty awful.

"These guys?" I gestured at Max, Adrian, and the kid that had Green's attention when the fireworks began, with a flip of my good hand for Grace, Phillip and our other vampires. I thought it was a stupid question, but I watched Green and Arturo exchange agonized looks.

"Our people first," Green said with a sigh, "But if we can, it needs to be all of them…" Arturo nodded slowly, not looking happy, but in agreement.

"I couldn't live well, with all this on my hands, brother." He said after a moment, wiping at his eyes. His sleeve came away smudged with red. I could have wept blood myself with the enormity of the task, until I took a better look around. "Wouldn't it be easier to lock up the place and sun-proof it?" I asked. It wasn't such a stupid question, really. Like most dive bars, this place had no windows, and much of it was solid, old-town Folsom brick.

Green grinned at me, and the pain lessened a minute bit. "Good idea, dearest." He said after a moment. "Excellent idea, in fact." He smiled tiredly then. "But first things first." He moved towards me then, and gestured towards my hand. Bracken held it up for me, because moving it myself did too many awful things to the twisted sinews and snapped bones inside. My fingernails were turning blue, I thought, almost fascinated by it. Ew. Green put his hand on my shoulder then, and I felt it trembling. He was sapped, I realized. Whatever had happened between all of us, it had drained him of energy. This close, I noticed that there were watery drops of blood starting from his eyes, his nose, and staining that lovely hair from his ears, and I shuddered for a moment to realize that whatever had been happening before the lights went out, it might have killed him, and he needed me now. I felt inside myself, for that huge force of a thing that I had been playing with all week, and realized that it was thin, transparent, like a dream of flying—for the first time in forever, I felt helpless. We stood there, awkwardly, trembling, and then he smiled, just a little with the absurdity of our bodies. He was so beautiful, I thought, so good. All of us needed him so much—how could he be powerless? It wasn't possible. Something quivered in me, through him, and a small noise came from his throat.

"So much faith in me." He murmured, looking to the side. Then his eyes met mine, and I saw, unbelievably, the same thing in his eyes that had been in mine. I felt stronger, just looking at him, warmer, even down to my blue fingertips, just knowing he felt that way about me. He bent down, leaned his forehead to mine, and smiled from that dizzying closeness. "Someday, Cory," He murmured, "I'm going to kiss you just to kiss you…but today…"

He would kiss me to heal me. "Just kiss me." I said gruffly. And then he did. It was warmth, and strength, and healing. I felt the tingle in my belly that with Adrian had been pure love and pure sex, but with Green was these two things and healing as well. It spread through me, coursing through my body, through my sex, up my spine and through my limbs. It hit my wrist just as the kiss ended, and I whimpered as bones re-knit, sinews re-attached, and muscles joined smoothly as though never punctured by bones. A scream welled up in my chest to be stopped by the weakness of my own body, and I fell backwards again, into Brack's arms.

"Oh, I see." Brack muttered from behind me, "He kisses her, and I catch her—fucking marvelous."

"Well, big brother," I murmured, trying to find my feet, "If I could stop getting hurt, we wouldn't have to do this anymore."

"You could always stay home." Arturo said with deep disgust. He was closer than I remembered. How long had I sat there in Brack's arms?

"You'd miss me." I said, standing up fully, hoping they wouldn't question my strength—it was pretty much gone.

"Just a little." Arturo said, flashing silver-capped teeth. Then we got to work. There were thick drapes over the bandstand, and the sprites ripped them down and nailed them to the doorways, getting them ready to be shoved into the cracks and the seals. The humans we dragged through the back door, leaving them in softly breathing heaps by the parking lot. Sweet dreams, I thought as Brack and I dumped an obviously under-aged goth-girl onto the pavement. She could have been me, I mused, if I had had the guts to try to crash a bar without my new crew.

We levitated our people out. Apparently our little kiss had worked wonders on Green, because it was his idea. He closed his eyes, said a few words, crossed his eyes underneath his lids (I'm guessing at that part) and then he reached for me and Arturo, and I reached for Brack, and Bracken held out his hand where the handful of pixies gathered and flickered as our power pushed through us at his command. Brack and Arturo must have been unphased by whatever had shorted out every power in the building, because I know all that was holding me in the circle was mule stubbornness and grit teeth. Suddenly our people—Max, Adrian, Grace, the kid, and the other five vampires who'd come with us, rose into the air, coming to a rest at about my waist.

Green let go of us then, and stood with his hand up. "Touch them," He said, "And they should follow you. Move them where you want them, tap them twice, their bodies should fall into place. Grace's mini-van will hold five, Cory, you'll have to drive three of them in your car—Bracken, you'll ride home with me on the back of the motorcycle.

I watched Brack doing the math in his head, and then glare at Green. "What about that damned cop." He asked after a moment.

Green swore, and Max almost dropped to the ground before I shouted "wait."

Green and Brack looked at me. "He was helping." I said. "We can't leave him in here—Sezan wasn't a vampire—heaven knows what's going to be awake here tomorrow morning."

Green nodded and sighed. "Can you find his keys, luv?"

It was odd to frisk *any* body, much less one that was levitating, but I slid my hands into the front pocket of Max's tight jeans and fished out the keys. I held them up, and Green nodded in satisfaction. "Right—you drive him onto my grounds, Brack'll take your car, and away we go."

And with that we began trooping bodies out the door of *the Granite Horse* bar. The place itself was on Folsom Dam road—a long time ago there would have been absolutely no one abroad at all—it would have been a perfect place for a murder then, and oddly enough, it was still one. The only thing different between twenty years ago and now was that the gas station next door to the bar was bigger and cleaner and tonight, it had shorted out too—I checked inside and saw that the clerk and two customers were out cold, so I turned off the pumps, in case anything got hinky when the short was fixed. After that, it was still a perfect place for a murder—it was quiet, it was secluded, there were about five acres of scrub and brush behind and to either side of the bar. Since the dam road had been closed after 9/11, any traffic at all was local, meant to turn off on the two small residential roads between the bar and the road block. As I guided a levitating Max to his car, I wondered if the locals were used to a lot of strange things happening in proximity to *the Granite Horse.*

Max drove a souped-up red Mustang, and the joy of driving a 409 V-8 was about the only thing that kept me from completely falling asleep on the long, quiet drive down Auburn-Folsom to Lincoln Way to Forresthill. It was on odd drive—I wondered if the others felt that way—coupled with someone who was dead to the world. It was probably worse for Arturo, I thought, smiling darkly—he had a mini-van full of vampires. But that was the only lightness I felt as we caravanned through the darkness and I followed my own car home. It was home, I realized as I rounded the final corner of Foresthill road and turned off onto Green's little slice of heaven. It was home in a way I didn't know a place could be.

Perhaps that's why, after I ditched Max and his muscle car immediately inside the hedge that bordered Green's power over the land and walked the good ½ mile to the house, I found I had mindlessly followed Green through to the darkling, where he was just depositing Adrian on his bed. Blindly I glanced around Adrian's room, thinking, not for the first time, that if you didn't know the guy was a vampire, you'd think he was a very nice, very old fashioned sort of man. The yellow tile winking from the bathroom still made me smile. It winked again, and I realized I was weaving on my feet, and I heard Green chuckle from the side of the bed where he was pulling off Adrian's shoes, jeans, and leather jacket. It was still pitch black outside, I knew, and Adrian and the other vampires hadn't stirred since the lights exploded in the bar. I could hardly say what I was thinking, but I had to.

"Are you sure he's not…"

Green looked at me, smiled wearily, and shook his head. "Vampires…they cheat death, yes?" Stupidly I nodded, even when he moved to my side and started stripping me of my own jacket, shoes, jeans and gun. "So when they die…it's like a rubber band that's been pulled back too long, and then snapped." He said this and snapped my bra through my shirt, unhooking it as he did so. With deft movements he pulled one side of the bra out through the sleeve of my T-shirt, then reached around the other side to do the same thing. I grunted a bit, in protest, and he swatted at my hands. "You know you can't sleep with it on…Anyway, it's a tremendous release of power, the death of a vampire. You would know." He set me down next to Adrian then in that enormous, plain wood bed and kissed the top of my head. "We would know." He whispered, and I was comforted beyond measure.

"Where are you going?" I said plaintively as he tucked the blanket under my chin and moved to go.

"I've got more vampires to safe up, luv—don't worry, I'll be back." He bent and kissed my cheek, and then each closed eyelid.

I should be helping with that, I thought, and then I didn't think at all.

Green crawled in with me sometime before dawn (I assumed—no windows!) and since I hadn't moved towards Adrian's cold flesh, it was only natural to turn towards Green's warm body by instinct. He folded his long body over me then, and I wondered when sleeping with naked men had become easy and natural and safe as breathing, and then I faded out again.

I woke again at what must have been mid-afternoon, to find Green's eyes fixed on me across the pillow. And suddenly his nakedness was neither easy nor safe.

"Been up long?" I asked, wincing with the pun when he grinned evilly back at me.

"Long enough." He replied, eyes glinting.

"Definitely." I said dryly. More than definitely. Apparently being a creature of sexual healing had some advantages. I would have scooted back, but both of us had scrupulously avoided touching Adrian so far. I remembered Green saying that he avoided the darkling in the day, and knew that the one reason we had both slept here this day was love. Love. We both loved Adrian. We both loved…

"What are we doing?" I asked. The heat between us was static and full, my body was changing with the strength of the sex and the need and the full throated desire to touch Green as we had only fleetingly touched before. He had seen me sexually aroused before, he had held me in his arms countless times, and what I felt for him now was perfect. Or it would have been if not for the lover lying lifeless at my back.

"Becoming lovers." He whispered, touching my arm at the shoulder, trailing his fingers from my shoulder to the tips of my fingers. I shuddered, and flexed my thighs together where the ache was building to become unbearable.

"But what will that make...ahhh..." His hand had moved to my hip, and his thumb moved cleverly to just brush the edge of my panties. My God, what want could do to a body.

"Lovers." He said, a smile to his voice. He looked arrogant, I thought, like it was a forgone conclusion. His hand moved up under my T-shirt to touch the curve of my stomach. I moaned. Well, he had cause to look arrogant, I thought, arching my back, practically pleading with him to touch my breasts, to touch my nipples which tingled and sang.

"All of us..." I tried again.

"Lovers." He said, firmly this time. His hand fulfilled its promise, cupping me, teasing me, and his gaze welded to mine. "All three of us will be lovers. You understand?"

I thought I did. And I realized that I could share Adrian with Green. And Green with Adrian. As long as I could have them both.

"And that will make me?" I needed his reassurance, as he had reassured me that morning after the garden. I needed to hear that our love would be good, and our sex would be clean. I am young, and human.

He had moved closer, so that our lips almost touched. "Ours." He whispered against my mouth, so that the word vibrated inside my skin, making all that was tender quiver as though stroked. "You will be ours." And then he kissed me, for real. I thought my skin would explode into a thousand stars, and I needed with all of my heart to embrace his body, his power, all of him, to take him into my skin, to be full of him, to bloom with him, to drive him into my body with force and power until the world shimmered with us. Our breathing grew ragged, and our hands caressed—they didn't wander, they moved with purpose, knowing exactly what and where we wanted them to touch. He groaned then, pulled me closer, crushed me to him and I twined my legs around him, trapping his hardness against my groin. A strangled sound came from him then, and he moved convulsively against me, a whim-per in his throat that made me laugh and then whimper back as our groins found contact. And then he was pulling away, holding his hands at my shoul-ders to keep me from following him blindly.

"What is it?" He called raggedly, and I realized that someone had been knocking on the door for heaven knows how long.

Arturo's voice, when it came through the door, was both amused and exas-perated. "Cory's cop is here—he's rather insistent about not leaving until he sees if she's okay."

Green sighed, and pressed his forehead to mine. We were both trembling, I realized. He pulled back again and answered. "Give us two minutes...we were...sleeping."

"Right." Arturo answered dryly, but he left, and Green rolled quickly out of the bed, and out of my grasp, I guess, because he backed away when I reached for him.

"I'll give you a few minutes to dress, luv." He said, searching for the jeans he'd worn last night. He found them and pulled them up, sans underwear and buttoned them over his amazing body.

I made a sound, of protest, of frustration, I wasn't sure which, but he ech-oed the sound with his expression and came back to the bed to kiss me hard and quick, then pull away. "You need to talk to Adrian. He wants this, yes, but we can't..."

"I know." I said, shakily. He was right. He was too right. How could I have thought...some of my dismay must have shone on my face because Green grinned then, all male. "He understands...don't worry...remember, the thing about vampires is..."

"No shame." I said, and his grin turned up a notch, before he turned and strode through the door.

If Max had been pissed and difficult in the beginning he was worse when I emerged from the darkling—I must have looked like hell. My cheeks had a little color—put there probably, from making out with Green just a few min-utes before. My eyes were heavily shadowed, and my hair was in need of washing. I moved carefully, as though not sure what was going to hurt next. In a heartbeat, Green was next to me, wrapping his arm around my waist and supporting my weight against him. Bracken was immediately on my other side with a can of trail mix which I started gulping by the handful.

"Thanks, baby." I said to Brack, who touched my nose in return and moved to perch on the back of the couch like a bird of prey. Max was probably feeling pretty mouse-like by now—there were several nymphs and three or four other high-elves besides Green, Brack, and Arturo standing in the room staring him down. I didn't miss this either. "Gees," I said, "I must look like total shit if you guys need to guard me from super cop here."

"You look tired." Arturo said honestly from across the room. "And worried. And super cop was threatening to break down the darkling door if we didn't bring you out."

I was appalled. "You threatened violence...in *here?*" I almost laughed with disbelief. "I would have liked to see you try to do that a little later tonight...asshole." But my voice softened at the last word, and I shook my head slowly. I went to move next to Max, and was mildly surprised when Green wouldn't let me. I turned to him, making our space personal instead of public, and reached up to touch his face. I felt his breath catch, and my next words were squeaky with that. "I'm fine." I said. "And I'm mortal, just like him...let us mortals talk, right?"

"I'm not leaving you alone with him." He said stubbornly. *Ours,* he'd told me. But in the daylight I was *his,* and he didn't want this mortal to touch me.

I smiled, and I must have reassured him. He knew he'd never have to fight for me because I was his. "So who's asking you to leave us alone?" My attitude made me stronger. "I'm just asking the rest of the house to back the hell off."

Green made eye contact with the other fey, and some of them winked out of existence, while most just sort of melted silently away, out the door, down the stairs, through the walls, until Arturo and Brack were the only ones left. I smiled at Green again, and the way he looked at me made my stomach clench with wanting him. He bent to me and whispered "tonight" in my ear, and felt my whole body quiver in response. His. I was his. I turned towards young Officer Max and reached out and touched his hand.

"I'm fine, Max." I told him throatily.

"Your wrist?" He asked, and I grimaced, then held it up and flexed my hand for him gingerly.

"Still hurts," I admitted wryly, "But Green healed it for me..." My smile grew ironic then. "We're getting my war wounds down to a science."

Max got mad then. "Dammit, I..." He shot a fulminating look over my shoulder to Green, who merely raised his eyebrows. "These people are not good for you...you do not belong here."

The thought hurt. "I do…" I do I do I DO!!!! I thought wildly. Then I calmed down…hysterics wouldn't help anything. "These people are my family." I said, my throat dry. "I'm like a new baby bird, found under a mushroom. I think I can barely walk and they know I should fly…these…" I flexed my wrist, touched my shoulder…I would have shown him the scar on my ankle if I could have, "These are a new baby's walking bruises…that's all…"

Max shook his head, denial? More anger? "They're serious scars, Cory…"

"But they're healed, Max. And my body is fine."

"You look like hell, you know that?"

I had to smile. "That's a shame, because you look *fabulous.*" His hair stuck up in clumps all over his head, his shirt was half untucked, and he was one of those men who had a face full of stubble if he went longer than twelve hours without a shave. His eyes were shadowed too. It surprised a laugh out of him, but he wasn't done.

"You've lost weight this last month."

I smiled, and it must have been the real kind because his face went slack. "Really? That's the best news I've heard in ages."

"Corinne Carol-Anne…" Green's voice was mild and I turned towards him in exasperation.

"It was an accident, Green." I said. "Have I really lost weight?"

Brack bust up laughing and Arturo put his face in his hands. Max was shaking his head to clear it when Green finally found his voice. "You have, dearest—I'll point it out to Grace and I'm sure she'll try to do something about that…" At that point a high elf dressed in really super-tight leather pants and a man's peasant shirt came and tapped Green on the shoulder. His face darkened, and he looked at me with worry, and something like regret. He sighed heavily, and came to take my hand. "The boy…the one from the bar last night—the one I found in Crispin's house…"

"The five second Oreo?" I guessed, and was rewarded by one of Green's brief smiles. How come Green's smiles made me think better, I thought, and mine just made people stupid?

"Yes…the five second Oreo…" He hesitated, touched *my* face now, and I guessed a little, what was needed from him. Suddenly I was flooded with the reality of what it would mean to be Green's—and why Adrian had always been looking for someone else. "He just woke up…he's lost, and alone, and he watched his girlfriend become a greasy spot on the sidewalk last week and…"

"I get it." I said, and surprisingly felt no bitterness. No jealousy. Nothing but sympathy for the poor kid who'd been dragged into my world with far less gentleness than I had been. I smiled then, and it was a little bit sad, but I'm pretty sure it still had the power to make men stupid. Then I raised on my toes to plant a kiss on Green's cheek. "No—really," I continued, "I get it. I understand. Go to work, baby." I murmured. "Adrian and me...we'll take care of you when you're done."

He raised my hand to his lips, kissed it, whirled and was gone.

Max looked at me, and I could feel his anger rising. "See...he's going to...to..."

"To what?" I asked, and found I was no longer tolerant of Max's blindness. "What is he going to do, Max? Can you put a name to it that isn't going to demean you by saying it?"

Max looked surprised, and then shook his head no. "But you...don't you want...an education...husband...children...a real life?"

I felt a bitter laugh welling up. "I've almost died three times in the last two weeks, Max. Any time I spend just walking on the face of the planet *is* real life. And husband...I'm all but married *now*...to two men, but good ones, men who would kill or die for me—how much more do you want for me?"

"Education?" He shot back weakly.

I had to laugh at that one, too. "This last month doesn't qualify?" I shook him off when he would have protested. "I know what you mean...I'm ready to register at three colleges, okay? I just need to pick one, all right?"

"But..." He looked away then, and I didn't know whether to kick him in the shins or laugh cruelly. I did neither, which made me wonder if I hadn't aged a decade instead of a month.

"You had your chance, Max." I said bluntly. "I needed a hero, remember? I needed a hero, and I got a cop, and maybe, if you can't be both at the same time, you should pick one and stick with it."

He looked at me then, in anguish. "Would that give me another chance with you, then?"

I had left Adrian, lying cold, still as silence, and while I'd been having this conversation a part of me was still hovering over his bed, frantic that he should stir, flutter a lash, **breathe, damn it all to hell...couldn't he even breathe?**

But I couldn't say that. "I have one lover who would like to eat you for breakfast and another who'd like to feed you to the first in a silver cup. Don't you think my plate's a bit full?" I asked instead.

Max looked at me, eyes narrowed, and a grim smile playing at his mouth. "That wasn't no." He said decisively, and before I could protest he turned on heel and strode towards the door. "Let me know what next, right?" He said over his shoulder to Arturo, who nodded. Then he was gone, and I was standing in the middle of Green's living room, munching trail mix. Abruptly I was too tired to do that, so I sat down so fast Brack blinked.

"You shouldn't encourage him." I said from the floor. "He's really happier as a cop, and you should leave him alone."

"Why didn't you just say no?" Arturo asked mildly.

"Would he have believed me if I had?" I returned, looking up at him.

Arturo shook his head. "Absolutely not." He agreed.

"Damn straight. I meant no. I feel no. Just looking at the guy pisses me off because I could be just that fucking stupid. How could he have not known that was no?" I said this last part to myself. Christ, I was tired. Because it was easier than getting up, I curled up right there on the floor around my coffee can of trail mix, and pushed a handful into my mouth, almost too tired to chew. By the time I had swallowed, Brack had hefted me into his arms and kissed the top of my head in true big-brother fashion.

"Officer Max was right." He said sweetly. "You have lost weight."

"Thank you." I mumbled.

"Wasn't a compliment." He returned smartly. "I mean it makes my job a lot easier, but you're going to miss your boobs eventually. Or someone in this house might."

"Fuck you." I said more clearly.

He snickered and turned left into my room. I made protesting noises, but he ignored me and set about stripping me down to my T-shirt and underwear again. But because he was Brack, he left the bra.

"Adrian…" I murmured.

"The darkling is no place for you right now." He said firmly. "And Green's bed is…"

"Occupied." I murmured resignedly.

"A third lover might not be a bad choice, Cory." Brack murmured, sitting down to tuck me in. "You need someone just for you. Adrian…well, he owes the day his soul. Green is needed to lead, and, yes, to pretty much love anyone of his people who needs him…you…you're high maintenance, sweet-heart. I bet you could handle ol' supercop with sex to spare."

"I was a virgin last month." I said distractedly. Sleep was so close. "Let me be in love, okay?"

"All right, little sister." Brack murmured, then kissed me safely on the forehead. He moved to go, and to my horror I made a little whining sound to stop him. He didn't say anything smart-assed, though. Instead, he grabbed a paperback from my little bookshelf and propped his back up against my headboard. "You won't wake up alone, right?"

I hope I murmured thanks. I meant to, but I was asleep too soon to know.

Adrian was next to me, warm, breathing, *alive,* when I woke up. I smiled when I saw him. "Hey you." I said quietly. He smiled back easily, happily, as though all were right with the world, and that was when the first sob broke out of my chest. I don't know who was more stunned—Adrian or me. He did okay, though. He wrapped himself around me tight, and held on for the ride. He showered my face with kisses and murmured nonsense things to me, and when I was done, and quiet, we stayed there, in bed, and he stroked my hair.

"Bad night?" He asked, at last.

I tried to laugh, but it threatened to break again, so I stopped because I had had enough of *that.* "You have no idea." I said finally. He pulled back from me far enough to take my left hand between his.

"Some." He said unhappily, "I have some idea…Arturo let me have it about this." He stroked my hand gently with his long-fingered, fine-boned hands, and it was hard to believe that these were the same hands that had held mine hard enough to crush it the night before.

"Did he call you a manky buggering git asshole fuckhead?" I asked, some tartness coming back into my voice. "Because those were Green's exact words."

Adrian grinned at me from across the pillow, a flash of teeth, of fang in that perfect fallen-angel face. "I missed that one." He said. "But I did catch goat-rutting prick-faced jerkwad."

Now I had to laugh, but this time it didn't clog in my throat. Adrian took this as a sign and leaned over and kissed me. It was a good, long kiss, but he pulled back after a moment, rubbing his tongue on his palette. "I know that taste." He said slyly, judiciously. Then he kissed me again, persistently, when I tried to back away and tell him. His smile, when we broke apart was dreamy, sly, anticipatory. "I know that taste very well." He murmured. "Where have you been, Corinne Carol-Anne?"

And I didn't know what to say, not at all. I know that a human in this position would be ashamed, or afraid, or deceitful. But I was not in bed with a human. "In your bed, with you." I said at last. "And with Green."

He chuckled, low in his throat, and I wanted to say something stupid, like "You're not mad, right?" But I knew he wasn't and I still didn't know how to reconcile that with what he *ought* to be. He stopped chuckling, and touched my face carefully, all fingertips and held breath. "My first woman…" He said after a moment, and I was surprised. I hadn't ever thought of Adrian's first *woman*. He smiled a moment. "You are so transparent, Cory." He murmured. "But only to me. I can hear your emotions…the mark, you know, but your thoughts…you're like your own television show…"

"*Buffy?*" I suggested facetiously.

"*Farscape.*" He replied, and I was flattered. "But now listen—you will listen, and I will watch my life, like a movie, on your face, okay?" He kissed my hand, then, the one he'd crushed, and I felt myself calm down. "Green…he…he thought I'd been deprived, I guess. I mean…me…I was a kid…I was…"

"My age." I said dryly.

"Too right." He grinned appreciatively. "I thought he was my world. He knew he couldn't be my world, because even then, he had people looking to him, right? And…" He sighed. "And he didn't want me to feel trapped, you know? By gratitude. By anything…He couldn't know…he couldn't know that after spending my life in a ship's hold, walking the street was freedom."

I understood more than he wanted me to, why Adrian was happy being a vampire. It made me incredibly sad.

"So Green bought a woman for me." He said it baldly, just to laugh at my raised eyebrows, I think. "She was a prostitute—all of sixteen, I'd bet, and he bought her contract and set her free. His condition—his only condition, was that he got to teach the two of us how to make love."

I blushed. I actually blushed. Then I got incredibly turned on. And Adrian read it all in my face.

"I was so scared, at first. She was like a whole other *species*, to me, yes?" I nodded. "I didn't even realize what women *looked* like, down there, right?…my hands were shaking, and I was almost too nervous to get it up— but Green—you know, Green? He taught me. He touched me. He touched her. He showed me and…bloody hell. It was amazing." He finished simply. "Women…damn…your skin, your faces, your expressions…they way you rub against a man like a cat…the sounds you make when I'm deep inside of you…your ferociousness when you come…all the gentleness to get you there…" He shook his head in wonder. "All of it…bloody fucking hell. But Green was there—he 's the one who made it that way because he was Green, and he was my sun and my moon and my stars and the world would have stopped spinning if he was ever to go away." He stilled for a moment, looked at me again, those blue eyes I could drown in, and that face that looked so proud and alone, unless it looked vulnerable. "I didn't know what to do with myself when she came back to me of her own free will, right?" He paused, read my wry expression. "Well I *learned.*" And we both laughed at that.

"But there never was a woman who could love us both. *Sleep* with us both, absolutely. Sometimes even at the same time—which was always a plus." I was blushing furiously now—had been for five minutes or so, and I loved to watch his nostrils flare as he scented the blood at the surface of my skin. "But never one who looked at me, and looked at Green, and thought *There you go…I could have them both, and we could all be one.* And it's been a disappointment, you know. Because I love women." He paused, he swallowed. "I love *you.* And I love Green.*" He waited then, and it wasn't as hard as it might have been, to find my voice.

"There you go." I said, watching his face light up. "That's two men of admirable parts, I could love them both, and we could all be one."

When he smiled like that, he looked like a little boy with a new bike. Well…*two* new bikes.

I wish we could have tumbled into bed then—I wish it with all my heart, but we had things to do, that had nothing to do with love and everything to do with war. First I showered (to the relief of the entire household, I'm sure) and then Adrian and I went out to the front room to eat—and to talk about the night before. On our way out, Green stumbled out of his room and he looked trashed—whatever had happened to the five second Oreo had been hell to fix, that was certain. Adrian had touched my shoulder, then moved to take Green's arm, and they both moved silently, grimly, into my room to talk, I assume. Although, from the looks of Green, I hoped Adrian was holding him close and making it all better. Funny how I could hope that, and not bat an eyelash. I still don't know if that means there's something wrong with me, or if I just subscribe to the blood deep conviction that love defies definition.

The living room was filled with vampires and high elves—the were-folk were huddling in the middle levels, I knew, keeping watch over Ray's bed to make sure Renny didn't rip him into kibble. It was almost comical, considering the fact the Renny, for the most part was a ghost child, pale, waiflike, hardly saying a word. But those of us who'd known her and Mitch together weren't laughing. The vampires in the room were more than a little upset. "It was like daylight—I was out cold." Phillip said, bitterly. I didn't blame them—whatever could put them out like that was a menace to them in any form. But I didn't think their being unconscious was the worse thing that had happened.

"You didn't see the fey." I said, walking into the room with a plate of ravioli in my hands. I was, as usual, ravenous...I didn't see how I could have lost weight at all with the way I'd been eating since I'd moved to Green's. The vampires all stood up when I walked in, and I blushed, as usual, and gestured for them to sit down. I felt like I'd married above my station or something, with the way they all deferred to me...gees, you kill a couple of vampires out of self defense and sleep with the leader of the pack...I mean really, who knew?

"What about them?" This was Marcus—Marcus used to be a stockbroker until he took a skiing trip and got caught in an avalanche and was found, freezing to death, at 3 a.m. by Phillip—another avid skier. He helped Green maintain his assets now, and woke up every evening and put on a three-piece silk suit. Green paid him enough to import the best—but it was always a crack up to watch him sit in the living room dressed like a corporate shark while he sipped blood from his were-cat girlfriend's wrist.

The living room was crowded with high elves and vampires, and suddenly even the high elves were paying absolute attention to me. Because the attacks had seemed so exclusively aimed at Adrian, we had taken mostly vampires to *the Granite Horse,* but all of a sudden the elves (always a bit elitist) were taking the whole night very personally. I looked sourly at Arturo and Brack, who had apparently not told them this part out of pure stinking machismo.

"They were bleeding." I said. "All of them—even Green—they were bleeding from their eyes and ears and nose...And they were weak, too."

"It's true." Arturo seconded. "While this Sezan was playing my body felt...it felt like I was being shaken apart, but not violently...like someone was using an electric toothbrush on my insides."

"It makes sense." Bracken said, speaking from the floor. He, too, was eating ravioli, and he patted next to him so I would have a place to sit. I sat next to Brack and he stole an extra piece of bread from my plate. I slapped his hand but let him keep the bread.

"What makes sense?" I asked, my mouth full.

"That the fey would be susceptible and the vampires wouldn't."

We all looked at him with raised eyebrows, and I chewed doggedly, until I could speak. "Well?" I said at last.

"This attack has been aimed *at* Adrian, but it's never been aimed *at* vampires—I mean, Sezan *couldn't* attack Crispin's crew, could he? I don't know what's wrong with Crispin now, that he'd let his kit be starved to the point of craziness, but at the beginning he could have taken Sezan out. So, whatever this is, he's using others of the Goddess' get—not vampires, but pretty much everyone else."

"Why wasn't *she* affected?" This was one of the elves—the one who liked really tight leather pants—I think his name was Gref.

"Two reasons." I said, thinking out loud. "One, I'm human, and most of the humans passed out when the vampires did—that's probably why I didn't get shaken apart."

"So why didn't you drop?" Asked Marcus. Marcus was way too analytical to get excited about any of this.

"Adrian was holding my hand—and Green's—you all know about that power surge thing we do, right?" At this there were several snorts and half laughs, mostly from the elves. I was going to say how that power surge protected me, but one of the smaller elves interrupted.

"You still haven't thanked us for cleaning up your mess." He hooted from the back of the room."

"You still haven't thanked her for cleaning up ours." Arturo said, shouldering his way through the crowd. He had Grace by the hand. "If not for Cory, we'd be hip deep in policemen after Mitch's death."

"Instead of one cop being balls deep in her." The same joker said from the back of the room. I winced, and was in the process of making Brack sit down when I heard a gurgling sound and turned to see the same elf—a short, wiry boy elf with extremely large hands and feet and lank, rat-tail hair down to the waist of his old running shorts—being held in the air by the throat. By Green.

"Cory's mine." He said. "And Adrian's. And since I'm pretty sure it was her power surge that saved us *all* last night, I suggest we say nothing about her that isn't nice. Right then, Cocklebur?"

There was silence in the room, and a now contrite Cocklebur was set back on his feet—he bowed twice to me and sank to his knees to press his head against the carpet. I was left speechless. Fortunately, the rest of the room had plenty of questions.

"How did she save us?" Phillip asked.

"What did she save the elves from?" This from Gref.

"Who was that asshole on the stage?" This was from Brack, and it was the question that shut down the entire room, because it was the question that had been plaguing us from the beginning. Who, exactly, was Sezan?

ADRIAN

Vulnerable

It's a good thing Green moved with faster than human speed, because I would have killed the fucker, and that's no way to be a leader. All Green has ever asked of me has been to be a leader—I can't deny him that.

Because if I weren't the Head Vampire right now, besides killing that bastard gnome, I'd be on a motorcycle ride with Cory, or inside of her, or inside of Green, living that fantastic promise of all that should be love that she had given to me not long before. My death would have been a lot more fun if I was that dissolute playboy I'd pretended to be when I first walked in that badly lit little station that she clung to like a weapon. Imagine— all that emotion hiding behind a pair of brown contacts, black dye, and about twelve pieces of metal sticking out of her ears and her nose and her eyebrow.

I watched as Green put Cocklebur back on his feet, and bared my teeth in his direction, letting my eyes glow and my face change. Little bugger turned blue he was so frightened, and that made me happy. For all of a second.

I looked back at Cory; she'd been pulled back into the conversation, and watching her face was more entertaining than any movie. But she looked thinner—not in a lean, predatory way, but in a stretched too thin way, and she was wolfing down that pasta crap that Grace makes that I would have loved when I was human but that made me queasy now.

"Red meat." I said, out of the blue, and I realized that the whole room had been looking at me before that, and the words had apparently been pulled out of my ass.

"Sezan's red meat?" Brack asked, moving his eyebrows like he was trying to shape the man out of the word. Fuck. Now I really didn't want back in the conversation.

"Cory needs red meat, moron." I said wearily. "We keep feeding her like an elf—she's a human, and occasionally she's dinner, and that's why she looks like she's going to wither up and blow away." I wanted to call to Grace, but she was too smart to throw back into the kitchen. I called for Renny instead—I'd fed often enough from her recently that she heard me quick, and changed shape when I asked. "Renny, luv—make Cory a giant steak, rare, lots of garlic and mushrooms, eh?"

"No garlic." Cory said from the floor—but her eyes lit up at the mention of steak.

"You love garlic." Green said in surprise.

She blushed. "No garlic." She murmured, looking at me under her lashes in a way that made Renny's blood rush in my body.

"No garlic." I agreed, and the rest of the room faded out of existence, until Arturo cleared his throat. Bless the elf—he loved me, I knew, like a son he'd never had—and he loved Cory too. But he was right. We had work to do.

"So…" Brack said dryly, "About that other thing…"

Christ. I didn't want to be here for this. Of all the things in the world I didn't want the world to know, it was what I'd told Cory, that night in garden.

"Sezan was a bad man." Cory said softly. "He's dead now." The elves looked at her, some with resentment, but most accepting. She was afraid of all that regard—I could feel it in our hearts—but you wouldn't know it to look at her. So good at deception, Cory my love—that's why she could blind a helpless old man with a genuine smile—it was like one of the fey, dropping their glamour. When she drops her glamour, like that whole punk-goth-bitch thing she had down when we met, when she drops that, she's blinding. I can't believe Arturo and I were the only ones to see beyond that. With a few exceptions, I truly loathe the human race—all those soulless bodies, when the soul was the only gift they had to begin with. All that fucking blindness. But not Cory. She could see right through me.

"He's dead now." I echoed. "Our git with the purple hair—that's his son." And of all the people in the world, it was Green who was most surprised.

"He's fey." Green said, his shock echoing through the house, louder than his words. "I'm not sure what kind—but he's not a vampire, and he's not a human, and he's certainly not a were-animal—he's one of us. How can he be Sezan's son?"

The room was silent for a moment, while they digested this, but Brack—who's incredibly smart, and has always loved me but will not leave any fucking detail hanging, asked the bad question again. "Who was the real Sezan..." He looked apologetically at Cory, then me, "Besides a real bad man." Oh, Jesus. Bracken, who had looked at me with worship in his eyes as a child, and now he was going to make me tell him this?

I swallowed, but Green interceded. "He was the captain of the ship that brought me over from England in 1849. I want to know how he managed to have a fey child—without dying before *I* met him." He looked at me now, and I wanted to die—and for a vampire, that's saying something, because we don't go out painless, and we don't go out pretty. I couldn't look at him, I was so afraid of his disappointment.

"I think she was a siren." I said, looking away. "I don't know—I never saw her. I just...I heard her...the men—they put wax in their ears, like that bloke in the story, and went into her cabin and raped her." It sounded awful enough. But I could still hear her screaming, in my head. It would have been bad enough if she'd been a human woman, but she was a siren, and I could have sworn her scream would liquefy my bones, turn my innards to jelly, and make blood come out my eyes. For a month I'd hidden under my blanket, my hands jammed in my ears. They'd forgotten to feed me then, but it didn't matter, because I would have sicked up anything they'd forced down my throat. You'd think more than a hundred and fifty years, and this would all just be a story to tell. But it was like I was still that kid. Hearing his name again, that night in the banquet room, and I was nineteen again, and that monster was my life.

From a hundred and fifty years away, I heard Cory gasp. I felt her horror, and her pity, and knew she could feel my helplessness, and I was embarrassed, for the first time, to know she was inside me, where my emotions dwell, because I did not like that person who had huddled under a filthy blanket and cried until I slept in my own snot. I hated the little bastard—who could be so fucking helpless? Who would have let that happen?

"It wasn't your fault." She murmured, and I glared at her. She stood her ground, which couldn't have been easy, because my hunting face was coming out but she didn't seem to care.

"What do you mean it wasn't his fault?" Corge said. He was a high elf and a sidhe, one of the more recent émigrés, and he liked to dress like a redneck—lots of jeans and T-shirts with foul slogans on them. I didn't know him well, but that was okay because now I could rip his throat out. "You let that happen to one of *us?*" Then he turned on Green. "And you brought him *here!* You made him a leader in your *house!*"

"It wasn't his fault." Green repeated, his face grave and sad, and I was suddenly tired of the people I loved standing up for me, and I was tired of being so fucking afraid of my past that I would hurt Cory *I broke her fucking **hand*** in my fear, and I was **TIRED** of that buggering cocksucker having more power over my life than I did myself.

"So it wasn't your *fault* that our people were bleeding out their eyeballs, now was it." Corge said to me, the sneer in his voice raw enough to flay my skin.

"I was a sixteen year old fuck-puppet locked in a closet, you buggering asshole." I snapped, relieved to finally get it off my chest. "Don't you get it? I was a *slave*—I was sick, starved, beaten and raped, and as much as I would think it a crime against goddamned nature after a century and a half of eating well and bathing lots, back then all I could think of was how goddamned happy I was not to have those fuckers banging down *my* door, all right?"

Goddess—fifteen people in that room, at least, and not a sound among them.

"No shame." Cory said, at last. "You have no shame." There were tears in her voice, then, for me, the jerk-off who broke her hand, and who almost got her killed not once but three times and she was ready to cry for me. Sometimes I hated loving people, because it could hurt like this. It could make your chest swell and your throat tight, and it could make you want to howl until your throat shredded and I *hated* that feeling, because it was overwhelming. Brack broke the silence, and I could have kissed him for it.

"How'd she get away?" He asked, all business then. Like I said, he loved me. "The siren—how'd she get away?"

I smiled, and it must have looked awful, because I saw several of the elves recoil. Good for them. "She sang." I said. "She sang, every day, when there was no one with her, and finally, the song got through the bloody ear plugs because one of the sailors set her free. He was ripped to shreds by the other sailors—but he did manage to set her free." Silence again. I was not used to silence in Green's house. "So, anyway, two or three years later, this little boy washes aboard…literally—a freak wave washed over the ship, and when it was gone, there he was, clinging to the mast. He had purple hair—ugliest kid you've seen in your life. Mean little bastard. They lock him up with me—forget to feed us, he starts taking bites out of my hand, right? Sezan loves this kid—nobody can bloody well touch him, right? He's got a shriek that bends metal—you'd rather be hit on the head than listen to him scream—swear to Christ, my eardrums went bleeding. Really bleeding—I spent most days passed out in the corner while the little fucker beats hell out of me. So, we get to port, he gets taken out of my closet, that's all. Green finds me about a month later…I don't give the little bastard another thought…"

"Until last night." Green murmured, looking at me with love, and sympathy, and I suddenly hated him too. God—who wanted to eviscerate themselves in front of a room full of people like this—it wasn't fucking fair. Then I looked at Cory, who had sunk to the ground and wrapped her arms around her head, and was rocking herself back and forth and back and forth, with the force of all I didn't say. I realized then, that it was all leaking out of me—my voice was flat, calm, offhand, but all that I wanted to scream to the heavens was seeping into her. With an effort that felt like holding my breath I blocked it off, only to have her glare at me.

"Don't." She said. I shook my head. "Don't." She said again. I glared back at her, stubbornly. I was *fucked* if my past would hurt her anymore.

Corge was looking embarrassed. Fucking bully for him. "Sorry, then, about…"

"Shut the fuck up." I snapped, and that godforsaken silence descended again. It was broken when Renny came in with a plate of steak. She looked at all of us with big, frightened eyes, then set the plate down in front of Cory. She took away the plate of pasta, which had virtually been licked clean, and I could almost feel the sob of hunger that gripped Cory 's stomach as she looked at that juicy, bleeding red meat.

"Eat." I told her, and she gave me this shining smile. I could hear her, then, thinking *arrogant bastard,* but she took her fork and knife and ate. I felt better. Love didn't always claw your throat out—good to know, that.

"Why didn't they die?" She asked through a mouthful of London broil.

"Why didn't who die?" Marcus asked stupidly. I'd almost forgotten my own people were there—and that's when I realized how much my embarrassment was aimed at the elves. That made me want to laugh—and not a nice laugh, either. Green would be appalled if he knew how high and mighty his people got around mine. But I didn't care, really, because we vamps kicked ass, and because Green loved me and mine and we took care of each other when it mattered.

"The sailors raping the siren…shouldn't they have died?"

I wanted to sink into the floor. I hadn't told her this was taboo to speak of—but it was, sort of. I didn't know why—but I knew that until I'd talked to Cory, what had happened to Sezan had been a secret only Green and I had known, and that neither of us had talked about. I was grappling for an answer when I caught Corge and Gref's exchanged look, and heard the other murmurings in the room. "How would she know about that?" Gref asked me.

"Because I told her, right?" I shot back. "Was it a big furry secret?"

That's when Green stepped up and took my bullet for me and I wanted to pop him a good one. God *damn* it, when did I get to step in front of my own bullets?

"It's not a secret." He said calmly. "The Rosetti sisters knew about it—I'm sure others have known. The point is that it's a good question." He looked at me then, eyebrows raised. "Any answers, mate?"

Oh. Well, apparently now was a good time to start taking my own goddamned bullets. "I think it was that it was so many, and so often." I said reluctantly. "When one needed her again, he simply took her—there was no moment to want, or to need. So that second taste of the fruit, you know, it came too easy." Everyone looked uncomfortable then, and angry, but not at me. But Corge would not let it go.

"I still want to know how she knew." He said after a moment. "She's awfully damn knowledgeable for someone who's been here a week."

I felt Cory's bubble of anger before it burst out of her mouth. "That's a month, ass-munch." She spat, "And you don't really give a shit about how I know, do you? You just want to watch him bleed some more for your personal enjoyment, right?" Corge looked startled, and I realized she was right. Cory knew people better than I did—I forgot that a lot. "Well fuck you and the high elven horse you came in on. You know what you need to, and he's done bleeding." I wanted to cheer. Suddenly love didn't hurt, and it didn't make me angry, and for the first time it didn't scare me. Green would take that bullet for me because I'd take it in a second for him. Cory would make my kill for me, because I'd die in a heartbeat for her.

"So now we know why the sailors didn't die." She continued as though she hadn't just ripped Corge a whole new arse, "But we don't know why the were-folk were dying, and why the elves *would* have died."

"Oooh ooooh!" Brack said facetiously, "I know, I know!" He had his hand raised and everything, and the rest of us had to laugh. It was a good laugh—it let Corge fade to the back of the crowd and let the tension drain from the rest of us. I looked at him with affection—like a brother.

"I know too." Said Grace calmly. Arturo had kicked one of the other high elves off the couch and pulled her on his lap. She looked at home there, plump and motherly with only one fang showing, because she was running her tongue over it out of habit, but she also looked like she'd rather be at the back of the pack. Too damn bad, I thought, a bit smug. I had seen so much in her, long ago, sitting on a porch, looking at the moon, and dying. She'd see it eventually.

"So tell us." This from the back of the room—a female elf named Sweet, who had tried with Green, Brack, Arturo, and even me, and been disappointed when we didn't sleep with her. What made her sweet was that she didn't hold grudges.

"Sound." Grace said quietly, "Isn't it obvious? If Sezan's a siren, like his mother, he can use sound as a weapon."

"*He* listened to him for a week and lived." Gref said, still out for my throat, and I didn't have an answer to that one, but Cory did.

"The sound equipment." She said thoughtfully. "I've been to concerts before in a small space—they didn't have all the crap he had on that stage—I'd like to know what some of it was."

"What about Mitch?" The voice was quiet and quavery, and came from behind Cory. We all looked at Renny in surprise—it was probably the most we'd heard her speak altogether since that first awful night after Mitch had died. "What happened to Mitch? We saw the concert the night before…and all day we felt this…thing, quivering in us, like a plucked string…and I changed right when it became unbearable, and he didn't…and why Mitch?"

Green's face—gods he felt his people's pain. And we all loved Renny and Mitch. "I think it's because you changed." Green said. "That's probably why Ray didn't die, and probably why there haven't been any more deaths since the concert. Renny—we don't know who all those bodies belong to—do you?"

"Maybe you should have asked her before this." Corge said, and I felt Cory's power building up in her stomach probably before she did. Before I could say anything, Corge was on his arse, looking dazed. As a whole the rest of the room looked at him; turned away; resumed our discussion. Brack stood up behind Cory, let her lean against him. I wished for the umpteenth time that I hadn't been standing equidistant from Green when our little pow-wow started—because between the three of us, Cory, Green, and myself, we formed a perfect triangle, a very powerful force of leadership, and I didn't want to break that. But, Goddess, did I need to touch her right now. And Green. I needed to feel them, under my hands. I needed to tell Cory that she was now officially my hero.

"I know that all of the were-creatures who're missing were there that night." She whispered. "They let us in free, because we were friends of the band."

Green and I shared a look. "That answers that." He said. It did—hiring Mitch's band that night had been a trap—and a very successful one—and it had been aimed right at my food supply.

"The were-folk must be affected differently because of their metabolism..." Cory said. "I mean—they replenish blood faster because they shape shift, and an animal's metabolism tends to be faster than a humans so the sound affects them, but it...it stays in their bodies, and if they don't change in time, it...well it needs a way to vibrate out...I guess he hadn't performed in front of elves until that night...we wouldn't know what would have happened if that short hadn't occurred."

We all shuddered. Cory, Arturo, and I had all seen what had happened to Mitch. The rest of the room could only imagine.

"Why did the short occur?" This from Phillip—he'd been knocked cold that night—I guess he deserved an answer.

"Feedback." Green said. "Sezan was pumping power into the air—mostly for us, I guess, so it was vibrating through me. Adrian grabbed my hand, which probably would have just grounded me, except..."

"Except he had my hand too." Cory interjected.

"Exactly." Green nodded. "This sound thing apparently doesn't work on vampires—or humans either—but the three of us..."

"We form a circuit." I was happy to have something contribute. Everyone else in the room was nodding, so we must have been making sense.

"So we had our love/sex/energy circuit going through us…" Cory didn't blush this time—she was too enthralled with the discovery process. I wished she would blush again.

"And then what happened?" Arturo asked. "Because this was the point when I was about to become vampire kibble."

"The boy—Oreo—he grabbed my hand." Green said. "He knew it was a trap—Sezan apparently blew-up the boy's lady friend, after I planted our little greeting—he grabbed me to take me from the room. He was trying to save my life." I was glad that got out—Green was wrecked over the girl's death, and Oreo's pain. It was cleansing, to have these things out in the open. I hoped.

"And that was when Adrian broke my hand." Cory said, and I winced. Then again, maybe that bit about things being public knowledge was bullshit. "And Max grabbed me to take me away from him.

"They were insulators." Green said excitedly. "It was like flipping a switch—one minute we're sucking in all the power Sezan was throwing at us, and the next minute…"

"It's all flowing back to him." Cory said with satisfaction. "It had to go somewhere—so it went into the electrical equipment." They sat there, smiling, in perfect simpatico, and I felt left out, just a little. I'm not bright. Green and Cory put me to shame.

"Why doesn't his singing hurt the vampires—they're preternatural beings." I asked.

Cory looked up, and I felt the sympathy crushing her chest. I wished I didn't. "Physics." She said quietly. I remembered her studies, and how I'd tried to talk her out of them. I'd wanted her attention. God, I was an asshole sometimes. "Sound needs a place to resonate…air space. Vampires don't breathe…no blood flow, no oxygen—you're kept sentient by sheer preternatural will, I guess, so you don't have air in your bodies in which the sound to resonate. No sound, no revenge."

"Did it affect any of the humans?" Green asked. "I mean…we know it didn't hurt Cory, but she was in an entirely different situation."

"No." Brack said decisively. "All of the humans we moved outside—none of them were bleeding like we were."

"Then why didn't he just go after me?" I asked. I wasn't hardly aware I had said it out loud.

"He couldn't, A'." Green returned gently. I felt a quick violence building up in me...I was suddenly so angry I could almost smell blood.

"No...he could have. There's a thousand ways to kill vampires—anything from a guillotine to a meat grinder—he just didn't fucking want to."

"It's like passing out." Cory said, out of the blue. We all looked at her, and she shrugged. "It doesn't hurt to pass out—I'm starting to look forward to it, honestly. It doesn't hurt to be dead. But watching your people go...that hurts."

I threw back my head and howled. I couldn't do anything else. My people were dying, to hurt me, and it worked, and I howled until Green threw up a shield around me to keep me from bringing the roof upon our heads. Then I turned and stalked out of the room, leaving the investigation and the discovery and the companionship to my people, sitting miserable in my wake.

GREEN

Three

Green was shaking when Adrian left the room, not just from the effort of shielding Adrian's howl, but from the pain itself. Green knew that pain—it was the pain Oreo (his real name was Owen—it looked like Oreo would be his non de plume forever) had spilled into Green with his sad release, and it was his own pain, as he watched Renny tremble and start and fear. Only Adrian, he thought wryly as he sat down on liquid knees, only Adrian would be so empathetic and self-centered in the same breath, to use that pain to try to tumble the house around their ears.

"That went well." Cory said dryly. She was sitting down again, at the foot of the couch, leaning back. Green had drawn on her, and on Arturo and Bracken who were also looking decidedly pale, to keep Adrian's shriek from rending the rafters.

"Peachy." Brack agreed, sinking next to her. They sat, shoulders touching, for a moment, before Green could draw enough breath to speak.

"Well," He said, "Now we know what we're dealing with. We just need to figure out what to do with it. Think on it, for the night, everyone—we'll talk again tomorrow night and develop a plan. I think we've damaged Sezan enough for now to take a breather." Privately, he wished he could stalk into downtown Folsom and rip the bugger's heart out—but he couldn't. He knew it. He was weak, and his people were frayed, and, dammit, they needed two days of peace before they gathered themselves into a small army and wiped the fucker off the face of the planet.

The room gathered itself to leave, all but Brack, Arturo, Cory, and Grace, and Green called out again. "Corge,Gref—a word please." Green smiled pleasantly, he thought, but he noticed that both elves looked uneasy.

"Gentleman—I believe you've met Cory?" They both looked at her, too nervous to be dismissive, then nodded. "Well let me formally introduce you. This is Corinne Carol-Anne Kirkpatrick. She is beloved of both the head vampire of this Kiss, and of myself. She has enough preternatural power to fry the hair off your testicles from two miles away, but she's very new at it, so her aim isn't quite that good...do you both get my meaning?"

"She's human." Gref said, strangling a little.

"She's power." Green corrected. "And she's mine."

"The vampire's screwing her!" Corge was indignant. In a whoosh of fluttering clothes and raven hair, Green pinned him against the ceiling.

"She's mine." Green said again, and his voice held the feral growl of a wolf, the shrill screech of an eagle, the yowl of an adamant tom. The noise pushed Corge's down-dark hair back, and crushed at his chest. "You will respect what's mine." Without warning, Corge plummeted back to earth to land face down on the sturdy wooden table. He bounced, coming to rest on Cory and Brack's lap. They pushed him off of them like a debutant getting rid of a dead rat, and he sat up, bleeding, dazed, and too surprised to be angry.

"The vampire's mine too." Green said into the silence. "You will respect what's mine."

Grefs hefted Corge up into his arms and backed out of the room in silence. At the entrance to the hall Grefs stopped, and made a formal, albeit awkward, bow before he disappeared down the hallway. Those in the living room remained silent for more than score of heartbeats, before Cory spoke.

"I thought you weren't a warrior elf." She breathed, eyes big. She was still backed up against the couch, brushing at her knees as though blood had spread there.

"I'm discovering all sorts of things about myself." Replied Green evenly. "For one, I'm discovering I don't much like the way my people treat Adrian's."

"It improves every year." Arturo defended mildly.

"That's not fast enough." Green snapped. "Especially not now." He looked down at Cory, then into his own shaking hands. "Our world—the preternatural world—it grows smaller every day. Crispin—he used to live in a cave, and his vampires used to be the hippies that hung out at Rattlesnake Bar into the late hours of the night. Do you think Sezan would have had a chance to fuck with his mind, if he was still in that cave?" He looked away from all of them. "It was a nice place that—like Tolkien's hobbit hole, really. I enjoyed eating dinner and drinking cheap wine there, with Crispin." He shook his head again, coming back to the present. "Our world is too small for us to treat each other badly. If the preternatural world is going to survive, it's going to have to survive as an entirety, not as just "High Elves", "Lesser Fey", "Shapeshifters" or "Vampires."" He met Cory's eyes, willing her to understand.

"It's too easy to minimize you," she said, "If you're just one or two. One or two is a freak of nature. A kiss or a hall is a people."

Green smiled. "Excellent—exactly." He sighed then, suddenly exhausted, and sank into the cushions of the couch love seat. Like the couch it was getting abused, he thought sadly, and would have to be replaced. Some of the springs were going. He watched then as Cory heaved herself to her feet and walked around to him and offered him her hand.

"C'mon baby." She murmured. "Let's go for a walk in the garden and see who joins us."

Green took her hand bemusedly and allowed her to help him to his feet. She had to put her weight into it, because he was so much taller than she was, and that, too, bemused him.

"He might not show." He said when he was standing by her at last, breathing through his nose so he could smell her shampoo and her skin and Adrian's must threading through it all. "He was pretty wrecked."

"We're all pretty shredded." Cory said frankly, indicating Brack and Arturo and Grace, who were all but falling asleep where they sat. "But a walk in the garden is a walk in the garden, and who knows how many of those we get, right?" With that she snagged a worn quilt that lay on the back of the couch and moved easily towards the door.

Mortals, he thought fondly, taking her hand and padding behind her out the door and down the stairs. Mortals knew all about living. That's what elves had been trying to learn from them for centuries.

Green was weak, and some of the balminess of the night around his faerie hill seeped through, but that was all right too. They wandered in around the giant rose bushes, careful of the thorns, then through the lime trees, that still smelled fresh, in spite of the lateness of the season. They came to rest at the crux of the rose bushes, the lime trees, and a stand of oaks that belonged to the original land, and which still stood, proud and full and green, unlike their sun-scorched brethren. In the crux of the meeting was a tree of each, surrounding a pool that was fed from a stream that encompassed all of Green's acreage. The pool was surrounded by grasses and wildflowers—the mustard flower and purple clover that usually besieged the foothills around March and then either died or turned into stickers around May. But these had stayed green and supple, and they were sweet to smell and comforting and crisp around the edge of the quilt when Cory spread it out.

"This is the Goddess' grove." Green told her, settling down on the blanket. He put his nose to a mustard flower, breathed gently, and with a thought the night was filled with the faint, sweet smell.

"I don't know Goddess." Cory said frankly. She sat cross legged, leaning back on her arms and bathing her face in the moonlight. "I know God—my parents used to ship me off the Baptist church around the corner every Sunday to 'get religion '...but I don't know Goddess."

"They were lovers." Green said, turning on his back to look at the pale big moon in the black sky. Cory snorted beside him and he turned towards her, an eyebrow arched.

"Isn't that blasphemous?" She asked, her hand over her mouth like a naughty child.

"Only if it isn't true." Green responded in kind. "No—you see—you have to know the whole story—there were three. God, Goddess, and the other. God was order, Goddess was joy, and other was all that made order and joy valuable. God sought to make worlds, Goddess set to give them joy, and the other sought to destroy them. It was a good system, I've always thought."

"It sounds a little cold blooded." Cory said thoughtfully. "I mean...look at us...love, passion, revenge...pain...it doesn't sound like us at all."

"It's not." Green agreed, running his long finger over her plump thigh. Still plump, he thought with satisfaction, but it would be lean eventually, with all the work she did. That too would send a shiver up his arm. "There's more to the story. Goddess was never really interested in the whole planning of the worlds thing, but by the time they got to this one, she was bored—she wanted her hand in."

"So she created you?" Cory said. She sat up and took his plait in her hands and began to worry at a lock of it, so she might have something to stroke between her fingers.

"No...she created the dinosaurs."

Cory burst into delighted laughter. "They all died." She said flatly, through her giggles.

"Not very practical, our girl, was she? No...she had the whole consumption to production thing wrong, but it was okay, because God had plans for this world. He let the other wipe out the dinosaurs, and made prototypes for all the creatures he planned to have on the planet."

"Adam and Eve." Cory supplied, looking thoughtful.

"Of course. But he needed to let them develop—you can't just go 'shazam' and start an entire species, right?"

"Evolution."

"Exactly right. But Goddess liked these new creatures—in fact she liked them too much. She would go down to earth, possess all of his creatures— enjoy their bodies, experience their pains. She hunted as a jaguar, screwed like a rabbit, and took long swims in warm oceans as a whale...but her biggest, best joys came from being human. She loved running, playing, jumping as a human...she especially loved the sensuality of human beings, and she took over many forms, male and female, to experience all that she could. And because he knew that God would not like it, the other joined her. And she conceived"

Cory was surprised. "As in...children?"

Green nodded soberly. "Yes—where else would you think the fey came from? We are truly the children of joy, and of chaos—but you can't really blame the Goddess for us. She loved God's children—she wanted some of her own. Because she used humans to 'sport with the devil' as it were, our basic shapes are human...but because she's *not* human...well, we came out with some...refinements."

"Refinements?" Cory asked, curious. She moved her index finger cautiously up the edge of his pointed ear, and down the line of his long jaw.

"Refinements." He affirmed, rolling to his back again and moving her hand to his flat stomach. "Powers, strength, pointed ears, long limbs, what-have-you...refinements."

"Mmmm."

"Immortality."

"Ahhh." She sighed. She stroked his stomach lazily, knowing her hand would go other places, but not minding. She could feel the differences, between's Adrian's mostly human body, and Green's inhuman one. Narrower torso, longer muscles…warmth. "That's a big furry deal, isn't it? That's what the vampires got, that humans didn't."

"Too right." Green nodded. "God wasn't too pleased with her—he's an authoritarian chap, and he wanted to dangle immortality, like a carrot—for the soul, but not the body. It made sense in its way—encouraged people to treat each other decently—but it was hard on them, too. So, she figured she'd just make her get harder to kill, and let their worship come as it would—that way, she'd know their love was unforced. He wasn't pleased, I think, when Titania and Oberon and Isis and Set and Zeus and Hera started mixing things up in their time—but He couldn't unmake what She had made. They really are equally powerful—she's just not so…"

"Aggressive?" Cory asked, flicking a little male elfin nipple with her finger.

"Ahhhh….I was going to say organized…So the Goddess' get thrived, unless they came in contact with God's children…he let word be spread that we were evil, and she, in turn, delighted in teaching her children how to ensnare his…sometimes kindly…" his hand moved slowly up her thigh again, then to her own stomach, flatter now, but still softly skinned and plump, "Sometimes not." And he finished with a quick tweak of *her* nipple, making her yelp and giggle.

"And, as always," he continued, cupping her breast, insinuating his hand under her bra, "There was the same undeniable, attraction between the Goddess' children and the God's that there is between the two deities themselves…"

"Except with us," She murmured huskily, "It's forbidden, because humans aren't supposed to know about elves and vampires and such…"

"And elves and vampires aren't supposed to desire humans…" He pulled her down then, into him, and touched her lips with his own, then pulled her closer, thrusting his tongue into her mouth, trying to devour her whole. Her mouth was warm, inviting, spicy still from dinner, and he wanted more of her. He wanted to sink in to her warmth, crawl inside her heart and curl up and be comforted by its beating. At the same time, he wanted to drive into her body, pound at her, until they were one, not even separated by skin. He heard her gasp, not with her breath, but with her voice, and knew, before he felt Adrian's cold hands against his, that Adrian had come silently behind her, and bitten her neck.

She made a sound then, a complete, drawn out moan of surprise, arousal, and eagerness. Adrian's bite was short—not long enough to bring either of them to orgasm, just long enough to let her know he was there. When he released her, she fell atop Green, hands trembling. "Goddess..." She bit out, wriggling against Green. "Goddess, I don't know if I can do this..." But she wasn't embarrassed, he realized, as she thrust herself against Green's body, just sensitive to the point of pain.

"Sssshhhh...." He soothed her. "Here.... let's just lay here a bit, then we'll go in, right?"

"Go in?" She asked, and he saw Adrian's arched brow as well. Green smiled grimly.

"Look my loves, my two, my own—I can't hold the three of us. The hill—it's spelled already, it will hold."

"Everybody else?" Cory asked anxiously, but Green's grin only deepened, became more sensual.

"Will have a very lovely night." He answered with satisfaction. They would need a very lovely night, he thought, if they were to cope with the ugliness that followed.

Adrian bent then and tumbled Cory into his arms easily—superhuman strength, excitement, love. She laughed a little, breathlessly, when Adrian lowered his head and kissed her, his mouth open, devouring her laughter and her gasps into his innocent, insatiable hunger. Her hands fisted in his moonshine hair, asking for more, and yet more, until Green could see that they, neither of them, had the presence of mind to make it to the darkling. To that end he came behind them and allowed the front of his body to cleave to the back of Adrian's, and he heard Adrian gasp as his arousal pressed through their clothing towards the cleft that met at the small of the back. He touched his beloved's neck with his nose, his lips, and then, savoring the vibrations of Adrian's throat as he groaned, and so close that he tickled the fine hairs on Adrian's ear, he whispered, "The darkling...hurry."

Adrian ran so quickly through the garage then, with Cory in his arms that Green practically had to blur his body to keep up with them. They were a whisper of sound, a whoosh of air up the stairs and through the darkling to Adrian's room. He chuckled low in his throat when, as he stayed back to lock the door behind him, Adrian dumped Cory unceremoniously on the bed and began to worship her with his own.

There was no other word for it, Green would reflect later, as he lay sated in his own bed, enfolding Cory 's naked, weeping body with his own. There was no other word in English or in Elvish for what transpired between the three of them besides worship.

Cory's body was so young, so inexperienced in passion, that both elf and vampire treated her delicately, respectfully, their touches almost demure, even when she cried out to them, demanding the hard and fast orgasm that her body craved.

Adrian undressed her with awe, his touches on her belly, her breast, her flank, her calf, all so tender as to be teasing. She shied, at first, when she realized she was completely nude in front of both men, but Green had thrown himself stomach down and naked on the bed, next to her, and pulled her hand into his own when she had pressed it against her breasts. He kissed her palm, the inside of her wrist, the inside of her elbow, and Adrian took his cues from his first lover, doing the same, but doing it with the teasing nips of fang that she had come to expect from him. By the time both men had worked their way to her upper arm, her shoulder, her breast, and the tender treasure of her nipple she was clutching at their heads convulsively.

Green looked up at her face, her eyes closed against sensation and realization and paused. "Look at us." He commanded, and flicked her nipple imperiously with his tongue when she whimpered in response. "Corinne Carol-Anne, look at us." She did then, with eyes wide and limpid and cool green and warm brown, and deliberately, still looking her in the eyes, Green bent his head to suckle at her again. She could see them both, he knew, Adrian's moonlight pale hair against her peach colored skin, and his own sunshine hair against them both. He needed her to know that she was theirs, both of theirs, that this coupling and tripling was a brand, a bond, which would not be easy to break. She murmured their names then, incoherently, and writhed underneath them, touching Green's arousal with her frantic movements. From Adrian's pained grunt, Green could tell she had done the same for him.

Adrian pulled back then, and allowed Green to possess her first, coming into her slowly, carefully, a tight fit in a fat satin purse. She made a sound then, a full sound, long and sweet, and when he began to move the sound increased in volume, warbling with this thrusts, convulsing around him in the little deaths that were building, building, rising in force and pressure to the crescendo of a sensual Omega. Green paused then, for a moment, pulling her up into his lap, keeping her joined to him as he swung his legs over the edge of the bed. Adrian moved behind her then, and Green watched her eyes, cloudy and vague with sex, widen in shock. He heard her gasp of complete surprise, and felt Adrian's member, next to his own, and separated only by the thin wall that was her. They stilled for a moment, shuddering, all of them sweating, breathing like sprinters at the line, and then Green's eyes met Adrian's, and an old, knowing smile passed between them. This they knew, but it had never been so sweet. They had never done this with a woman they loved, that they would die for, and whose little death renewed their life and their heart. When they moved, it was in tandem, and Cory's voice rose to a high, shrieking wail as her body coped with nerve endings and sensations and her mind coped with being possessed by them both.

When the first shudder of raw, primal Goddess-born power ripped through the three of them, Green was the first to recognize it for what it was. And even *he* was too far gone to halt what they had become. He saw the glow surround their heaving bodies, and felt their power circuit charging, changing, growing with the power that raw sex built through the three of them. Cory 's wailing increased in pitch until it rivaled the Siren's sound that had almost destroyed him the night before, but this sound, instead of shaking the blood from his bones, strengthened his heart, poured power into his soul until his soul spilled over, and Adrian's too, to fill the fragile human vessel between them. Cory's head fell back, onto Adrian's shoulder, and he cried the stripped, bleeding, animal sound of a man roused beyond endurance, on the edge of climax. With a groan that Green could feel in the place where their bodies almost touched, Adrian dropped his lips to her neck and sank his teeth into her flesh.

Her mouth fell open as she came, and sunshine, blessed, deadly sunshine poured from her, missing Adrian's fair, suckling head by fractions, tickling the hair on Green's throat as his own head rolled back with his climax, and spread, poured, penetrated through the ceiling of the room, permeating the very earth that surrounded them, saturating all it touched with power, unbelievable power, and burgeoning life.

As the shudders of body, power, and soul that rocked them all quivered to completion, Cory bit her lower lip softly, then hard enough to draw blood, and the three of them melted, dissolved, poured across the bed, and reassembled in each others' arms.

CORY

Powerful

I awoke the next morning in Green's arms, and tried to reconcile what I had become to what I believed in the world. A year ago—a month ago—and I would have dismissed myself as a whore or any number of awful names and degrading ideas that mortals in America are raised with. But this morning, wrapped in Green's body, draped in that wheat-gold colored hair, and smelling of the sex of two men, every time I tried to call myself one of those words two things stopped me.

The first was the power. It had filled me, made me weightless, formless, lovely, and it had spilled out of me in a way that defied orgasm or release and was, quite simply, beautiful. How could I dismiss that as animal, as base, as common? It was impossible...and so it was gradually settling in to my brain that maybe I should rethink my vision of sex and love and all that I was until it wasn't dirty anymore.

The other thing that wouldn't let me degrade the night before happened about an hour before dawn. I awoke alone on Adrian's bed, and looked up to see Adrian emerging from the shower in the gloom, and Green moving past him to get in the bathroom. The two men stopped in the darkness, arrested by each other's presence, and then, slowly, they had reached to touch each other. A hand to the chest, to the forearm, to the neck, to the flank, to the groin. I watched, entranced, by their lovemaking, and could not, even though I had been mesmerized by them, say who had mounted who in the end, and who had spilled himself on the ground and who had spilled himself in the other, but I could say that it had been beautiful. It was beautiful, and they were mine, and that beauty, and that passion was mine to hold in my hand, and to kiss and to suck and to swallow, to lave and to touch and to tremble at—they were mine. I couldn't renounce them. If I wanted to I could call myself horrible, mean and petty names, but I couldn't degrade them. Green and Adrian were all that was perfect. They belonged together. They belonged to me. I couldn't reduce them to sex words. It would have been a wrong larger than any sex act I knew—and this morning, laying in Green's arms, I knew a lot more than I had when I'd first let Adrian sink into me, and welcomed him.

"You're awake." Green said into the sunlight. It must have been around noon.

"I am." I murmured into his arms.

"Regrets?" He asked carefully. I could hurt him, I realized, shocked, thrilled. That was why he'd made me look at him, at the beginning. He needed the right answer to this question.

"No." I said, securely.

"Embarrassments?" He asked, and now his voice was playful.

"Some." I mumbled. Because I did. Logically I could accept the three of us…but embarrassment didn't just go away with logic.

In a move, Green was on top of me, kissing my chin, my neck, my breast. "Let's take care of those, shall we?" He said, then progressed his way down to my stomach. I tried to stop him, then, because I hadn't showered, and because…well, I knew what he wanted to do, what he wanted to kiss and to lick, and I knew what had happened down there and…

"nah ah…" He murmured, spreading my clenched thighs and breathing in deeply, "We did this, Adrian and I…the least we can do is clean up…" And then he was there, with his tongue and his clever, clever fingers, and all I could do was call out to him and cry out and come. And when I had, he lifted himself up and came into me, and kissed me, and I tasted us, all of us on his tongue, and any of the doubts I'd had to begin with were kissed away, because we were wonderful, the three of us, beauty as I hadn't known, pleasure, hunger, satiation, love, and how can you refuse that, how can anyone refuse that when it's inside them, moving, moving, moving and glory was just a heartbeat away.

Afterwards, we lay, breathless, happy, for a moment, and then Green kissed the skin directly between my pubis and my stomach, and whispered silently "no, no, not today…"

I looked at him surprised, and then, both delighted and appalled…"Was I…am I…"

He smiled, kindly, and, for the first time in forever, older than trees and stone. "You can not have Adrian's child—that is truth. But you can have mine. I simply asked the child to…wait." He stopped then, looked out through the sunshine of his bay window, an unfathomable look in his old, old eyes. "There will be a child." He said, then turned so I could see the track of a single, happy tear. "If we live, one day, there will be a child."

I was dumbstruck—I didn't know to ask if this was rare or wanted, but I wondered how he knew. "A hope?" I asked.

"A vision." He murmured. "A true one." He roused himself, quickly then, and chided me into the shower. We were too sated to make too much out of the shower except to be naked and wet and happy, but that was okay, I thought dreamily, soaping his back. It was all okay.

It was all okay right up until Arturo knocked on the door while we were dressing. Green opened the door and his second strode into the room, shaking his head with exasperation. Green turned to shut the door, and without warning Arturo's hand snuck out to whack him on the back of the head, like a mother might do with a heedless child.

"Her…" He said, his voice strangled. "Her, I could understand…. Adrian, I could understand…"

"Understand what?" Green asked, sounding as stupid as I felt, which was reassuring.

Arturo shook his head again, and at that moment Brack strode in the door, took one look at us and giggled. "Have you showed them yet?" He asked through chortles of laughter.

"Showed us what?" I asked, this time being the stupid one

"You're going to *love* this." Said Sweet and Blissa from the doorway. Green and I looked at each other, and both of us made a run for the door before anyone else could come in. Arturo led the way, and the rest of us followed as he made his way to a granite staircase next to the hallway that, hello, **hadn't been there the day before.**

"What the buggerfuck is this?" Green asked, and Arturo gestured us up. The staircase was apparently carved out of the very living rock of Green's hill, and it led to a door of oak and lime and rose wood that again, seemed strangely living, that was mounted in what, in any other house, would be the attic crawlspace above the living room. Green's house didn't have an attic crawlspace—it was roofed by the scorched top of his fairy hill—and so the new magic door opened right up into the top of the hill itself. Which was scorched no longer.

"Buggerfuck." I echoed as we came into the sunlight, because it was a very good word. The landscape had changed completely. It had been a very average hill top in Forresthill/Auburn—scorched grass, sentinel oaks, dusty pines as the hill progressed. Now it was a fairy land. Literally. Wild roses, lime trees, and oak trees—not the Sentinel Oaks that are easily found anywhere in the foothills, but the Bur Oak, the kind that's found up North—Oregon, Washington, Canada—generous oak trees, willing to share their space, and not sucking up the moisture and the land like the greedy Sentinel Oak. The grass was no longer scorched—it was ankle length, green as velvet, crisp and sweet, fed, no doubt, by the spring that burbled up, defying logic, from the center of the crown of the faerie hill itself. I tried for a moment, to wrap my brain around how that spring could have rerouted itself to spill out over the hill like a long, clear ponytail and feed into the stream that circled the hill itself, but was left only with an impression of an Ourobouros of water, that fed on itself, and grew, sustained by its own liquid flesh. The flowers that grew by the spring were the same that grew by the goddess spring—mustard flowers, lupins, purple wildflowers, clover.

I had time to notice all of this, just before I got a *really* good look at the boles of the trees themselves, and I felt my knees give out.

"Jesus, Mary, and Joseph." I murmured, aware of the blasphemy and unable to stop it. "Buggerfuck." I tried again, and this was embarrassingly closer to truth. "Green...." My voice was strangled, and I had to fight the urge to run down that impossible staircase and hide under his bed.

His knees gave out too, and he sat abruptly next to me. "I see them, Cory luv." He said nervelessly.

"But that's so *wrong!*" I wailed, one hundred percent human now, with a human's inhibitions and a human's mortification.

"Looks damned good to me." Said Sweet from behind us, and I buried my face in my hands.

What I wasn't looking at were the boles of trees that had been created in the force of a night, twisted into the forces that made them. Twisted and gnarled into *us*. I couldn't see faces, but I could see forms, I had my memories of the night before, flashing before my eyes in erotic, cinematic detail, and every position, every quiver of my body and of Green's and of Adrian's, had an echo throughout this grove of trees and thorn-less rosebushes. Trees grew together, split, and merged again, in the shapes of nude, cavorting bodies— more often than not, two men and one woman. Us.

"They're beautiful." It was a rusty growly voice, and I turned to see Renny, in human form yet again, wearing hardly more than an oversized sun-dress of Grace's. I wanted to weep, and even Green's arm around my shoulders couldn't ease my complete mortification. Oddly enough it was Brack who made me feel better about the whole thing.

"Looks like fun." He muttered, sitting next to Renny. "Can I play?"

"Sorry, hon…its members only." I shot back, irritated.

"Thought so." He said easily. And like that, I realized he was right. Members only. A love that could create this much power—that was pretty god-damned exclusive, wasn't it? I didn't do these things with the whole entire freaking world. Just my entire world.

We all sat there for a long, nameless pause then, letting the sun sink into us and marveling at what had been created out of love and magic and pure sex. Damn, I thought reluctantly to myself, if you had to put your private life on display, this was the way to do it. We were disturbed only by the growl of my stomach, but when I would have gotten up to go get some food, Renny patted me on the shoulder and flitted away down that amazing granite stair-case, into the cool of Green's home. A thought occurred to me then, and I was compelled to break the silence.

"Did anyone see this…I mean, anyone not here?" I asked hesitantly.

Green shook his head—and I noticed, for perhaps the first time—that he looked more substantial, more real, than Adrian. Maybe it was sunlight, I mused, but the planes of his face—finely etched, true—were broader, of more flesh than my night lover's, and his hair was warm and supple, silky and coarse and almost alive as it dried beside him on the grass. His texture was somehow appropriate…Adrian was always a creature of the Goddess—his very existence was an act of magic and will. Green…Green had always existed…just sort of under human radar. Green was a fact of nature, Adrian of the preternatural.

"We were not seen." He was saying, and I pulled my attention back to him completely. "In fact…" He frowned, and little lines bridged between his eyebrows as he concentrated. "In fact, my shields caused some of this...here, close your eyes." I did, and I saw, as Green had taught me, the cool green that marked his boundary of magic for his faerie hill, and on it, splashed boldly, vividly, the darkest purple, green the color of violet leaves, and azure and sunset colors in wildest, most amazing patterns. I gasped, and, unbelievably, felt the flush of arousal flood my body. Hurriedly I opened my eyes because I knew I couldn't do that again, not so soon.

"That's us." I breathed. "Us. Our power...it poured out of me...it hit your shields and it...it saturated the ground...Holy shit..." I stood, restless, panicked. "What would have happened if your shields hadn't been in place?"

Green opened his eyes and blinked thoughtfully. "I have no idea." He murmured. "That's an amazing amount of power we created...it's an amazing thing we did with it..." His eyes met me, all the greens of the magic around us, and their gentle brown center, "Cory—you, me, Adrian—I think we need to be very, very careful together. Careful indeed."

I was saved by answering then by Renny, who arrived with a bucket of trail mix and a hamburger, extra rare. As we ate, I noticed more and more of Green's people coming out to dine, or to simply sit and marvel and what had been completed. Their looks at me, I noticed, had gone from skepticism and doubt to awe, and a certain grudging respect. The pixies and sprites formed a glowing, humming, circle around Green, Brack, Renny and I, as we sat at the center of the reverent fey. I didn't know what else to do when I finished, except lean against my sunshine-soaked lover, and fall asleep, surrounded by all I had become.

I learned how to control our power that night—the three of us together were magic, and magic could be controlled. I learned to focus on the flesh of us, the whisper of skin together, the nerve endings pulsating from blood, from pressure, from friction, the firings of dendrites to places that sang, the simple, the animal pleasure of the body, and only when we were collapsed, laughing, in each other's arms, did I allow the joy of love, of celebration for what we were to fill me. I know that most people have been so much in love that their skin felt like it glowed. Mine did for real—pretty fucking amazing.

During the days, I was either practicing with the gun until I wasn't a bad shot, or once again training in the garden, until I could make light and sound and pain come at my will. My evenings were filled with vampires and elves and tactics and strategy. Disturbing, all of it—especially when I realized that when we stripped away the elves and the vampires, the Goddess and the power, essentially we were Officer Max's worst nightmare: A giant preternatural gang, and we were about to bang in a big scary fucking way. But what else to do?

We thought of everything from kidnapping Sezan and getting him to see reason to grand speeches in public venues, but every time we even tried to call up his people on the telephone, we were met with mocking laughter, obscenities, or worse. After the first dead sprite, we could think of no other way of sending messages. Confrontation was our only answer—and even I, a frightened mortal, could see that in spite of uneasy discussions of peace, or alliance, anything of the sort would always be tainted by Green and Adrian 's righteous anger over the death and assault of their people. We couldn't make peace. They wouldn't let us, and we could not try anymore.

So we set about making plans to stage a sort of preternatural high noon (or high midnight?) and we debated hotly who to send with the message and how to protect them because a beeping light on an answering machine just didn't seem appropriate, and the sprites were already mourning those we'd sent to parlay. Adrian or Green were always present during the debates, but around one or two in the morning, I would slip away, with one of them, and we would honeymoon, in our fashion, touching and touching again, until we screamed with it. And always, before dawn, there would be the three of us, and I was filled with a love so fierce, so consuming, for what we had become, that war with Folsom seemed reasonable to me—because I would kill and I would die, to protect the two men in my bed.

On Friday, the twentieth, we decided that on Saturday night, Litha, the day before Midsummers Eve, we would to send Arturo and Phillip to Folsom, in the daylight, to leave a message that we would meet Crispin and Sezan's people by the slag heaps and rock quarries below the railroad, Midnight, the day after Litha. Green had told me that Litha was the ancient celebration of the sun—and a re-welcoming of the Goddess as the nights once again began to lengthen. Litha was a dangerous time for vampires—it was their shortest breath upon the earth, and that breath was all but human. All secondary powers, such as shape-shifting, turning into mist, breathing fire—whatever—were practically non-existent—about all they could do, and they had to be well fed at that, was fly.

However, as detrimental as Litha was to Adrian's people, Litha was a **very very** serious time of power for Green's—when they invoked the Goddess at sunset, they were filled with sort of "power squared"—and that would continue until the moonset in the afternoon of the following day. Green tried to explain the whys to me—but I was up to my teeth with how's and why's and explanation—after a week of living as we had been, my whole life rotated around sunset and sunrise—joy and fear. So the night after Litha would be our best bet—our most powerful time, and Litha night itself would be the weakest. Since we had heard nothing from them, we would choose for ourselves.

So it was with sort of a dreamy reality, that Litha morning, that we put Adrian to bed, sleepy and sated, and practically glowing with love and shadowed with worry. And that same dreaminess pervaded our fear when his eyes, resting on Green and I as we backed out of the door hand in hand, opened wide and frantic as he shouted "Fuck it all…Renny…goddamn it…they've got her…" And then the clock clicked from 5:39 to 5:40 and Adrian died the great death of sunrise, leaving Green and I gasping in shock.

GREEN

Litha

Stupid stupid stupid.... Green cursed to himself as he and Cory started the search for Renny. How could he have *been* so blind? He had assumed that everyone under his protection was safe—but Renny hadn't been staying in his protection as a were-cat—she'd been wandering afield, taking solace in her solitude, and although they had repeatedly warned her, they hadn't had the heart to enforce their warnings. She'd been so lost without Mitch. And now she was in danger of being lost to them forever.

Cory was thrusting her head into various rooms, waking people up and telling them Renny was missing. Her face was taut and white and grim, and Green mourned, once again for the innocence they'd taken from her. At the same time, he felt a tremendous pride in her—she was so much his lieutenant, now, after such a short time in the ranks of the preternatural. How had he ever taken a breath without her?

The elves started streaming out of their doorways—most of them completely naked, and many of them in pairs—all of them looking angry and upset, but not at Cory.

"Renny's missing." Green said shortly. "Adrian's been taking a lot of her blood—they 're pretty connected right now—right before sunrise, he told us 'they've got her...'—and then it was sunrise, and that's where we are now."

"Fuck its early..." One of the high elves grumbled loudly—his name was Grit, and he was sleeping with one of the vampires—a quiet girl, recently brought over. "I hate fucking Litha…" Green didn't have the heart to chasten him for his blasphemy—he was feeling too much the same. Whatever would happen, would happen that night—when Adrian and his people were at their weakest and Green's patrician lot would be forced to fight instead.

"Yes, it is Litha." Cory said from next to Green. "And that means that if we meet tonight, Adrian's people aren't going to be at their best—and that means that all of us here are going to have to fight for them—does anyone have a problem with that?"

Green tried not to smirk out of shock. Trust Cory to lay it on the line like that without flinching.

"You expect us to die for a bloodsucker's feud? Just because you're banging him?" Cory's eyes narrowed at the speaker, but she couldn't place him. Corge and Gref, he noticed, remained silent and tight lipped, making furtive eye contact only. Apparently the amount of power it took to carve that staircase had made its impression.

"I'm not just banging the head vampire; I'm also banging your boss." Cory said pleasantly. "This makes him my boss too—and our boss wants your co-operation." *Jerkoff…*She whispered that last part to herself, but Green still heard it and smiled thinly.

"I'm your boss?" He asked, loud enough to carry, but phrased only for her.

"Well, I don't work at the Chevron anymore." She replied, shrugging. They both looked up when they realized they were being flanked by Arturo, Brack, Sweet, Blissa, Crocken, Grit and a number of other elves who were either staunchly loyal to Green, friends with Adrian or one of the other vampires, or who had come to love Cory all on her own. The shape-shifters were all there as well—including Ray, who had been up and talking quietly to Renny for the last few days, both of them grieving for Mitch and for their other friends who had been lost in that first attack.

"And this is for Renny." Cory added, trying very hard to look like she had expected such an obvious show of support. "And for Mitch, because we all loved him."

"And for Ratso." Arturo intoned, "Because he was a friend."

Two or three others shifted to look at an increasingly small number of elves. Corge and Gref were not among them. "And for Janine, Jake, and Gary, and Jon Greves, who were our friends." Said Ray, speaking up.

"Look…it's not that we didn't love these people…" Said one of the few elves on the opposing side. It was Cocklebur—now that he was without the support of the masses, Green could place him.

"It's just that you don't see what this has to do with you?" Cory asked sympathetically. Cocklebur nodded and smiled, relieved, he thought, to have such a sympathetic ear. "Hmm…yeah." Cory pretended to consider. "But then, technically this doesn't have anything to do with me—right? I mean, like you said, I'm just fucking Adrian—we all know I'm not his first bed mate, right?" The others nodded, looking wary. "Yeah—quite right—I mean, really, Green's taught me a lot, this month—I could protect myself from attack after attack—I could move to Bum-Fuck-Saskatchewan and really, nobody could do a thing about it, could they?"

The opposing elves looked eager at hearing their own logic spoken back to them, and a few on Green's side were looking alarmed.

Cory nodded again. "Well, I could do that—I mean, I am pretty powerful, you know." She smiled conspiratorially at the resistant sidhe. "I mean, if I wanted to…if I got good and angry…I could fry your asses right where you stand, couldn't I?"

Everyone's eyes got really big at that, Green noticed, and his people started to smile.

"I could do that, right, Green?" Cory was saying.

"Right luv…too right, that." He affirmed.

Cory smiled wolfishly. "But I'm not gonna…" She said, and somehow, no one looked reassured. "I'm not gonna, because that wouldn't be right, now, would it? And if Green's taught me anything, it's what's right…right?" She asked them.

They all looked at Green sideways, considering. "Right." Cocklebur mumbled at last, and the others nodded, not looking at Green.

"So…as your leader, he's taught you right…right?"

"Right." The others mumbled, not liking where this was headed.

"And he's treated you right—yes?"

"Yes." The mumble was downright ashamed now.

"Sooo…." Cory continued, her smile completely unpleasant now, "If Green's your leader, and he's taught you right from wrong, what the fuck are you doing over there?"

Silence. Complete silence.

"Well…" Cory drawled, enjoying herself now, "I'm going to assume you're going to ask your captains or whoever, exactly how quick to step, what to fetch, and whose ass to kiss to make us forget I even had to have this conversation…am I right?"

Cocklebur made eye contact, finally. Green noticed he looked the definition of sheepish, and he felt his own mad coming on.

"We will do it because we all live here, and we all protect each other, and we all care about each other, and that's what makes us different from Crispin's get, and Sezan's, and from any other sidhe or vampire or shapeshifter who believes that only the biggest, meanest, and most amoral buggers make it to the top." He snapped, and in that moment he knew that his eyes went cold, his face remote, and he knew that as he stood there he had become the chill of discarded love, the dark shadows of a regretful heart, and that even Cory was watching him and shivering.

Cocklebur and the others dropped to their knees, and shivered and wept as they crouched. Without another word Green gathered Brack, Arturo, and Cory to him with a glance, and they swept out of the living room and down the hallway to the underground, leaving the others to prepare as they had planned.

When they got to the bottom of the staircase, Cory's knees went out, and she sat shivering on the second to last step, while the others gathered around the table to look at their map of Folsom and the lists of personnel and strategies they had devised over the last week. "We'll need someone free to snag Renny if they see her in the fray." Artuuro said at last, and the others nodded sightlessly, not wanting to think about the alternative.

"Bracken." Green said decisively. "He's quick, strong, and she knows him." And that was it—the last decision they had to make. The three of them stood there for a moment, saying nothing until Cory spoke up from the stairwell.

"That's all moot now, isn't it? Your plan?" she said softly. The others looked at her. "I mean, we made a good exit and all, but Renny's missing, and they've got her, and now it's all them, isn't it?"

Green thought about it, bit his lip, shook his head negative. "No—not at all. The sprites have still volunteered to confuse the enemy, the vampires will still flank the elves to keep Sezan from blowing them up, the shape changers will still go on the front lines—it's full moon tonight, so they should be able to shift in and out at will, in order to counteract the music. It should still be hard to take out the teams with guns or swords—which shot will they use? Silver doesn't work on elves, lead doesn't work on vampires, and as far as we know, Sezan is the only elf in his mix. All that's changed is that they choose the time—but even then, the only place left for this battle is by the slag heaps—the lake is too public, especially on Litha. No." Green shook his head in certainty. "Their only advantage lies in knowing we want Renny back alive."

Cory nodded, but she still sat at the foot of the staircase, arms wrapped around her knees, trembling. Arturo and Brack looked at each other, then looked at Green, and he moved closer to her. "What's wrong?" He asked gently. Cory shook her head, and laid it against the banister, closing her eyes tight. Green moved closer to her, touched her shoulder, and she moved into his touch completely. In spite of their audience, in that touch, they were all that existed on the planet.

"People may die, tonight, Green." She said, her voice wobbling. "People I know, and I like…and…I just talked them into it."

"No." He said gently. "No—no…you reminded them of why they should do it, Cory—you were magnificent."

"But I know why I'm going." She tried to hold back a hiccup, failed, took in a breath that shook her entire body. "I'm going to protect Adrian, and you, and Brack, and Arturo, and to help Renny, and I'd die for all of you…but they don't…they don't…"

And she gave up and rested her head on her knees and gave into the tremors that took over her slight shoulders. Green gathered her up in his arms, and found to his surprise that Arturo and Brack were gathered around her too, whispering, touching, murmuring to her that it wasn't her fault, that they were only scared, just like she was, and that she had helped them, all of them find their courage. After a moment the shaking stopped, and she said in a small voice—but a strong one—"Green can put me down now. Aren't I supposed to be Queen of the Undead or something? This is embarrassing."

The three men laughed, and Green nodded to Arturo and Brack, who faded away—presumably to talk to their sources about where Renny might be, and about mundane things like transportation and who was to stay behind and hold down the fort. Medicine, also, was discussed—many of the lower sidhe were better at healing than they were at fighting, and they, too, needed to be placed near the injured. Cory and Green sank into chairs and Cory reached up to touch Green's face, anxiously, as though she were trying to explain something without words to him. He looked at her, concerned, and waited until she spoke.

"You shouldn't go tonight." She blurted at last. "I know you want to—you want to protect Adrian, and me, and the others—but…"

And for the first time ever in front of her, Green felt the bitterness of who he was wash over him, and he knew she saw it on his face because she looked away. "I'm not a warrior." He said after a moment. She nodded. "Neither are you." He pointed out, and then almost wept because the look that she gave him was older than he was, and it didn't belong in the human child he loved.

"You know that's not true." She said gently. "You know it, Green—this thing I've been given—whatever it's full potential, it's a weapon as well as a blessing."

"No." He denied, feeling foolish, because he'd agreed, all those weeks ago to use her as a weapon and now did not like what he had done.

"It's not your fault." She said softly. "No." When he would have denied her again. "I knew what I was doing—Green, I think I knew what I was getting into that first night I saw Adrian's ex-girlfriend dead in the bushes…no—before that even. Arturo touched my hand and the world exploded into a meaning and a life and a color that I had never dreamed of—how is that not going to come with a price? Maybe I knew the first time I watched Adrian pop his bubblegum around his incisor and realized that he smelled like blood—and that I was attracted to him. And I'm a fighter by nature—I've fought my whole life—I've fought my teachers, I've fought my parents, I've fought the destiny everyone thought I should have—I can't fight this thing inside me, Green. I've killed two vampires with it—to save my life, yes, but I've killed. I smiled at an old man because I didn't know what power was and he went out and got dead, and that same power kept me alive—I don't know everything about me, but I know what my power is and what it isn't—and it isn't always peaceful."

Green's smile was truly bitter now. "And mine?" He asked, wondering if two millenniums of hurt looked any different than a fresh wound.

"Stop." She snapped, in tears. "This is hard for me—I worship you, you know, and so does Adrian and Arturo and Brack—we love you more than life and I fear for you tonight. Don't you understand? Sezan shot at us and you gave him the mother of all boners…" She snarked through her tears, but wept still the same. "I mean, it's beautiful and ironic but *it won't save your life…*"

She clasped his hand, carried it to her cheek, and he wondered if she realized that she hadn't worn mascara in a week, because it wasn't smearing all over his hand. Ah, Cory, he thought—so much of everything has changed for you. For us. For all of us.

"I won't stay home and tend the sprites." He said after a moment.

"We can't afford to lose you." She countered.

"I can not be a leader if I don't risk what I ask others to risk." He responded firmly. "And if you think being a leader in a warrior society without any warrior skills is easy, you've been watching the wrong movies, luv."

"I know that." She squeaked, and he knew that it must piss her off to lose her eloquence now, when it meant so much to her. "Do you think I don't know that? Do you think I don't know that's why you bind everybody to you with sex—so they can't fight you when their very natures cry out to defeat you?"

"Not everybody." He smiled gently.

"Arturo's different—and you offered him sex—not yours, but one of yours…and don't try to sidetrack me—this is serious." She sniffled a little, and he stroked her head with his hand. Her hair—red now, in a way he hadn't suspected when he had first seen the roots under the black—had started to curl a little as it grew out, and it felt sleek and alive under his hand. Her face, which had been plump and solid, that first night he'd seen her with the power hose, and later, weeping on his couch, was thin and pointed—both with strain and exertion, and with a purpose she hadn't had before. Yes, he thought somberly, it was serious. She was serious—and she was a warrior. The power surging through her had nothing to do with sex, as his did, although sex and love roused it to a formidable force—it had everything to do with her person, and her way of attacking the universe until it formed to her specifications. She used it to move things, to change color, to force growth where none had been before, and to wreak transformations that lived in an object's soul, but not in its form—she was right on all counts—she was both a blessing and a weapon. And he was not a weapon.

"You're a blessing." She said quietly, leaning her face towards his until their foreheads touched. "You're all the blessing many of us have had—you can't risk that."

"I didn't know you could read minds." He murmured, feeling stubborn and wretched and knowing he would still win because he was one thousand eight hundred and two years old, and if there was another advantage of being that old instead of nineteen he couldn't think of what it could be.

"Only yours…because I love you." She whispered.

He smiled a little. "Have you ever actually said that before?"

She laughed a little, hysterically. "Always implied, never stated, always felt, never announced—and we, all three of us—knew I would love you from the moment I woke up on your couch."

"And I love you." He murmured, because it was true, and he cursed English because it only had one word for love, and he couldn't differentiate it even from what he felt for Grace, or Blissa, or the sprites or Sweet or even Adrian. But it didn't matter, because she wouldn't have heard that one word of differentiation, not with what he had to say next. "I love you, and I love Adrian, but I will go tonight, and no one must die for me."

"Who would lead us?" She asked, turning a puffy, swollen, stricken face to him.

"Adrian, Arturo, You, Grace—pretty much in that order." Green assured her.

"But…"

Green smiled, self-deprecatingly. "Apparently, Adrian has been living much in my shadow, until these last weeks—when you shed light on both of us. I didn't know, right, how good a leader he could be. I've watched him rip himself apart to protect this community—I've watched him work with the elves in a way I didn't think he could. No—Adrian was here long before Arturo, and even Arturo recognizes his greatness and his right to lead here. He will do fine."

"Stop." She ground out, standing up and moving restlessly around the empty banquet hall. "Stop talking like it's a foregone conclusion—stop talking like you're going tonight to die."

"Then you stop." He retorted out of patience. "You stop assuming that just because I can't kill with a mighty push of my psychic warrior muscle that I am helpless and that this is hopeless." He stood and moved towards her, enfolding her with his arms. "You, me, Adrian—we're a big deal. We're a power source I don't think any one has reckoned with—give us a chance, have faith, right?"

She nodded her head at last, and he kissed the top of her hair. "You know," he said after a moment, "You've not slept in over twenty-four hours." She had been up early the day before for target practice—it was mid-June, and it was ninety degrees by ten o'clock in the morning—morning was the only time to go.

"I want to go look for Renny…" she mumbled, and then he caught her when her knees went out. "Ahh…fuck you, Green, stop doing that…" And then she was asleep, and he didn't feel particularly guilty about it either. She was getting too powerful on her own to let him do that, if she was properly rested and had all her wits about her. Gently he took her up the stairs and put her down in her own room. He had a meeting with Owen, later, and then one with Ray, and he did not know how either one would need him. He didn't want to have to move her while he conducted his business as a leader. And even as an ancient elf, a part of him quailed at that, that his business involved making love to people to fill the empty spaces they had in their souls. Because he had never thought sex should be just about business. But Cory had been right—he had needed to bind people to him—his strength was formidable, but he wasn't a warrior. He couldn't kill people with force or even with force and a weapon, as she had. He had to rely on loyalty, and for people to be loyal, they had to feel safe and protected, and that was what he gave them. For one hundred and fifty years it had worked. He would not let it fail him now.

CORY

We're Off To See the Bad Guy

Bracken woke me up at three, after a full eight hours sleep. I was completely pissed off, and he was the only one to bitch at, so I was pretty fucking merciless.

"Food?" I barked, blinking awake and glaring at him.

"Pretty demanding, aren't you."

"Food, moron." I sat up quickly, almost giving him a facer because he was bent over the bed to shake me awake.

"You did that on purpose!" He accused.

"Yes, I did that on purpose." I bitched back. "I'm in a foul assed mood—now fight back, asshole, or I'll take it out on someone who can't."

His hand shot out, smacking me on the side of the head. "Get over yourself, heifer." He growled. "It's not me you want to beat to shit, and you're not going to pull this crap on him, so save it for someone you can kill."

Deflated, I sank to the bed and turned my face towards the wall. The silence ticked by with the sun. "Two months ago I was a working student who couldn't even manage to graduate." I murmured to the window. "Everyone thought I was stupid white trash and I thought I had it bad. Six weeks ago I saw Mitch vibrate like a plucked guitar string and spatter all over the side of the Chevron and I felt helpless and useless and wondered where it would all end." I turned to Brack, feeling weak and dumb. He had eyes the color of sea and sea weed—grayish, greenish, brackish, and I realized that he had become a confidante in the last month. I couldn't ask for better. "Tonight I've got two kills under my belt, I can shoot pretty damn straight, and I can move the world around me in a way I should not be able to believe, much less do—and I will still be stupid, useless, and helpless if I can't protect two men who are older and more powerful than I've ever imagined. Who do I get to kill for the sheer stinking injustice of that?"

Bracken laughed in spite of himself, and it was a grim, dark sound. "There will be plenty of people to kill, dear." He said with assurance. "Just make sure you point that sunshine of yours in the right place, and watch death grow. I'll have Blissa fix you something, right?" He turned and left the room, and I showered and changed. I wore a .38 on my ankle holster, and a .45 strapped to my shoulder harness. I knew how to use them both, and the knowledge that the breath that filled my body and the blood that coursed through my veins made me a deadlier weapon than either gun was somehow not reassuring at all.

We left for Folsom at 6:30 in the evening—although the shadows were just beginning to lengthen and sunset was nearly three hours away. It was ridiculously hot, and I realized that this was one element we had not reckoned on—vampires regulated their own body temperatures, but most of the elven émigrés had been born and raised in cooler climates. Arturo had come from South America, and Bracken had been born and raised in the Foothills, but for the most part, our people were fatigued and sweat-drenched the moment they first stepped foot out of the assorted cars and minivans we'd driven in, into the parking lot of the clothing outlet.

When Brack had first suggested the outlet stores as a place to meet I had convulsed with giggles at the absurdity of a giant cosmic battle happening at an outdoor mall. But Green had looked at me with sorrowful eyes and said "It used to be all oak trees and long grass—there were good times there." And I abruptly remembered how very young I was, and how what was absurd to me was tragic to the others in the room. "Besides," Green had gone on, "The gravel quarry is not far away, and *that* is a very good place for a battle. The landscape is scarred anyway, and there's no residential area for a bit—it will keep the innocent safe, yes?" Bastard. He'd better not get hurt in all of this stupid insane crap—Adrian neither. My irritation at the two of them for putting themselves in danger was a good thing, I thought. It put me on edge and kept my power surging, right at my fingertips where I needed it.

We got out of our assorted cars and started to shop—ostensibly, that is. The idea was that we would work our way down towards the quarry, but wide enough through the little shopping village to be able to sight our opponents and gauge their strength. We would meet at the quarry shortly before the vampires would wake. It was a good plan, but as I moved restlessly in front of J Crew for the fifth time, catching a narrow eyed look from the security guard inside, I realized that we had a little too much time on our hands.

Green grinned at me, looking at me slantwise from those amazing, tranquil eyes of his. They weren't always tranquil, I knew—sometimes they were as passionate as spring, dark, like water bubbling up from a deep pool, or forceful, like a gust of wind through a field. But now, hours before we went to battle, they were tranquil.

"Calm down, darling." He murmured. "Here's an idea—we're at a mall—lets go shopping?"

My mouth fell open in surprise, and he used that to his advantage. Within moments, he had dragged me into The Gap, J-Crew, The Burlington Coat Factory and Linens and Things. He bought everything I looked at, everything I liked—lots of stuff for Adrian, like a new leather jacket and a couple of new pairs of jeans and black leather boots with flashing silver buckles, but some things for himself as well—mostly business suits and shirts and slacks. And the things he bought for me…

There was nothing punk. No men's t-shirts. No 501 jeans. He bought me those gauzy little dresses that the rich girls always wore in school, and at my inelegant snort he touched my hand and looked into my eyes and I could *see* myself in them, strolling down a college campus, looking like I had every right to be there. He bought me bras that weren't cotton, panties that weren't white, shirts that weren't two sizes too big. There was nothing too lacy, certainly nothing in pink—just clothes that let me see that he saw something in me I hadn't known was there. But the first time I came out of a dressing room in a short skirt with a spaghetti top, and saw the way he looked at me, I knew that he still saw me. *Me.* Not the façade I had worn so long. This girl, I thought, looking in the mirror with Green's eyes glowing as he scoped me out, *this* girl could have two lovers. This girl could draw a gun and throw a kick and conjure wind that could shriek the trees. This girl could walk away tonight alive and well, with her two lovers by her side. Green came up behind me, put his hands on my hips, lowered his lips to my neck, and I felt my nerves still, and the trembling that had followed me since that morning, when we found Renny gone and I had realized that tonight was inevitable, still. This girl, the girl who could wear these clothes and love this man, could protect her own. I met his eyes in the mirror, and saw that knowledge reflected back at me, except Green looked like he had always known, and I looked shocked with self-discovery.

"So, luv," he murmured in my ear, "Do you want to wear this tonight? It would be devastating you know…"

"I don't know…" I whispered, unable to find my real voice. "Stealth Cory always seemed to work for me."

"Quite right." He replied, amused, tender. "But remember that Glam-Cory is always right underneath the jeans and t-shirt, right?"

I grinned then, suddenly comfortable in my own skin again. "Right." I murmured. Then we both stilled, and the moment grew somber. "Time." We murmured together. Time indeed. I changed and we put our purchases in my little car. Then we trotted quickly down, past the McDonalds to the corner of Iron Point Road and Folsom Blvd, then turned right. This stretch of road, in places, still looked old and rural, full of oak and tall grass and hiding the monster of new businesses and new residences just around the corner. We took our lives into both hands then, and ran across the atrociously busy four lane road, stopping in the center divide and laughing slightly, because we'd forgotten, in the dash, what we were running towards.

The gravel pits of Folsom were part of the landscape. Ravaged earth, piles of rocks—you ignored them on your way to the outlet stores, car dealerships, and Intel. But they were there. We climbed the levy of stone in the beginning twilight and surveyed an industrial waste land, much the same, I think, as J.R.R. Tolkien had always envisioned Mordor. And on this summer day, it was hellishly hot.

I looked around and realized that Green and I were the only ones visible—as it should be, I guess. Green nodded slightly. "They're here." He said reassuringly. They *were* wood elves and high sidhe right? Who else could disappear in plain sight? It was okay, then, I thought. About half the were-folk were still at Green's for dinner—in both senses, since they had to eat well, too. I did see some shifting shadows, a few wolves, but mostly the giant tabby cats and horses and pigs that I had encountered those first wild nights at the Chevron station. Good, I thought with satisfaction—if anyone deserved vengeance, it was Mitch's people. And seeing their shadows made me feel not quite so alone.

Arturo suddenly materialized next to me—I had no idea if he walked fast, blurred in hyperspeed, as I'd seen Green do, or if I'd just been that distracted by scoping out the practically negative cover that we had once we ventured out of the surrounding oak trees, over the rise, and into the slag heap—but I was startled, and let out an undignified squeal when I saw him there.

Bracken heard me as he came up on Green's other side and snickered— and I loved them both, suddenly, so much that my chest hurt, and I wondered if I could breathe. I felt Green's hand on my back, and felt him moving through me, and knew he was breathing for me. Breathe in, breathe out, breathe in, breathe out…repeat if necessary, right?

"What kind of entrance do you think they'll make?" I asked, staring off onto the opposite rise of slag from where we stood.

"They will make…an entrance." Arturo replied, but with emphasis.

"They are a rock band, after all." Brack stated obviously.

I looked at Green, with anguish in my eyes. "He'll set up—you know he will—he'll have the mother of all amplifiers back there and turn all of you into elf-jam."

Green shook his head. "No—I mean, he will try, but not right away. Remember,—this is Adrian's enemy. He'll wait until Adrian's people are here and then try to defeat us. And remember, too, that most of his people are vampires—they will have to fly here, much as ours—and when you're coming across the lake, there' s not that much difference in the length of the trip."

"Then why are we here so early?" I asked. Why would we give our enemy the upper hand?

"Because we can." Green said mildly. "The lot of us can be here in the daylight, and Sezan is the only one of his party that can—it makes us stronger. Sezan will not like a reminder of that—not from what I've seen. We're here early to watch him set up—he will have to do that in front of us, while he waits for Adrian. We're here early to see if we can't spirit Renny away from him, before the actual fighting starts, just in case he's careless. Lot's of good reasons to be here early, Cory. Your nerves don't count as a strike against."

I smiled thinly. "Silly me." I murmured. We stood there, then, and watched the sky turn brilliant gold, casting shadows and fire on the faces near us. Arturo and Brack looked fearsome, and staunch, but Green, in a miracle of irony, looked simply young, and, when he smiled warmly at me in the glorious light, happy. The light didn't fade rapidly, it divided itself, between shadows and flame, and there was nothing you could look at on that rock quarry that would not send sunspots and shadow blindness dancing back into your eyes. My eyes, anyway—because I saw between my blinking and squinting that the men around me were unaffected. It figured, I thought irascibly: eyes that were meant to exist in shadows were probably made to function in the vagaries of light.

Then the light grew grey, and I heard Brack's sudden intake of breath and felt Green grow almost languid with relaxation, while Arturo on the other side of me grew taut like a drawn bow. There was something on the other side of the quarry that I could not see in my own sun blindness and it did not make them happy at all.

My eyes adjusted to the twilight, and I saw three things, all of them bad. The first was the purple-haired moron himself, Sezan, and the second was his keyboard, all set up, appearing, for real, by magic. I assumed there would be amps out there, probably surrounding us—but I saw Arturo smile ruthlessly and thought, maybe many of them had been disconnected. The third thing I saw was Renny, curled up in the fetal position, shivering like a wild animal in a cage. She was all shiny, shimmering with a twisted, odd pattern...the end of which was plugged into his keyboard. I gasped too. "A silver net." I murmured. Silver hurt lycanthropes and vampires. Silver wouldn't let were-animals change or vampires heal. If Sezan decided to play his little techo-pop of death, and Renny was right there, all decked out in silver, she'd suffer the same fate as Mitch and the others. Except worse, more painful...like having your body explode through swords.

Green didn't move so much as lean, brushing my arm with his. Then he whispered "Alchemy" under his breath, just loud enough for me to hear, and I knew what he wanted. He shook his head—from across the quarry, it would have looked like the faint breeze had simply caught a strand of hair from his braid and whipped it in his eyes, but I knew what else this meant. Change the silver into something else...but not yet. Sezan didn't know what I was yet. I had been an object to kill, a decoration on Adrian's arm, a plaything in his bed. He may not have known my name. But I was a weapon, even better as a secret, and I realized that while Green and Adrian danced with this psycho, I would be changing the beat.

"You've got a friend of mine." Green called after another breathless pause, during which the wind died down to nothing, and the absolute stillness of twilight descended with choking grey weight. "I would like her back."

Sezan spoke, and his speaking voice was surprisingly ordinary. "She smells like Adrian." He said mildly. "Let Adrian ask."

"Adrian will, when Crispin shows to parlay." Green responded. "But she's also mine, and if you breathe a little deeper you will find she smells like me too. I at least deserve to know why you've taken my people—and why some of them are dead." I remembered all of the time Green had spent with Renny, when she had first been brought back to Green's place—and less and less could I object to his propensity of sleeping with everyone he loved.

"But she was Adrian's last." Sezan insisted, but even I could see his eyes widen a little—I don't think he realized who all he had been dealing with.

"You still haven't told me why." Green continued pleasantly. How could Sezan have missed that threat of iron in his voice?

"That's between me and the bastard who killed my father." Sezan spat suddenly.

He had a temper I realized. Temper makes people ridiculous—not anger, but temper—losing your cool when it's not controlled. Suddenly Sezan lost some of his glamour, if that's what it had been. He looked less ominous, more small-town. More like us.

I realized that Green's eyebrows had nearly hit his hairline in honest surprise. "Adrian didn't kill your father." He said, clearly. "Your father killed himself."

"That's a lie." Sezan's voice was certainly not magic right now.

"I was there, little man." Green replied his face hard and not nearly so young now. "Adrian was no more to blame for the death of your father than he was to blame for the rape of your mother." This entire conversation was carried across a rock quarry, and yet Green managed to sound as though he were speaking across a drawing room to the opposite couch.

Even from across the quarry I could see Sezan's jaw drop. "My mother was a slut." He said, automatically, as though he'd been forced to memorize those words.

"Your mother was a captive." Green responded. And I could sense, underneath the seriousness of the situation, an honest puzzlement. Five of his people dead, one held captive, because this man had been poisoned with lies as a child, and was, after all this time, still a child.

"She gave me up." Sezan responded, his voice hurt. "She gave me to my father…"

"Your father gave you to her." Green said gently. "It was not a…welcome giving. That is not your fault. But it wasn't Adrian's—it certainly wasn't his people's fault. And yet you attacked us anyway."

Green and Arturo and Brack had bled from their eyes and ears and nose. Mitch had exploded like a water balloon on pavement. Adrian's very undead soul bled at the loss of his people. I knew all this, and it was still hard not to feel sorry for the small half-bred elf across the quarry whose every expression betrayed a deep confusion. Then the expression hardened on Sezan's swarthy, ugly face, and I realized that we would get no mercy from him, and, as though to prove his point, he hit an idle key, and at the sound (smaller than he'd expected, I could tell by his frown and his glance around the trees— good, did he think we were stupid?) two human men—drugged or bewitched or both—both wearing little more than cut off jeans and sneakers—walked out from behind a small rise of rock, carrying a bound and furious Officer Max between them.

Brack breathed "Fuck me…" and earned a withering look from Arturo, but I was glad he said it, or I would have.

"Is this one of yours?" Sezan asked maliciously. "He smells like one of you…vampire I think, but I'm not sure. So hard when you don't keep your people straight, now, isn't it?"

I wanted to know who had been chewing on Max Johnson—I felt a pang somewhere around my chest, and then another, and realized that I was feeling oddly protective of this dickhead cop. At the very least, I realized unhappily, he did not deserve to be served as lunch or turned into goo, simply because he had tried to help me.

"He's mine." Green said in a pained voice, casting a disgusted look at me. I wrinkled my nose at him. Max was mine—my problem, my fault— but everybody had been so damned determined that I not make myself a real presence until I'd done my whole "secret weapon" routine that I felt like I'd be letting them down even more if I spoke up now. Silently I vowed that the next time we had a confrontation like this, everyone would damned sure know who I was, and why I was there.

"And that should mean something to me?" Sezan was preening. I no longer felt sorry for him—looking at Renny's absolute misery, and Max's fury and confusion, I simply wanted him dead.

"It will." Green responded mildly. "Of course you might not remember the last time you tried to harm something that was mine…although, it was probably a hard and painful lesson to forget."

Sezan paled, then blushed. We could see it from fifty feet away because his hair turned color—weird. I mean, I was standing on a hill top surrounded by elves, with at least fifty lycanthropes at my back, and watching his hair turn from magenta to a sickly Pepto-Bismol color, and back again to a bright purple was definitely weird. And he said nothing for a moment, leaving us on the crest of the gravel pile, trying not to smirk.

"Does that make you happy, then?" Sezan sneered. "We all know a real man would have at least cut it off. Or sucked it off…either way, you fell short, didn't you, elf?"

I felt something wash over me then that I was powerless to stop…a rage, a fury, a protectiveness that would tolerate no reason. He said those things to *Green…Green,* who had held my hand as I learned, my shoulders as I'd wept, and my body as I came. I was unprepared for this moment, when I realized that love was a ferocious, hungry, bestial thing, and that it had taken over my body, and I thirsted for our enemy's blood.

I'd been concentrating on changing the nature of Renny's silver chains, so that's what happened first—they changed to water, then steam, and ordinarily I would have felt awful for the steam burns that made Renny squeal, but she was just so happy to be free that she changed immediately into a big brown tabby cat, and any burns she had healed. While that was happening Sezan's hair caught on fire. He was occupied with Renny, and didn't notice until our people started to laugh. They were mostly hidden, so it was a muffled, insidious laughter, the kind I was sure had surrounded me in high school but could never prove.

Sezan stopped then, suddenly, his eyes narrowed and angry and watched as Renny vanished around a pile of rocks, disemboweling one of Sezan's pretty puppets with a swipe of her paw, tracking blood as she padded off. Sezan took a deep breath, then and he put his hair out with a damp wave of his hand. Water siren, I remembered dimly. His mother was a water siren. And then, like an infant revving up for a tantrum, he prepared to scream.

Oh, fuck. He was going to scream. And we had no vampires to protect us, and this wasn't planned, it was honest fury, and he might not kill all of our people, but he would kill some. I had practiced for two months, almost daily. Before all of the implications of his scream could pass through my mind, the

.45 was in my hand and I fired a warning shot over his head. For the rest of my life I would regret not firing into his heart.

But it was enough for now—he froze, looking at me in honest shock, and then we both gasped. Our eyes widened, and I know that for a moment our expressions were identical—awareness, pleasure, and an evil sort of anticipation.

The vampires were awake. They were heading this way.

ADRIAN

Summer Wind Through a Cotton Dress

I was in the air, coming in low over the lake with my kiss, when I realized Cory was in danger. I had felt her tension from the moment I had awakened, and the wash of magic anger that blazed through her almost made me fall into the lake. I laughed when she set the miserable bastard's hair on fire, but I could feel her fear, for Green, for Renny, even for that cop who wanted her body...and for the first time ever I cursed not being able to rise until the sun went down. Minutes, I thought, moments...

Our entire kiss was a fearsome thing, flitting between trees like giant bats—probably why we all wear black, just to keep up that illusion. Ordinarily, I loved flying—I loved the wind in my hair, and my freedom. Perversely enough, I even loved that this was a place that Green and Cory would not often come. I loved them—with all of me I loved them. The thought of their deaths—impossible. Unimaginable. Absurd. But I had so little of me that was mine. My redemption was Green's. My conversion was Lucien's. My salvation was Cory's. Flying was mine. Sometimes I thought that my flying and my pain were all that made me enough of a person to be loved. But tonight, flying was not fast enough, and I was *needed* to be there with them. I felt weak, knew it was the power of Litha, and fought against it.

By the time I'd flown from oak to oak along the roadway, then looped into the gravel pit itself, I had left my kiss far behind.

Cory was standing on the far side of the quarry, up on the rise of facing East. Arturo, Brack, and the entire compliment of elves were on the opposite rise, staring across at them. All of their attention was on Cory, and, right next to her, that damn amplifier of Sezan's. She was in enemy territory, face to face with the little bastard—I almost dropped out of the sky when I saw her there.

Green was about ten feet behind her, and he had a long suffering look on his face. She had done something, I was sure, to put that there. I could have told him, I *should* have told him, weeks ago, that whatever they planned, whatever sort of sixteenth century parley he had in mind, that Cory would bollix it up—for the better, I'm sure, but bollix it up just the same. As I topped the gravel ridge, I was close enough to hear him ask her who the fuck she was. I wanted to rip out his spleen for that alone—but I could see the others, Crispin's lot, winging in behind Sezan. Something looked odd about Crispin, but I couldn't put my finger on it. It didn't matter, I guessed—compelled, bespelled, or free-willed, Crispin had somehow allowed this to happen. It had to be stopped.

"I'm nobody." Cory said pleasantly, insincerely. I felt Renny nearby, and since no one had seen me yet, I dropped behind the edge of the gravel pit—Cory was out of sight, but Renny was there, in were-cat form, hiding behind a large oak tree with others of her clowder. I smiled when I saw her, then arched an eyebrow, and she rushed into my arms in a flurry.

"Hullo, little sister." I said softly, "You gave us a scare."

"I wandered too far, hunting this morning." She confessed. "They put a silver net over me before I could even smell them…they were only humans…" She stopped, and looked at me, unhappily. Her language had been slipping, I realized, in this last month. It's what happens when you spend too much time as a giant house cat. "Cory changed my silver wire for a moment and I escaped…but it was too soon, Adrian…they didn't know who she was…And now they know—she doesn't think they do, but they know she's important…they're going to kill her first. As soon as you show up…that silver wire…it's important…it's hooked up to the amplifier and Sezan 's voice. What it did to Mitch—it can do to anyone, even…"

It would have been "even you." That's what she would have said, but I didn't hear the rest. It wouldn't have mattered if I had. Cory, Green, Bracken—they were all I've ever had in the world. Even Arturo, who loved me in his completely obnoxious paternal way was my family. And they were all standing right there. If I had known what that silver net would have done to me, I may not have picked it up—but that still might not have changed what happened that night. There were so very few choices, all in all.

So, when Renny warned me, I was already motioning to Phillip and Kurt and the others to fly by and distract Sezan, while I got my girl the fuck out of the way. I wouldn't have done a damn thing differently. Cory could die and Green didn't know she was their target. I had no choice. I hope Cory knows that I had no choice.

It happened so fast—Phillip, Kurt, Chet, all leapt into the air and I followed them—the granite quarry looked dim and grey under a sliver of moon, but I could see Cory, trading amiable insults with Sezan.

"Adrian? Adrian's a *vampire?* Really? And that's *bad?*" She was saying, wide eyed. I had no idea what she was responding to, but I wished I could hear the entire conversation. It was such a pleasure to hear her battle with her very sharp, very savage wit. "So…being a screeching psychopath is a *good* thing," She said, as the others did their fly by. Their wind ruffled her hair, I could see that, but I didn't really see much else. My whole attention was on that deadly silver net, attached to the amplifier.

As I swooped by to grab it, I heard her gasp, all worry pain and loss, right to my toes. It ripped through me, more painful than the final note that ended me.

Someone, not Sezan but someone, pressed a key on the keyboard, and I was gone. I don't know what happened to my body—it was suddenly not there.

My soul, however—ah, Goddess—my soul blew through Cory's like a wind through a cotton dress, but worse, because her heart had just been ripped in two. It left a bleeding fabric, a wounded wrap. *I couldn't change, it, Cory, luv—I wouldn't change it if I could. If it were a choice between me and you, it had to be me.* But I didn't have time to tell her that. I didn't have time to tell Bracken to care for her. I didn't have time to tell Arturo that I knew why he was so hard on me, and it was okay. I didn't have time to tell Green that he was the sun and the moon and the stars. The Goddess gave me just enough time to feel her pain, to let her know I loved her. I had just long enough to say goodbye.

CORY

Blood Like Rain

I knew what the silver net would do, even before he touched it...but I felt
him coming, and I was so happy, because I was just terrified standing there,
talking to Sezan. I thought when Adrian got there, it would all be okay.

I mean, who am I? I'm a stupid little mortal, and there I was, trading
insults with the guy who had killed Mitch, and the others, Ratso, and that
poor little sprite with the tiny body like a broken light-bulb. And he could
have destroyed me in a minute, but he wasn't—he was just talking to me,
waiting. I thought *When Adrian gets here, it will begin.* How can one person
be so wrong? Adrian arrived, and everything ended.

He saw me—I could tell. He had his hunting face on, and was snarling
with extended jaws and burning eyes at Crispin, and I could feel inside him
the need to protect me, the need to keep me and the others safe. I thought he
would settle down and parley, or attack Sezan as he stood, but Adrian had
just enough information to save our lives and lose his own. I saw him reaching for the net and the whole world condensed to what must not happen—
and it did, and it was like Adrian was in slow motion and my agony was in
hyperspeed. I knew, before flesh touched element, what would happen, but I
couldn't seem to make him understand.

As he grabbed the net—one of the vampires—I think it was Crispin, but I
never found out for sure—giggled weakly and pressed a key on that fucking
keyboard, and my life and heart exploded into the air around me. I can't

remember what it looked like. I can't. No one can make me. No one has tried. All I know is one moment, I was happy, and Adrian was there, and the next moment I was covered in a gentle mist of blood, like a fine, warm rain. And he blew through me. It was the best and the most awful, that last kiss on my mind, the last stroke on my heart, the apology, the farewell. I could smell him, his hair, his sweat, his sex, *him* for weeks, just by remembering his mind merging through mind, for that simple, devastating kiss goodbye.

I stood there, in shock, covered in my lover's blood, unable to comprehend anything more or less than that my world had just been ripped asunder. While my mind and my heart tried to put this together, I watched as Green, who knew death and recognized loss immediately, did something truly horrible.

One moment he was behind me, making a strangled moan of devastation, and the next he had both Sezan and Crispin by the throats, they were held high in the air, with their legs kicking feebly beneath him, and he was…grieving.

There was more to it than that. There was a sound—a beautiful, awful sound, like a tornado must make when it rips up a house, or a volcano makes as it heaves ash and lava and smoke effortlessly into the air, or a flood makes, as the water rushes from the dam. His mouth was open in fury, and that sound was pouring from his throat, and Crispin and Sezan were begging for their lives.

They said it was an accident. They said I was the target, and Adrian shouldn't have died like that. Sezan said that Crispin was a fucking moron who couldn't hold his wad. And then their words died in gurgles, as Green's grief tried to rip grief out of them. They didn't have any—they had no grief, no compassion, no understanding, and Green's power, unsatisfied with what they didn't have, settled on their flesh instead. Sezan would have screamed then, his fatal, toxic scream, but he couldn't, because his throat was full of blood, and it was gushing out past his mouth, and down Green's arms. Crispin's slow, borrowed vampire blood was vomiting out of his mouth too, and the blood ran thicker and more awful and more full of things that should never come out of a person's mouth ever, until Green dropped them both and turned to me, holding their fluttering hearts in his hands.

I couldn't even be horrified. I just stood there, unable to even think "Adrian is dead." How could I think Adrian was dead? It was like looking down at my body, and finding air instead. I breathed, without breathing, and then inhaled further, but it wasn't oxygen. In the back of my mind I heard the sound of fighting, of a fearsome battle, but I didn't hear it. All I could think of was "breathe" and even though my lungs were moving in and out I was still inhaling, like a child getting a shot, taking that long pull of air before he unleashed a howl that would shatter glass and hearts. I was nowhere near ready to unleash what was in me, but the pressure grew greater and more explosive and my breath got mightier and mightier and stronger and I wanted my flesh to fly from my bones I hurt so badly so I didn't know what would happen when I...

GREEN
Just Breathe

He felt what she was doing as he turned around. It's the only thing that kept him from chewing Crispin's and Sezan's still beating hearts and spitting the bitterness on ground that would never, ever grow, not for a millennia, not for ever.

But he felt the power, the pressure, and turned, and saw what her grief was doing—it was plain as the blood on her face, and left him with very little time to save them all. He blurred towards her, and picked her up from behind. That was a mistake, he thought, as he felt their bond, their magic, snap through him, and even though Adrian was only there in memory, he still worked as a catalyst. His presence was just as strong as if they were all linked in sex, and it coursed through Green and then Cory, and he knew it was beyond stopping, and maybe even beyond control. She struggled but he was physically stronger at least, and he held on tightly as he called, in an awesome voice that he didn't know he had, "My People, Our people, leave **NOW. NOWWW.**"

Later it was reported that his great, terrible voice had carried even to the lake and beyond, but all Green cared about were the people in the center of the quarry who were now fighting and bleeding, but who might not live another heartbeat if they didn't get the fuck out of Cory's way. His voice worked, because as Green wrestled Cory facing inward, towards the center, he saw only Crispin's vampires, and Bracken, making a rolling dive towards

Cory's bound and frightened cop. Brack was moving fast enough to blur, and they ended up on the far side of the quarry, skidding through the gravel, just as Cory's grief exploded from inside, covering the gravel pit with searing, boiling, terrible sunshine screaming.

In less time than it took for Adrian to die, nearly one hundred vampires disappeared in a blast of sunshine and a hiss of vapor. Not even their shadows remained. It wasn't enough—her pain streamed out of her, into the bowl-like center of the quarry until it boiled through the rock, turning it into magma, bubbling through until Green felt the earth under their feet start to tremble, as the foundation under them turned molten.

He was shouting at her, screaming, begging her to stop, because the pit was widening, farther—it would take Bracken and Max next, and although he was sure his people were on the other side of the opposite ridge, he didn't think they were safe either. But he felt her weakening—even a howling infant must draw another breath, and as she stuttered, and went to pull power again, he blurred backwards until they topped the ridge and literally fell over backwards, tumbling head over heels, battering and bruising until he was sure she was far too physically hurt to wield power any more.

They had become separated during their fall, and as they stilled, Green heaved himself to his knees and crawled towards her. He saw her breathe deep from the chest again, and stopped, for a moment, confused and frightened that she would kill him, now in her grief, and she would never survive that knowledge, ever. Then she let out the cry she'd been holding, and it was a wail of grief, horrible and anguished and sad, but it was human grief now. It shredded her chest, made the air around them thick with pain, but it would not kill him. In a moment, he was at her side without thinking, cradling her, rocking her, weeping with her now as he could not before, for their lover, for themselves, and for what they had wrought.

Cory

How To Keep Living Without Really Caring

I don't know how we got home, or who carried me up the stairs. I don't think it was Green, because I remember weeping with him on the gravel pile, both of us coated in blood, and I remember the tremble in his body, the weakness in both of us as we clung together. We were wrecked. We should have been wrecked.

So I don't remember how we got home, but we awoke wrapped together in a sleeping bag next to the spring that I had created only weeks before. Someone had bathed us, probably in the spring, and we were naked.

I awoke with a gasp, and reached automatically for that link—that tenuous, magical, fragile link to Adrian, to my beloved, and found only a void of darkness. Oh, no. Oh Goddess. No. I didn't remember. You couldn't make me remember. But it was there—the look on his face, the deadly silver net, his blind reaching for his own destruction. Oh, Adrian. You bastard—you were supposed to be immortal. How could you leave me alone like this? The pain was devastating, obliterating, too huge to even contemplate, and yet it was there, crushing the breath out of my chest. I inhaled on purpose, and my very breath hurt. I screamed, sobbed, felt that amputated link between us, and knew that Adrian wouldn't be there and never would again.

I reached automatically for Green, and he for me. There were no words. There didn't need to be—we had both lost our lover, and he left the same nightmare void of pain in his wake. Green was the only person on earth who would understand what it was I missed. I sobbed on him, I screamed, I howled, I pounded on his chest, and he just held me, held me and wept until I thought the spring around us was running with tears and it still was not enough. It would never be enough.

But there comes a time when your body won't let you grieve like that, because the grief will kill you. Eventually we stilled, and were sitting, naked, and together in the sunshine, and missing Adrian so badly that the only place we could find solace was in each other. I needed comfort. And then I simply needed Green. For the first time I realized—truly realized—what it was that Green did, in his room with his people. I had an emptiness, a void and the need overwhelmed me and, just like that he was hard, and inside of me, and the void was filled, and I welcomed him. For just a moment, that moment that he was filling me, I knew Adrian was gone, but I remembered that I was here, and that I'd have to live, and that Green could fill me whenever I needed him. It was the best comfort I could have had, and for Green too, maybe, but we still cried Adrian's name, in our climax, and still wept into each other, as our bodies shuddered, and the sex was gone, and we remembered again that Adrian was gone with it.

But it was worth it. And important—for just that moment, as we gave each other solace in the most physical way possible, I realized a that for a moment I knew what it would be like to be Renny, or Owen, or any of the people who went into Green's bedroom in shadowy afternoons, and came out closer to whole. As Green clutched me, and wept, I thought brokenly that perhaps for the first time, Green had been like them too.

Our breathing eventually calmed, our heartbeats eventually resumed their usual rhythm, and the sun soaked through the sleeping bag, making us drowsy. We had no more tears, and only the simplest of words to greet the empty day.

"I don't know what to do." I said after a moment.

"Get up, eventually." Green replied. "Get dressed—eat—Goddess, we need to eat. Talk to the others. Sleep."

"I mean...after..." I murmured. I looked at him, trying to find words, and saw his true age, for maybe the first time. And seeing it, etched into his perfect features, into the sadness of his shadowed emerald eyes, for the first time his age was a comfort. Age was no shield against grief, I realized. Age didn't keep you from pain. My hand shook, and I traced those lines around his eyes. "I feel so lost, Green." I whimpered.

He stroked my hair, then, and nuzzled my cheek. "So do I, my lovely. So do I."

We followed plan A. First we slept a little more, and then awoke, numb, ravenous, and found two coffee cans full of trail mix and clothes, stacked neatly near the sleeping bag.

"We're being handled." Green murmured, wryly, through a mouthful of trail mix.

"We're being loved." I corrected him.

"That too."

We descended down from our grove, from our erotic memorial to Adrian, and to the two of us when we were innocent. I didn't realize how much of my innocence had been lost until I came down the stairs and saw Bracken, his back towards us, leaning bare-chested over the counter and stealing food from the bowl in front of his mother. His braid had been singed off, from the backs of his knees to his shoulder blades. I almost ran into him, trying to touch it, the curled ends, the coarse, melted texture, and I felt tears, again, sliding down my face. The night came back, and I saw him sliding, to save Max. I would have killed them both, I realized. Like I had killed...

Green caught me when my knees buckled, and Bracken whirled and took me from him. "I'm sorry..." I mumbled, "I'm sorry...sorry...Goddess, I'm so sorry...."

Brack held me close to him, clutched me tight, bent forward, kissed my forehead. "I'm fine." He said.

"Your hair." I said helplessly, "Your lovely, lovely hair..."

"Will grow." He murmured kindly.

"But..." I hiccupped, "I could have...you and Max, I could have...Oh Jesus, I *did...* " And it flooded back—everything I had forgotten in my grief about Adrian and it was there, dumped over my head like iced acid. Crispin's vampires, oblivious to everything but the fact that their enemies had blurred, flown, raced away so suddenly that not only did they have no foes, but they had no purpose. And then the sunshine, my grief, my power, the surge of Adrian's memory, Green's attempts to control us both...

And they were gone. All of Crispin's people...all of them. I went limp against Bracken, and he scooped me up, cuddling me against him, giving me forgiveness and redemption, if I would take it. I didn't know if I could. "How many?" I murmured weakly.

"Cory…" Brack said, weakly, not wanting to tell me.

"How many?"

I heard Arturo's voice, then, felt his hand on my face. "Cory…" He murmured.

"How many?" I said again, my voice getting stronger every time. "Green…" and I sounded plaintive, even to my own ears. "Green…make them tell me, how many people I killed?"

There was silence in the room, then, and I realized that it had been full when I came down. It was still full, but now they were reverent, respectful, in awe. They were in awe of me, cowering Bracken's arms, falling apart on him, stroking his beautiful, beautiful, ruined hair. They were in awe of me—but they wouldn't answer my questions. Arturo finally broke the silence.

"We guess a hundred or so—we didn't really have time to count, Corinne Carol Anne."

That silence, that stillness sat over the room. And it was still reverent. I thought of Adrian again, of the big, gaping hole in my heart, where Adrian should be. "I'd do it again." I mumbled. "I'd watch out for Bracken's hair, this time…" I choked, and I saw a very small smile that didn't make me feel better at all, "But I'd do it again."

Green took me from Brack then, and I felt myself falling, falling, sleeping like he said before I'd planned to sleep. "No…" I murmured, but I didn't really mean it.

"Yes." He said. "We know you'd do it again. He bent down, kissed me, on the lips this time, so I could taste him, his sincerity, his life. "That's why we love you, Cory. Because you'd do it again." And then I was gone.

Green was right about the rest. I got up, I ate, I talked, I slept, I cried. Green and I were exclusive to each other for this time, but I could feel the pull, the anguish, not from him, but from his other wounded. The shape-shifters had lost their own. The vampires were in mourning. The healing that I was given by my lover could not be exclusive to me—Green's people needed him. Finally, one afternoon I couldn't take Owen's anguished silence anymore, and I pushed Green in his direction. Green turned a face to me then, that I had never seen, and I recognized that this was a job. Sometimes it was a job he loved—hell, often, it was a job he loved—but it was a necessity to who he was. I had known that, practically, I had even forgiven him, if that was the word. But finally, I think, I realized that he had never been unfaithful to Adrian and I. It was a final doubt, a final acceptance. I had lost Adrian, and I grieved. But Green was still mine, and I rejoiced. And I could do both.

Things got easier after that.

There were still days when I couldn't get out of bed, and days when I was pretty sure Green only got up in order to make me get up. We still wept in each other's arms every night, missing third lover in our bed like we would miss a third of our flesh if it were hacked off.

One day my mother called and asked if I could bring my young man over for dinner. I didn't know what to say...I told her we'd broken up. Then I curled in the corner of Green's couch and mewled like an infant until Bracken picked me up and put hauled me up the granite stair case into the erotic grove above ground. He plunked me down and sat next to me in the blessed coolth and silence.

"I see Adrian here." He said after a moment.

"You see a lot of Adrian here." I cracked weakly, looking at one of the thorn less rose bushes, whose bole formed Adrian, leaning back against the oak and the lime trees, each wrapping their limbs around him. There was an unmistakable protrusion from the bole, with small tendrils of oak wrapped around it. It was raw, and erotic, and I remembered that moment so clearly I could smell him against my skin, and feel him, splashing against my hand.

"No." Brack said, talking past my wisecrack. "I mean he's here. He's in this place. You can't wipe him out of existence by a well meaning lie, Cory. It's okay if you don't tell them now. You'll tell them when you can. When it won't hurt them quite so much."

I swallowed, hard. "I was supposed to go to school." I murmured. "Then I was supposed to be with Adrian and go to school. I don't know what I'm sup-posed to do now."

Brack smiled, leaned against me companionably. "It sounds to me like you're supposed to go to school."

"I can't." I murmured.

"I don't see why not."

"I can't leave Green." I said baldly. It had been a month since that night in the quarry, a month of wandering around Green's home like the undead, of watching him drag the torn bleeding parts of himself together and make him-

self work for his people. He needed me, I thought, and thank Goddess someone did.

"How can you leave Green?" Asked Bracken, completely surprised. "I've
seen you—the three of you were amazing, magic, but the two of you are the
same, only two. It's like you both grew, to take over the space that Adrian left
in your hearts. You can't leave him—he'll always be here, and you'll always
come back to him. You haven't been in our lives long, Cory, but I can't imagine the world any other way."

And he was right, I realized. Green and I would always be bound together.
But it still hurt.

"I don't think I can." I said, brokenly.

He hugged me to him then, and we sat alone on top of the hill for most of
the rest of the afternoon. After that, Bracken let the question of my future
alone, but eventually Arturo started asking, then Grace, then Green. They
wanted me happy, I realized, and I told myself that it was my job to make
them think that I could be happy again. That's why I eventually decided to
go to San Francisco for school—to make them think that I would heal. It
wasn't a good enough reason, but it was the only sense of purpose I had.

GREEN

Never Goodbye

It was damned hard to let her go, even if he knew she'd be back every week-end. Green would pay her way—she had tried to argue, but he had silenced her with a long-suffering look. She was his now—a part of the giant preter-natural co-op that he'd devoted his life to—he would have done it for any-body, but most especially for her. And for Renny—Renny was going with her. They would room together, in an apartment Green reserved for business trips, and commute to school.

He helped her pack, in that last week of August, noting with comfort that her grandmother's quilt, and her pictures, and many of her own things stayed in her room. Their room, since he only used his to work in now, lately. He would stay in here, he thought forlornly, and sleep on her bed when she was gone. Suddenly she stopped throwing her new clothes into a new suitcase and turned towards him, practically bowling him over.

"I can't go." She whispered brokenly. "I can't. I'm so lost, and here is the only home I'm found."

"You don't have to go." He murmured. "I can't make you. I'd love to have you here—I'll miss you like I'd miss breathing…but, Cory…"

She was weeping, openly now against his chest. "I know. I know…" she sobbed, then she stilled herself with an effort, forcing herself to breathe. "I won't be happy here until I go get something for myself. Then I can be who-ever I want, whatever I want—but I can do it here."

Green smiled, barely, because he felt like crying too. "Please do." He said, choked. "I'm forever old, Cory, but I don't think I can make it through one more mortal lifetime, without you by my side."

"I'll be here." She promised. "I won't leave you, Green. Not for real. Not forever."

He tucked them into a new car, a big one, with air conditioning and cruise control and air bags, even though Cory could probably stop anything in her path and Renny could go through the windshield, change forms, and walk away. Renny looked lost—a tiny brown-haired girl wearing a sundress and a look like wind. Cory wouldn't let go of him, in their hug good bye. Cory was clinging to Green, balling his shirt in her hands like a toddler in the effort not to let go when Officer Max drove up. He looked lost when he saw the full car, and hurt, and almost permanently puzzled.

Cory was still clinging when they both heard Max's hesitant cough behind them.

"Where are you going?" He asked, puzzled.

"School." She said shortly. "San Francisco State—the have a good humanities department."

Max's eyebrows rose, but he nodded.

"I'm glad you're okay." Cory said after a moment. "I'm sorry—about dragging you into this…about almost boiling you like soup—about everything."

"I still don't know what you mean by 'everything'." Max said after a moment. "There was blood, everywhere; I still don't know whose. Then Bracken was tackling me, and then there was light, and heat…and no one ever explained it to me. They just let me go, when it was over, and I drove home."

Cory stood there, stunned for a moment. Green couldn't even answer. How do you explain that your world ended, and you're only pretending to be around to talk about it?

"Adrian's dead." She murmured at last. "That was his blood," Her voice hitched, "Coating us all like…water. And then Green killed Sezan and Crispin, with grief alone. And then I killed…well…" She looked at Green helplessly. "I killed everybody else who wasn't us."

Max's jaw dropped open, and Cory's knees obviously wobbled. There it was—the enormity of what she'd done to defend the people she loved. It would never go away. She swallowed, leaned back against Green, and looked at Max. They were lost together, in that look, two mortals, striving for balance on immortal grounds.

"Are you going to arrest me?" She asked at last.

"For killing people who were technically dead? What's the charge?" He asked, genuinely puzzled.

"Murder." She answered simply, then shook her head. "Don't say anything, Max. I'll be back—I won't ever leave here, not really." He was still bemused, so she pat his cheek and smiled a little, then turned and kissed Green one last time, memorizing his taste, his smell, his texture. "I won't ever leave." She murmured, for his ears alone. "I love you." And then she ran to the car and skid out of the driveway.

Max stood there for a moment next to Green and watched the car disappear. They could tell when it reached the end of Green's property, because it started to kick up dust.

"She really loved him—true love. I'm so stupid."

"Blindness is a handicap." Green said cryptically. "And we both loved him."

"She would have killed me, if not for Brack—thank him for me."

"If it's any consolation, she couldn't have lived with that."

"It helps a little." Max conceded. And still they stood there, watching, wishing futilely that there was something they could do to call her back.

"She's not ready to go." Max said at last.

"I'm not ready to let her go." Green replied.

"Then why are you letting her."

"Because I don't know what else to do." Green said at last. He turned to Max and shrugged, feeling alone and old and foolish. "I don't feel much like company." He said after a moment, "But I bet Arturo would offer you a beer."

Max nodded. "Thanks. I'll take him up like that."

Green gestured for Max to precede him into the house, and he watched as the once reassured police man walked hesitantly up to the open front door and knocked. Then he turned and looked towards the road again. She'd be home every weekend, he told himself. And he could visit too, for a day or so.

"Come back to me, my mortal heart." He murmured, and did not move for a long, long time.

0-595-33746-5